MYTHICAL MENACE

A DRAGON RIDER FANTASY ROMANCE

TALES OF THE VANIR

BOOK IV

Cover Design by 100 Covers
Formatted with Atticus

Thanks to the beta readers and editors who helped make this a better book:
Cindy Ray Hale and Keele Publishing
Kaitlin Slowik
Keeya Marquez

And perpetual thanks to my alpha reader, Cynthia Davis

DEDICATION

To anyone who's been trapped in a hole so deep,
they feared they'd never see light again,
and then they did.
This one's for you.

Ziselaer's song is *Digging My Own Grave*
by Five Finger Death Punch

Content Warning

This book is intended for adults only, and contains subject matter that may be difficult or disturbing for some readers.

Sensitive material includes, but is not limited to: frequent profanity, violence, torture and killing of people and dragons (but not the cat; nobody messes with Thor), emotional abuse, socio-economic power imbalances, frequent mentions of blood, and genocide (of elves).
Mythical Menace also contains explicit, open-door sexual content.
Reader discretion is advised.

Contents

Glossary

Ætt: Clan/Fhord's people

Dragon's-Length: Unit of measure; sixty feet

Draikana: Female of a mated dragon pair

Drake: Male of a mated dragon pair

Draugr: Undead

Drott: Chief/leader

Dróttning: Queen

Kastali: Castle

Konungr: King

Male's-Height: Unit of measure; six feet

Meistara: Lady

Meistari: Lord

Seiðr: Ability to predict the future

Thunder: Group of dragons

Valkyrie: Shield maiden/female warrior

Vekter: Guards/police

Viku: Unit of measure; one mile

MAP

TALES OF THE VANIR
NJORDHEIM
BARRIER
TRAINING GROUNDS
NORTHERN NEST
VANATIA
SOUTHERN NEST
REVALLE
TRAINING GROUNDS

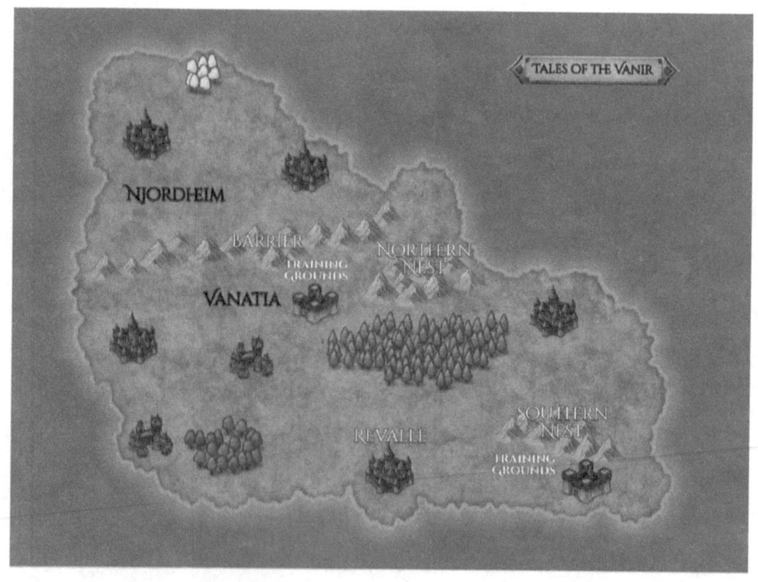

Recap

What Happened in the Last Book?

In *Divine Dilemma*, Fhord and Sifa are running again, this time, with both of their dragons. When they find a place to hide for the night—giving Fhord and Tindera time to heal—Dani shares news that shakes the group to their core. The blue dragon that raped and beat Khirta, who appeared and fought Vulryn during the rescue, is Vulryn's drake, Ziselær. The copper dragon is determined to go after him and try to turn him against the Dróttning.

The group finds the strength to travel to the healing waters in north Vanatia, and then to an island, Lumaria, that the elves Joralf and Fróðr lead them to. When the group lands, the emissaries who greet them drop to their knees to salute Fhord. Fhord reveals that he discovered this island a century ago, and that every drop of water that flows through it is imbued with magic similar to the water in the north. Fhord turned it into a sanctuary for rebels two years after Sifa appeared in Vanatia and, without realizing why, created a cavern for Sifa—a private space for his mate.

But they're not safe, even in this sanctuary. A group of rebels is convinced that all dragons and their riders belong to the Dróttning. They shoot Astarot with a dragon bolt, leading to the discovery that Aksell (the paltry-penised male who appeared early in Sacred Struggle), is fomenting that hatred. Fhord and Sifa return to Vanatia to punish Aksell but Dani doesn't join them. She and Vulryn will chase Ziselær and his rider to try to win their loyalty. Before everyone leaves the island, we learn that Mikkael is obsessed with Dani, despite his hatred toward her. Sifa tells Mikkael about Johan's death, leading him to decide to go to the mainland with them, then chase vengeance.

Dani and Vulryn present themselves at the Nest and are placed in cells. Vulryn and Ziselær spend time together, as Vulryn uses her influence to try to improve Dani's treatment. When Dani is attacked by a guard, Matthias comes to her rescue. With the Dróttning's consent, he moves her to a private room, where he demands that Dani convince Vulryn to eat gruel that the dragon refuses to touch. Dani learns that the gruel—which Vulryn calls "slop"—is made from a plant in Njordheim and that those who eat are pliable, subject to even the most extreme demands from their leader. Vulryn pretends to eat the slop, ultimately convincing the Dróttning that Vulryn is now in her control and can be trusted to fly with her drake.

In Revalle, Mikkael encounters Ziselær and feels compelled to follow him. They find each other in a park, where Mikkael realizes that he's fated to ride the blue dragon. Ziselær's rider, Matthias, orders his dragon to kill Mikkael but Ziselær refuses (which we'll later learn is because his pairing with Vulryn pleases the dragon, and he doesn't want to harm his draikana by killing her rider's fated mate—yes, Mikkael). Mikkael tries to get Dani out of his mind but he can't. He decides to leaves Revalle behind in search of the plant the Dróttning uses to create slop, which Bevin thinks might be found in Vanatia.

Vulryn and Ziselær fly to the cove where the dragons encountered each other. Vulryn contacts Astarot and Tindera, asking them to come and stand with her when she leaves Ziselær. Matthias and his dragon fight to force Dani and Vulryn to leave and Matthias is injured in the process. He and Ziselær have no choice but to stay, and Dani and Vulryn decide to join them. Dani and Matthias grow closer as he heals—a more gentle male emerging when he's away from the Dróttning—leading to an intimate connection between the riders.

When Dani and Vulryn leave the cove, Matthias and Ziselær join them. After offering penance to Khirta for the harm he caused her, Ziselær and his rider travel with the group of rebels. But to Matthias's disgust, they encounter Mikkael trapped by a ferocious ghost pig. Ziselær saves Mikkael, who joins their group long enough to drop him off somewhere safe. Matthias's old, cruel self starts to emerge, leading to conflict between Dani and Matthias. Before the group can drop off Mikkael, an earthquake drags him and Dani into an underground cavern. They grow closer as they spend time together, while Toffer helps them find a way out. Still, when they emerge, Dani immediately leaves Mikkael's side to go to Matthias.

The group is attacked by the Dróttning's dragons as they travel to a place to leave Mikkael, leading Matthias to abandon them. Khirta is killed, devastating everyone, but the others survive. Dani assumes Matthias left because he doesn't want the Dróttning to know his loyalty is wavering, but when the cruel rider returns to his liege, we learn that he betrayed the rebels, advising the Dróttning about when to attack. He had a moment of weakness in the cove but realized when he returned to Vanatia that his loyalty is to the Dróttning. He punishes Ziselær for the dragon's weakness toward Vulryn—something he does regularly, we learn—by carving off the beast's wingtips.

The rebels join with others who've broken the Dróttning's control by pretending to eat the slop and attack the dragon "training" grounds to free the beasts chained there. Matthias appears during that assault, revealing his commitment to the Dróttning. He commands Ziselær to land when he realizes Mikkael is there and the males fight. When he orders the dragon to kill Mikkael, Ziselær is forced to decide between fate and the Dróttning. He chooses fate, killing Matthias. But his connection to the cruel male was too strong to go unscathed. Matthias's death shatters him. The dragon rejects Mikkael, angry at his fate-chosen rider, grabs Matthias's body and flies away.

Ziselær isn't the only one who hurts Mikkael. Although Mikkael was injured in his fight, when Ziselær killed Matthias, Dani went to the dead male. The pain of those rejections devastate Mikkael and he pushes Dani away when she tries to comfort him. They leave the training grounds successful in their mission, taking most of the dragons with them.

Mikkael's victory, though, is more bitter than sweet. He leaves knowing he'll never have the dragon or mate fate chose for him.

CHAPTER ONE

DANI

WE FLEE

*T*HEY COME.

Vulryn's unexpectedly worried voice pulls me out of a dream I wish I didn't remember. I hate that Mikkael sneaks into my head at night. *Who comes?* I ask when I'm awake enough to focus my thoughts.

The wyrm's soldiers approach. The snow dragon found them as she flew watch. She and her rider race back to the cavern now. Our male is deciding whether we will fight or flee.

I yank on my clothes under the covers then throw my blankets off, standing to start shoving everything into my packs as I look up. If Vulryn hadn't woken me, I wouldn't have any idea what's going on.

Everyone moves in silence, as if they're afraid noise will draw our attackers here more quickly.

Does Mikkael know? Is he up yet? My thoughts spear toward Vulryn as I stride to her and start strapping on our packs.

The sun beast wakes him now.

And Toffer and Thor?

I woke the troll.

Before you woke me?

The feline grows ... frustrated ... when he is forced to move too quickly in the morning. The troll needed extra time to prepare him.

I can't help myself. I tighten the final strap and then stalk to Vulryn's front to stare her down. *You woke the troll first so the cat wouldn't be grumpy?*

The feline is a ferocious beast, she reminds me with a huff, her gaze flicking toward the pissy little cat for a moment. *We all suffer when the feline is unhappy.*

Well, fuck me. I've never heard of anything as ridiculous in my life as a troll and a bunch of grown-ass dragons catering to a gods-damned cat.

They come, Vulryn repeats, lifting her eyes toward the kitchen gear that still needs to be packed as her tail whips back and forth. *I will carry more.*

We're not done talking about this. You can't let a little cat push you all around.

They come, she says one more time, a puff of smoke spouting through her teeth.

Fine, I say as I pat her snout. *I'll pack but we'll talk about this again.*

She tosses her head but can't seem to stop herself from glancing at the precocious cat with the barest smile.

My dragon is pussy-whipped, I realize with a laugh as I head to the makeshift kitchen and start packing.

"Fhord doesn't want to fight," Sifa tells me as she strides over. "We're going deeper into the cavern. He thinks that's the safest option. Once we leave the caves, we'll split up. When they're healthy enough, I'll enter each of their minds to confirm we can trust them, and we'll send them to Lumaria. They'll all be suffering soon without the slop. The water should help them get through it."

"How in all the worlds are we going to move through Vanatia with this many people? And dragons?"

Sifa smiles as she surveys the massive cavern around us. It's the group we started with—Mikkael, Sifa, Fhord, Toffer, Thor, our dragons, plus the four new dragons and riders who joined us right before the attack—along with more than a dozen beasts who followed us from the training grounds. Half of them are badly injured, and it's a miracle they made it this far. But they did, and they'll be with us as long as they need to recover.

"Carefully," she responds at last.

"Why don't we go north, to the pool near the border?"

"Fhord and Tindera flew up to see if it's safe and almost got caught. The Dróttning has too many patrols flying in that area." Sifa's whispering now and I realize I should have done the same. She doesn't know yet that we can trust all the beasts who joined us. "We can't risk leading them there and being seen."

"Why would the wyrm waste resources patrolling the border? If the Monarch sends someone across, a dragon won't notice a random soldier."

"Fhord suspects it's because of your dragon," Sifa tells me with a smile. "Vulryn is fucking with the Dróttning's mind. She's terrified of another northern beast coming here and adding to the chaos yours has already created."

Vulryn's purr drops into my thoughts, a mix between a growl and a hum that erupts from her when she's particularly pleased. I spin my head to look at her because it's the first sign I've had of a break in the miserable mood she's been in since Ziselær left. *You deserve to be proud of yourself, my magnificent dragon.*

The wyrm knows I am her greatest threat. As she should. But there are no other beasts like me in the north.

Of course not. It's still nice to have her so afraid of the possibility.

"Vulryn appreciates the wyrm's fear," I relay to Sifa with a smirk, "although she's convinced no other dragon in Njordheim could fuck with Vanatia the way she has."

"I've no doubt of that. Your dragon is singular. Thank the gods."

"Thank the gods, indeed." I glance toward the tunnel we're about to follow. "Fhord was captured and Johan died the last time we tried hiding from the Dróttning in a cave. Why does he think this will be better?"

Sifa sucks in a deep breath, glancing at Mikkael as her eyes start to water. She stares at him for a few seconds, her hands growing still, before shaking her head and looking down again to focus on the things we're packing.

"Sorry," I mutter, dragging my gaze away from my fiercely handsome mate, the muscles in his broad chest rippling beneath his tunic as he lifts a large pack onto a dragon. His long dark hair is tied back with a leather strap, like always, a single rebellious lock falling onto his tawny skin. My fingers itch to tuck it behind his ear. Focusing on what matters, though, I turn back to my friend. She loved Johan as much as she does Mikkael. "I shouldn't bring up Johan's death like that," I add with a grimace.

"No, you're right. It was bad last time. This cavern plummets, though. Fhord can stick with us as we all descend. We'll get far enough away that the Dróttning won't be able to sense him. That's the hope, at least."

"Can everyone make it? Some of the dragons had a tough time getting here."

"That's why we can't fight. They're better but still too injured for combat and we don't have enough beasts to defend them and ourselves. This is our best option." She pauses, her gaze finding mine for a moment. "There is a potential problem, though. Toffer thinks part of the path is treacherous, especially for the dragons because of their weight in an area too narrow for them to fly. He's not sure yet what we'll find. It's still what we need to do."

"Alrighty, then." We can deal with a treacherous path if it gets us too far away from the Dróttning to be tracked. *We flee,* I tell Vulryn, glancing at her. She's next to Toffer and Thor, the cat glaring at my dragon as Toffer murmurs something in his ear. Vulryn's tongue reaches out to try to caress the little monster but he slashes at her, nails fully extended, with a hiss. *Why's he being such a dick?*

The feline is grumpy. The troll will help settle him before we must leave.

Grown-ass dragons tip-toeing around a little cat. Ridiculous.

It only takes a few more minutes to pull everything together. The injured dragons won't carry supplies but the rest have split our gear between them. The three extra sheep we herded into the cavern last night will go with us to feed the most desperate along the way. They'll need more than this but it's all we've got. Hopefully, Toffer can lead us to an exit within a few days.

The first few hours are fairly easy. We're following a steady slope down in caverns large enough for two dragons to walk side-by-side. The injured dragons move at a decent speed, only occasionally pausing to catch their breath or rest tattered wings. All the beasts from the training grounds are clustered in the center, and I suspect they're sticking together to support each other. Vulryn says they created a strong bond in their shared misery.

Fhord's thoughts constantly billow out—probably searching for hints the Dróttning is following us—but he doesn't seem worried yet. Toffer drops to the ground every ten or fifteen minutes, digging his hands into the earth or resting them on the rock beneath our feet, then mumbling to himself about something as he stands and continues leading us forward.

My mind isn't so disciplined. It keeps dredging up images of Mikkael during those final minutes in the cave—reminding me of everything he suffered and how badly I fucked up when I ignored him and went to Matthias. I've made a lot of mistakes and have a ton of regrets, but I don't think I'll ever forgive myself for that one.

"Are you okay?" Sifa's soft voice drags my gaze toward her, away from the grieving male I didn't realize I was staring at. I was so lost in my thoughts, I didn't notice her walking over to me.

As I look up, though, I see what everyone else does. Mikkael's eyes, sharp as glass and dark as obsidian, stare at me from the other side of the cavern. The emotions that cascade through me at his hatred just add to the rock that's been sitting in my stomach since we left the training grounds. The others in the cave look between us, their glances never lasting more than a few seconds whenever they land on one of us.

"Do you think he'll ever come back?" I ask. I don't have to tell her who the "he" is. We both know it could only be the heartbroken dragon who's fucking with everyone's moods.

"Eventually. Whatever happened with Matthias, Vulryn and Ziselær still belong together. He won't be able to stay away. Even if right now he'd rather turn his back on everything and everyone. Especially his rider. I think Mikkael is almost as devastated as his dragon."

My gaze lifts for the quickest second, searching for my mate. I'm always looking for him. I wish I could stop but I can't. "And then I made it worse, going to Matthias instead of Mikkael."

"I've wondered about that. You must have sensed that Mikkael was hurt. Why did you go to Matthias?"

Shaking my head, I glance at him again, then focus on my feet. Anything to stop myself from staring at the male who despises me. "I didn't realize he was hurt," I tell her at last. "You know how it is with our dragons and our mates and their mates. All the emotions are fucking confusing. Add to that an extra rider for Ziselær and that dragon's tortured feelings about both males. I had an overload of chaotic emotions bouncing around in me."

"So, you didn't know Matthias had stabbed Mikkael?"

"I had not a single gods-damned idea. I wish I'd known. Maybe I'd have reacted differently and he wouldn't hate me quite so much." Sighing, I find myself looking up yet again at the sable eyes still glaring at me. I hold his gaze as I tell Sifa, "I suspect he was so focused on Ziselær, he didn't even think about his own pain. I'd have at least gotten echoes of the agony he must've been in if it dominated his thoughts."

"And you felt Ziselær's pain over Matthias." It's not a question. She knows the answer.

"I couldn't feel anything else. From the moment Matthias demanded Mikkael's death, Ziselær's conflict raged through his draikana. We nearly lost our own battle because Vulryn was so torn and preoccupied." The memory washes through me, spawning a host of butterflies in my stomach, just as it does every time I think about it. "Maybe if we'd been able to break away, we could have stopped it."

"This was going to happen," Sifa growls, her hand capturing my cheek to swing my gaze toward her. "One of them had to die, and Ziselær alone could make that choice. When he chose to let Mikkael live in Revalle, he forged this path for himself."

"There must have been another way. We could have figured something out."

"Stop telling yourself that." Sifa's voice is firm, commanding. "Maybe if Matthias really had changed, they'd have found a way to live together. But Matthias was a lying bastard. He tolerated Mikkael while he had to, so he could pretend to be sympathetic to us. Once he abandoned that charade, he didn't have any reason to let Mikkael live. His loyalty to the Dróttning—and his own overblown ego—demanded Mikkael's death. It was *always* going to be Mikkael or Matthias."

I nod, letting her words sink in. She's right. Matthias is the one who made Ziselær's impossible choice inevitable. And I can't deny that Ziselær chose right. My stomach clenches a bit as I let the thought settle in my gut—because Vulryn's drake may never recover from this trauma—but it's true. Mikkael may be an asshole, but he's a far better male than Matthias was. If Ziselær ever forgives himself and embraces his bond, he'll be happier than he could have been with the Dróttning's cruel and abusive lackey.

"Still doesn't make it any easier," I say at last.

We trudge along in silence after that. Hours later, we reach the part Toffer felt from our cavern, with a slope so steep, it's practically a cliff. Fhord tosses a torch down—which falls a long time—to give us a better view. It's too narrow for the dragons' wings to extend and several of the newcomers wouldn't be able to fly anyway. We'll be scrambling our way down.

How are we going to protect the dragons with injuries? They can't make it down this.

Help, Vulryn responds vaguely.

I spin to look at her. *And?* She's usually more talkative.

You will see, she tells me, her voice dismissive as she moves toward the other dragons.

Shaking my head, I watch as the dragons reposition themselves, the larger healthy dragons moving to spots just behind each of the injured beasts, Vulryn among them. There are bigger dragons than my beast but none with her strength and resolve. Whatever they plan to do, there's no way she'd be left out. And then Fhord and the other riders—everyone but Sifa and me—start to tie cords between them.

"Fhord says they've done this before," Sifa tells me as she appears by my side, gesturing toward Astarot and the enormous gray dragon they're tying him to. "It's one of the things they practice in training, for some reason."

"I guess it'll work. But why is Vulryn joining if she hasn't trained on it?"

Sifa barks out a laugh, one eyebrow jutting up as she stares at my dragon. "Because your dragon does whatever the fuck she wants to do. She won't be included among the weaker dragons, who aren't helping the others."

"Of course she won't."

"But you know that, better than anyone."

"That I do." I watch her for a moment, a bit of relief filtering through me as I see hints of the old Vulryn in her raised snout and firm stance. "She likes being useful. After all those years alone, she wants to be everything to everyone. I think she's afraid the others will turn on her if she's not enough—although she'd never admit it, and she'd be very angry with me if she knew I'd just suggested that to you."

"I'll never tell her," Sifa assures me with a smile. "You should know by now, though, that you're both part of us. We're not letting you go, no matter what you do or don't do."

"Even if Mikkael and I never find a way to tolerate each other? He's been your friend for a long time."

"He's one of my best friends and always will be. I hope you two work it out. I've come to believe the fates know what they're doing. Fhord and Astarot are as perfect for me as any two males could be. The gods may be assholes..."

"That they are," I interject with a laugh.

"They really are," she responds with a smirk. "The fates, though ... I think they've planned a better world. Maybe if we're really lucky, this is all coming together at the right time. Maybe we can fix this fucked up land for everyone, or at least, make it better." Her smile as she says this is effervescent, full of light and joy.

"I think you should let this thing between you and Mikkael play out," she adds. "But know that I would never push one of you away because of the other. Even if you don't accept your mating bond, you'll figure out how to exist with each other in your lives. And you'll both always have a place in ours."

Something in me settles with her words, a knot unfurling deep in my gut. I've gotten close enough to Sifa to know she feels this way, but hearing her say it helps. Vulryn would never forgive me if I did something to fuck up this family she's found. I don't think I'd forgive myself either.

"They're ready," Sifa tells me as she points her chin toward the dragons preparing to descend.

"Do we just slip-slide along behind them?"

She nods. "They'll descend before us so they don't take anyone out if they start to fall. It's too far to go down individually, and we don't want to split up for that long. Fhord and I can sense beings of some kind beneath us, in a lower cavern. Toffer can't find any pathways between here and there, so he's confident they can't get to us, but we're still concerned enough to want to stay together as a group to the extent we can. The dragons decided on an order, with the weakest beasts—those most likely to slip—going first. Fingers crossed it works."

They stride into place, Astarot last in the line of dragons, Vulryn and her partner fourth, and Tindera with her beast at the beginning. She's beginning to feel the effects from not eating the Dróttning's mash and worried about her strength if her dragon slips. Even with that, though, she's one of the strongest dragons.

I don't know if I've ever been so nervous about something my dragon does. The slope is intense, and they struggle to get down it. As they descend, the weaker beasts keep losing their footing, often dragging along the other for a male's-height or more as they try to slow down. Tindera and her partner nearly are taken out by the beasts who go behind them, sliding more than a dragon's-length while struggling to find a grip.

My stomach clenches when it's Vulryn's turn. The beige dragon she's helping, Akupa, drags herself up and stumbles to the path as Vulryn whispers encouraging words to her. I feel Vulryn's confidence as they start their descent. It's a boldness that many would call arrogance, but I know is my beast's way of drawing from the strength she's always needed to survive.

Four different times, Akupa stumbles and falls forward, with Vulryn straining to stop the two of them from tumbling down the slope. Each time, I can feel stabbing pain from where the bindings wrap around my dragon's shoulders and legs, digging past her feathers to embed in her skin. Before they're halfway down, Vulryn's bleeding in a few places, splatters of her resolve dripping to the rock below.

They're more than three-fourths of the way down when Akupa slides too hard and fast for Vulryn to control. I can only watch, my stomach flinging itself into my throat, as Vulryn loses her fight to stop Akupa's tumble, and they drop together the ten or twelve dragon's-lengths to the bottom. But they don't stop there. The ground beneath them collapses. Both dragons disappear as they fall to the cavern below.

I don't think. I barely breathe. Before I've even willed them to go, my feet are flying toward the slope and I'm sliding down it. Astarot reaches out his tail to slow my fall as I slip past him, but he doesn't try to stop me, thank the gods. I'd hate to stab Sifa's dragon, but I would if I had to. I'm tumbling by the time I get to the bottom but I don't give a fuck.

I do have the presence of mind to shift away from the gaping hole that sucked in Vulryn and Akupa, throwing myself to the side at the last minute. I slide another dragon's-length or more, the momentum from my fall too much to slow quickly, and barrel into a wall on the far side of the cavern.

Fuck me. I hurt everywhere.

My thoughts spear out, finding my battered dragon and confirming she still lives. My gut churns a little less, but my *need* to see her is visceral—a living thing that writhes inside me. I push myself up enough to look around and realize I have no idea how I'll ever move again. Every single part of me aches.

That was so gods-damned stupid.

Vulryn would haul me back from Helheim and kill me herself if I let myself die from slipping down a hill.

"Dani, are you okay?" Mikkael's bellow breaks through the fog in my head as I pull myself up into a seated position.

"All good," I rasp out, somehow lifting a hand to wave at the riders peering at me from the top of the cliff.

Tindera stalks forward—freed from the bindings somehow—and nudges at my side, extending her snout toward my arm.

"She'll help you stand," Fhord shouts at me, a chuckle in his voice he doesn't try to hide. "You're gonna need help after that disaster."

"Thanks, asshole," I gripe under my breath, drawing a snort that sounds a lot like a laugh from his dragon. "You know it too. I love your rider, but he can be a real dick."

Tindera spits out another snort, her tongue reaching out to gently lick my arm, and pokes me with her snout again.

"Okay, okay. I'm getting up. Just give me a second here."

I grasp a few of her feathers, my side blossoming with pain as I do, and drag myself up slowly.

Are you okay? I've gathered my thoughts enough to reach out to my dragon.

The sand beast's wings are injured. She will not be able to fly up.

Is there a way for you to get back up here?

I believe so. I will need light to assess. But the sand beast will not be able to fly. The others will need to come here. We will find our path out from this cavern.

I'm coming to look. We'll talk to Fhord and Toffer about it once they get down here and can see for themselves.

I lean on Tindera as she leads me forward, watching from the corner of my eye as Astarot makes his way down the slope. The fifth pair are just getting to the bottom, skirting around the massive hole created by Vulryn and Akupa's fall, to join the other dragons on the far side of the cavern. Tindera pauses two male's-heights from the hole, shifting her chin to urge me forward without her.

"She's worried about the ground near the hole," Fhord yells down. "We don't need another dragon dropping in before we decide what to do."

I nod with a muttered "Thanks" to the sun beast and stumble forward a few steps—because holy fuck, do I hurt—before dropping to my knees to crawl the rest of the way.

"What do you see?" Sifa's worry seeps into her words, which quiver just a bit.

"Not much yet," I shout back. "It's dark. I need more light." They're starting to come down the slope but taking longer than I did—because they're not reckless idiots like me—and I'm too anxious to wait for them to get here.

Dragging myself to my feet, the pain receding a bit as my body finally gets its shit together and starts to heal itself, I lurch toward Tindera to dig into her pack for the torches Fhord stowed there. Then I drag my ass back across the cavern to the flame Fhord threw down and back to the hole. Within a few minutes that feel like an hour, I'm laying at the edge watching light drop into the cavern, my heart sinking as I realize Vulryn's right. There's no way Akupa could get back up here.

Vulryn could fly, although it would be close getting through the hole. Akupa wouldn't be able to follow her. The beige dragon's wings already were badly injured, but they're worse now. One is bent nearly in half. I'd be screaming in pain if it were me, but she's stoic, her snout a thin line, eyes dull. The other's a little better but not much. She'll need to heal a few days, at least, before she can fly again.

And there's no way to climb back. The cliff Vulryn mentioned only rises half the distance. Even if Akupa could drag herself up it, she'd be stuck there.

"Fuck," Sifa groans as she kneels beside me, Mikkael dropping onto his belly on her other side. "We're going down there, aren't we?"

"Will everyone be able to make it? Looks big enough for them to extend their wings, but I don't know if all the dragons can fly."

"They can make it," Fhord answers as he lays down next to me. "Only two have injured wings, but none as bad as Akupa. That fall really fucked her up. Their wings might not be able to lift them, but they can extend far enough to slow their descent after they drop into the hole."

"So we go down?" I ask. "Continue our trip from there?"

"I don't see another way," Sifa agrees. "We're not leaving Akupa behind and we can't get split up."

Is the cavern big enough for all of us?

It is large. It will hold us.

And there's a way out?

Three tunnels lead from this cave.

Please move to the side and ask Akupa to do the same. We're coming down. Toffer will figure out where we go next once he's down there.

Vulryn shifts closer to Akupa, positioning herself under the beige dragon's most damaged wing to lift it as they move, while I look for Tindera to ride down with Fhord. In a few moments, they're out of our way and we're assembled by the hole. And then we start dropping in, the stronger dragons going first to hover in case one of the injured dragons isn't able to fly down. They make it, though. Barely thirty minutes after Vulryn and Akupa fell into the hole, we're all with them, Toffer's hands digging into the ground as he reads the cave around us.

We don't expect the net that drops onto our entire group, trapping us beneath a material so heavy, I don't think even the dragons could lift it away from us. I plunge to the ground, a gust of air rasping out of me as I try to budge the weight digging into my back. But I can't move. I can't even lift my head to look at whatever or whoever is cackling from the cliff high above our group.

Worse—much, much worse—I can't push myself away from Mikkael, who somehow landed beneath me, his harsh breaths tickling the skin on my neck as he stares at me with a mix of anger and desire in his black eyes.

Chapter Two

Mikkael

A Mind of Its Own

Of course, Dani landed right on top of me when the net crashed down on us.

I've spent this entire trip keeping my distance. I can't be near her. It fucks with me because my body responds to my mate, even as my brain reminds me of her betrayal. That she chose the traitor. That she will never be mine. But she fell, and my *need* to check on her pulled me to her side along with Sifa. Then, I had to walk past her as I was trying to get to the other side of the cavern and at that very moment, something tossed an impossibly heavy net on top of us.

Fuck if I'm not getting hard, just feeling her body lying across mine.

"Really, Mikkael?" she demands in a voice loud enough for everyone to hear, breaking the shocked silence around us. "We're trapped by who knows what and your cock's decided to make an appearance? Now?"

"Bastard has a mind of his own," I growl, the blood rushing into my cheeks. "How the fuck do we get out of here?"

"You don't," the asshole laughing at us declares. "That iron heeds my command. It could control Jörmungandr if he ventured into these caves."

"You don't know who you're fucking with," Fhord snarls from a few feet away. "Release us. Now."

"I know your name, dragon rider," the stranger tells him. "The iron speaks to me and I listen. You are the sole son of the witch who rules the land—the secret she's spent three centuries hiding because of your elven father. Nothing escapes the minerals that live in these rocks. And those minerals hide nothing from me."

I hear a few gasps at his words but can't lift my head enough to look. It must be the riders who joined us recently. Almost nobody knew about Fhord's connection to the Dróttning before he revealed it to us in Lumaria.

Dani's trying to shift away from me—driving even more blood into the cock that really wants her to stay—but even that is nearly impossible with the net splayed across us. I leverage myself to shove out from beneath her, struggling for a few seconds before I manage to put some space between us.

Thank fuck. Because I would have burst—in the most embarrassing way possible—if she'd stayed on top of me any longer.

"About time," she murmurs as she tries to push herself even farther away, creating as much of a gap as possible.

"I wasn't going to bite you," I mutter as the part of me that craves our mating bond flares—the loss of her body on top of mine opening a chasm in my gut—and the dull ache of rejection reminds me to reinforce the wall I've built between us.

"It's just ... tough ... to be so close to you," she tells me, her eyes growing soft for a moment.

The response that starts to bubble out of me—an apology I don't want to let myself voice—is cut off as Sifa cries out, surprise and a hint of anger in her voice.

"What did you do, dwarf?"

"Stay out of my thoughts, elf. I won't be swayed by your mind tricks."

"Then don't give me reason," Sifa demands. "I won't be so gentle next time, and you won't be able to withstand me. Tell us what you want, why you've trapped us."

"You come into my caves—my home—and dare to ask what I want?" His voice is shrill now, anger warbling the last few words. As he speaks, the net tightens around us, squeezing everyone together. I feel it tugging me closer to Dani, her arm digging into mine as the net tries to force her on top of me again. And I realize that if it gets much tighter, I won't be able to breathe.

But I can't bring myself to give a fuck whether I live or die. All I can think about is Dani and our dragons. My heart is clenching even more tightly than this trap, the realization that they've had hardly any time together buckling the hate and anger I've worked so hard to fortify.

I'll never find the kind of happiness they have, but that's how it should be. I don't deserve it. I hurt Z and I will suffer whatever punishment the fates dole out. It kills me, though, that Dani and Vulryn are going to die having spent so little time with each other and Z. That their vast love for each other—Vulryn's utter devotion to her rider and my dragon—will disappear as if it never existed.

It seems profane, ungodly, for the gods to be able to snuff out flames that burn so brightly.

"I want you not to have come," the evil dwarf continues, the pitch of his voice rising with every word as the net continues to crush us. The dragons start to keen, even their strength no match for the iron as it heeds the dwarf's commands. "I want my caves to be undisturbed by the evil witch who rules the bright spaces above." He's silent for a moment, then adds in a low tone that somehow bounces off the walls, "I want the death of the witch and all of her coven. And I'll start with you."

"We are on your side," Sifa chokes out, each word a struggle. "We're working to defeat the Dróttning. Free us so we can follow the path the fates have set for us."

"Liars," he yells, his tone somehow even more piercing. "You came to my cave with the witch's spawn and here you will stay until Hel opens her gates to you."

"Have you never betrayed a being who shared your blood because you discovered and despised their evil?" Sifa's voice is a whisper now, but she still finds the strength to imbue it with persuasion. I've heard her use this approach on humans, but not one of this land's magical beings. "No son or brother to whom you swore allegiance, but then were compelled to drive your blade into his back?"

"I told you to stop, elf. I will not say it again."

"I will not be silent," she bellows, the net responding with a clench that feels like punishment, every part of me being compressed into itself. I inhale sharply, wondering if it'll be my last, as Sifa somehow finds the strength to continue. "You've trapped us, and now you demand our silent surrender? I know your name. I know your story. And I tell you, we are allies in our fight against the Dróttning."

"You do not know my name." His response is indignant, each syllable warbling through the cave around us. The net clings even more tightly, digging into my skin to draw out little crimson drops, which splatter to the ground next to me.

"You are Mótsognir, the father of the dwarfs," she breathes, her voice wavering, "and you've been separated from Niðavellir for too many centuries to count. You've survived here, far from Asgard and Yggdrasil's magic, for all those years. I too come from those worlds. I've walked Niðavellir's dark fields, but I can't return to them either."

Our captor gasps at Sifa's words—the net pausing and releasing enough to let me breathe—and then is silent for a long time. Finally, his words float through the air. "How can you know this? None in this land hold such knowledge."

"I'm not of this land, either. I'm of Álfheimr but I've walked through Asgard, Niðavellir, Midgard, and the other worlds. For ten years, I've searched for a way home. Do you seek a path back to the dark fields?"

"I've been here too long to return. But I would know what became of my sons and daughters. Do they thrive?"

"Free us. Let me tell you what I know."

Again, Mótsognir's response is slow in coming. But the net isn't compressing farther. I can breathe freely and might be able to move if I tried. When the dwarf answers Sifa, his voice holds an uncertainty I haven't heard from him before. "You intrigue me, elf. I would speak with you." He pauses once more, the silence growing heavier with each second. "Are there others who come from our worlds? Midgard, perhaps?"

"The troll who travels with us is from Midgard, and I spent many years in that world. Perhaps you sense its influence on me."

"No," he declares sharply. "I recognize the troll, but there is another. You will tell me who or I will crush you all."

"Me," I announce, the word leaking out of me before I even realize I've spoken. I'm not sure why—I've never considered the possibility that I came from another land—but as I speak the word, its truth washes over me. "I don't belong here either," I tell him. "I can't remember my childhood, and I have no idea how I got here, but I'm certain I was born and lived the first half of my life in another world."

"You shall come with me," he proclaims, his voice a little closer than it was before I spoke. "Know, though, that if you test me, my iron will stop you. You have no power here sufficient to defeat me."

Before I can acknowledge his words, the iron shifts, links releasing each other and pulling back to reconnect beneath me.

A shiver rolls through me. That was some creepy shit. And then my gaze falls to my mate.

"She comes too."

I have no gods-damned idea why those words just spilled out of my mouth. I hate Dani. I don't *want* her to come. But the part of me that won't stay buried—the bond that pulses deep inside and *needs* her to be safe—can't stand the idea of leaving her trapped here.

"I will not kill them. Yet." The dwarf's voice echoes through the chamber and I spin to look at him, at last. He's taller than I would have expected—perhaps Sifa's height—and as thick as the stumps of the trees that grow in the northern forests. With hair as black and shiny as the stones they quarry near the border to Njordheim and skin as pale as the winter snow, he looks like one of the specters that haunts children's dreams.

His clothes are surprising—a dark tunic and thick trousers, probably wool, held up by thin leather strips over his shoulders. He's had enough contact with humans to wear clothes I could buy in any town across Vanatia.

It's his eyes, though, that capture my attention. They're as red as my blood. And I can see them clearly, despite the darkness enveloping us, because they glow as bright as the sky over the ocean when the sun falls beneath its waves. I want to look away, but I can't. I'm mesmerized by his gaze.

"Come," he beckons, stirring my legs, which start to pick their way through the bodies around me, moving in his direction.

"What the fuck? What are you doing to me?" I can't keep the tremble from my voice because seriously, what the fuck?! I spin my head to find Dani, still bothered with the idea of leaving her behind, but she nods at me, her chin dropping just a bit beneath the weight of the net.

"Just go with it, Mik," Sifa tells me as she reaches my side, Toffer right behind her. "She'll be fine, and we'll be better once we get away from the net."

"How do you know she'll be okay?" I cringe as I hear a tremble in my voice, my irrational fear of leaving Dani behind on display. Because I can't control shit where she's concerned.

"He's not going to hurt us. I promise."

She's so certain. Her words settle my nerves, and I'm able to drag my gaze away from the female I don't want to give a shit about. Instead, I force my thoughts to focus on something else.

"The iron's doing this?" I murmur, unsure if we should let the dwarf hear my question.

"Dwarf magic runs through the metals they manipulate," she tells me, her voice normal. "Iron's always been a favorite because it can hold and wield so much power. This dwarf is very strong."

"How do you know this?"

She turns to me, a smile brightening her face. "I remember all you've forgotten from our worlds, although if you lived only in Midgard, you probably never knew of the magic of the other worlds."

"And you did?"

"I'm an elf and I've lived a long time. I know dwarf magic well."

"And him? How did you know his name?"

"That was a guess, although I had some information to guide me. The peek I got into his mind before he shoved me out hinted that he ruled Niðavellir centuries ago. With the other creatures from our worlds starting to show up here, I'm beginning to see that this world's been connected to ours in more ways than I realized."

"That massive eagle that plucked us off Astarot, and the wolf who took Thor?"

"That's them," she tells me before growing quiet, turning all her focus to the dwarf. We reach the edge of the net—my legs finally becoming mine again—and stride toward the dwarf.

And then he smiles—his teeth misshapen and yellow like an overripe banana—and really creeps me out. "Elf," he says to Sifa, holding her gaze. He hasn't acknowledged me yet, but I'm good with that. I hope he ignores me completely.

"Dwarf," Sifa responds, no hint of fear in her voice or her gaze.

"How did you come to this world?"

"I've spent the last ten years trying to figure that out," she tells him with a shrug, "although I've realized recently that I'm asking the wrong question."

His eyes brighten, a smirk lifting his lips. "And what question should you have been asking?"

"How did the Dróttning get here?"

I feel my eyebrows lift because that is a gods-damned good question. I've been around Sifa and the others long enough to realize that nothing else in this world has the kind of magic the Dróttning and Fhord do. She must be from Sifa's world ... and mine, I know now.

"That is an important question," he tells her with a nod. "But not quite right."

"No? What do you think I should ask?"

"I believe we must ask what gives her power. But first, tell me what you know of the dark fields."

"Will we return to our questions?"

I sure as fuck hope so. This weird dwarf may hold pieces of the puzzle that formed in my mind when I realized I'm from Midgard too. Like how in Helheim did I get drawn here? If I'm just human, why do I have a mate and a dragon? And does this mean I have magic too?

"I may give you some answers," he responds as his lips lift into a smirk, "if I decide to let you live."

"You won't kill me or mine." Sifa's voice is steel, her shoulders thrown back as she glares at the dwarf. "I'm more dangerous than I look. But I'll humor you because we want the same thing. What do you need to realize I speak true?"

"I can sense your home. I know you are not of this world. And that they are not," he adds with a quick nod toward Toffer and me. "Yet you brought the witch's spawn and beasts who have fought her battles into my cave. Why shouldn't I kill you?" Now his gaze is focused on Fhord. If he could spit flames from his eyes, Fhord would be burnt to a crisp already.

"He's mine," Sifa barks, moving to stand between the dwarf and Fhord, drawing his attention back to her. "He rejected the Dróttning and fights with those who rebel against her. Even before me, though, he worked behind her back. He created a place for rebels to meet and plan. He's been trying to defeat her for years."

"You are his mate?"

"I am."

"And do you ride the red dragon?"

"I do."

He leans forward, his scarlet eyes piercing as they study Sifa's face. "Has the time come, then?"

"What time is that, dwarf?"

"The time to liberate this land."

"What do you see?"

"I see a melange of paths from here, an ever-shifting array of options. Evil has gripped this land for too many years, and it may yet prevail. But in every path that leads to the witch's defeat, you walk with your dragon and another I do not see here. She is silver, young but powerful enough to defeat the witch."

Sifa's quiet for a long time, watching the dwarf with a wrinkled brow, one hand rising to the back of her neck. She knows this silver being well enough to fear for her, and I wonder how many other secrets my friend holds.

"She's not ready yet," Sifa whispers at last, her words barely loud enough to reach my ears, although I'm only a few feet away.

"She will be ready. She must be." The dwarf's gaze hasn't left Sifa's, his eyes little slits of molten lava.

"I won't put her at risk."

"It is your only hope."

"There has to be another way." Sifa's angry now, her tone strident. I'm not sure who she's talking about, but I've never seen her more protective of anyone.

"Have you spoken with Konungr Erik?" His demeanor changes as he asks this, as if he knows something Sifa doesn't.

Sifa's eyebrows slam together at his odd question. "The draugr?" she asks, her voice tight.

"Have you spoken with him?"

"I have. Fhord took me to him shortly after we met. He told me the story of the elven war and the Dróttning's victory." I hear confusion in Sifa's words, a little warble I recognize only because I know her so well.

"And have you talked to him of the silver one?"

"No, why should I discuss her with him? He wouldn't know anything about her."

"He has your trust. I do not and fear you will not heed my advice. You must hear it from someone you know and believe." He turns his intense gaze toward me. "You also need his wisdom," he declares, before looking again at Sifa. "Go to him. Ask about her. And when he tells you, as I have, that she will be ready when the time comes, accept the fates' call. She must be with you. There is no other way."

"What have you seen, dwarf? Me walking with my dragon and the silver one is hardly an answer to my question. You must have seen more."

"I've told you all I can. The rest must come from Konungr Erik. Your destiny will reveal itself in the days ahead if you follow the path the fates demand."

"And why should I trust you, even in this? You hold my people and their beasts captive and speak in riddles."

"I hold your mate because he has served the witch for many years and I do not trust him. But I will free him when I'm sure he can cause me no harm. You believe he stands with you now and I believe you are part of the destiny the fates have planned."

He pauses, stepping closer to Sifa as his gaze grows more intense, his crimson eyes sharp and focused. "I am of the dark fields. You know my kind. You know we long have been friends to the elves. I ache with their misery in this land. Their pain is my pain. I would help you liberate the elves and defeat the witch. And then I can rest."

"Release my friends, then. You have no more reason to hold them."

Mótsognir scoffs, his red eyes flaring. "I may accept that you believe him, but I do not. He has proven nothing to me. I will not give him a chance to turn on me, as the witch does to all who trust her." He throws his shoulders back, his fists clenching. "Tell me of the dark fields and I will go. When you can no longer reach me, I will call back my iron."

Sifa's silent for a few moments, just watching him, until Toffer's voice breaks her out of her reverie.

"Dwarfs dream of destiny," he says in a low voice.

Now it's my turn to scoff. "You don't believe him, do you? You're gonna go chase some draugr—whatever the fuck that is—because he tells you to?"

"Toffer's right," she responds, glancing at me for a second and then back at the dwarf. "Dwarfs can see things we can't. The most powerful dwarfs can see the future, or parts of it. Mótsognir is a powerful dwarf."

"You would do well to trust me. Now tell me of the dark fields, or my iron will start taking lives."

"Stop being dramatic, dwarf," Sifa mutters with a smile. "If you wanted to kill us, you would have already. I will tell you of the dark fields."

"Who rules those lands?"

"Sigurd, the grandson of your grandson Hreidmar, has governed the dark fields for many years. He is a benevolent king and his dwarfs are happy."

"Hreidmar does not live?"

"They gave his body to the forge and he passed into Valhalla during my youth. I don't know how he died."

"But the dark fields thrive?"

"They do. Sigurd is a good dwarf. Your people could have no better leader. They would welcome your return."

"These caves are my home. I have lived here too long to ever return. I will see the elves liberated and then I will give this body to the forge." He spins suddenly, his gaze lifting to the rock above us. "The witch grows near and the rocks between this place and the surface are too thin. She will sense your presence if you linger. When I release my iron, follow the large tunnel to the river that crosses its path. The water will carry you back to the witch's lands."

"I have more questions," she insists. "Like, how have you survived for so long this far away from Yggdrasil?"

"Return when you have defeated the witch," he tells her. "When she no longer lives, we can talk of our homes and the magic this world holds."

Sifa's quiet for a few moments, her gaze never leaving him. Finally, she nods. "Thank you, Mótsognir. We are in your debt."

He lifts his chin, turning to Toffer, me, and then back to Sifa. "Go to Konungr Erik. Trust that the silver dragon will be ready. Free the elves and then return to share your tale. When we've talked, I will finally rest. That is how you will repay me."

He spins but before he can go, I reach out, grasping his arm. "Why did you bring me here with Sifa?"

He inhales deeply, every part of him relaxing as the barest of smiles plays across his lips. "This land called you here, as it did the elf, the troll, and the silver dragon, but Midgard pulses through your veins. Even Asgard lives within you, although you carry but a hint of that magical place. I feel those worlds in you and I am soothed."

I drop my hand, his words echoing through me, and watch as he turns and strides away.

CHAPTER THREE

DANI

LET'S NOT TEST IT

THANK FUCK.

That's the only thing I can think as this gods-damned net finally lifts away, floating through the cavern like a butterfly on the wind. Pushing myself up, my limbs still heavy, I find my gaze drawn to Mikkael, who's striding toward us by Sifa's side, before I look for my dragon. I breathe out a sigh of relief when I see her standing at the edge of our group. Her gaze finds mine, eyes flaring at the indignity of having been trapped by a dwarf.

He was wise to leave before releasing us. I have never tasted dwarf and might have been tempted.

Ick. That dwarf's been alive a very long time. I suspect he'd be tough and gristly.

Most meats improve with age. Perhaps I could catch him still. There's a laugh in her words now as she spins her head to inspect the tunnel he walked into.

Sifa would be angry. She seemed to like him.

The starry female likes everyone. She would forgive me.

Let's not test it.

She huffs, a small burst of flame flickering from her snout, as her eyes narrow. *As you wish*, she says after a moment. She likes to give me these little meaningless victories every once in a while. We both know she wouldn't have chased down the dwarf, but she can pretend she compromised on this the next time she demands my compromise on something that actually matters.

She's crafty like that. My badass bitch of a beast.

Everyone's walking toward Sifa, Mikkael, and Toffer, so I join them as Sifa points toward a large opening to my right. "He said we'll find a river there that will carry us out of the caves."

"And he's sure the Dróttning's getting closer?" Fhord's lips droop on the sides, his head cocked toward Sifa. "I don't sense her and I would if she were near."

"I suspect his senses travel through the rock better than yours. He sounded certain. I think we should follow his advice."

"You don't think he was trying to trick us?"

"I'm sure he wasn't." Sifa's gaze dances across the group, assuring everyone with her bright, clear eyes. "I was in his thoughts long enough before he kicked me out to sense deception if that was his intent. He used the net to protect himself because he hates the Dróttning even more than we do."

"I doubt that," Fhord spits out with a sneer. "Why did he call you up?" he asks as his gaze spins to find Mikkael. "And why haven't you ever told us you're from Midgard, like Sifa? What other secrets are you keeping from us?"

Mikkael lifts his hands, palms up, as he throws back his shoulders. "I didn't even realize it myself. I've told you, I don't remember anything from my childhood, and I've never felt at home here. It's always seemed like I'm different from everyone else. Except Sifa," he adds with a quick grin at her. "It just ... came to me ... when the dwarf asked who else. Fuck if I know why."

"He was probing us as he asked," Sifa explains. "I felt the whisper of his thoughts. He may have triggered a memory you buried a long time ago."

"But why would I have done that? I had a rough child-hood, but everyone in Vanatia's slums does. Nothing bad enough to hide from myself."

"If you'll let me, I'll dig a bit when we get someplace safe. See what I can help you uncover."

"Yeah, maybe. If I'm from a different world, I should figure that shit out. Not that I'd go back," he adds as he glances up at me, almost too quickly to notice. "Z's here, and even if I'll never ride him, I won't leave him."

Sifa turns toward Fhord. "He has the sight and told us some things we should discuss when we get away from here. We need to go see the draugrs again."

"Why would we go back there?"

"Let's talk about it when we're out of here. If the Drót-tning's coming closer, we should go."

Fhord watches her for a moment before dipping his chin. He spins to search for Akupa and then beckons to Tindera to join him as he strides toward the beige beast. Within a minute, the other riders are gathering straps and helping Akupa bind her wings above her so she can walk on her own. She's silent as they work, but pain ripples across her face, her eyes widening at times as her snout sets into a thin line.

This is the dragons' lives in these lands. The Dróttning and the Monarch have destroyed the family structure they all need and crave—in different ways, but just as effectively—and fed them such pain and misery in their efforts to control the majestic beasts that the dragons have learned to accept it. If I wasn't committed to this fight before, I would be now. They deserve to be free.

It doesn't take them long to get Akupa ready to travel. She moves to the front, Vulryn right ahead of her to protect the beige beast from anything they might not expect. Vulryn and Akupa lead the dragons into the tunnel as the rest of us follow along. Soon, I lose most of the dragons to the murk, our torch not bright enough to reach beyond the last few, but I know Vulryn's sharp eyes can pierce the dark cave. She's a constant reassuring presence.

The river is broad, she tells me sooner than I would have expected. I doubt we've walked more than an hour. *And it moves slowly. I will go ahead of the others and determine whether it will be safe for the sand beast.*

Wait until we've caught up, I urge as I quicken my step. *I'll go with you.*

I will go alone and return when I've confirmed the risk of harm is low.

"Stubborn beast," I complain, slowing down to walk with Sifa. "Vulryn found the river and went in. She wants to make sure it doesn't move too fast for Akupa."

"She's going alone?"

"Of course she is. I asked her to wait but Vulryn is not an obedient beast."

Sifa scoffs, glancing my way as she laughs at me. "Thank the gods. The Dróttning's dragons are obedient because they have no choice. Astarot and I debate *everything* and he wins more often than I do."

"Tindera tells me Vulryn's in the river," Fhord bellows as he stalks toward us. "We agreed not to let ourselves be separated."

I shrug, smirking at the uptight male. "Tell her. I tried to stop her, but Vulryn does what she wants to do."

"Is she coming back?"

"That's the plan. Unless something keeps her from returning, she'll be back soon."

She's not back soon. We decide to wait for her because we need to know what to expect. Fhord won't admit it, but he's glad she went. Somebody needed to. Still, I have to talk him out of giving up on Vulryn three different times. I can sense her—I know she's alive and unafraid—but he grows more and more frustrated with the delay.

Finally, I feel her drawing closer. "She's coming," I tell the impatiently brooding bastard.

"It's about gods-damned time," he mutters, staring down-river as Sifa walks up and wraps her arm around his waist.

They're so good together. A little part of me twists knowing I'll never have that, but I shove it down deep inside, hoping it doesn't rear its jealous head again. I've got more than I ever could have hoped for in Vulryn. Anything else is wishful thinking. People like me don't get happily-ever-after.

My dragon's presence—a soft caress across my psyche—reaches me before I see her. She's pleased with herself but hasn't told me why yet. I suspect she figured out something that will help Akupa and the rest of us and is eager to share her news with everyone.

When I see her, I know I'm right. She's got the smug look she gets when she's done something praise-worthy—which, I have to admit, is a lot because my dragon's a badass. She soars into the large cavern and settles next to Fhord and the others, then beckons me over to share her news.

"The river splits in two," I tell them as she fills me in, "and Vulryn followed both branches far enough to figure out that the tunnel on the right leads to a cavern too narrow to get through. The one on the left is wide the whole way, with deep but gentle waters. She didn't sense anything dangerous within it and thinks it'll be safe. Regardless, it's our only option so we need to go left."

Fhord nods and barks out a few orders. The dragons lead the way in the same order—Vulryn at the front again—but with their riders this time. The river is just as gentle as Vulryn reported, a mild current that carries the group with little effort. It would be enjoyable if we weren't running for our lives. And if Mikkael wasn't a few dragons away, avoiding me as stubbornly as I'm avoiding him.

I have no idea how long we've traveled when we start to get hints of our exit. At first, it's elusive. I know we're getting close, but I'm not sure how. The air feels different—a little warmer, perhaps; a bit more humidity pressing against us. When the cave begins to brighten, a soft glow that bounces off the rust and browns lining the walls, I start to feel like I can breathe again.

Finally, the river carries us into a broad lake, its cyan waters lapping against the nearby shore and the distant songs of birds the only sounds that disturb the quiet day. It's calm and peaceful and I feel like the fates may finally be pushing us in the right direction. I could use a little downtime.

Attack! I snap my head up at Vulryn's scream through our bond. My gaze follows hers as it whips to our right, where two enormous dragons are barreling toward us. For a moment, I can't move, ice spearing from my spine into every finger and toe, filling me with a chill so deep, I think I'll never be warm again.

We can't escape her. The Dróttning will always be there, waiting for us to make any mistake.

But that dread lasts just for a moment.

Then I remember who the fuck I am, and that I ride the only beast in either kingdom the wyrm fears.

"Who are they?" I hear myself screaming before I've even decided to ask the question.

"Scatter," Fhord yells, Tindera lifting from the water to move as far away from the plummeting beasts as she can. Astarot follows close on her heels, the others right behind them.

But in their fear for each other, they must have forgotten that Akupa can't fly. Vulryn didn't, and she won't leave a helpless beast to fend for herself. She throws herself directly into the beasts' path, hovering just in front of the beige dragon as she watches the attackers shooting toward us.

What the fuck are you doing? I can't keep the frantic edge from my words.

Would you have me desert the sand beast? She's calm. Of-fucking-course. Nothing frightens my reckless dragon.

No, I tell her, my voice a little more measured. *Just be careful.*

I am always careful.

I scoff—to myself because Vulryn would not appreciate my sentiment—and hold on as she hovers in front of Akupa, watching the plunging pair aiming directly for us. I feel her stiffen beneath me as she prepares for her assault, my body responding as my heart starts to pound in my chest and my hands grow clammy. At the last minute, the first dragon swerves to the right and I find myself too stunned by its beauty—its feathers a mesmerizing blend of silver and gold, shimmering in the soft light—to wonder why.

The second dragon, an enormous black beast, his feathers so dark it seems like even the night would get sucked into them, doesn't veer from his path. Across the shrinking distance, I can see his eyes light up as he focuses on Vulryn, probably realizing he's about to strike one of the Dróttning's greatest enemies.

Out of the corner of my eye, I notice Tindera, Astarot, and a few of the other beasts racing back to join Vulryn in protecting Akupa. Vulryn realizes it too, hissing something at them—probably a command to protect her charge—before giving a huge flap of her wings and throwing herself at the ebony beast.

He didn't expect her attack, and I almost laugh as he spins frantically to the side, trying to escape my dragon. Because she's already established that she's the baddest beast in this land. Vulryn twists with him, shooting directly for his neck. The other dragon turns at the last minute, though, barely avoiding her strike. And then he uses a maneuver these southern beasts must have learned from Vulryn, ungrateful bastards.

Flipping in the air, he positions himself perfectly to dig his claws into the bases of Vulryn's wings. Trapping me just below his massive stomach, he uses his much larger body to control my dragon.

She screeches, struggling to spin away just as his feet come up to try to leverage himself on her and pull.

Fuck. No.

Fuck no.

I'm plucking my knives from my belt before I think about what I'm about to do. Releasing my grip on Vulryn—and praying to our mercurial, vengeful gods that the black beast doesn't do something to send me flying to the ground—I scramble toward the closest limb and grasp it, dragging myself up to the belly of this beast. And then I plunge my knives in.

He squeals, releasing Vulryn as his huge wings pound at the air around him, tossing both of us up and away from my dragon. I'm hanging on for my gods-damned life as this asshole completely abandons his attack on Vulryn and starts soaring away from the group. Like he's never coming back. Taking me with him.

Fucker.

What are you doing? Vulryn screams at me, her tone a mix of fear and frustration as she swivels in the air to chase after us.

Saving you, I respond, unable to keep the quiver from my voice. *I think.*

I do not need to be saved, Vulryn yells, anger the only emotion in these words. *Hold*, she adds, a hint of calm creeping in.

But this dragon is fast, even with my knives plunged into his belly. He's shooting away from the other beasts and I can tell already that Vulryn won't be able to catch him. The others are too far behind to even try.

My stomach is in my throat as I look at the waves writhing nearly a viku beneath us, and the edge of the lake getting closer. Once he crosses onto the land, I'll be even more fucked. Maybe I'd survive a drop into the lake but he's soaring higher. I'd be dead before I hit the ground. I'm not getting away from this beast unless I do something drastic.

Sucking in a deep breath, I dig one shaking hand more deeply into the ebony feathers and wipe away the sweat dripping into my eyes so I can see what the fuck I'm doing. Then I grab one of my embedded knives, stretch and thrust that blade as close to the heart as I can, wresting a tremor and an angry shriek from him. Inhaling one more time as I tighten my hold, I yank out the other one, then shift back toward the dragon's leg. And I start sawing.

He doesn't react at first, as my knife works its way through the feathers packed tightly into this sensitive and important area. When I reach skin, though, I know I've got him where I want him. He yowls at me, his head spinning to spew flames in my direction, and starts to spin.

Fast.

Within a few seconds, we're twisting like the cyclones that erupt when winds collide, and I'm clinging for my life. I can't attack. I can't do anything except hold on and hope the dragon doesn't find some way to fling me aside.

Hold, Vulryn commands, her voice more normal than it should be. I'm terrified, and she's cool and collected.

She really didn't need to be saved.

I should think a bit more before I start acting like I'm as badass as my dragon.

Nobody's as badass as my dragon.

When she strikes, the black beast is flung to the side, his furious cry echoing around us. The spinning stops as the beast tries again to attack Vulryn, pivoting with an open maw aimed for her neck.

She's ready for the bastard now, though. Before he can reach her, she grasps the roots of his wings, digging in as she leverages her feet against his back. And shoves.

The black dragon trembles when Vulryn throws her weight into her assault, an angry groan seeping from his snout. He tries again to spin—hoping to throw her from his back, I assume—but she's got the leverage now. Her wings alone hold us up and this dragon is fucking huge. I have no idea how long she can do this. We'll all be tumbling to the rock soon.

Let go, Vulryn says, her tone infuriatingly calm.

I won't survive this drop! She knows this. I don't know what the fuck she's thinking.

Do you trust me? This question is soft, not a hint of fear in it.

Always.

Let go.

So I do. I have no idea what she plans, but it doesn't matter. I trust her in everything.

My heart beats a dozen times as I plunge to the ground, pounding through every part of me. I can't see Vulryn. I'm twisting, my gaze scanning the air as I fall, but she's nowhere to be found. I can only catch glimpses of the sharp tips of the nearby mountain, wisps of snow covering their peaks, and the stark colors around me.

This land is so fucking beautiful. If I'm going to die, at least I'll be surrounded by its splendor.

I don't think I'm going to die, though. My stubborn dragon won't allow it. She'll save me.

I'm no more than three or four dragon's-lengths from the rock when I start to wonder if she'll make it. But just as my confidence starts to waver—a rock forming in my gut as some masochistic part of my mind drags up an image of Mikkael—Vulryn glides beneath me. And then she plummets along with me, our bodies touching just enough to help slow my descent. When her wings snap out, sending us soaring just above the ground, I collapse onto her back.

A burst of joy ignites within me, rippling out to bathe every inch of my body in the warmth of my beast's devotion. I suck in a deep breath, trying to calm my racing heart, and dig my hands into her feathers.

What did you do to the black dragon? I ask when I'm pretty sure I can keep the tremble from my voice.

He will not bother us again, is her only response.

Is he alive?

The night beast will not see another night.

Thank you for saving me.

I will always save you.

I'm so fucking lucky. Leaning down, I wrap my arms around my beautiful beast.

What would I do without you? I ask, wonder filling my soul.

That is a foolish question, she tells me, her tone that of a teacher scolding a child. *I am yours and you are mine. You will never be without me.*

Maybe I was wrong. Maybe elves like me do get more than we deserve sometimes.

I'll never have Mikkael, but Vulryn is so much better than I ever could have imagined.

CHAPTER FOUR

DANI

HE HATES ME

"**W**HAT THE FUCK WERE you doing?" Mikkael stalks toward me as soon as Vulryn lands, his dark eyes flashing in a face that's more pale than it should be. I feel a hint of fear deep in the mating bond I can't seem to escape, but it's almost completely drowned out by the anger he's spouting at me.

"What the fuck does it matter to you?" I demand, pushing at his broad chest before he can get too close, then turning to give him my back. Fuck him. He hates me. He doesn't get to attack me like this.

He grabs my arm, though, pulling me closer to tower over me as he spins me around.

Vulryn takes a step forward, a single burst of fire spilling from her nose.

It's okay, I tell her as I ignore the asshole in front of me and look at my dragon. *I've got this.*

He may not treat you this way.

Which is exactly what I'm going to tell him. Just ... let me handle it.

She puffs out another flame but drops to her belly, watching us with a fierce gaze.

I turn to my asshole mate, a smirk twisting my lips, and yank my arm away. "You're not allowed to touch me. You're not allowed to question me. You're not allowed to act like you give a fuck. Because we both know you don't."

He leans into me, his shoulders back as he puffs out his chest. "And you're not allowed to throw your life away," he yaps. "Like it or not, we're connected through our dragons. Z needs Vulryn if he's ever going to drag himself out of this desolation. If you die, she won't care about anything else. She'll never go to him. So stop doing stupid shit."

"Gods, you're infuriating," I yell, throwing up my arms as I take a step forward. He needs to know he doesn't intimidate me. "I will not answer to you. Ever. When the time is right, Vulryn and I will go to Ziselær. Alone. I don't know if he'll ever be yours and I don't give one little fuck. Stay away from me and stop nagging me about him."

"The time is now," he barks, clenching his fists as he leans into me. But then he inhales deeply, looking down as he flicks out his fingers. They're straight as arrows, like he's struggling to stop himself from making another fist. "I feel his desolation," he rasps, "his wish he'd died along with Matthias. Or that he'd killed me instead." Now his gaze lifts, dark, stormy eyes holding mine. "We need to go after him. Before he does something drastic."

"We need to give him time." I do my damnedest to soften my voice and respond with some emotion other than the anger he was throwing at me. He may be a bastard, but he's hurting, and I don't want to make it worse.

"I think I know my dragon a little better than you do," he growls as he narrows his eyes and scowls at me. "I can feel how lonely he is without Vulryn or his ... a rider."

"*His* rider," I point out in a calm voice. "That's what you were going to say, right? Ziselær doesn't have his rider and he can never have him again. They've been together for a century. He won't get over Matthias's loss this quickly. We need to give him time."

"But that's what's killing him." A hint of a plea sneaks into Mikkael's voice and his eyes go flat as he seems to realize it, shaking his head as if to dispel that impulse before he utters his next words. "He hasn't been alone for a hundred years. He's always had Matthias, and now Vulryn. He's trapped in his thoughts, unable to drag them away from the moment of that bastard's death. We need to help him break away from all the macabre images flipping through his mind."

"Like it or not, Vulryn knows him better than you. She thinks he needs time and that's what we're going to give him. He may be your dragon, but you need mine to get to him, and she won't do it."

Mikkael spins his head to look at Sifa.

"Don't even think about it," I spit out, pulling his gaze back toward me. "Astarot and Tindera—all of the dragons—will heed Vulryn on this. They won't go without her. And it wouldn't matter anyway, because nobody knows where he is. Vulryn could use their bond to find him. It would take a while, but it would work. None of the other beasts could do that. Vulryn and I will go alone when the time's right. That's the best way." I snarl the last few words, pushing past him as I stride away.

"You're wrong," I hear him call behind me. "When you go to Z, I'm coming with you. I won't be left behind."

I respond with a wave of my middle finger and walk toward Fhord and Sifa. They're smiling, like my drama with Mikkael is amusing them.

"It's not funny," I mutter as I watch them try—unsuccessfully—to stifle their laughter. They look at each other and cackle like children, then make one more attempt to smother their grins. This time, they're able to control themselves, wiping the glee from their expressions.

"He's such an asshole."

"Yes, but he's your asshole," Sifa responds with a wink. "I can't wait until you both figure it out."

I shake my head, letting them enjoy their moment. I'd deny it but it doesn't matter. They'll give up in a few months, when Mikkael and I still can't stand the sight of each other. Instead, I open my mouth to ask the question they must expect, because Fhord responds before the words spill out.

"That's Slata," he tells me, his gaze lifting to find the silver and gold dragon who rocketed into our midst. "She's defecting. The black dragon, Kotlo, suspected something. He chased her down and demanded to be told where she was going.

When she couldn't convince him she was just flying, he tried to kill her. She had no choice but to race to us for help."

"Did he say anything?" I ask. "The Dróttning was close, but was she close enough to hear a report from Kotlo?"

"I don't think he told her, for some reason. I would have heard him, and I didn't. He was a cocky beast and may have thought he could take one of our dragons out and carry the rider to her. Maybe he didn't want to give others a chance to interfere and steal his prize."

"That doesn't make any sense." I shake my head, looking around the large group he attacked. "There's a lot of us and only one of him."

"He was the fastest beast in the Thunder," Fhord tells me. "If you hadn't slowed him down by hurting him the way you did, he'd be gone. Nobody could have caught him."

"So, I wasn't completely crazy to do that? Because it felt fucking crazy."

Sifa smirks. "Not completely crazy."

"How did Slata find us?" That's what scares me. "If we're that easy to track, we're in deep shit."

Fhord cocks his head toward the new dragons, a little frown playing on his lips. I get the sense he didn't like what they did but knows it probably was the right call. "Vyara and Slata are close. They were hatchlings at the same time and have flown together often."

"Vyara told her?" My stomach sinks at Fhord's nod and the realization that while we might be able to trust the riders, the dragons are another story. I glance at the light blue dragon who might have exposed us, standing with Fhord's friend Nalani, a rider we all trust. "Why didn't their riders demand secrecy? Who else have they told?"

"They've all spoken with their dragons now. They assure me Slata's the only one. And it's good she came. She has news about Ziselær we needed to hear."

"Is he okay?" Mikkael barks from behind me, triggering my embarrassing jump to the side and into Sifa. Holy fuck, this male is going to drive me nuts. He's worried about his dragon, and I can't blame him, but it makes him even more frustrating than usual.

"He's struggling," Nalani responds as she strides toward us, her kind eyes focused on Mikkael. "The guilt about killing Matthias is eating him alive."

"How does Slata know? Where did she see him?"

Nalani looks up, her brow crinkling. "Let's get out of the open. I know where we are. Fhord showed me a place nearby. It'll be perfect."

Mikkael grasps her shoulder, more gently than he did my arm, and I can tell he's holding himself back. His hand shakes a little, his free hand curling into a fist.

"Please," he murmurs, a plea in his tone. "Just tell me he's alive. I need to know he's safe. For now, at least."

Nalani lifts her hand to his cheek, her dark eyes solemn, and my gut gives an unexpected—and unwanted—twist in response. That spot inside me that belongs to Mikkael doesn't like other females touching our mate.

"He's alive and safe," she tells him. "I promise you."

Mikkael dips his chin as he releases a soft breath. When he lifts his head again, his eyes shine more brightly than normal, which prompts another twist to my gut. Because he's so fucking beautiful and it kills me to see him this sad. "Okay," he tells her. "Let's go."

She nods and turns to stride toward her dragon, her shoulders tight and her back straight. Whatever she's going to tell him can't be good. We all mount our dragons and follow, flying just above the ground as she leads our group into the forest.

My jaw drops when the clearing opens in front of us. It sits in front of a massive kastali, its walls crumbling under the weight of the vines and branches that have forced their way into it over the years. It must have been stunning in its day.

Large windows face east and west, remnants of the patterned glass they probably all held still clinging in jagged shards along a few edges. The structure is mostly a mixture of beige and brown stone but accented with rock from a nearby quarry—alabaster white with threads of copper and gold running through it. It's the design of the building itself that's most stunning, though. High towers connected by sweeping bridges surround a complex made of sharp peaks and soft lines.

"It's been empty for centuries," Nalani tells us as we dismount and walk through the gaping hole that probably once held a door, big enough for even our dragons to enter.

"Tindera and I have used it a few times when we wanted to hide," Fhord agrees. "Other than when we brought Nalani and Vyara here, we've never seen, or even sensed, anyone else."

"How old is it?" I don't recall seeing anything like this in Njordheim. I find myself striding forward alone, fascinated by everything.

"I don't know," Fhord responds. "I've never asked anyone about this place because I didn't want to reveal it to the Dróttning, if she somehow doesn't know or has forgotten."

I turn to see Nalani nod and shrug. "I've also never asked. It's Fhord's secret, not ours to share."

Vulryn snarls under her breath as I start to climb a staircase that curls above us, leading to what I assume are bedrooms and libraries and other wonderful spaces. I spin, my eyebrows slamming together.

Do you not wish to hear news of my drake? She sounds hurt and I don't blame her. Of course I need to follow Nalani and the others.

I'm sorry, I respond, abandoning the search that is far less important than my dragon. *I don't know what I was thinking.*

She huffs, her eyes narrowing. *You may leave if you want*, she says in a tone that tells me leaving is the last thing I should do. If I ever want to ride her again.

I got carried away. I'm desperate to hear what Nalani has to say about Ziselær.

As you wish, she says with a snort as she follows the group to wherever Nalani and Fhord are leading us.

And now I'm glad I've come—beyond my need to be here for my dragon—because this place is fucking amazing. It's a ballroom of some kind, enormous and made almost entirely of marble and crystal. I spin in place, my gaze dancing across the room as I inspect the silver chandeliers and sconces, their curves seemingly too delicate and intricate to have been forged by mortal hands. The broad windows still have most of their glass, which sends a mosaic of light and color across the room. Absolutely amazing.

"We'll need to put someone on guard, but we can rotate," Fhord says as he starts to tug packs from Tindera. "Everyone should be able to rest here as long as the dragons need."

Mikkael's voice draws my gaze to him. "Now will you tell us what's going on with Z?" His back is tight and straight, hands clasped at his ass with his feet spread apart. I think he's trying to be as non-threatening as possible, but he's so uptight and anxious, he can't pull it off. It also doesn't help that he stands a foot taller, with a chest that's probably two feet wider, than Nalani's much smaller form.

Nalani smiles and I understand why Fhord cares so much about her. She's open and kind. "Let's sit," she says, gesturing him toward a spot in the sun. He responds with a sharp nod and strides over, dropping to the floor to watch her approach. She settles half a male's-height away, her expression growing more serious as she catches his gaze.

"Slata came across him by accident," she says as I join a few others striding over to sit with them. "Ziselær always has been … difficult … and she's avoided him whenever she could."

"Matthias was a gods-damned bastard," Mikkael growls, his hands clenching in his lap.

"That he was," Nalani agrees in a light voice. "The dragons who've known Ziselær since his hatching believe he deserved a better rider. They think he wouldn't have become such a cruel beast if he'd been paired with a kinder male. I always doubted them—what he did to Khirta was horrific—but now I wonder whether they're right."

"He's got a gentle heart," Mikkael declares in a stern tone. "He'll prove it to everyone now that Matthias is gone."

"With you as his rider?" Nalani's question is soft but piercing.

"I'll never ride him," Mikkael says, his gaze dropping to the floor. "I know that. He killed Matthias because of me, and he'll never forgive me. But that's okay." Now he looks up again, his eyes shimmering with tears he hasn't yet shed. "I don't need to ride him. I just need Z to be happy and well. If I can do anything to make that happen, I will."

"So, if he wants you to go away and leave him alone, you'll do that?"

"If that's what he wants, that's what I'll do."

"And if he needs your life to assuage his guilt?" Nalani's voice is intense and even more penetrating.

"I've offered him my life more than once. If it will help him to take it, I'll give it gladly."

I've heard Mikkael say this before but never with such resolve and resignation. I feel his determination in my gut, which clenches at the thought of Ziselær taking Mikkael's life. Not because I care about him, I assure myself—I don't have a single fuck to give about that asshole—but because it would hurt Ziselær, which would make it even harder for Vulryn to reach her drake.

"If Slata's right, I fear he'll take you up on that offer if you find him," Nalani whispers, her gaze holding his.

Mikkael leans forward, the corners of his lips tipping up. "I'm not afraid," he tells her. "If that's what he needs to start to heal, that's what he'll get. And as I said, I'll give it gladly." He watches her for a moment, then turns to the window, taking a deep inhalation, and then another. "Part of me needs to give that to him," he says at last. "My penance for weaseling my way into his heart, or whatever it was that took over and killed Matthias instead of me. If I'd left him alone, he'd never have been so conflicted. Matthias would still be alive. Z would be okay."

Mikkael shakes his head, sitting up straighter as he turns back to Nalani. "Just tell us what happened. Then we'll decide what to do."

"He's ... struggling," Nalani says, looking at Mikkael and then Vulryn. "I think he needs you," she tells my dragon, "even if he won't admit it."

"Why do you think that?" I ask before Vulryn prompts me.

"He's so alone," Nalani tells her, tears forming in her eyes. "Slata never imagined she'd feel sorry for him, but she did." She gives Vulryn a sad smile, then continues in a voice full of compassion. "She was flying alone in the area, looking for him or any of you. Of course, she didn't report having found him. She'll keep your secrets."

"We're grateful," Fhord responds with a nod of his chin toward the silver-and-gold beast. He's sitting behind Sifa, his arms wrapped around her as she rests her back against his chest. They're so good together.

"Slata says she wanted to ignore him, just report back to the rebels so others could go find him. Like I said, he's always been a cruel beast, and she didn't want to risk being alone with him. But something about him spoke to her. She decided to stop."

"What did she learn?" Mikkael's leaning forward now, his focus shifting between Nalani and Slata.

"He's already lost weight. She says she doubts he's moved since he landed there. He didn't seem to have any energy. Slata tried to talk to him about what happened, but he wouldn't say anything to her other than insisting he doesn't deserve to live, and wishing he'd chosen Matthias. He said that more than once, she told me."

"I felt that from him as soon as he killed that bastard," Mikkael rasps out.

"For now, at least, he still feels that way."

"Does he want to see Vulryn?" I ask, shivering a bit as she rumbles her displeasure. I don't think my dragon wants to know the answer to this question, but she needs it. We *have* to go to him, regardless of what she thinks right now. I'm as certain of this as I am that Sifa and Fhord have an unbreakable bond. And that Mikkael and I ... don't.

Nalani turns to find my beast, two of the tears I saw in her eyes now rolling down her cheeks. "Slata didn't ask him about you, and he didn't say anything. But she's convinced he needs you, and I agree with her. He won't admit it right now, even to himself, but we think your bond would help pull him out of this."

"She's right," Sifa says, her gaze also focused on Vulryn. "His guilt over killing Matthias would convince him that he doesn't deserve happiness with his draikana, and while you're so far away, he can ignore your bond. If you go to him, he won't be able to do that. He'll have to confront his feelings. It'll help him get past this desolation."

"Then I should go too," Mikkael interjects, drawing everyone's gaze to him. "He needs to confront his feelings about me just as much."

Nalani's face somehow grows even more sad. The corners of her lips tick down as her soft eyes shimmer, reflections of her compassionate soul. "Hate and love are two sides of the same coin, Mikkael. Ziselær can't let himself love you. Not so soon after Matthias's death. So he hates you. Fiercely. Because if he allowed it, he'd love you just as fiercely. I don't think he's ready to see you yet."

"That won't change until I'm there," Mikkael declares, flinging his shoulders back and sitting up as he turns to Sifa. "Tell her," he demands, his gaze flicking over to me and then back to Sifa. "Tell her he needs to confront his feelings about me too."

"I'm not sure if he does, Mik," Sifa murmurs. "I agree with Nalani. It's too soon."

I'm nodding, because I think so too, when Fhord speaks up. "I fucking hate agreeing with Mikkael about anything," he mutters, "but he's right. Ziselær needs to feel the bond he chose. Mikkael needs to get close enough to awaken the place inside Ziselær that belongs to him. The dragon needs to be forced to remember why he saved the life of his fated rider. That's the only way to drag him away from his certainty that he fucked up."

And now it's Mikkael that's nodding. "I can feel it," he adds, leaning toward Nalani again, his palms raised to the roof above us. "The part of me that belongs to Ziselær is screaming for my dragon. I don't want to eat. I don't want to sleep. I just want to go to him, wherever he is and whatever it takes. And I know, deep inside, he feels the same way too. But he won't let himself acknowledge the reason, so he wallows in his guilt."

Mikkael looks at me again, no hint of uncertainty in his steely gaze. "Vulryn won't be able to convince him alone," he tells me. "You'll leave defeated and might never try again. And we'll lose him. I can't let that happen. I won't."

I'm not sure what to say. I don't know the right answer. So I nod to acknowledge his words and say the only thing I can. "I'll think about it."

"You're not leaving without me," he tells me again. Then he stands, his shoulders stiff, and turns away from all of us, stalking deeper into the kastali. Part of me wants to follow him. But I shove that shit down. He hates me. The only reason he's even talking to me is that he needs my dragon to get to Ziselær. I can't let myself forget that.

CHAPTER FIVE

MIKKAEL

SO FUCKING WEIRD

WE'RE GOING TO ANOTHER gods-damned haunted forest. This time, to chat with beings who died centuries ago that Fhord and Sifa call draugrs. Everyone's acting like this is a normal thing.

My life has gotten so fucking weird. I'm not sure if I love it or hate it.

I knew this world held magic. Even before getting to know Sifa—and then joining her and Fhord on this suicide mission—I'd seen hints of it. People whisper about the power of the elves hidden in the Dróttning's prisons, the reason they can't be allowed to walk free. And we all know that wyrm uses her fucked-up magic to control the dragons ... and everyone else.

But undead, wandering around a haunted forest.

So gods-damned weird. Even weirder than a ghost pig. And that was seriously weird.

What the fuck have I gotten myself into?

At least it gives me more time with Dani and Vulryn before they abandon me to chase down Z. The forest is on the way to where Slata found my dragon, so they're tagging along for now. Maybe I can convince them to take me when they go after him.

I hate the idea of being alone with Dani. Of riding her dragon at her back. But I can't reach Z any other way. I just need to make sure I don't let her get to me again. She showed me exactly who she is and how she feels when Z killed Matthias. Nothing could ever change that.

For now, though, I'm riding with Sifa—maybe my favorite person in this strange world we occupy—on her dragon. We spent a few days at the abandoned kastali to give the dragons a chance to heal, Dani keeping her distance from me the whole time. Now we're splitting up. The new dragons and riders all are going to Lumaria. Nalani knows the way and will take them there to rest and prepare for the war we're about to wage.

The rest of us are traveling together, flying low to hopefully evade patrols. Toffer and Thor ride Vulryn with Dani since Z's draikana refuses to trust the cat with anyone else, even Tindera.

We're heading in Z's direction. Life is good. Better than I deserve.

And the trip is surprisingly quick. We stay in a cave overnight and are flying again in the morning. Three times we have to change direction to avoid the Dróttning's soldiers, but nobody gets close enough to cause a problem. Before I know it, we're at the edge of another haunted forest—which Fhord and Sifa insist isn't haunted, despite the dead beings lurching through it—ready to go interrogate someone who lived hundreds of years ago.

So fucking weird.

I've never been here before, I realize as the dragons land in the midst of an area that looks more like jungle than forest. The enormous leaves that adorn hundreds of trees in front of and all around us stand between the sun and the ground below, turning cover I assume is a deep green into shadows and dark contrasts. Flowers decorate the area, their bursts of sun and fire and even some blood adding muted color. A shallow creek bubbles its way through the forest in our path, its soft murmuring a pleasant background to the cries and songs of the birds swooping above us.

But not across the creek. I don't see any life there. Which means that must be our destination. Because we're fucked up like that.

"There's one rule in this area," Fhord announces from behind me as Tindera stalks to the front of our merry band of rebels. Fhord's staring at Toffer and I'm not one little bit surprised. He's about to be surrounded by death. Who knows what that'll do to the troll's bloodthirsty urges.

"Do not kill the draugrs," Fhord continues, finally looking at the rest of the gang. I snort at his command because they're dead already, but he throws a glare my way and then ignores me. "No matter what they do to you or how they make you feel, you are not allowed to end their existence. You can damage their bodies, cut off an arm or leg if you must, but not their head. Never the head."

"Why the fuck not?" I demand. "They're dead. They probably want to rest."

"They belong to the gods," Fhord snarls as his gaze snaps toward me. "Those bastards resurrected the draugrs to preserve knowledge they alone hold. They bound their existence in spells that will destroy anything or anyone who harms them. They value some draugrs enough to give them extra protection. If any one of those draugrs is ended, every living being in this place will be killed. None of us would leave here."

Fuck, this world they dragged me into is bizarre. "Well, when you put it that way," I gripe as Sifa turns to laugh at me. "No killing the dead guys," I add. "Got it."

"I'll go first," he says, because of course he wants to lead us into the shit we're about to face. "We'll stay together. I think they'll leave us alone since we're riding dragons, but I don't know. Many rode dragons in their day, and their curiosity may draw them toward us."

"And if they attack?" My voice doesn't waver, thank fuck. I'll be damned if I'm gonna let this schmuck know how freaked out I am about this place.

"They shouldn't. Sifa and I have been here before." Fhord's gaze catches hers for a moment and the barest smile lifts lips that rarely bend up. "Our first job together, before she met Astarot," he says as if to her alone. And we all just sit there for a moment, waiting for Fhord to stop ogling his mate. My eyes want to find Dani, a need to experience this with her pulsing through me for a moment, but I shut that shit down.

"They should recognize us, let us pass easily," he continues as he finally drags his gaze away from Sifa and I win my battle to keep my gaze right where it is. "But if they do attack, we leave. We'll walk in—I need to attract one of the draugrs to me and I can't do it from the sky—but nothing stops us from flying out. Sifa and I will dismount to talk to this draugr. The rest of you stay on your dragons unless they call you to them."

Tindera turns and strides toward the creek. At one point, she hesitates, swinging her head as if she's waging an internal battle while Fhord sits up straighter on her back, his fists clenched tightly. But she continues on, her steps more determined as her wings flex to lift her across the creek.

When we get to that same place, I understand. I want desperately to turn around. My insides twist as a need to avoid this place erupts within me. A swarm of fireflies buzzes in my gut and my legs start to bounce restlessly, like they'd carry me from here if they could. As we approach and then fly over the creek, the anxiety grows and I wonder if I'm going to get sick.

The moment we cross the creek, that feeling goes away, something even worse settling in its place. Desolation. Hopelessness. Loneliness. Above all, though, I feel desperation. They need this empty existence to end. They're trapped in a shadowland from which there is no escape. Solitary beings who barely interact any longer with the others captured here with them, their only desire is release.

I want to help them. The fireflies that danced in my gut a minute ago have been replaced by a fire that burns so hot, I don't know if it will ever be quenched. It feels like I will live my life desperate to return here and free these beings from the Helheim in which the gods have trapped them.

"Fuck," Sifa whispers in front of me. "I'd forgotten how strong the drive is to end the gods' hold on them. It's harder to resist now than it was the first time, maybe because the desire never fully left me."

"I want to risk the gods' wrath," I utter. "I can't even find my bond with Z, my need to get back to him. This urge to help them shoved everything else aside."

"Ride it out," she tells me. "It'll get worse, but we can outlast it. I promise." She pauses for a moment, then turns with a smile. "Well, I hope. I'm pretty sure."

"That's encouraging," I groan. But I tighten my grip on Astarot, resisting the urge to drop to the ground and race deeper into the trees, find the draugrs more quickly.

Nobody speaks as Tindera leads us on a winding path. She goes forward, but she seems to be resolved to cover as much land as she can along the way. Sifa must notice it too, as she turns to me with a forced smile. "Fhord and I meandered like this when we came last time. I didn't ask him why. I think covering more ground helps the draugrs sense our presence before they see us."

I don't respond, other than a grunt and a sharp dip of my chin. It's all I can do to keep my raging emotions in check, and I can't risk letting any part of my brain concentrate on anything else. Sifa responds with a knowing nod as we continue in silence again.

And then I smell them, and my focus shifts to stopping myself from barfing all over Astarot. I've been near dead people before—more often that I like—but this is far beyond any odor I've come to expect. It's the waste of a thousand cities after years of festering; a legion of soldiers gutted and left in the sun to decay; the rotting, green flesh of a hundred wounded before it's sliced away.

I force my breaths to slow—loathe to draw any of the fetid vapors into me but struggling to hold down the meager contents of my stomach—and wrap my legs tighter around Astarot. Now, the urge isn't to race toward them. It's to escape this Helheim while I can, because the worst torture in the worlds would be getting trapped here, to inhale this stench forever.

When I see them, my need to drop to the ground and run from this Helhole magnifies. Except, I'd have to go through them because they've surrounded us. There's no escape now. But the idea of getting closer to any of them is almost enough to force out the retch hovering at the back of my throat.

They're walking corpses, the causes of their deaths forever displayed in the festering wounds they each bear. Head gashes revealing decayed brain matter. Chests ripped open to expose putrid entrails, some bulging out of the open cavities. Gaping holes in necks, leaving little to hold up their heads. These males and females should have dropped to the ground ages—eons—ago, but the fucking gods decided to animate the corpses and keep them here for their pleasure. Bastards.

One of them steps forward—the largest of the group from what I can see. His clothes, what little remains after all these years, suggest a high rank. I see hints of gold and silver on his chest. The material once was a heavy fabric, worn only by a leader. He carries himself with that same authority too, even in death. My gaze is drawn to the gaping cavity in his chest but I drag it away. I don't need to look at that shit.

He stops when he's a dragon's-length away, staring at Fhord. And I'm not sure how, but I sense something that feels like surprise emanating from him. He glances at Sifa and then me and Dani for some reason, then looks again at Fhord. *Have you come to release me from my pain?*

I shake my head, wondering how in the fuck those words appeared in my thoughts. The voice is rasping. Wretched. Hopeless. I've never heard such utter despair in my life.

"I cannot yet do that," Fhord responds, his voice low and full of respect, "although I am closer than ever to gaining that power. We need more of your knowledge if we're to succeed."

Another wave of anguish, desperation, washes through me, and I have to stop myself from dropping to the ground and striding over to shove my blade into his head. It shouldn't work. Beings with massive head wounds surround me. But somehow, I know it would. And I want it more than I've wanted anything, even my bond with Z.

These things are fucking with my head. I need to get a grip.

This is the worst haunted forest ever. The pig forest doesn't even come close.

The lead draugr is quiet for a long time, and I feel his conflict. He doesn't trust Fhord, but he's starting to. It's as if he's examining Fhord's black soul as it turns gray, watching him become a better being as he sits astride his dragon, waiting for the corpse to render his judgment.

Finally, the undead being nods his head, gesturing to Fhord and Sifa. They dismount and start to walk toward him but pause as agitation, unease, ripples around us. *There are others who need my knowledge.* Again, the guttural words drop into my mind.

"Call them and they will come," Fhord responds, glancing back at us.

The draugr dips his chin again, watching Fhord for a moment before looking at Dani. I don't hear whatever he says for some reason, but she responds as if he's spoken to her, her eyes widening in surprise as she leans back and into Toffer. After a moment, she puffs out a breath and climbs down from Vulryn.

And then the corpse turns to me. *I have knowledge to share with you, dragon-rider.* These words also drop into my head, but now I understand why his message to Dani didn't reach me. He's communicating with me alone.

"I don't ride a dragon," I correct him. "He rejected me."

The sympathy that washes over me almost draws tears to my eyes. *It is your fate to ride a dragon,* he tells me, *and ride him you shall. Come to me.*

So I do. I've never felt such a strong compulsion to heed another being's order. It's as if he's seized my mind, compelling my legs to move without my consent. I'm reminded of the dwarf's net, and his use of my legs to propel me toward him, but this is different. The dwarf took control of my legs, which moved without my intent; this draugr has taken control of my thoughts, commanding my movement.

Fucking weird. Just … really fucking weird.

As I walk toward him, he turns to Fhord. The forest is quiet—not even a bird or bug disturbing the silence—as they converse entirely within their minds. I wonder if Fhord's magic allows him to respond without speaking words and if I'll know how when my turn comes.

More than anything, though, I wonder what he meant when he said I'll ride Z. Whether he's going to tell me something that will help me and my dragon get through this fucked up time.

I also want to know why the fuck this undead being cares enough to call *me* over to talk. I'm nobody, a mundane human who somehow has gotten mixed up with the most powerful elves in the country.

I can only watch in silence as the draugr finishes with Fhord and turns to Sifa. Their conversation is also silent, but Sifa—and Dani—have mind magic too. I'm just an ordinary human, somehow dragged into this extraordinary cast of characters. I'll never understand it, but I gave up trying.

When he turns to Dani, I can't drag my gaze away from her. There's something respectful and unassuming about her stance. The shield she always seems to wear is down, as if this being, despite the guts and gore, poses her no threat at all. She's just as quiet as the others until her gaze spins toward me and she snarls—actually fucking snarls—before looking again at the draugr. Now she's pissed. If she could kill me, I think she would. She's never-been-more-furious-in-her-life pissed. About me, for some reason.

When the draugr's gaze turns to me, Dani's does too. She spits in my direction, her nostrils flaring, then growls something under her breath and turns to stalk toward her dragon. Fhord and Sifa watch her, their eyes wide, as Sifa's mouth drops open and then jerks shut.

"What the fuck was that?" she mutters.

And then his words drop into my mind. They're hoarse, as all his words have been. *Your mate did not care to hear my words.*

She hates me. I ignore her. I don't speak out loud. When the draugr turned his attention to me, the knowledge of how to communicate with him appeared within me. It's unsettling, but I manage to take this oddity in stride. It's no stranger than anything else in the fantasy I'm currently living.

Yet, she is your mate. And she must be your ally if Nerthus's reign is to end.

You mean the Dróttning? That's Nerthus, right? I vaguely recall learning her given name, but she's always just been the Dróttning.

Yes, I understand she has gained that title. But she does not deserve it. I will not give her that honor.

Happy to call her Nerthus too, I announce, unable to hold back the smile. Because I agree. That bitch does not deserve one little bit of honor. *But I think you've got the wrong guy. I'm just a human. I'm tagging along with them, but nothing I'm going to do will change this world.*

His expression doesn't change—I doubt it could—but I feel the laugh that ripples through him. A moment of joy in an otherwise painful existence. *Perhaps not just human,* he declares cryptically. I feel my eyebrows hike up, but he starts talking again before I can ask what the fuck that means. *Even so, humans who would challenge gods rarely believe they might prevail. But those who appear weak can be the strongest among us. Your humanity is your strength. Never doubt that.*

Am I not human? This question hovers in the air around us, weightless despite how heavy it feels in my gut.

Midgard birthed you, yet I do not fully recognize your essence. Something inside you is ancient and elusive.

What is it? What am I? The last few days have been full of revelations but as with the dwarf, this one feels right.

I sense a grin that doesn't emerge on the draugr's face. *I would tell you if I could. I do not recognize whatever exists within you.*

I nod, wishing I had answers I may never find, and focus on what I can ask. *Were you human?*

I was. For a time.

What does that mean?

That, you will learn if you follow the path the fates have set before you.

What could I do, though? I have no powers. I don't even have the dragon I'm supposed to ride.

You alone can change your fate and his. If you do, the fate of the world will follow.

I need to go to him. I'm not asking. I know the answer.

You do, he confirms. *It will not be easy. Your beast is not yet ready to release the guilt that consumes him. He may not listen to your words. He may choose to end you as he ended the male who tried to take your place. Yet must you try.*

And you told Dani this?

She did not care for my words. But she heard them.

And you're sure this will matter in the war ahead?

I cannot see the future. I know only what I see within you. The draw of the fates in your life and to this land.

You think the fates want me to ride Z?

I know you would not have been brought to this world if your presence here held no import. I believe you will ride your dragon, but even if you never do, you are here for a reason. Follow the path the fates have chosen for you.

The calm certainty that fills me is unlike anything I've ever felt before. I know he's right, in that place where I know that Z is mine—and Dani too, although that part sucks. *I will,* I tell him. *Thank you.*

You and the others can thank me by releasing me from my pain when the time comes.

I promise we will return for that. When the time is right.

He drops his chin and turns abruptly to shamble back toward the trees.

While I spin and smirk at Dani.

She flings her middle finger at me, her mouth a thin line that looks like it'll never open again.

And I just smile more broadly. Because now she's stuck. She's taking me with her, and there's not a single thing she can do about it.

Maybe fate isn't a bitch after all.

CHAPTER SIX

SIFA

THIS IS MY HOME

As we leave the draugr's area in silence, I can't stop thinking about what Konungr Erik told me. The reality I feel deep in my gut that I'm supposed to stay here. I spent my entire life in Midgard and its adjacent worlds. Yggdrasil has given me more years than any human ever had. If Freyr survived Ragnarök—and I desperately hope he did—he's still there with Freyja and their father. But I belong here. And I will never leave.

When I first met him, Erik asked me about home, and I thought he was helping me find my path back. But his words were vague. He never told me to return. Instead, he gave me information to continue my search, which kept me with Fhord long enough to find Astarot. To fall in love with Fhord. To tie my life to theirs.

Erik saw fate's influence within Fhord and me. He helped push us down the path that brought us here. I still have no idea how Toffer and I can regain the long lives we had in Midgard, and he didn't have an answer to that pivotal question. But there must be an answer somewhere. I can't imagine the fates would call me here to kill me after only a few decades. We'll figure it out. We have to.

And now Erik's pushing us down another path. He told me what the dwarf said he would. I need to go retrieve her. He said she's in this world because she belongs here too. Her mate is here and they must find each other when the time is right. None of us will return to Midgard.

Here, in our home, she and her mate are key to what we need to do: defeat the Dróttning, and make a better life for everyone. They won't fully bond—she's too young—but something in her will unfurl when she gets close enough to him. She's ready for whatever's going to happen. I don't like it, but it's no longer my decision. We'll go to Revalle and do what we must.

First, though, we have to travel north to a city I've never visited, Nerthwaite. Fhord got word from Torsten that the Ætt, Frida, and Liv are there. We'll need them all as we prepare to take on the Dróttning. They'll go with us to Revalle and then on to Lumaria.

A weight lifts from me as we cross back over the creek, and I feel Mikkael relax at the same time. He's been a jittery mess since he spoke with Erik, desperate to talk to Dani. She's doing her best to shun him. I haven't asked what they were told, but I can guess. Mikkael's going with Dani in search of Ziselær.

As soon as we land on the other side of the creek, Mikkael releases the tight hold he's had on Astarot and me. "Are we staying here long enough for me to dismount?" His voice is tense.

"Give her some time, Mik. She needs to come to terms with whatever Erik said to you both."

"But what if she leaves? She was pissed. She doesn't want me to go."

"So he did tell you to go to Ziselær? That she should take you?"

"He did. He said it'll be important. We can't win the battles ahead if I don't reach him. And ride him."

I manage to hold back my laugh, barely. "Yeah, it'll take her a minute to accept that," I tell him in the gentlest voice I can muster. "You've been a real bastard to her."

He sighs, rubbing his palms against his pants as he leans away from me. "I can't let myself get close to her," he mutters after a few seconds. "Not after what happened in the cave."

"That doesn't mean you have to treat her like shit. I wouldn't want to take you either."

"Fuck, this is hard. How'd you deal with the draw of the mating bond before you and Fhord got together?"

"Not well. He was even worse than you, if that's possible. He knew, but I didn't, and he didn't want me to know. We got through it. You'll get through this."

"I just want to get to Z and get away from her. I know what she thinks—how she feels about me—but the bond keeps telling me I can trust her. That I want her. It's fucked."

"Give it time. You'll learn to live with the bond even if you're not together."

I feel Fhord's caress across my thoughts before I see Tindera land beside us. He's smiling. I'm not sure what Erik told him and suspect it's something he desperately wanted to hear. But that secret's his. For whatever reason, Erik insisted again that his words to Fhord and me are to us alone. We're not to share them, even with each other.

Where to now? I ask Astarot as he spins his head to look at his draikana.

A nearby cave, he tells me. And I think my jaw drops to my chest as he spins his head to catch my gaze, almost as surprised as me.

What did you just say?

We will go to a nearby cave. His voice—which has somehow responded with a full sentence instead of the single word that typically drops into my thoughts—is full of wonder.

"He just spoke to me," I yell at Fhord as my gaze finds his.

He stares at me like I've lost my mind. Astarot's been speaking to me for months. "And?" he asks, one eyebrow cocking as the corners of his lips tip up in the beginning of a smirk.

I laugh, my chest filling with warmth as my bond with my dragon somehow grows even stronger. This is how it's supposed to be, I realize. It's how dragons and their riders are meant to speak with each other. "I mean," I tell Fhord with a grin I can't seem to control, "Astarot responded to my question with a sentence. Like Dani said Vulryn speaks to her."

"Impossible." Fhord's voice is firm, as if he doubts me.

"It just happened, Fhord. He spoke to me in a sentence."

He stares at Astarot for a long time, a muscle in his jaw twitching, then turns to Tindera to say something to her before looking at me again. "Does he know why?" The tension I feel surging through him makes his words crisp, demanding.

Do you understand what's happening? Why you're responding differently now?

Astarot looks at Vulryn, his gaze fierce as they try to figure out what's changed. And we wait as patiently as we can. Finally, Dani answers Fhord's question.

"Vulryn thinks Astarot is finally completely rid of the Dróttning's control, which was what led them to communicate as they did," she explains, and the truth of it filters through me. It's one more thing that bitch screwed up in the dragon-rider bond. "She's not sure why. Maybe to protect their conversations from her, if she heard only the word, and not the nuance you've all described that comes with it. Whatever it is, she's convinced the limited communication is something that grew out of the Dróttning's hold on the dragons and will disappear for the other beasts when they're fully free of her, like it just did for Astarot."

"Holy fuck," Fhord breathes, his gaze finding mine as a smile splits his cheeks. My responding grin does the same. I'm lighter somehow, as if a balloon that had created an empty void inside me just popped, filling me with a connection and understanding of my dragon I should have had from the beginning.

"It would make sense," he adds after a moment. "The Dróttning is limited as Vulryn suggests. She can speak to them and hear their single-word responses with a hint of the full meaning, but she's never had the complete mind connection—the exchange of ideas and information without words—that forms between dragons and riders with their bonds."

"How long have they spoken with just a single word?" I ask as my mind searches for a reason the more limited form of communication would have developed.

"As long as I recall," Fhord tells us. "But she took control of the dragons before I was born. Before any of us were born. If our dragons were hatched into this kind of dialog, they wouldn't know anything else."

"Now I want to go back to Erik and ask him." I spin to glance again at the forest, wondering if I'm curious enough to put up with all of the desperate emotions that come along with a trip across the creek.

"It's not safe to go back again so soon." Fhord's voice is low now, a warning. "Every time you go, a little bit of their need to escape this existence stays within you—their way of trying to draw you back to end them eventually. The desire to help them will build on that feeling, which is still too fresh. You might give in. I might give in."

Fhord's right, so we don't go back to Erik. Instead, we follow Fhord to yet another cave he's identified across the country. With a hot spring, thank fuck. I desperately want a bath right now. Fhord gives me a teasing kiss that promises more to come and a slap on the ass as he sends me away and starts preparing our meal.

By the gods, I love having a male who cooks. And everything else.

Dani joins me, sinking in with a sigh I recognize. It slipped from me more than once when I hated Fhord and couldn't wait to be rid of him.

"Fate's a bitch sometimes, isn't it?" I gripe as I glance at her. She's leaning her head against the wall, eyes closed and lips a thin, angry line.

"The next few days—or weeks, or whatever it is—are going to be so gods-damned miserable." She gives me a half-smile as she shifts forward and glances my way. "Maybe you and Fhord could come, carry him so Vulryn and I don't have to? Run interference for us?"

I smirk at her, because I know she's only half joking. "Fate's got other ideas."

"But fate's a bitch. We don't have to listen to her, do we?"

"Yeah, we do." I whisper these words, because sometimes the truth is tougher to hear when it's loud.

"You're right, I know. I can still be pissed about it though."

"Fuck yes, you can. We don't have to embrace fate happily. We can moan and groan our way into it, cursing the gods and everyone around us. But we have to go along." I pause, wondering what I can tell her about Erik's words to me. "Fate's sending me to do something I hate almost as much as you. It's fucked but necessary," I tell her after a moment.

"I guess we'll deal with that shit tomorrow," Dani says as she rests her back against the side. "I'm gonna pretend for the next few hours that I don't have to leave this place with the asshole fate paired me with. Maybe get a good night's sleep."

We're silent after that, lost in our own thoughts until we drag ourselves out and give the pool to the guys. After a quick, quiet meal, we find our blankets, searching for the sleep we all need. Fhord holds me, murmuring his love into my ear as we both drop off, letting the dragons protect us from anything that might come.

Nothing does. We're still alone when I awake in the morning after a ridiculously good night's sleep. Fhord's already up and starting breakfast. I lay there as others begin to move, suppressing a smile as I watch Toffer navigate Thor's morning moods. The cat's an asshole, but thankfully, the troll has the patience of a saint. Once they bonded, they became inseparable. When Vulryn wanders over to help brighten Thor's mood, Dani laughs and smiles at me. Her dragon's got an enormous heart.

We eat a fast meal, again in silence, then clean up. I try not to stare or laugh at Mikkael and Dani. They're stubbornly ignoring each other, as if they might be able to avoid the days or weeks ahead. I can't wait to see what this time alone does to them.

"Any advice?" Dani asks as she helps me strap the rest of my packs on Astarot. "I think I'll need it."

"He's getting what he wants. He'll be better now. He might even be nice to you."

"I'll believe it when I see it," she huffs.

"When are you leaving?"

"Now. We're packed, and it's a two-day flight. Fhord's given us a place to stay along the way, but it'll take eight or ten hours to get there."

I watch her for a moment, the strange evolution of our friendship playing out in my mind. "I don't know what we would have done without you and Vulryn. And not only because she's saved our asses more than once. Like we told you in Lumaria, you're family. Be well, my sister. Come back to us soon."

She smiles, but tears are forming in her eyes. "Be well, my sister," she echoes, before giving me a swift hug and turning to stride toward her dragon. I watch as she mounts and glares at Mikkael, then waits in silence as he pulls himself up behind her. He sits as far back as possible, digs his hands into Vulryn's feathers—not an inch of their bodies touching—and sighs. And then they're gone, Vulryn's strong wings carrying them toward her drake.

We're on our way within a few minutes after that for the shorter trip to Nerthwaite. And we again have no problems with the Dróttning's soldiers. We're less than a viku from the town, spiraling down to leave the dragons in a cave Leif directed us to, when the realization hits me. They should be blanketing the country searching for us. We should have had to fight our way past them at least once. But there's been nothing.

It makes me nervous. If her people and dragons aren't here, she's got them focusing on something else. I can't help but wonder what she's planning.

We should be back soon, I tell Astarot as I pull off the packs to stow while they're here. *Fhord told Tindera about a nearby herd. Just ... be careful that you're not seen when you go.*

I almost laugh at the side-eye he gives me and the response he can now fully express. *Do I look as if I need instructions on how to hunt safely?*

I can't hold back the smile. *Of course not. I'm just nervous. More about what we're going to be facing as we try to sneak into the town than what you'll be doing here. Sorry.*

I will forgive it, this once, he tells me with his dragony smirk. *We will be careful. As will you.*

As will I, I assure him with a scratch behind his horn. *Enjoy your time with Tindera.*

We cannot fly so close to this place, he reminds me. *We will rest.*

Then enjoy your rest. I give him one more scratch, grab the bag I'm taking with me, and stride over to Fhord and the others.

"It's clear," he tells us as he starts to walk toward the cave's entrance. "We'll run into people soon, but the Dróttning doesn't generally keep many soldiers in this area, so we should be able to get in without notice."

"From your lips to the gods' ears," I plead as we leave the cave.

And the gods are listening. Nobody gives us a second glance as we stroll into town, reaching the house holding our friends within an hour of leaving the cave. Striding in behind Fhord, the rock in my gut dissipates, hope and ripples of happiness finding their way into my soul.

We're together again. We've lost Johan—which still breaks my heart—and Dani, Vulryn, and Mikkael are suffering along with Ziselær, but we're alive and safe. I'm gods-damned grateful for this moment in time.

I'm also frisky. I hug everyone and settle down next to Fhord as he starts to tell them all that's happened since we left them. The Ætt pepper him with questions about our fight, while Liv and Frida dig for information about Dani and Mikkael's botched mating bond. But it's been too long since I had Fhord to myself and he's talking too much. So I decide to start fucking with him—not literally. Yet.

He's recounting Vulryn's fall in the cave when I reinforce my shields to make sure Fhord can't go digging around in my thoughts when he realizes what I'm doing. Then I lean over, my lips close enough to his ear to ensure my words will only be for him, and purr, "When are you going to come in my cave?"

He pauses, his brow creasing as he turns toward me. "What?" he asks, reaching out for my hand.

"I didn't say anything," I respond with a shrug, shifting my expression into the feigned innocence that's always served me well with males.

He shakes his head, his lips dipping into a small frown for a moment, then turns back to the others to continue his story. And I wait for my next chance.

This one comes soon. Fhord's telling them about the net the dwarf trapped us in and I lean forward to breathe, "Will you cast your net over me?"

This break in Fhord's story is accompanied by the smallest twitch of his lips. Because my mate knows me well and he's onto my game. "Did you say something, rabbit?" he asks, turning toward me as his thumb caresses the back of the hand he's holding.

"I think you're imagining things, Fhord," I proclaim with a glance around the room. "You didn't hear anything, did you?" I inquire in the most guileless tone I can muster. The others respond with shakes of the head and smiles they're trying to suppress, but nobody outs me. They see my game too.

Fhord smirks, leaning forward to mutter, "Troublemaker," before giving me a quick kiss and turning back to the others. He's relaying our visit with the draugrs when I lean forward again, lick his ear—because I'm getting impatient—and sigh, "I wish someone would put me out of my misery."

"What did you say?" Fhord rumbles this demand, but it isn't anger I feel rippling off of him.

I bite my lip, because fuck, do I love this version of Fhord, and throw my shoulders back. "Are you okay, Fhord?" I ask in a voice full of concern. "You seem to be hearing voices." From the corner of my eye, I see Jorunn roll her eyes as she turns toward Astrid to say something in her ear. But I'm much more focused on my sexy mate.

Fhord's grin is vicious. He doesn't move for a moment, eyes flashing as he holds my gaze. "Run, rabbit," he drawls as he rises to his feet.

And I do. I've never been here before, but this place must hold a bedroom or two. Racing down the hallway, I open one door and then another, finding a closet and a bathroom, but no bed. Before I can reach the third, Fhord's there, gripping my waist and tossing me over his shoulder. I can't hold back the squeal as I kick in protest—just a bit—while he takes me to a small room with a large bed.

He slams the door, dropping me to the ground, then yanks his shirt over his head and kicks off his boots, a wicked smile on his face. "How long has it been since I fucked you, rabbit?" he demands, catching the hem of my blouse to pull it over my head and toss it aside.

I don't answer right away, watching his pupils blow wide as he stares at my bare chest. He lifts his hands to grasp my breasts, drawing goosebumps from my sex-starved skin. "So fucking beautiful," he says, leaning down to take one of my nipples into his mouth, sucking on it for a few seconds before giving it a little nip, sending a shiver of pleasure through me along with the pain, and doing the same with the other hard peak.

"Too gods-damned long," I finally respond as I tug the ties on his pants, loosening the string enough to push them down his thighs and release the dick I haven't touched in days. "Too fucking long," I repeat as I drop to my knees, ignoring his frustrated groan when my nipple breaks free from his lips, and lick the length of the vein that's pulsing his arousal.

His next groan is not one of frustration. He fists my hair as I swirl my tongue around his head and then suck it into my mouth, my hand circling the rest of his dick to stroke up and down while I lap at the vein that throbs underneath. He tastes so good, the salty precum dancing on my tongue as I slowly take him deeper and deeper. When his hips start to move, thrusting toward my throat—sending a pulse of fire straight to my core—I release my hands and let him fuck my mouth, opening to him as I savor everything about this male that belongs to me.

But that's not what he wants to fuck. As abruptly as I dropped to my knees, Fhord's out of my mouth and reaching down to draw me up next to him. His lips devour me, his probing tongue tangling with mine as two fingers catch the waist of my pants and shove them down to my ankles. Breaking the kiss for a moment, he pushes me onto the bed, his gaze focused on me as he drags my pants the rest of the way off and then kicks his to the side.

"So fucking dangerous," he grunts as he strokes his dick, lidded eyes heavy and a teasing smile on his lips.

"Fuck me, Fhord. I want you inside me."

"Not yet, rabbit. You got to taste me. Now it's my turn."

"I wasn't done," I remind him, lifting myself to spin on the bed, laying down with my head right next to his raging erection. "Let's taste each other."

"I fucking love you," he moans as he crawls over me, then grips my hips to flip us both, landing with his back on the bed and me on top.

His tongue finds my clit immediately, sending a burst of pure pleasure rippling through me as I drop my head and wrap my lips around his dick. The next few minutes are a hurricane of sensations, as I luxuriate in the feel of my mate in my mouth—loving the way he vibrates with every suck and lick and stroke—while he feasts on me, fucking me with his tongue and then his fingers.

I want this to last. I want his mouth on my pussy, his fingers deep inside me, all night. Until the end of time.

But I want to fuck him more. And I'm the one on top. Before he can stop me, I pull my mouth away, swing my leg over his head—ignoring the "Not yet, rabbit," he croaks—and throw my other knee over his thighs. Holding his gaze, I position him at my entrance and smile. When he thrusts his hips up, I feel him everywhere, the bonds that connect us lighting flares as they flow from our joined bodies to every single part of me.

We find our rhythm instantly, our hips rolling together as we give and take from each other. When I feel him release his shields, I do the same, letting all our thoughts, each sensation, the weight of our desires, blend to become one. It's as if two universes have come together, stars colliding as a million points of light combine to create one perfect kaleidoscope in the sky.

I know exactly what he craves—what he needs—and want it as much as him. I send my thoughts in search of his savage, inviting him to come play, and can't hold back the smile as I see him shimmer toward the surface, anxious to feed his bond with me too. The physical change in Fhord is barely noticeable: feral hunger in his eyes; a shift of his lips as his canines descend; a broadening of his chest, the tattoos rippling as they stretch; a dick that somehow grows even larger.

The emotional and mental change, though, opens a door within me I never knew existed before our bond. I belong to the beast that shares Fhord's skin and he belongs to me. I am feral and ravenous and untamed. Nothing, nobody, can contain the being I am with him.

Fhord flips us over, our bodies never losing contact as he throws me on my back and shifts me to the end of the bed, standing between my legs. He pushes my ass into the air, his arms beneath my thighs, and drives into me again. A satisfied smile emerges as he watches himself thrust, his balls slapping against my ass with every rub and scrape of my swollen clit. He gazes back up at me as his thumb finds that nub, spinning around it in circles while his hips drive both of us toward the explosion we need like air to breathe.

My world is upside down and inside out, the only anchor him and the ecstasy of our joined bodies. When I don't think I can hold on any longer, he drops me back to the bed, laying on top of me as he continues to fuck me like he may never have me again. I feel the wave cresting within me, all the little fires he's lit growing into an inferno that will burn both of us to the ground. And then his mouth is on mine, his hips shifting just enough for his dick to find that spot inside me that always—every single time—rocks my world.

He breaks our kiss long enough to snarl, "Come for me now, rabbit," and then takes my mouth again while I fall apart, my orgasm pulsing through my body in one surge after another, each more powerful than the last. He comes as I do, his dick throbbing inside me as he roars my name.

When Fhord has nothing left to give me, he falls to my side, pulling me over and onto his chest. His hand pushes the hair away from my face, and he strokes my cheekbone, his caress gentle. "Sometimes," he says after a few moments, his voice soft, "I wonder what the gods will demand of me as tribute for giving me more than I deserve."

His worry whispers across my skin as my heart slows and then starts to race. But I refuse to fear those bastards. They've fucked with our lives too much already. "That's not the question," I growl as I lean up on my elbow to capture his gaze. "The question is what we will demand of the gods, for keeping this from us for so long." I pause, running a finger along his bottom lip and watching him shiver beneath my touch.

"This is what fate intended," I remind him as I tug on his lip. "This is right and real. The gods tried to prevent it, but they lost. We will never let them win again."

His answering smile is savage. "Never again," he promises, his hand cupping my cheek.

"Never again," I agree, before laying down to let him draw me closer to him with a sigh.

My last thought before sleep takes me is that he's right to worry. The gods kept Fhord from me and they'd take him again if they could.

But I won't let them.

He's mine and I'm never letting him go.

CHAPTER SEVEN

DANI
NOT AGAIN

"DO YOU HAVE TO sit so close?" I bitch, shoving my shoulders back into the male who cannot seem to stay away.

I've never wanted to escape someone so much. Every touch is agony. Because it feels so fucking good to have him at my back, and I can't let myself enjoy this. That path only leads to misery and disappointment.

"Do you think I want to be stuck to you like this?" he demands as he tries, again, to push himself away from me. "Your dragon's back is sloped. I keep sliding forward."

"I've carried other riders. None drapes themselves around me." I'm not being completely honest—okay, I'm not being even a little bit honest—but I don't give a fuck. Toffer's hold doesn't trigger these kinds of sensations in me. He can be clasped firmly at my back, arms clinging to me, and my body will be as calm and cool as a winter morning. Mikkael's touch is fire, and I hunger for the heat I know he would bring.

He manages to get far enough from me to eliminate any contact between our bodies, his legs gripping Vulryn so tightly she rumbles into our bond. "This flight cannot be over soon enough," he complains, before falling into silence.

As I said, my dragon tells me, frustration in every word, *he is the angry male. Are you certain we must take him? I do not think he will convince my drake of anything except that he is right. He made a poor choice.*

Matthias was a bastard, but I don't remind her of that. She only cares about Ziselær's feelings, and she's terrified bringing Mikkael will fuck up our only chance to reach him. I don't know what in all the worlds I was thinking, taking the advice of a corpse who's been trapped in an ancient forest for centuries. *It's too late*, I gripe. *We're stuck with him. Let's just get to Ziselær and get this over with.*

And if we are forced to stay with my drake for days or weeks, will the angry male remain with us the whole time?

Yes, I think? I'm not really sure what we'll do if it takes that long to reach Ziselær. *Let's take it day by day, let your drake guide our decision.*

As it should be. We will do as my drake wishes.

We're silent after that, my thoughts bouncing over everything that's happened and how much remains to be done if we're going to defeat the Dróttning. Anything to keep my mind off the male that has again slid forward, his thighs grazing against mine every few seconds as he leans back, trying to keep the rest of his body away from me.

Days later—well, hours that felt like days—Vulryn lands outside the cave Fhord pointed us to. It's hidden, like they usually are, but I recognize all the markers. This better be it. I don't think I can fly any farther today with Mikkael's occasional touch driving me mad. I need to get away from him.

He must feel the same. As soon as my dragon's feet hit the ground, his leg flings over her back, pushing me forward as he leans over and drops to her wing, then scrambles down. "Thank fuck," he mutters, glaring at me before stalking toward the cave's entrance to start pulling at the shrubs.

"You're gonna help with the packs, right?" I demand, watching from astride Vulryn as he battles the bushes, losing more often than he wins.

"Of-fucking-course I'll help," he yells, his words harsh and cold. "Don't get me confused with the usurper who used to ride my dragon. I don't know what the fuck you ever saw in that lazy bastard, always disappearing when trouble showed up. I'll get the bags when I don't have to be right next to you to do it. Just ... get down, go take a bath, whatever. I'll take care of it."

Fuck. Me.

Sifa was wrong. Horribly wrong. As wrong as any person could ever be. Mikkael is somehow worse now than he was before. This is going to be such a long trip.

I shake my head, watching in silence as he finally wrestles all the plants away from the entrance, creating an opening large enough for my dragon to get through, and turns to stride back toward Vulryn and me. Before he can reach us, I start unstrapping the bags and dropping them to the ground, ignoring his glare when I don't obey his command to let his manly self take care of it. Because I'll be gods-damned if I let him do one single thing for me.

It is not too late, Vulryn tells me as she swings her head around, her beautiful crimson eyes wide. *If you send him into the cave, you can tie the bags on me again and we can leave before he stops us. Our journey will be much more pleasant without the angry male.*

I laugh and slap her neck—drawing another look of utter scorn from that same angry male—and climb down from her back. *You have no idea how much I'd love to do that*, I snort. *But that draugr-thing said we have to take him. If this is what Ziselær needs to come out of his depression, it'll be worth it.*

I do not trust the corpse, Vulryn declares dismissively. *My drake will not be swayed by such a churlish rider.*

We'll see. Let's get to Ziselær and figure it out from there. At least we're here. We can stay away from him tonight, let him be a bastard on his own.

As you wish, Vulryn responds with a shrug of her shoulders—a strange movement she must have picked up from humans, since I've never seen another dragon do it. It's cute, and I love her even more for it. She turns toward Mikkael, her disdain for him displayed in brittle eyes and a tight snout, flicks her tail, and struts past him into the cave.

Glorious bitch that she is.

He grumbles something under his breath as he watches her go, then turns toward me, his palm stretched out toward the bags I'm standing next to. "What are you waiting for?" he demands.

"What are you waiting for?" Bastard.

"Grab whatever you're going to take and go," he barks, flinging his hands into the air. "I'll get the rest."

"Are you afraid to get close to me, Mikkael?" I ask with a slow smile and a wink. "Worried I'll bite?"

"I've had more than enough time with your scent in my nose," he snarls, before pausing to take a breath, his chest expanding and then deflating as the fight seems to whisper out of him. "I'm sorry," he groans.

And my guard goes up. Because he's the most stunning man I've ever met, perfect for me in every way. I love his dark skin, such a contrast to my pale features, and the muscles that ripple under his tunics and leather pants. I've only ever seen hints of his tattoos and have dreamed more than once about shoving his clothes out of the way, finally seeing what he hides beneath the garments he's never without.

Worse, I *like* him, much as I wish I didn't. When he's not being an asshole, he's charming and sweet, and I find myself getting drawn into him. I can't let that happen. Not again.

"The gods-damned mating bond is fucking with me," he says after a few seconds. "That ride was ... hard. So fucking hard," he adds with a smirk and a glance down at the erection I've been trying to ignore since it formed between us hours ago. It's not like he could hide it. We both know exactly how hard the ride was for him. "I'm gonna need you to go, take a bath or something, before I bring everything in."

"I get it," I tell him with ... not a smile, but less of a frown. "My skin's been itching since you mounted Vulryn behind me." Itching isn't the right word, but it's better than the truth—that I feel every single touch in my core. "Let's just make it through tomorrow, get to Ziselær, and decide from there if we ever share a dragon again."

"Yeah, that's all we can do." He stands there watching me, one eyebrow quirked, as I find myself entranced by this slightly nicer side of him. "My stubborn spy," he murmurs, almost to himself, when I don't move. "I wasn't kidding," he adds with a smirk, that playful, flirtatious grin he shared with me freely when we were stuck in the cavern together. Before I gave him reason to hate me even more. "My cock will be stiff all night if I can't escape from your scent. Because it is driving me absolutely nuts."

I can't help myself. My gaze flicks down to said cock, which has formed an impressive bulge in his pants. "Sorry," I tell him as I try to pretend I wasn't ogling him, focusing on his eyes instead. "But you'll need to move or you won't be able to avoid my scent when I go into the cave."

He responds with a sharp dip of his chin, turning to stride far—really far—to the side. He watches as I snatch half the bags, smirk at him again because it's really too much to carry in one trip, and stride through the opening, my spine straight and my shoulders back. I even flick my hair before I pass into the cavern, just to let him know he's not getting to me.

I'm such a liar.

I'm plopping my bags next to the far wall—giving him all the room he needs to get as far away from me as possible—when he walks in with the rest of our things. I watch as he pulls shrubs and bushes back into place, protecting us while we're here. His umber skin is warm in the light that filters into the cave, hints of the tattoos he never shows peeking out beneath the long sleeves of his tunic. I stretch my fingers and puff out a breath, shoving down the urge to tug off the band that always ties his long, dark hair and run my hands through it.

"Fhord said there's an enormous pool in the cavern at the end of the largest tunnel," I tell him, dragging my thoughts back where they belong. "Big enough for Vulryn. You go bathe first. I'll get dinner started, then she and I can take it after we eat. We prefer bathing right before bed anyway."

"Thanks," he grunts, dumping everything next to the fire pit and grabbing his pack before tramping deeper into the cave.

The air lightens without his anger and misery weighing it down. I suck in what feels like the first deep breath I've been able to take since we left the others this morning. Setting up my sleeping pads and blankets quickly, I stride to the bags he dropped and dig for what we need.

As I start to chop the root vegetables I'll use for our stew, I let the relief I've been holding back wash over me. We're finally going to Ziselær. I don't know what will happen, but I know it's necessary. And that eventually, Vulryn will bring him home to us. He won't be able to resist her.

Mikkael's gone a long time, thank the gods. When he comes back, he sets up his own bed—on the other side of the cave from me—then walks over to the fire. "What can I do?" His voice is soft. Whatever angst or anger was bothering him is gone, for now at least.

"Nothing," I tell him. "It's nearly done."

He turns and drops onto a rock more than a male's-height away. For a few minutes, his gaze dances about the cavern, the attempt to avoid looking at me so obvious I have to fight to hold back my laugh. That would not go over well, and this ride will be more pleasant if we're not sniping at each other the whole time. Eventually, he gives up and watches as I finish our meal.

"It smells good," he says after a moment.

"It'll be enough. Simple but filling."

He's quiet again for a long time, his gaze never leaving me. When he finally speaks, he looks down at his hands and doesn't look up again.

"I'm sorry I've been such an ass," he mumbles. His voice clears as he continues. "I'm not normally this miserable to be around. The thwarted bond with Z has fucked with me more than I could have expected."

I'm silent. I think he just wants to talk and I don't know how I'd comfort him. Nothing I can say would help.

His eyes are haunted when he glances up again. "It's worse since Matthias died. When Z's bond was shared between us, I sensed it less inside. It was a constant presence but only really flared to life when I was near Z. And then Z killed that usurper and it felt like my bond expanded, demanding the dragon who no longer was tied to another rider." He spits out a rueful laugh, smirking as he adds, "It was not happy when he left."

He sighs and my bond to this heartbroken male twists inside me, the demanding bitch. It's all I can do to stop myself from running over there and wrapping him in my arms. I'm only dealing with one fucked-up bond, and I've got Vulryn to keep me sane. I'd be going nuts if both of my bonds were as broken as Mikkael's are.

"Anyway," he tells me, his eyes clearer, "I think that's why our bond is bothering me so much. They share the same place in my gut, and when I'm close to you, I can't tell them apart. All I know is that everything I am craves the connections the fates decided I need, for whatever fucked up reason. But I'll control it, stop being such an ass. I promise."

Now it's my turn to sigh. It's so gods-damned tough to remember that he hates me when he's this nice. "I'll be better too," I assure him. "I know I can be a bitch. I need to be a little more understanding." I smile and wink. "You are my mate, after all."

His responding grin releases a knot in my gut I've been carrying around all day. "It's the least you can do for your mate."

"That and a good meal," I amend.

"Well, that's a given. You're supposed to feed me, right? It's a mate thing?"

I let my face tell him how much I hate that suggestion.

He smirks. "Not a mate thing?"

"Not mates who don't like each other."

"Okay, good point. I'll help with the cooking."

We're quiet as we eat. We said everything we needed to say. Maybe tomorrow won't be quite as miserable as today. "I'll clean up," Mikkael says as I stand to wipe out my bowl. "It was a good stew. I'll store it for breakfast. Go get your dragon and bathe. The pool is nice."

"Thanks, Mik." I nod and get my things, anxious to wash off the day.

I'm going to the pool, I tell Vulryn as I stride down the tunnel. *Join me.*

I am in the pool. It is pleasant to be away from the angry male. He makes me question the wisdom of the fates.

He's not that bad.

He is.

I don't respond because the tunnel opens in front of me to reveal a pool shimmering a soft aqua in the light Mikkael left for us. It's quiet and calm and I wonder if I could just stay here all night. I drop my things and pull my knives from their sheaths, then take off my shirt, pants, and underwear, folding them next to the fresh clothes I brought. When I step into the pool, I feel the tension leave my bones.

Fuck, this feels good. I might stay here all night after all.

Vulryn's shriek yanks me out of the haze I let myself fall into. My eyes slam open and I watch—my heart skipping and then racing in my chest—as my dragon fights to stay afloat. *WHAT THE FUCK?* I demand, pushing from the rocks to swim toward her, as if I could do something about whatever the fuck is happening.

Stay away, she responds, her voice much calmer than it should be. *I am being attacked. I will fight it.*

Fuck! Fuck, fuck, fuck. I drag my gaze away from her toward my clothes, realizing that if I'm going to do anything, I'll need a weapon, and my knives are close. Fighting the *need* to go to her, I swim to the edge and drag myself up. I'm halfway to my things when Mikkael emerges in the cavern, his eyes angry.

And I don't even give a fuck that I'm naked in front of him. "Something's attacking Vulryn," I scream as I grab my largest blades and spin back toward the pool, running to dive in and toward her.

The water's churning, and I can barely see her head above the frantic waves her wings are creating. I feel the disturbance to my side when Mikkael jumps in next to me but don't turn to look at him. My entire focus is on my struggling dragon. My heart is galloping in my chest, my body so cold, I wonder if I'll ever be warm again. None of that matters, though. Vulryn is fighting for her life, and I'll be damned if I'm going to let her fail.

When I'm half a dragon's-length away, I pause to get my bearings and suck in a deep breath, plunging down to try to see what the fuck is attacking my beast. I vaguely sense Mikkael doing the same and swim away from him, hoping he gets the hint and knows we should attack from different directions.

And then I catch a glimpse of it, almost sucking in the water around me. My shock at what's surrounding Vulryn's feet is so stark, it feels like a dream. It's an enormous tail, the end of a snake or serpent, attached to a body so large I can't find all of it despite the clear water in the depths of the pool. I can see two or three dragon's-lengths into the water, and there's no hint of a head. It looks like it goes on forever.

Vulryn is still fighting it, her massive wings fluttering frantically as she tries to pull away. I kick myself up to the surface and take in a deep breath as I swim to the other side of my dragon, then drop again, pushing myself deeper toward the monster trying to take Vulryn from me as she submerges and attacks it with her beak. I find a spot out of her way and cling to it, trying to shove my knife into its thick skin.

I can't. My blades are sharp, but this is the strongest hide I've ever encountered. From the corner of my eye, I see Mikkael doing the same, his arm encircling part of the beast as he searches for a place to stab it. He's as frustrated as me.

My heart is pounding in my ears, my chest cracking wide open as I search desperately for some weakness. But there's not a single fucking one. This gods-damned monster is impenetrable. I'm growing weak from my need to breathe, but I can't let go. It feels like I'd be letting go of my dragon to release this beast, even for the air my lungs urgently need.

And then the serpent starts to plummet. I realize it's been playing with Vulryn so far—more than capable of dragging her to its depths whenever it chooses—and has decided to put an end to the game. With a strength even my dragon won't be able to resist, it yanks her into the pool, towing her fully under the water, even as her wings scramble to find some escape. There is none.

Go, she commands. *You will not die with me.*

I sure the fuck will, I spit back at her. *You will not die without me.*

I forbid it, she declares before spinning her head toward me to gently—so fucking gently—take my arm in her snout. Before I can stop her, she tugs me away from the monster and flings me to the surface.

I fight to slow my ascent, spinning in the water to push myself back toward her—my lungs screaming at me—but it's too late. Vulryn is dropping so much faster than I could ever swim. I can only watch, horrified, as she grows smaller and smaller, and then disappears.

My chest cracks wide open, the pain of her loss so great, I reflexively open my mouth and suck in the water that will take my life too. I welcome it. I can't live without her.

I barely notice Mikkael grasping me around the waist and kicking us both to the surface as I struggle weakly, trying to stay with Vulryn. To die with my dragon.

I'm too weak. I can't fight him. I can't fight anything.

Vulryn's gone.

Nothing will ever matter again.

CHAPTER EIGHT

MIKKAEL

I COULDN'T STOP IT

I FINALLY MAKE IT to the surface—dragging a motionless Dani with me—and gasp for air, pulling her up and onto her back to give her a chance to breathe too.

She doesn't. She's still as death, her skin ghostly pale. For a moment, I'm terrified she didn't make it. Gasping to fill my aching lungs, I lift her on me—her back to my chest—and start to kick while I search for that spark inside me that belongs to her. I cry out in relief, tears erupting in my eyes, when I find it. I don't know what I'd do if I lost her too.

The thought lands in my brain with a thud, shattering all the lies I've been telling myself about my feelings for this beautiful, precocious, funny female. As I propel us toward the nearby shore, desperate to reach it and force the water out of her lungs, I cling to the flame we share, doing everything I can to feed it, to make sure it stays lit.

I hear my heartbeat pounding in my ears, feel the vise clamped to my chest, as my arms pump frantically through the water, legs kicking as hard as they can without dislodging my mate. I'm throwing everything I have into the swim, but that's not why my heart aches. Dani must live. And it's not just because fate paired us. That's physical, and I've realized since Ziselær killed Matthias that I can distinguish between the compulsion that comes from the mating bond and my own emotions and desires and needs.

I need Dani to live. Not the mating bond. *Me.*

We'll never be together. There's too much hurt and distrust between us. But I can live without that. I just have to know she walks this fucked-up world somewhere.

We finally make it to the shore, my breaths rasping in my throat, and I haul myself out of the water, then drag her up behind me. I've never done this before, but I've seen someone bring a drowned sailor back to life. I know what I have to do. Alternating between pushing at her lungs—trying to force out the water she swallowed—and breathing air into them, I chant a prayer to gods who probably don't exist. Mythical beings who couldn't give a shit about me even if they did.

Long seconds or minutes or maybe hours pass as I fight fate or the gods or the monster that snatched Vulryn away, in my desperation to save Dani's life.

And then she coughs, and everything in me relaxes. I realize I was bound up in a thousand knots—running up and down my back, squeezing my lungs, clenching around my throat, weighing down my limbs—and that every one disappeared with that single sign that Dani still lives.

I roll her over, patting and rubbing her back as she coughs up water and food and whatever gunk fills her lungs and stomach. My mate is gasping and spluttering and puking, and she's never been so gods-damned beautiful.

I'm very, very fucked.

"Vulryn?" she chokes out when she's finally able to suck in a breath.

"I don't know. I'm so fucking sorry. I couldn't do any-thing. I couldn't stop it from taking her."

Her sob binds all the knots inside me again. I lay down behind her and pull her into my arms, giving her whatever comfort and warmth I can. "Can you feel her?" I whisper. "You'd know if she died. Does she live?"

She sucks in a deep breath and holds it, her eyes focused on the wall ahead of us as she lets herself relax into me. When she coughs out a hiccupping laugh, grinning as she turns to look at me, I smile too, every coil releasing in me again.

"I can feel her. I have no fucking idea how, but she sur-vived."

"It must have taken her to an underground cave where she could get air. Can you speak with her?"

Dani's quiet for a few moments, her eyes lifting to the cavern above as they often do when she and Vulryn talk but she can't see her dragon. I doubt she even realizes she's doing it. I see her, though. I know all her little quirks, every strange and charming thing she does.

"I can't reach her," she says at last. "I think she's uncon-scious. She can't be out of range. Not yet."

"How do we find her? Can you feel that string that connects you? Follow it, maybe?"

"I've never tried that. Never had to."

She looks down then, sees my body wrapped around hers, my arms holding her close to me. And a touch of pink flows into her cheeks.

"I ... I'm sorry," I mutter. "You were cold and hysterical. I thought it would help."

"It did," she sighs, her eyes casting ahead for a few seconds as she continues to lie in my arms. "Thank you." She shrugs against me now, and I release her, rolling over to disentangle my top arm and leg from hers. "I need to sit up," she tells me as her hands lift to cover her breasts. "I think it'll help me search for that thread, see if I can follow it. Can you ... get me a blanket, please?"

I lift her slightly to tug my bottom arm from beneath her, then sit up and help her do the same. As I stand, my gaze focused on her face, she hugs herself and lifts her knees—hiding as much as she can—then sucks in a deep breath. "Fuck, I hope this works," she murmurs before closing her eyes and going still.

I drag myself away and stride into the other room, grabbing a blanket and returning to her as quickly as I can. She's quiet while I cover her, so I sit and watch her face for any sign of success. I see none. Dani's brow is wrinkled when she begins, her fingers resting against the base of her throat, her bottom lip tucked beneath her teeth as she chews at it nervously. As the seconds pass, though, her lips settle into a frown and everything about her droops. Her head cants forward as she falls toward her knees and her shoulders slump.

"The thread's there, but I can't follow it. It stops somewhere deep beneath us. I don't know if it's because she's too far away, or something else." Now she looks at me again, shadows in her eyes. "And I don't know how the fuck I'll be able to reach her."

"I wish I knew how to contact Fhord and Sifa," I respond as my thoughts bounce around our options—none of them good. "They might know what to do."

Then I feel him.

Z's coming, and he's frantic. Desperate. Angry.

He's not close yet—probably vikus away—but even from this distance, I can tell he's flying faster than he ever has before. He needs Vulryn to live as desperately as Dani does.

I lift my gaze toward the cave's entrance, as if I could see him from here, with so much rock and space between us. "Z knows," I tell her. "He'll be here soon."

"Ziselær's coming?"

"He is," I answer with a nod and the barest of smiles. "He'll help. He's as bound to Vulryn as you are."

Dani's eyes shine, bright and crisp as the sky on a sunny day, as tears fill them then slide down her cheeks. "I love your dragon so much."

"He's fucking amazing," I breathe, my lips lifting into a full grin. "I can feel his emotions. He's still so traumatized, grieving Matthias with everything he is, but he loves Vulryn more. He won't let her die."

"Let's go greet him," she says as she pushes herself to her feet. For a moment, she hesitates, as if she's not sure what she'll do next. Then she extends her hand, her gaze finding mine.

I can't move for a moment, my chest expanding as I watch her. It feels like a crossroads. An offer to try to set all our bitterness behind us and join together in this one thing. We'll work together to find Vulryn and then we'll go our separate ways. Nodding, I lift my hand to hers and let her haul me up.

"Fuck, you're heavy," she says with a laugh as she releases my hand and turns to stroll toward the cave's entrance. "Don't know what in Helheim I was thinking."

"Neither of us is thinking straight right now," I respond as I follow her out, breathing easier than I did a moment ago. "Hopefully Z's head is a little clearer." I grimace, adding, "Although it doesn't feel very clear right now. His thoughts are as scattered as mine." I pause, hesitant to leave her behind.

"I'll be quick," she promises, glancing down at the blanket she needs to shed to get dressed.

"You're safe," I remind her—or maybe myself—and turn to leave.

Exiting the cave, I shift aside the bushes to create enough space for him to enter, then stand in silence to wait. Dani joins me a minute or so later, reaching for my hand, like I'm the one who needs to be comforted. Then I see him, a dark blue speck in the cyan sky stretching above us, and take the first full breath I've managed since he left. I can tell from here that his feelings about me haven't changed, but it doesn't matter. He can hate me all he wants. At least he'll be near.

Ziselær's black eyes are focused on me when he's close enough for me to see them. But they're narrowed and I get the feeling he still can't stand the sight of me. That if he could go back in time and kill me in the park the first time we met, he would. He's coming for Vulryn alone. It's still more than I could have asked.

His gaze shifts away after a few moments, resting on Dani. She relaxes under his inspection, her shoulders settling as she exhales slowly. I think she was as wound up as me, anxious for him to get here and help. If he can.

Move! His barked command drops into my thoughts. He doesn't want to risk touching me and is asking—no, ordering—me to move away from the cavern's entrance. I lift my chin, trying unsuccessfully to capture his gaze again, and stride a dragon's-length away. He lands next to Dani, nuzzling his snout into her side. He's trying to comfort her. And I think he yearns for the comfort of his draikana's rider.

She leans into him, a single tear sliding down her cheek as she reaches behind his horn to scratch his favorite spot, her other hand stroking his cheek. I want to drag my gaze away from them, but I can't. I've never seen them together like this. Vulryn's always been between them in some way. My gut twists as I watch the female and dragon who are supposed to be mine, but both chose a male who didn't deserve to wipe their asses. And now they're grieving his death.

The fates are so fucked.

"I can't talk to him," Dani says as she looks up toward me. "Sifa said she and Tindera can exchange words, the way the dragons do with the Dróttning, and Ziselær and I should be able to do the same. But I've tried reaching him. I can't."

"Maybe it's because he rejected my bond," I offer. "Or because you and I rejected our bond. Or both. It might require the kind of connection Fhord and Sifa have embraced for the riders to be able to speak with the other mate's dragon."

"How are we going to speak with him, then? I get the feeling he doesn't want to talk to you."

"Oh, he definitely doesn't want to talk to me. He hollered a command at me when he got here, but he was angry about that." A sad smile lifts my lips as I finally capture his gaze. "He'd rather ignore me completely, but he can't. We'll have to talk. He'll have to talk to me."

Ziselær spits out a puff of smoke, which settles around Dani's legs before dissipating. I feel his anger spike, a rage so potent it takes my breath away, spilling into me.

"I'm sorry," I tell him, my chest growing heavy again as his grief and anger take root in my gut, as if they'll never leave again. "So fucking sorry. I didn't want you to kill him. I was ready to die. It would have been an honor to die by your flame. If it would help you to take my life now, do it. End me and take Dani to find your draikana. She's all you need anyway."

He watches me for a long time, his eyes as black as the starless night but still so full of life. They're a dark, deep sea, no light to display all that dances and thrives beneath the surface. I feel the weight of the decision he's making, and how brutal it is for him. He's trying to hide from me, but I can sense the guilt that's nearly drowning him and his desperation to escape it. Maybe my death would help, even if only for a moment.

I don't move—I can't—while he decides. Finally, he snarls at me and pulls his snout away from Dani's embrace, his tail flicking angrily as he looks into the cavern. *Draikana*, he bellows. He wants to see the pool where we lost Vulryn.

"Look at me first, Z. Please."

Ziselær, he responds, his tone flinty, uncompromising.

"I won't call you that. It's his name for you. I'll call you anything else. Not that."

His head spins and his gaze finds mine again, but he doesn't speak. Instead, he lets the fury in his eyes tell me exactly how he feels. *Draikana*, he repeats at last.

"Okay, we'll take you there," I tell him with a little smile. "My offer to you stands, though. My life is yours. Take it whenever you want—whenever you need—if it'll help you get through your grief."

He snorts again, this one a bitter laugh. Nothing I can do will help him.

I nod, striding for the cavern's entrance as he rears back, giving me the space I need to pass without touching him at all. It's like he fears contact, and I wonder if he does. But even as the question filters into my mind, I understand, as if the answer lives within me somewhere.

Dragons and riders bond through touch. Nobody's ever told me that before, but I know it as surely as I know that Z is mine. He refuses to bond with me, and that starts with avoiding me at all costs.

I have no clue how the fuck we're going to get through this. I'll need to ride him when we go in search of Vulryn. It's not like he can carry me in his claws the whole way.

Although I suspect that's exactly what he'll want to do, if I can convince him to carry me at all.

As soon as he sees the pool, Z plunges in, his wings undulating to help him dive faster than I would have thought possible. In a few seconds, he's gone. The water is crystal clear, but he's so deep, I can't see a hint of him.

Dani's shuddering breaths from beside me echo my fear. What if he's chasing her this way and doesn't come back? He didn't say he'd take us to find her. He didn't say shit. He came in response to Vulryn's distress, demanded to see where she'd disappeared, and then followed her down.

"I don't know if he's coming back," I mutter when I finally find the courage to voice my fear.

"What did he say to you?"

I sputter out a laugh. "As little as possible," I tell her. "He told me to move when he first arrived so he didn't risk touching me. Ordered me to call him Ziselær instead of Z—which is the one thing I won't give him—then demanded to know where Vulryn was when she disappeared."

"Why won't you call him by his name?" Dani's voice is gentle. I suspect she realizes how much of a sore spot this is for me.

I turn to look at her because I need her to see my truth. "That usurper had what's mine, for a long time." At her grimace, I clarify, "Not you. That's not what I meant. Z. He rode my dragon for a century, since he was a hatchling. Matthias was all Z's ever known and Z's identity was tied to him. To being Ziselær *for* him."

I inhale, picturing Z's wings when he flew into the training grounds, thinking about all Z suffered under the usurper's hands. "The bastard turned Z into something he's not. My dragon was cruel because the rider the Dróttning chose forced him to be. He committed travesties—like that bullshit with Khirta—at his rider's command. But that's not who he is. When Z finally lets go of Matthias, and he will, I don't want anything to connect him to his old self."

I nod, knowing as I speak the words that this is how it must be. "He'll be the dragon he's supposed to be. It's fitting that his name would change too. That he'd let go of everything that ties him to his former life—the usurper, the Dróttning, the Nest, and even his name. I know I won't ever be his rider. Even if he agrees to carry us, it'll be temporary. But I'd like his new life to be fully free of the pain of his time with Matthias."

Z flings himself from the water, startling both of us as he lands on the other side of the pool and shakes out his heavy feathers. *Alive*, he announces. I can tell he doesn't want to speak with me but he's realized he has no choice. He has to communicate information, and he doesn't have the bond with Dani he needs to do it.

I'm so fucking glad Toffer isn't here. It's a salve on my battered soul to hear Z in my thoughts, even when every word vibrates with anger and hate.

"Z knows she's alive," I tell Dani, although my gaze never leaves my dragon. "But like you, he couldn't follow their thread. Wherever she went, it's too deep for him to chase this way."

"What do we do?" Her question is to him.

Alone.

"Fuck, no." My response to him is immediate and angry.

"What?" Dani's startled question shifts my gaze toward her.

"He wants to chase her alone. He doesn't want to be ridden by anyone else."

Now, she turns toward Z. "Please don't go without me," she whispers, so much emotion in her voice, I have to fight my *need* to assuage her pain. "I have to go, search for her too."

Alone. His response is firm, unwavering.

"He said 'Alone' again," I tell Dani as I turn back to stare at Z. My next words are for him. "You know that's not an option," I insist. "What if she's captured someplace you can't reach? Or if you need to speak to a human to get information about her? Are you going to give up? Come back and get me? I have to be there. You know it's true. And Dani needs to come too. Your connection to Vulryn will be stronger together."

Never! This word is a shriek, full of a host of emotions, all of them so strong, I actually stagger back a few steps. He's not ready. He may never be ready. But I think he's realizing he has no choice.

"I won't say a word in your mind," I promise him. "I know that's the problem—me communicating with you that way created a bond you couldn't resist. I won't do anything to enhance that bond. I'll only talk to you out loud, and only when we must to exchange information about Vulryn. I won't touch you except when I'm on your back, and I'll throw a blanket between us so we don't have any contact. I can even use gloves so you never feel my skin."

He's quiet, listening as flames filter through his teeth.

"Whatever you ask," I continue, feeling his resolve weaken. "Anything you need. And when we find Vulryn, I'll go. You'll never see me again. Just ... take us with you. Don't force Dani to face this alone. She's as devastated as you. She needs Vulryn as much as you do."

When Z turns to Dani, his eyes soften. She shares his pain, in this at least. And he's a kind beast. He would never intentionally hurt his draikana's rider. *Together*, he says at last, the word a grouse in my mind. And I nearly collapse, the relief at his agreement stealing all my strength.

It's not much. He still hates me.

But it's more than I had dared hope.

Better than I deserve.

And I'm so fucking grateful.

CHAPTER NINE

FHORD

A GOOD PLAN

HOLY FUCK, I LOVE waking up next to Sifa.

It's early and her soft, even breaths whisper over my chest, reminding me that I need to let her sleep. Regardless of what the cock digging into her leg—which is charmingly splayed across me—might think. It would like to wake her up and fuck her until the entire house hears her scream. And then fuck her again for good measure. But I'm in charge here, and my cock and I are going to let our mate rest.

Her hand is fisted, lying on top of my chest, as it usually is when she sleeps. I've often wondered why but never asked. I think it's the warrior in her, always ready for battle, even in slumber.

Dragging my mind away from Sifa for a moment, I cast out my thoughts to the rest of the house to see who else is awake. We'd only spoken for a few minutes—many things left to discuss and decide—when I carried my rabbit into this room last night, desperate to taste her and then sink into her. It had been too fucking long. I need to make sure that shit never happens again.

My breathing hitches in my throat when I sense two extra lives in the house. It should contain Sifa and me, Toffer, Thor, the Ætt, Liv, and Frida. That's who was here when we arrived. Someone must have shown up overnight. I was so lost in my mate, I didn't even realize it.

I need to make sure that shit never happens again, too. There's too much at stake for me to get sloppy.

I don't want to leave Sifa. My cock sure as fuck doesn't want to leave her. But I need to find out who's here and why. So I drag myself out from under her, rubbing the throbbing erection that won't be dropping anytime soon, and pull on some clothes. Throwing one last glance at the female I wish I was balls-deep in right now—her dark curls wrapped in my fingers instead of splayed across the bed—I open the door and slip out.

Bevin and Ulfhild are waiting for me in the kitchen, along with Liv, Frida, and every member of the Ætt. Toffer and Thor must still be sleeping, thank the gods. The cat's a real asshole in the morning.

"Good fucking morning," I grouch, letting my gaze rest on each of them for a few seconds. They're tense, ready for battle, and I suspect we'll be leaving soon. So I stride over to the stove and pour myself a cup of coffee. I'll need it for whatever we're about to discuss.

"Your timing getting into town is perfect," Bevin tells me. "We have a chance today to capture someone we've been chasing for months. You can get us in."

"Is the Dróttning in the area?" I demand. "I won't use my power if she is. We need more dragons on our side before we face her again."

"She's close, but we can get away before she reaches us. If we plan it right."

"I already don't like whatever the fuck you're trying to drag us into."

"You'll like it when you hear what it is."

Bevin's too gods-damned confident. I hate it when he gets like this. "Let me get Sifa. Whatever it is, she needs to hear it too."

"And the troll," Bevin yells out as I set my coffee on the counter and turn to stalk down the hall. "We'll need Toffer too."

"Fuck me," I mutter as I open the bedroom door and slip back in, my cock twitching in my pants at the naked female still sleeping on the bed. She's so gods-damned perfect, and I wish we could disappear somewhere. Ignore all this shit. Just be together.

But that's what we're fighting for. It's why we're here.

Sitting on the edge of the bed, I smooth a curl from her forehead and cup her cheek, smiling as she wrinkles her nose, lets out a low, slow breath, and finally opens her eyes. "Back to work already?" she asks, her hand lifting to rest on top of mine.

"Bevin and Ulfhild are here. Bastard's got some ideas about our day. Thought you'd want to hear them too."

She doesn't respond right away, her hand dropping to caress the bulge I've been trying to ignore since I left this bed. "That is not how I wanted to start this morning," she says as she squeezes me, drawing out my groan.

"I had some other ideas too," I respond as I reach out and cup her breast, leaning down to suck one of her nipples between my teeth and give it a little nip. "He seems to think it's important, though."

A knock on the door confirms his impatience. "Troll's in the kitchen. We're waitin' for ya'," Torsten gripes before stomping down the hall. I suspect he knew we'd be a while if he didn't give us a nudge back to the others.

"Later," I vow, leaning forward to take a kiss, then standing to find her clothes. She dresses quickly and takes my hand to follow me down the hall and join the others, smiling with a quiet, "Thanks," when I pour a cup of coffee for her.

"We've been trying to figure out how to neutralize the Dróttning's medallions for months," Bevin explains as he looks at Sifa. "The bitch has been focused on them, trying to manipulate them in different ways to fight back against elves. Against you."

"They nearly fucked us when we attacked the training grounds," Sifa confirms with a nod. "Dani and I had been planning to sow some confusion with Dani's memories, but they figured out a way to wield the medallion at a distance. We were three or four dragon's-lengths away from the closest trainer when they hijacked my thoughts, used my magic against me."

"We heard about that, which is one of the reasons this mission has become so critical." Bevin's quiet for a moment—strange for him—then steels his shoulders as he holds Sifa's gaze. "First, though, I know where you plan to go from here," he tells her. "Revalle's no longer safe. The Dróttning realizes you lived there and suspects you left something you value in the city. She wants it." He pauses again, adding in a soft tone. "She wants her. She's been tearing the city apart trying to find her, or any of you."

"She won't find her," my ferocious rabbit snarls, her hand squeezing mine. "She's protected in Revalle, but we're going to need her. We plan to get her and take her someplace safe."

"I don't know if you can get to her," Ulfhild says, her tone solemn. "Perhaps one of my girls should retrieve her, bring her to you."

Sifa shakes her head, throwing her shoulders back as she glares at Bevin and Ulfhild. "I won't risk it. We *will* get into the city. I won't send someone with no offensive magic after her. She'll need our protection."

"Sifa..."

I cut off whatever Bevin was about to say. Sifa doesn't need to hear this shit. "This isn't a matter we'll discuss. She's important to Sifa. She's gods-damned important to all of us. *We* will get her."

Bevin dips his head, casting his gaze down for a moment, but then he looks up again, the fire back in his eyes. Because the bastard is nothing if not resilient. "The elven prison closest to us is receiving Einar, the male responsible for creating the medallions," he tells us, his eyes sparkling.

"Einar's being sent to prison?" I'm guessing my eyebrows just slammed into my hairline. I never expected him to say that. "Did he finally piss off the Dróttning enough for her to decide he's not worth the trouble?"

"The Dróttning concluded she's gotten all she can from him. She can recreate the medallions and his efforts to extend their reach have been ... half-hearted. He's unhappy with his work in the Kastali."

"He's been unhappy since he appeared on her doorstep offering his services a hundred years ago. He's a fucking asshole, and she hates him. But he's necessary. The medallions made it possible to keep the other elves in line. Problems at the prisons disappeared overnight when she introduced them." I glance at Sifa, who knows the medallions too well. "And not just at the prisons," I add after a moment.

"How many elves does the Dróttning put to work, instead of sending them to prison?"

"Not many," Bevin tells Sifa. "The Council claims to despise the hypocrisy, but they recognize the need in a few cases. They control the elves they use carefully. None ever leave the area set aside for them in whatever Nest holds them."

"Fucking Dróttning," Sifa moans.

"Fucking Dróttning," I agree. "What changed?" I ask Bevin.

"She found someone more powerful—a possibility I never considered. This male appeared weeks ago and wormed his way into the Dróttning's trust. I've seen what he can do. I've felt it. Einar's amulets deliver debilitating pain. But this male, Jarl, can kill people with a touch after paralyzing them with the most ungodly pain I've ever experienced." He pauses, a tremble rippling through him. "He demonstrated for me. It lasted only a second or two, but it's given me nightmares since then."

"Fuck me," I mutter. "Where did he come from?"

"That, I do not know," Bevin tells me, his tone more serious than I've ever heard it.

"I've tried to reach him through my girls," Ulfhild adds, "get him talking. He's never said a word about himself. He's an enigma."

"Is he an elf?"

"We don't think so. We're not sure what he is, but he doesn't appear to be elf, or dwarf, or any of the other races that walk this world. We think he's human with powers that exceed the elves' gifts."

"Like the old gods," Sifa murmurs, a pensive expression on her face.

"Like the old gods," Bevin agrees.

"In my worlds," she tells the others, "a tree called Yggdrasil gives people who were once human their powers. Few were allowed access to the tree, but those who ate its fruit lived forever. They're powerful—like the Dróttning. Much more powerful than other beings. People grew to revere them as gods. They ruled for more than a thousand years before going into hiding."

She sighs, and her shoulders slump as if a weight fell onto them as she turns toward me. "As Asgard prepared for Ragnarök," my little rabbit adds after a moment, "the gods shared its fruit with a few humans, who grew even more powerful than the gods. One of them was Jonathan, the asshole who trapped and tortured me in Midgard before I was brought here. As bad as the medallion was, Jonathan's touch was ten times worse. And now we've got someone like him here—another male with magic capable of destroying elves."

I lift my hand to caress her cheek, wishing I could take her pain—or destroy the bastard who hurt her so badly. She smiles, leaning into my touch, before turning to the others.

"Some of those old gods have been coming here from my worlds in recent weeks," she says. "First Hræsvelgr, who tried to take Mikkael and me, then Sköll, who couldn't capture me so decided to take Thor, hoping to draw me away. It can't be a coincidence."

"Not a single gods-damned chance," I growl.

"We'll worry about Jarl next," Bevin interjects. "Today, we have a chance to capture Einar, maybe use him against the Dróttning for a change. We can't lose him to the prison. We'll never get him back."

"So we intercept the transport?" Leif's smiling. He loves this shit.

"He'll be arriving late today. It gives us time to get there and get into place."

"Why do you need me? And the troll?" So far, I haven't heard any reason to expose us to the Dróttning, to tell her exactly where we are and give her a chance to start chasing us again.

"The contingent will be enormous," Bevin explains. "My people tell me five hundred soldiers will guard Einar. She fears his power as much as she fears her enemies. She's not taking any chances."

"But you think Toffer and I can reach him?"

"We'll attack in the Gorge. It holds a mish-mash of uncharted caverns. Toffer can get us into place in an area where the rock is narrow enough for you to move it. You'll open the earth near Einar and whoever guards him, and then take him and disappear into the caves."

I watch him for a moment, letting my thoughts bounce around that area, weighing the risks. I fucking hate to admit it—because he's an annoying little shit who's managed to grow on me anyway—but the troll and I make a good pair. "It could work," I say at last.

"It will work," he promises, no hint of doubt in his tone.

"Where's the Dróttning?"

"I received word today she's in the northern Nest."

"And you trust the source?"

"With my life." Bevin pauses, his lips lifting into a smirk. "Well, with your life, but I do value your life enough to not risk it if I wasn't sure. You're the key to our success. You and Sifa and your dragons." He glances at my mate. "Thank you, by the way," he tells her. "I realized after Fhord and Tindera's escape that you must have manipulated Knut's memories. He had no recollection at all that I helped you."

Sifa nods, her shoulders lifting again as she shakes off thoughts of her worlds. "I remembered as Astarot was carrying us away, got to him before anyone else could."

"Ever resourceful," Bevin praises.

"Are you saying you won't be going with us?" I demand when Bevin watches Sifa a little too long. I know he doesn't view her that way, but it will always annoy me to see other males give my mate too much attention.

"There's still value in my connection to the rebellion remaining hidden," Bevin replies as he turns toward me. "And Ulfhild's. I won't risk exposure until the time's right. We're leaving as soon as this conversation's done. I want to be back in my bar—Ulfhild in her brothel—when you attack."

I glance at Liv and Frida. "Are you staying or going?"

And Frida looks at Leif, a question in her eyes.

Torsten stares at his friend—who now wears the barest smile, his eyes bright—then dips his chin. "They're staying," he declares.

Sifa notices it too. One eyebrow is cocked when she turns toward Frida, a half-smile on her face. "It's about time," she says to her friend, who responds with a blush.

I'll ask Sifa about them later. Leif's been hurt before, but he needs and deserves love more than anyone I know. "You ladies stay here with the cat," I tell Liv and Frida as Toffer grumbles behind me.

"Thor will thrash my throat," the troll mutters. "My pal is petulant when we part."

"You can handle the cat," I tell him. "He's not coming. Just ... make him understand." My next words are for Bevin because I'm still not sure if I can trust him, despite what he sacrificed and risked to free Tindera and me. "If you've fucked us on this, I'll kill you myself."

"Ulfhild and I are on your side, Fhord. You'll realize that with time."

I dip my chin as Bevin takes Ulfhild's hand and leads her toward the front door. I'm trusting him on this, and we'll know soon if that's wise.

"We leave in three hours," I tell the others. "Less if we can manage it. I want to be in place before the Dróttning's soldiers get close. The dragons will stay where they are. The caverns in that area are too small for them."

"Guess it's time for my gift, then," Torsten tells Sifa, his voice rough.

"Your gift?" Sifa looks impressively surprised. She's always been a good actor.

"We weren't able to toast before you left us the last time, what with Harald fuckin' things up the way he does. I'm just gonna give this to you without the whiskey we're supposed to share with these gifts. I've seen you drink it. You won't miss that part anyway."

My rabbit's smile lights up the room. "What did you get me, Torsten?"

"When I got Dani's horse, I picked up one for you too. Hilde's been a good beast, but her best days are behind her. You need a mount worthy of your fight."

She strides over and wraps her arms around him, resting her head on his chest and drawing a rare half-smile from him. "You got me a horse," she whispers, hugging him tight.

"It's just an animal," Torsten grunts, his cheeks growing red as he awkwardly pats her back.

She leans away from him to rest her hands on his cheeks. "Will you introduce us?"

I almost laugh as the tension leaves his shoulders and he releases a huge breath. Shit like this—feelings and emotion—always makes his skin crawl. He jerks his chin at the back door. "She's in the barn, through there." Dropping the arms he'd rested against her back, he turns to stride out, Sifa and me following close behind.

She's a glorious beast. Golden like the sun with chestnut hair along her legs, tail, and ears. Her body is muscular but sleek. She'll be able to carry everything she must but run as fast as Sigurd. And she's smart, I can tell at once. Her ears perk as Torsten and Sifa approach her, soft eyes gazing at the male who bought her and the female who will ride her.

"Does she have a name?" Sifa's stroking the soft fur along her neck as the horse nuzzles into her hair.

"That'll come from you," Torsten grumbles. "Name her well. Can't be bringin' bad luck on us."

Sifa's quiet for a minute or more as she gazes at the horse. "One of my favorite flowers from Midgard," she says at last, "is the morning glory. I've never seen it here. In that world, it comes in many colors, but the yellow glory is the prettiest. Some consider it a weed because it's so persistent and durable, besting other plants in the fight for survival. I value it for its fight. I suspect this horse carries those traits. We'll call her Morning Glory, Glory for short."

Torsten nods. "A good name." Glancing at the barn, he says, "Let me show you the saddle."

"You bought me a saddle too?" I think I see tears in Sifa's eyes.

"Can't ride a horse without a saddle, can you?" he demands, turning toward the open door to lead her in. "I think this'll suit you well. Let me know if not and you can use something else until I replace it."

"It looks perfect." Sifa reaches out to take Torsten's arm. "Thank you. Truly."

"Ain't nothin'," he responds as his eyes drop to the ground. But then he looks up, holding her gaze. "Welcome to our family, Sifa," he tells her.

"Thank you, Torsten. I am more grateful than you could know."

"I still think we need the drink," Leif offers from behind us. "We can't just skip over that part. It wouldn't be right."

"Oh, we'll do the drink," I assure him. "She's not getting out of that."

"When Dani and Mikkael are back," Sifa suggests. "I'd like them to be part of it too."

"Alrighty, then," Leif agrees. "When the whole family's together again."

The rest of the morning is a blur. If this group wants to get shit done, it gets shit done. Leif, Astrid, Liv, and Frida pack food, water, and other supplies we'll need if this little outing goes awry. Sifa and Toffer prepare the horses—reminding me again how gods-damned handy trolls can be, because those horses would do anything for Sifa's sidekick—and Torsten, Jorunn, and I gather our gear.

Well, weapons. That's the gear we gather. We load blades of every size and shape, a dozen bows with hundreds of arrows, and enough explosives to blow up the cavern if I sense the Dróttning and decide not to risk moving the rock with my powers. We'll still use Toffer to get us into the gorge and find the right place, but we haven't decided yet what we'll do once we're there. We're going prepared for anything.

Two hours after we got started, we gather outside. I inspect everything—because that's the kind of uptight bastard I am—and grin when I see we're ready to go.

"Time to go fuck up some of the Dróttning's soldiers," I proclaim, turning to look at each of them.

"My favorite thing." Leif smiles as he swings himself onto his horse and leads us out of the yard.

CHAPTER TEN

DANI

I GET IT

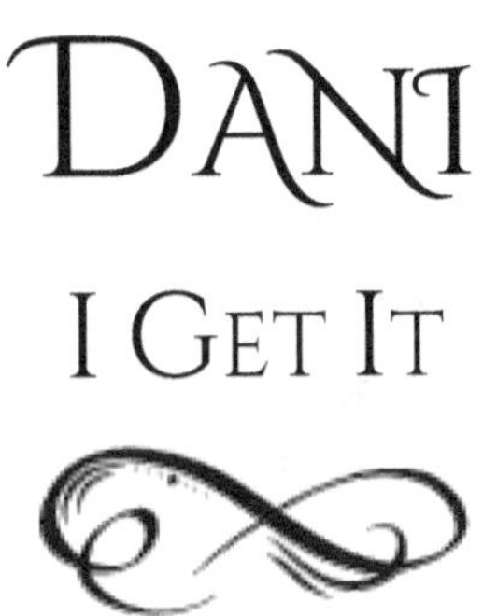

"**I** GET IT." I'm sure Mikkael can see the tears in my eyes as he looks over, but I'm not hiding from him. He'll see plenty before this is over.

"No wonder you've been such an ass," I explain when one eyebrow rises. "You've been living with this for a long time. I'm a couple of hours in, and I'm ready to strangle someone." I glance down, a slow sigh trickling out. "I'm incomplete, utterly lost." When I look up, a sad smile lifts my cheeks. "I'm gonna be a bitch until she's back."

"Now you tell me," he declares, throwing his hands up with the smallest tilt of his lips. He turns toward Ziselær, who scowls at him as he always does when their eyes meet. "Forget it," he says. "We can't take the sassy spy if she's gonna be so sassy."

"You think I'm the one he'll leave behind?" I smirk at him because we both know if one of us stays here, it'll be him.

And then I marvel for a moment that I can smirk at all. My heart's been lighter since Ziselær got here. Vulryn's alive and her steadfast, ferocious drake broke through his agony and despair to come help us find her. I'm still empty—like half of my insides were ripped out, leaving a gaping void—but I'm not hopeless.

"I mean, if we were smart," Mikkael responds, "we'd both leave your sassy ass behind."

"He's a dragon in love. He knows how pissed Vulryn would be if he arrived without me. She might send him away, tell him to come back when he's fixed his shit."

"That, I'll concede," Mikkael tells me with a wink. "Z's smart enough to stay on your beast's good side. Which probably does involve bringing you along."

"Glad we agree about something," I murmur, although I suspect I don't hide the smile that emerges as I look down. "When are we leaving?" I ask when the silence has lasted a bit too long.

"Z needs to hunt first," he tells me, his voice low enough to evade Ziselær's sharp ears. "He won't admit it, but he's been starving himself and he pushed hard to get here. He'll need a couple of large beasts and a night of rest before we go."

"Fuck." That's not the sense I'm getting from Ziselær. He's restless, and I'm sure he wants to leave as soon as we tell him we're ready. "Is he willing to wait that long? He seems anxious to go now."

"We won't give him a choice. We'll convince him we need a sheep to dress for our trip—which we really do. He'll go with me to the herd Fhord told us about, and he won't be able to resist feeding when he sees the animals. I'll dress the carcass in the field while he eats, and you can be asleep by the time we get back. Or at least pretend to be."

"You're a manipulative bastard, aren't you?" I grin because I'm not bothered. He's right about his dragon, and we need to do whatever it takes to convince him to eat and rest. Much as I *need* to go find Vulryn, I know we won't get far on a depleted dragon.

"I'll be whatever I must to help Z. Even if he doesn't want my help."

"Okay. Should I ask him?"

I almost laugh at Mikkael's responding nod, his eyes wide. "Yeah, definitely. 'Cause he'll tell me to fuck right off."

He's right about this too. Standing, I stride over to kneel in front of Ziselær. He's completely still and quiet as he watches me approach.

"We need your help," I tell him before clarifying, "I need your help." He doesn't move, so I plow forward. "We don't have enough food. There's a herd of sheep nearby. It's one of the reasons Fhord sent us to this cave first. Will you go with Mikkael to the herd? He can kill and dress a sheep, but without horses, he'll need you to bring it back."

He doesn't respond for a long time, watching me. Finally, he lifts his snout and dips his chin. Then his gaze shifts toward Mikkael, and he turns into the raging beast again, his eyes narrowing as flames trickle through his teeth. But he lifts himself to his feet and stalks out of the cave, leaving Mikkael behind.

"Guess I better go," the not-so-angry male mutters as he grabs and sheathes his knives and rummages for the bags he'll use to store the mutton, tossing a wink back at me before racing after his dragon.

I watch the cave's opening for a long time, letting myself adjust to this new, nicer Mikkael. I've seen him before—he made an appearance when we were trapped together underground—but it's rare. Usually, he's a dick and it's easy to hate him. Not so confusing. This Mikkael makes me forget he hates me. Wonder whether his feelings have softened. Because I've never hated him, much as I've hated being around him sometimes.

But I have to put all that shit to rest. He's made his feelings clear. When he's nice, it's a temporary thing, and always for a reason. Like now. He needs me. Ziselær won't take him alone. He's lucky the dragon deigned to go hunt with him. Mikkael doesn't want to piss me off, so he's on his best behavior. The real him, with his true feelings, will return when we find and free Vulryn. When he doesn't need me any longer.

I lie down after an hour or so, realizing that my near-death experience and all the emotions surrounding Vulryn's capture and Ziselær's appearance have drained me. When I wake up, the cave is dark and I hear the gentle snores of a sleeping male, along with the much louder snorts and snuffles of his snoozing dragon. They're breathing in unison, as if the mating bond has drawn them together in rest, even if it can't when they're awake.

There's something comforting about it. Hearing Ziselær and knowing he's going to help us find Vulryn calms the terrified part of me. I let their gentle—and not so gentle—breaths soothe me back to sleep.

Mikkael's making breakfast the next time I wake up, quietly stirring a pot that smells like it holds the porridge popular here in Vanatia. I watch him because I can't drag my gaze away from his broad chest, the muscles too pronounced to be hidden by his clothes. I don't fight it this time like I normally do. The Monarch and the Dróttning have fucked up so many lives. He and Ziselær should be bonded and happy together.

He and I should be bonded and happy together.

I know he doesn't want it and never will. I blew it in so many ways with him. I chose Matthias again and again, thinking that was best for Vulryn and Ziselær. But I've realized how right the fates were when they joined us. He and I would have fit perfectly.

His head turns toward me with a smile, and my heart jumps. Literally pumps more quickly in response.

Traitor.

"How'd it go last night?"

"Z ate three sheep," he tells me with a laugh, "and drank so much water, it's a wonder he could get into the air again." The grumpy dragon sniffs in response, his narrowed eyes focused on Mikkael. "I brought back enough mutton for us to eat well while we chase after Vulryn."

"Thanks for doing that."

"It was good for me." He turns toward Ziselær. "He didn't want me with him, but I needed to be there anyway."

"When will we leave?" I'm rested and suddenly anxious to go. Vulryn's probably already taken control wherever she ended up. I imagine she has her captor wrapped around her smallest claw, and I can't wait to see it.

"As soon as we can," Mikkael tells me. "I'll pack our stuff while you eat, then I'll eat while you store it on Z. He won't let me get that close until he has no choice." He turns to wink at the angry dragon, who growls in response.

This is going to be a long trip.

The porridge is delicious. He added cinnamon and another spice I don't recognize. I eat more than I would have thought possible, the warmth coating my stomach and helping me feel ready for the long flight ahead.

We're in the air within a half-hour, following the tug Ziselær and I both feel toward the ocean. It's trial and error, as we find ourselves going off course—her lifeforce drifting farther away—and backtracking to find and follow the draw. Ziselær is willing to communicate through Mikkael but not happy about it. The messages he relays are perfunctory, each with an edge of anger Mikkael doesn't try to hide.

And for some reason, it's easier riding Ziselær with Mikkael than it was Vulryn. Ziselær's bigger, with a straighter back where we sit, so I'm not constantly sliding into my mate. We still touch occasionally, but the spark that always lights between us has settled down. Or maybe I have more important things on my mind, like a kidnapped dragon, and I'm not letting my broken relationship with Mikkael bother me as much. Whatever the reason, Mikkael and I don't fight at all today.

The sun is dropping below the horizon—reflecting fire above and on the rough waters ahead of us—when the string to Vulryn leads us to a cave facing the ocean. It's the only opening in a small cove that looks like it's never been walked by man or beast. I suspect it's flooded most of the day, as the tide moves in and out, but not now. In the final rays of daylight, it's an abyss that appears eager to swallow anyone foolish enough to enter.

Like us. Since that's exactly where we're going.

"I don't think we should go in yet," I suggest. "If it floods at high tide, we could be trapped. We might want to camp here overnight and explore it with a little light."

Mikkael shakes his head. "It'll flood again soon." He points toward the plants above the entrance, still dripping from whenever they were submerged, and the ocean already starting to advance on the cave. "It rests lower than other caverns in the area. I suspect we have a very small window to get into it. It's now or we wait here until tomorrow morning."

But then he turns to Ziselær, his expression softening. "Z wants to go now," he tells me, his gaze never leaving his beast. "We made him wait all night, and he flew fast to get here. I think he's done being patient."

"I guess we're going in, then." I look at the demanding dragon, my head cocking to one side as I plant my hands on my hips. Because this is a bad idea. A really bad idea. "If we can't find a place to breathe, you're in charge of getting all of us back out here safely."

Ziselær glares at me and tramps into the cave. He doesn't look back at us. He's going, whether we follow or not. So we follow.

Mikkael lights a torch within the first couple of male's-heights because it's almost immediately too dark. Ziselær should be fine. His dragon eyes see much better than ours. But we'd be stumbling aimlessly without it.

My abs are clenched, waiting for the deluge, and my breaths already are starting to quicken. This is such a bad idea. Caves don't usually freak me out, but I'm realizing the idea of being trapped underground as water rises terrifies me. My mind keeps drawing up images of Vulryn being dragged down into the pond's depths. Remembering how fucking useless I felt. How much I wanted to die with her.

But she's alive and I don't want to die. So I cling to that thread between us, a sigh of relief whispering through my clenched teeth as I realize it's growing stronger, and I focus on that. As my breathing slows, I replace the dread with images of my ferocious, fearless beast. She always wins. She always survives. The bastard that carried her away won't beat her.

We've walked more than an hour—all downhill, to my dismay—when I start to feel the water lapping at my heels. Memories of Vulryn being sucked down and out of my sight start to force their way back in. I'm again struggling to take a breath, gulping air in as deep as it can go but still feeling like it's not enough.

And then Mikkael slows and reaches for my hand. My first instinct is to pull away, but I realize I need his touch. It calms me. I grasp onto him and my breathing slows.

"We've got you," he murmurs. "We won't let the deep take you the way it did Vulryn."

I don't respond. He knows from my touch that he's helping.

We're still going the wrong way while the water starts to move more quickly, filling the cavern as it rises to my knees, and then to my ass. But we're committed. We've gone too far to turn around and can't do anything except plow forward and hope we find air. My gaze is flitting about the tunnel we're walking through, searching for someplace we can escape. I can't see shit, though. We're trapped in this cave until we find a way out.

Even with the comfort of my mate's touch, my breaths start coming in short rasps again, my chest tight. I feel everything—water lapping at my hips, mist clinging to my brow, dripping in heavy lines down my cheeks, the occasional touch of fish or whatever else lives in this place as they dart past us.

When Ziselær snaps at us, I nearly jump out of my skin. I am on-edge.

"He wants us to mount him," Mikkael tells me as he tugs at my hand. "It'll get us above the water, maybe enough, but he wants to start running. He'll go faster than we could."

I grunt my thanks and let him pull me toward his dragon then push me up. His hands are on my ass for a moment, but I don't give a fuck. I'm gods-damned terrified. I've never feared anything the way I fear drowning in this cavern, my dragon alive and waiting for me somewhere at the end of this tunnel.

We settle on Ziselær's back, and I wrap my arms around Mikkael. Because in this moment, I have to *feel* him. I don't care what he thinks, how much he hates me. I *need* the comfort his touch brings.

He doesn't flinch from me, thank the gods. Instead, he holds his dragon with one hand and rests the other over my fingers, threading them together on his stomach. "Z will protect us," he promises.

Ziselær doesn't waste any time. He launches himself forward, plunging through the water with a speed and strength that finds the hope in me I thought the ocean washed away. He'd have left us behind within seconds if we weren't riding him. For now, we're high enough to not feel the waves, although that won't last long. They're rising quickly, and we'll be submerged soon unless he can find us someplace safe.

When I feel the water lapping at my feet, rising even faster than it was before, my chest tightens again and I start fighting for air one more time. I've never experienced anything like this before—nothing scares me, gods-damn it—but I'm spiraling into panic so fast, I think it'll kill me even if drowning doesn't.

And then I feel Mikkael's caress across my thoughts, his hand tightening on mine. "I've got you," he reminds me. "Z's got you. He won't let us die. He's much too stubborn for that."

I spit out a laugh because his dragon is almost as stubborn as mine. If anyone can keep us alive, Ziselær can.

"We're gonna be completely underwater soon," Mikkael warns a few minutes later as the water rises to our chests, Z's snout pointed up as high as it can go. "I'm gonna release your hands and hold on tight to Z. He can swim fucking fast, and that's what he's gonna do. When I tell you, drag in the deepest breath you can get and cling to me. I won't let him go, and you don't let me go."

"We're gonna survive this, right?" I demand, a catch in my throat.

"Fuck yes, we are," he tells me. "Vulryn needs us. We won't let her down."

I focus on my ferocious, never-say-die dragon as I force my breathing to slow down, getting myself as ready as I can for what's coming. When Mikkael barks, "Now", I take a deep inhale and hold it.

Ziselær plunges under the surface, throwing everything he has into swimming. And he is fucking fast. For a moment, I'm mesmerized by the pulse of his wings and tail, which work like fins propelling us. Everything else on his body is still, but he doesn't need his legs to increase his power or speed. He's streamlined, an arrow racing through the air.

Too soon, my body's demand for air captures my focus. I try to drag my mind away, realizing that the more I think about it, the more I need to breathe. I can't see shit, so I have no idea if we're going to find air in time. The only thing I know is that my dragon will track me down and kill me again if I die in this tunnel before we find her.

That it would destroy her to lose her rider and her drake together.

My head is woozy, my thoughts slowing to ... little ... drips ... through ... my ... brain when I feel Mikkael's caress in my mind again. I have no fucking idea how he's doing it, but I'm grateful. It gives me something to focus on other than our imminent death. Or the heartache of my dragon, losing us both in one devastating moment.

And then Ziselær flings us out of the water, soaring up into a massive cavern. I suck in air as a sob bursts from me.

We're alive.

He saved us.

I rest my head against Mikkael's back, grasping the thread between my dragon and me.

And I fill again with hope that we'll find her. That we'll save her.

CHAPTER ELEVEN

MIKKAEL

SELFISH BASTARD

I KNEW I WAS about to die. I've never been so sure of anything.

And fucking selfish bastard that I am, the thought that kept flipping through my brain was at least I'm gonna die on my dragon, my mate clinging to me.

I know it's bullshit, but I can't deny what I feel.

Vulryn appeared in my mind for a second, her devastation at losing both of them bouncing in and then out just as quickly. Because in that moment, the dragon underneath me and the female at my back were the only things that mattered. My loyal, heartbroken beast, and the sassy, sultry, so-fucking-sexy spy the fates paired me with. I think that's the way it always will be.

Z soars toward a massive ledge high above us—much too far for the water to reach it—and lands, shaking his feathers a bit before his gaze jerks to the riders on his back.

Off, he barks at me.

"Z wants us off," I tell Dani as I turn to look at her. She's bedraggled, soaking wet, her thick auburn hair plastered to her shoulders, little drops falling from thick lashes surrounding wide eyes. And she's never been so fucking stunning. She wears her joy—probably at still being alive—in a grin so broad, I can't help but smile with her.

"Well," I amend, "he wants me off. He'd probably be fine with you staying here, but I can't get off with you wrapped around me. I'd need you to move a bit, then you could hang out up here. It's the safest place in the cavern, I'm sure."

"I'm guessing whatever he said was aimed at both of us. He probably needs to stretch out these feathers. We're all drenched." She lifts her leg over Z's back and drops to his wing then walks down, her legs a little wobbly. I follow after leaning forward to scratch Z behind his horn. "Thank you for saving us," I murmur, prompting an angry snort.

As soon as my feet are on the ledge, Z stomps to the other side and shakes. Vigorously. Splats of ocean spray the rocks, many landing on us. A laugh bursts out of me as I stare in his direction. I can't see anything. It's as dark as the coal we burn in winter. But I can hear the pounding and then shuffling of Z's steps, smell the musky scent of his wet feathers along with a hint of Dani's citrus and sandalwood, feel the patter of water Z sends toward us.

For a moment, it feels like the old Z is back. But then he snarls and I realize I'm imagining things. I slam my lips shut and drop my head, hiding the smile that won't go away quite yet.

We're there at least an hour, maybe more, while Z and Dani chase the thread that leads to Vulryn. Once I lit a torch, it was clear we had lots of options for leaving this cavern. Eleven tunnels lead away, and it's not obvious to them which one is best. I relay their messages to each other while I inspect the vast space around us and the shadows that dance along the wall from the small flame next to me. It's beautiful here.

Finally, Z decides to explore on his own. Growling *Stay*, he launches himself into the first of three passages they'd been debating through me for the last several minutes.

"He's getting better," Dani tells me with an encouraging smile.

"Liar," I respond with a smirk. "He's a very emotional beast. It's like Nalani said, he can't love me so hate is his only option. And it's a fierce, stubborn hate."

"But he's talking to you more. Working with us. He could have just left instead of letting me have a say. And I could tell he wanted to leave. He's a good beast with a big heart."

"He is."

Dani's quiet for a moment, watching me, and I'm wondering what question is bouncing in her mind. Finally, she asks it, her crystal gaze still holding mine. "I felt you in my thoughts, when I was getting close to panicking."

"Yeah, that was some scary shit." I could tell how freaked out she was—something I've never felt from her before.

"How'd you do that?"

I smirk again because I don't have an answer. "I have no fuckin' idea. I sensed your terror and wanted to soothe you.

It happened on its own. I knew I was doing it, but it was like breathing—although I realize that's a fucked comparison, since that's the one thing we couldn't do. I don't have to think about how to convince my lungs to suck in air. I just do it. That's how it felt to comfort you in your thoughts."

"Well, thank you. I've never been panicked like that before and I hope I never am again. It helped."

"You're welcome." I don't turn toward her because I can't. These times when we're nice to each other are dangerous. I can't risk letting her in again.

We're silent after that, waiting for Z to return. He's gone a long time but eventually soars back toward us, frustration evident in the tightness of his snout, his rigid shoulders and snapping tail.

Fail, he reports, this time with a little nuance. He thought Vulryn's thread was getting stronger, but far into the tunnel it shifted left, and he realized he'd lost her.

"We need to take the tunnel on the left, he thinks," I tell Dani before turning back to him. "Do you want to explore without us, or should we all go together?"

Together.

"We'll go together," I relay. "I think he's realized he'll be flying for a while, so better to bring us along."

He dips his chin briefly—agreeing with me reluctantly, I can tell from the emotions wafting off him—and extends his wing. I climb up, and Dani does the same, settling in behind me. And it strikes me for the first time that when we ride Vulryn, she's in front, where the dragon's rider always sits, and I'm in front on Z. I wonder if she and Z recognize that I belong first on him because I'm his rider. Or if I'm trying to find meaning where there is none.

Z takes off with a huff, aiming for the passage he and Dani hope will lead us to Vulryn. And again, we're silent. It's hard to speak on a dragon—the wind is loud, especially in a tunnel where everything echoes—and I'm too lost in my thoughts to try to draw her into conversation.

Hours after we left the ledge, we enter a shaft too narrow for Z's wings, that looks to be shrinking. It might be too tight for him to go farther into the cavern. He lands when he runs out of room to fly, and we drop to the ground. I light another torch and take the lead, my stomach in my throat as I wonder what we'll do if he can't make it through.

After fifteen or twenty minutes, we're at the spot I dreaded. A narrow passageway that Z would have to squeeze through. He's a big beast, and I'm not sure if he'd make it.

"Is she still in front of us?" My question is to either or both of them. I imagine they'd have stopped me if we weren't going the right direction, but it's always better to put thoughts like these into words.

Yes, is Z's response as Dani murmurs, "As far as I can tell."

"Before you try to get through this, let me scout ahead. If it's narrower in front of us, we probably should just give up now." I turn to Dani. "I'll light our other torch and leave it with you and Z."

"I should go with you. If nothing else, so I can confirm we're still following Vulryn's thread."

For some strange reason, a nervous energy inside me soothes at her response. I don't want to leave her behind.

"You good with that, Z?" I can't imagine he'd disagree but better to ask. It's another excuse to talk to him, which I'm gonna do every chance I get.

He flicks his head toward the narrow opening.

"Okay, we'll be back soon."

I throw a smile his way as we trudge forward—one he doesn't return, although I didn't think he would—looking back one last time before we turn a corner. But I don't let go of him. I can feel his presence and cling to it like a drowning man to the chunk of wood keeping him afloat.

We've traveled a few dragon's-lengths into the cavern—which expanded again, giving Z room to walk if we decide he should come here—when I see the barrier that will stop us more effectively than any rock. A massive spider web hangs in our path, stretching from the ceiling to the ground and wall-to-wall. It's an elaborate mosaic that would impress me if I wasn't scared out of my mind. Because I fucking hate spiders.

And there isn't just one spider on this web. Hundreds, maybe thousands, of the little ghouls hang between us and Vulryn. Their beady eyes focus on us as soon as we turn the corner, bringing them more light than they've probably seen at any point in their miserable existences. There can't be much food down here. We must look really fucking tasty to the horde now staring at us.

I stop in my tracks, feet refusing to carry me a step farther, as Dani strides forward. "I wouldn't get that close," I warn her, a tremor in my voice I can't seem to hide. "They'd probably love to trap us in that massive web. And hold us there. And slowly digest every bit of flesh and bone and blood."

As I speak the words, I can almost feel the spiders. My skin crawls as if I'm already snared by their web and they're exploring my palsied body as they decide where to start their meal, crawling into my mouth and nose and ears, paralyzing me along the way so I can't fight back while they feast. I feel nauseous—like I might actually get sick—and I'm sucking in deep breaths to keep myself from spewing at my mate.

She turns to look back at me, one eyebrow rising as she cocks her head. I can't imagine being foolish enough to turn my back on the monsters just waiting to attack, but she's too gods-damned blasé about the bastards. "Are you frightened of them?" she asks, a little giggle in her voice.

"Come over here. Please. You're making me nervous."

"You are scared," she laughs, her eyes wide. "It's just a bunch of spiders. They're so small."

"And so creepy," I point out. "And so many. And probably so very, very hungry."

"I'll clear it," she says, pulling out her sword to stride forward.

"Wait!" I yell, my voice higher than it should be. "You'll just piss them off and they'll attack. Let's figure out something else."

She looks at me, her eyes soft. "It's okay, Mik. They're not going to hurt me."

I think that pisses the assholes off, as if they understood her and decided to prove her wrong. Without warning, they glow—they fucking glow—and launch themselves at her.

Dani's shriek is nearly as loud as mine.

All of them.

Cover her.

From head to toe.

Fuck. Me.

Seriously. Just ... fuck me.

For a moment, I can't breathe. My heart is pounding so frantically, I'm sure Z can hear it. My palms are covered in sweat. I feel like I've just run a dozen vikus. Because this is my worst nightmare. I don't know why I'm so fucking terrified of spiders, but I am *so* fucking terrified of spiders.

And the fuckers are already starting to weave a web around her, working in unison. She'll be covered soon.

If you can get through that opening, come! Please! Dani needs our help!

Coming. Thank fuck. I don't know what Z can do, but Dani needs every bit of help she can get.

I launch myself at my mate and her thousands of spiders, kicking and tossing as many off as I can, stomping on any that land on the cave's floor. Not many do. They're stubborn little fuckers, concentrating on the web they're quickly trapping her in.

Most stay focused on her—they're probably gonna wrap her up, then attack me—but a few launch themselves at me now. Their massive pincers look even bigger when they're crawling over my arms, working their way toward my neck and face. I bat them away, but for every one I get rid of, three more take its place. There's an endless gods-damned supply of spiders, and I'm fighting a losing fucking battle.

I think I'm losing my mind.

This is every one of my worst nightmares all bound together in one terrifying moment.

Because it's not me I'm freaking out about. It's Dani. And that frightens me more than the spiders.

Then they start biting me. In unison, in the same way they attacked Dani. I've got a dozen or more of them swarming me, and it fucking hurts. Like they're ripping bits of skin out, then shoving a white-hot poker into the hole. Every exposed piece of skin on my body erupts in agony. I'm still trying to focus on Dani, but I've never felt such pain in my life.

"Go, Mik," she rasps, her words a whisper I barely hear. "No reason for both of us to die here."

"Fuck you, Dani," I shout—because screaming at her is exactly what she needs right now, selfish bastard that I am. "If these little shits are taking you, they're taking me too."

Z's angry roar rattles my bones. I spin to stare into blazing eyes, forgetting for a moment that my skin is on fire. *Move!* I don't know what in all of Helheim he can do, but I get the fuck out of his way. He's much more confident in whatever he plans than I was in my half-assed attempt to help Dani.

The fire that shoots from him is unlike anything I've ever seen before. It's a narrow stream, like a rope attached to an arrow and shot into the sky. I forget about the vermin eating me alive as I watch him destroy the web and then attack every spider on the ground. But then one digs into my neck—right next to my gods-damned pulse—and I focus on what matters.

I need to get these fuckers off of me and then I need to help Z save Dani.

They're stubborn bastards, but within a minute, I've killed everything that was attacking me. No others take their places because Z's got them on the run now. *Can I help take them off Dani?* I squawk at him, unable to keep the terror from my voice.

Yes, is his response. He's so much calmer than me.

I love my dragon.

He shifts his flame as I throw myself at her, doing everything I can to not smack her every time I toss one of those little fuckers away from her head and neck. I catch one just in time to stop the little demon from forcing its way into her mouth as two others try to wedge her lips open. 'Cause these bastards are fuckin' smart.

When they're far enough away from Dani, Z shoots flame at them.

Not a stream like he's been doing. These are little darts of fire, precise and deadly. Every single one strikes a single spider, turning it into ash. And he doesn't miss. He's a gods-damned marksman, here to save the day.

Holy fuck, do I love my dragon.

And then they're gone. As if they're one being driven by a single mind, every spider abandons Dani at once. One second they're there, and the next they've vanished.

I fall next to Dani, grasping at the web to yank it away. It's sticky and attaches to me as soon as I tug on it, but there's not shit I can do about that. She needs to get free, and I'll clean this shit off my hands eventually.

She's silent while I work, her eyes huge as her gaze bounces around the cavern. Probably looking for the gods-damned spiders. Bastards might have just gone to get reinforcements. But they don't come back. We're still alone when I pull the last of the web off her and wrap my arm behind her back to help her sit up.

"Maybe next time I'll listen to you about the spiders," she croaks, barely loud enough to hear.

"It's always wise to listen to me," I respond with a grin. "For future reference."

She smirks, the horror on her face finally giving way to relief and a little bit of joy, eyes that were wide and shadowed now bright. "That was the most fucked-up thing that's ever happened to me," she says, her voice flat. "I've never seen such aggressive spiders. Didn't even consider they might attack like that. Thank you."

"Thank Z," I mutter, turning toward him. "I wouldn't have been able to get rid of them. We'd both be spider food." I smile because I feel good. I'm covered with holes where those bastards took bites out of me, but they're gone and we're here.

"That was so gods-damned amazing," I breathe. "I've never seen anything like that before."

He snuffs, dismissal the only emotion rippling from him. *Hands*, he tells me.

I lift my palms toward him, unsure what he plans. And he licks them. His abrasive tongue drags along my skin, removing a little bit of web with every lap. "Doesn't it taste horrible?" I ask, a little appalled at what he's putting himself through. "I'll get it off. You don't have to do that."

Yum, he tells me. And I nearly plop onto my ass. Because Z just talked to me. And he didn't have to.

"He likes it," I tell Dani, unable to keep the wonder from my voice. "Whatever's in this web is really tasty to dragons. He couldn't get it off you without spreading it around too much—and he didn't think you'd want him licking you all over—but me wiping it off you created the perfect little treat for him."

"Well, that's fucking amazing," Dani breathes, watching my dragon as raptly as me.

"What the fuck were those?" I ask when Z takes his final lick. "They seemed to move together, like they were able to talk to each other."

Wolf, Z responds, again with detail in his answer.

"The dragons know of them," I tell her. "They're wolf spiders—they hunt in packs like wolves. And they do talk to each other, just like it looked. The dragons think they have a mental connection, drawing from the land's magic, but they're not positive."

"Will they be back?" I hear a hint of fear in Dani's question.

And now I'm freaked out again. Because they could be going for reinforcements.

But Z's confident in his answer. *No.*

"Z says they're smart enough to avoid dragons and wouldn't have bothered us if he was here. They were in a frenzy by the time he arrived, or they'd have stopped when they saw him."

"It's good to have a dragon," Dani responds with another smirk.

"That it is," I agree. "Let's go find yours."

"Let's," she says with a nod.

Z snorts and strolls past us, leading the way to his draikana.

CHAPTER TWELVE

SIFA

MORNING GLORY

I LOVE THIS HORSE.

Morning Glory is unlike any other mount I've ridden. She anticipates my moves almost before I do, following Sigurd like she's as entranced with the stallion as I am with his rider. She's running when she needs to run and generally doing everything she must to be a perfect steed.

"This is such a good horse," I tell Torsten as he rides over to check on me when we stop to let Toffer follow the path of a cave. I've got an enormous smile on my face, but it grows even broader when Torsten's lips twitch up at the ends, his expression as close to a smile as I've seen on this stoic male. "I owe you."

"Fuck, no," he declares, the caterpillars above his eyes pulling together as his lips turn down. "We fuckin' owe you. Fhord needed a kick in his ass to tell the gods-damned Dróttning to fuck off. We all did."

"Our chances aren't great," I remind him. "Fhord and I could be leading us all to death."

"Then we'll be dead and we won't give a shit no more. If we're not living the way we should, we're better off dead." He spits, his gaze tracking toward Fhord, then back to me. "He agrees. We all do. We're doin' what's right. And it's about gods-damned time."

"We'll turn in here," Fhord yells to the group as Toffer stands, shaking the sand off his hands. "Toffer thinks this'll take us to the Gorge."

"The cave connects to the canyon," Toffer agrees. "The fight can be found on this footpath." His gaze finds mine, and he nods, then strides over to Hilde, who's carrying him today. Torsten had offered to let him take Dani's new horse, who we're calling Bob until Dani names him—a tribute to the dragon Vulryn killed before we captured her. Toffer refused. "The rebel will return to ride," he'd said.

I'm happy to see it. Hilde's still got some fight in her and she loves my troll. She'll give him everything she has to give.

Within a few minutes of entering the cave, we're stalking through a narrow cavern that leads to a tunnel too tight for our horses to pass. We dismount and tie them off, then load up, everyone carrying as much as possible. I've got weapons strapped all over me and a pack on my back with half my weight in explosives.

"I could take more," Fhord says as he watches me adjust the straps around my shoulders.

I laugh because he's already packing twice as much as me. He's strong, but I am too. "You've got plenty," I tell him. "I'm good."

"You're not good," he whispers into my ear as he steps behind me to help adjust my pack, his voice dropping into that sultry purr that sends fire straight to my core. "You're perfect. And I can't wait to worship every perfect inch of you tonight."

Holy fuck, this male. "Promises, promises," I murmur as I back up just enough to push my ass against his growing erection. "Next time, wake me up," I tell him, turning to find his green eyes, which are smoldering in the dim light. "I don't need sleep nearly as much as I need you inside me."

"You'd never sleep if my cock had any say in it," he tells me, his hand resting on my stomach to tug me even closer. "But when we're done, I'll make up for this morning with my tongue, then my fingers, and then my cock."

"That's enough," Torsten mutters as he stomps past us. "Keep that shit to the bedroom."

Fhord smirks at the retreating form of the grumpy male and grabs my hand to drag me along behind them. Before long, we're single-file, squeezing and even crawling through a few places. I trust Toffer but still can't ignore the fear that he misjudged this cave. He seems confident, though, and we follow along behind him.

It takes an hour or more to reach the cavern he identified, but we make it in plenty of time to get set up. And we wait. And wait. And wait.

This is always the worst part—sitting silently, knowing lives will be lost today, with nothing to do but worry about who will live and who will die. It could be any one of us. We're strong, but as we usually do, we face impossible odds. Five hundred soldiers march to this place, and we have a handful of rebels, only two with magic. At least the Dróttning's far enough away for Fhord to use his powers without much concern.

And we do have powerful magic. Much more importantly, we have a cause. The Dróttning's people fight because they must. Few soldiers in this land are committed to her. Most, like Dani in her country, have no choice. It kills me that we have to end their lives. But that's the price of war, and we have to win to stop the futile deaths. To save lives—human, elf, and dragon—we have to take some first.

Hours after we arrived, Fhord's expression changes. He senses them, I can tell. Everything slows down as my thoughts shift from waiting to preparing.

I've been sitting here the entire time without paying attention to my surroundings, so I'm not prepared for the wave of emotion that crashes over me when I start to ready myself for the fight ahead. An angst erupts from nowhere, dragging me back to the caves adjacent to the Nest and the tunnel that always led to pain and degradation. Ache and emptiness spill into my gut, but I shove that shit aside.

I will not let the Dróttning fuck me up.

Memories from that time belong in a hole, buried deep, and that's exactly where I push them.

If I give her space in my mind, she wins. But I won't let her win. I can't.

Instead, I think about the warriors sitting or standing by my side. This is how I prepare. How I pull my attention back to the here and now and focus on what we're about to do. This is how I ready myself for war. I look around and really see where I am today. Who I'm fighting for.

Toffer, who's been with me for so many years, sits with his hands resting on the ground, as he often does. He's been my rock for a decade. We've helped each other through so much—the trauma from the Nest, losing our home, and learning to love a new one. I fight for him to return to Thor and live the life he loves. That cat needs him as much as I do now.

I let my gaze rest for a moment on each of Fhord's Ætt, the family I never knew I needed. Jorunn's unflinching devotion. Torsten's quiet, steadfast strength. Leif's happier, more optimistic view of the world around us. Astrid's unquestioning faith in the kin who are also new to her. Each of them has welcomed me, helped me see the life we can live.

And Fhord. Half my soul. Well, a third of my soul, since the other third belongs to Astarot. They're the best part, by far. This land sucked me into it so that I would find them. All the torture, every bit of pain, brought me to these males, and I wouldn't go back for anything. First Astarot, then Fhord, gave me a reason to live, a reason to fight. The sun rises and sets with them, and my world would be dark and destitute if they didn't share it. I don't know how I'd survive if something happened to my mate or dragon.

Fhord turns as if he can feel my eyes on him, and his lips lift into that sexy smile that always sets me on fire. I'm ready for this fight to be over. He owes me an orgasm. Or two. Or three. And I plan to call that debt as soon as we're alone again.

When he raises his fist, I concentrate on breathing, trying to steady my heart in these final few moments. Prepare for what's coming. Everyone's eyes are on him. We fight when he tells us to fight. As it should be.

And then he slashes his arm down and I feel his will punch out. The wall next to us succumbs to his power, the rock breaking apart and then pieces flinging out as if shot by catapults. For a moment, we can only watch as he uses his magic to take as many lives as possible, turning scores of rocks and boulders into weapons. My heart aches for all the lives lost, but it's them or us. It will always be us.

When he turns to me, his thoughts reaching out to mine to urge me over, I cross the short distance between us and rest my hand on his neck, opening myself to him. The tug on my power is gentle and so familiar, I sigh into it. And then our magic joins together and I watch as he starts to create a barrier between our target and the surviving soldiers.

This was always the plan. Kill who we must but then stop others from interfering as we isolate Einar and take him. If Fhord still has the strength he'll need, we'll close the cavern behind us; if not, we'll do it in a smaller space on our way back to the horses, bringing rocks down to stop anyone from following us.

Neither of us expected the spear of pain that shoots into us as Einar turns in our direction. Fhord was certain he'd be wearing the manacle; that the Dróttning would never risk transporting him without it. But as Fhord continues to rain boulders into the area near the elf prized for his ability to torture, that elf goes on the attack.

I drop to my knees—the pain waning when I lose contact with Fhord's skin—and watch, my gut twisted, as Fhord bends over and clenches his jaw, trying to do as much as he can before he's forced to give up.

It's a devastating few seconds. His pain bounces in his thoughts, expanding as it consumes all it can, leaving nothing but agony in its place. When Fhord falls onto his ass, finally releasing his magic and collapsing next to me, I wrap my hand around his neck again, letting him draw from my magic to restore his strength.

"He's done," I yell to the others, standing to drag Fhord up next to me. "Let's finish this."

They respond with shouts and action, raising their blades and running into the morass of bodies and soldiers in the Gorge.

"Be safe, rabbit," Fhord tells me, grasping my jaw to spin my lips toward him and pressing his against mine.

"You owe me that mouth. And fingers. And dick," I remind him. "You sure as fuck better survive to pay that debt."

"Always," he growls with one more kiss, then turns and snarls at the soldier stupid enough to walk into our cavern. With one swing of his sword, the male's head goes flying and Fhord looks for his next victim.

I follow him out, my blade swinging behind him as I focus on an enormous male who thinks he's gonna attack my mate from behind. Groaning as I fling up my blade to stop his—Fhord tossing a wink behind his back before turning again to the male trying to take his head—I lose myself in the fight.

Within a few seconds, my heart starts skipping and leaping as it tries to catch up with the sudden burst of activity. Sweat drips down my face a minute or so after that, but I can't let myself get distracted. This male is more than a head taller than me and he's powerful. Every swing pulses through my back and limbs, the muscles required to stop or push it back already screaming at me.

But we're evenly matched because what he gains in weight and height, he loses in speed. He can't move the way I can. His thrusts would kill me if they connected, but every time one gets close, I'm able to bend or shift or jump out of the way. And then he makes the mistake I need. He over-extends as he chases me after a leap back, thinking he has an advantage when I struggle to gain my footing.

My blade slides into his chest like it's butter. I fucking love this sword. His eyebrows slam to the top of his brow for a moment as he realizes I've just killed him. His heart hasn't stopped yet, but we both know it will. And then his gaze shoots to something behind me, giving me just enough time to withdraw my sword, twist, and thrust it into the female behind me. I give myself a second to enjoy this kill, then jump into the midst of the worst of it.

The next ten or fifteen or twenty minutes are brutal. Fhord did what he could before Einar twisted his mind, but there are a lot of soldiers left, and only five of us.

I'm dripping everywhere—an enormous gash above my eye that forces me to wipe away blood and sweat way too fucking often, rips on every limb, and a puncture in my chest that, thank the gods, didn't go deep enough to do real damage. I don't even feel the pain, though. The only thing that matters is the next thrust or swipe or parry, and the glance up whenever I can to make sure everyone still lives.

Finally—fucking finally—I shove my knife into the neck of a female who was too gods-damned good for my comfort. Twice, she nearly had me, but each time, I bounced away just before the killing strike. And I look for my next battle.

There is none. Fhord's about to end the life of a wiry male and the rest of our group stands in a small circle around Einar. They've donned the gloves that will let us touch him but are still keeping their distance. They've heard our stories and aren't taking any chances.

Now, I hurt. Waves of agony start to rush into me from each wound, reminding my brain that it should be bawling its torment. Because I've taken a lot of hits. Bending over to work my way through the onslaught, I inhale slowly for a minute or more. I'm an elf and I'll heal, but this part always sucks.

Fhord's hand on my back draws me from my reverie. "You're fucking magnificent," he rasps as I stand. Taking my cheek in his hand, he tugs me forward. "I've been wanting to do this for the last ten minutes. I've never needed to fuck you more than I do right now."

I smile as his lips take mine and lean into his kiss. He's ravenous, plunging his tongue into my mouth, sucking on my lip and moaning as he clings to me.

"That's just a taste of what's coming," he promises before stepping back and turning his attention to Einar. "Let's get him to the horses before others get here," he grunts. "He'll ride with me."

Jorunn and Leif, who are standing closest to the elf, shove him in the direction of the cavern. He resists for a few seconds, his gaze bouncing all around us as he searches for a savior who isn't coming. But then he glares at Fhord and strides into the cave.

We move fast now. Halfway through the cavern, we set enough explosives to bring it down behind us, since Fhord is concerned about using his power again. Leif stays behind to light them, and I hold my breath as we wait for him to join us. When he does, a grin on his dust-covered face, we turn and run toward our horses, dragging Einar behind us.

They're where we left them—thank the gods—and we're mounted and racing back to the city in seconds. It's a nervous ride. The Dróttning's soldiers who survived our attack are spreading out, searching every place they can. But that was the beauty of Bevin's plan. We started on the other side of the mountain. Their chances of reaching us before we're back in hiding are slim. The vekters will have gotten word, so we need to watch for them, but there aren't many in this little town. They shouldn't find us either.

At least, that's what I keep telling myself.

When we reach the gate that leads to the barn, it feels like we all heave out a collective sigh of relief. The hard part is over.

Liv, Frida, and Thor come out as soon as the gate closes behind us. "Leave the horses with us," Frida says as she stares at our mark. "Just get him inside before the vekters are pounding on our door."

"They'll start in the barn," Fhord tells her as he drops from Sigurd and drags Einar down with him. "Do only what you must to make them look like they've been stabled all day, then join us in the house."

They both nod, taking reins from everyone and leading the horses toward the barn. Toffer goes with them, his skill with horses more useful than anything he'd do inside since we want Einar to live. I watch Glory for a moment, unreasonably happy with Torsten's gift as I let myself enjoy a mission that's given us what we'd hoped for, then turn to follow the others into the kitchen.

Einar's already strapped to a chair when I enter. His chin's up, and he's not shrinking from Fhord's glare.

"You've caused my mate a lot of pain," Fhord snarls as he steps into Einar's space, forcing the torture elf to look up to hold his gaze. "Fucked up our plans too many times. I should kill you now, but lucky for you, you're gonna come in handy."

"Fuck you," Einar responds, spitting at Fhord as he straightens his spine. He's got the look of a male who's placed too much faith in his magic. He seems to think he can piss us off without being punished.

He'll realize soon just how wrong he is. Fhord's not the forgiving type. Einar will survive, but the number of fingers and toes and teeth he keeps depends entirely on him.

Fhord gestures to Torsten, who picks up the dining room table and drops it in front of Einar, one leg barely missing his foot.

"That would have hurt," Fhord points out with a smile. "We're not ready to really fuck you up. Yet. But if we can't get what we want, we will."

"She'll destroy you for this," Einar vows. "She'd have taken my life if she was done with me. She wants me where she can get me back when she realizes how much she needs me."

"She's got a new toy," Fhord responds, spinning a chair and dropping into it as he rests his forearms on its back and his chin on top of them. "He's gonna give her more than you ever could."

Einar spits again, although he turns his head this time. At least he's smart enough to realize spewing in Fhord's face would be a bad, bad idea. "Jarl's a passing fancy. Fucker isn't loyal to anyone but himself. The Dróttning will soon realize I'm the only one she can trust."

"Why would you stay loyal to her?" I ask. "She's sending you to prison and she's been a cruel master. Why not take this chance to help us? Get away from her?"

"You think you can win this?" Einar demands, his voice rising. "You think you have a chance in Helheim of defeating the Dróttning? You don't know what the fuck you're dealing with. It's not just the Dróttning. She's got allies you'd never imagine."

He turns to Fhord, his eyes flashing as he grinds his jaw. "Jarl doesn't belong here, and he won't stay. He came with the others, and there are more of them, more powerful, that will heed her call. I'm loyal to the Dróttning because she will never lose. And when she puts you down like the dogs you are, and Jarl goes back to his world, where he belongs, I'll be back at her side."

The pounding at the side gate leading to the barn drags my attention away from Einar. Away from all the questions bouncing around in my mind. He has the knowledge we need. But then the bastard squeals—a stuck pig in our little house—and captures my focus again.

Fhord slams his hand over Einar's mouth, reaching for a scarf Astrid's handing him. He shoves it between Einar's teeth, but before he manages to tie it on the back of his head, two vekters kick down our front door, bows raised.

The arrow that slices through Einar's throat surprises all of us. For a moment, everyone's still as we watch our best chance at fighting back against the Dróttning's medallions—this elf who has some of the answers I've been seeking for a decade—slump onto the table. Dead. We just killed all of those people for nothing.

And then all Helheim breaks loose as the vekters turn their bows on us, and Fhord's Ætt attack them.

CHAPTER THIRTEEN

DANI

I WATCH HIM

"**W**E'RE GONNA HAVE TO figure out what to call you," I tell him as we trudge deeper into the caves a few hours after we escaped the super spiders. "If you're not the angry male anymore, who are you?" Mikkael's so much better around his dragon. It almost makes me forget what an ass he is when Ziselær's not nearby.

"I'm a fan of the wanton male," he responds with his characteristic smirk as he glances back at me. "I can't think of a better description."

"You're the least wanton male I've ever met," I tell him with a laugh. "I think sex is the last thing on your mind."

When he spins, his dark gaze finding mine, I stop in my tracks. "You know better than that, my saucy spy," he drawls lazily. "My cock gets hard from your scent. I can think of nothing but fucking you when we're astride your dragon, your ass pressed into the erection that always—every single gods-damned time—fills the space between us."

I can't say a word. I force a gulp down my throat and watch the tic in his jaw as his gaze follows it and then he looks at me again.

"But I wouldn't fuck you, Dani. If I took you, it wouldn't be because of the mating bond. Fate wants us to fuck so desperately, I dream about sticking my cock into you every gods-damned night. I won't give into that bullshit." His words are fierce now. Resolved. "This bond won't control me."

He takes a single step closer to me, and I don't know if I want to retreat or advance. My chest is tight, my breaths growing shallow as his eyes drink me in. He's so fucking confusing. Everything about this is so fucking confusing.

"No," he tells me, his tone sultry as his gaze roves down my body, then back up to my face. And fuck if my core doesn't respond, his lidded eyes and sexy voice spilling fire into me as my nipples stand to attention. "If I were to take you, my seductive spy, it would be because I've fallen for you. Not the mating bond. Me and you. And then I wouldn't fuck you. I'd make love to you. I would worship the body this bond keeps telling me was made for my touch alone. I would never be wanton again. I'd be yours." He pauses, his hands clenching as if he's fighting some battle he must win. "And you'd be mine," he rumbles at last.

Now, he winks, his gaze never leaving mine. "But today—and I suspect forever—I'm the wanton male. It's the perfect description for me. Let's tell Vulryn to go back to that. I just need to find some females other than the mate I can't let myself fuck."

He spins and strides away, leather pants molded to a perfect ass teasing me as he disappears around a corner. And I will myself to calm down before I kick my legs into gear, chasing the flame he carries because I have no choice.

When we find a river that flows too fast for us to cross, slicing across our path in a cavern too small for Ziselær to extend his wings, I know we're fucked. We can't swim and he can't fly.

I reach out for Vulryn, my string to her stronger than it has been since that monster took her. I still can't talk to her—and it scares the fuck out of me, because we should be close enough to exchange some words—but I know she's alive. And that an impassable river stands between me and her.

"We need to get to her," I mutter, tears filling my eyes as I look helplessly at the water standing between me and her. "We can't let a gods-damned river stop us. Not when we've come this far."

"We could use a couple more dragons," Mikkael declares in a surprisingly matter-of-fact tone. He points to the narrowest part of the river. "It's not *that* wide. If we had other dragons, they could stretch across." Mikkael opens his mouth as if he's about to say something else but then spins and cocks his head at his beast.

His grin when he turns back to me lights up the dim cavern. "He's talking to me," he explains in a voice full of wonder. "Since the spiders. Not just the single-word response I'd been getting before that. He's telling me things with detail."

"So, maybe he hates you a little less?" I realize I'm smiling too. His joy is infectious.

"He still hates me," Mikkael responds with a laugh. "That hasn't changed. But he's realized we need to talk if we're going to reach his draikana. I'm hearing him in my head, and everything feels right." He pauses, fierce eyes staring at me as he adds, "Well, almost everything."

So fucking confusing.

"What did he say?" I ask, determined to ignore the mix of emotions—a fire in my core and clench in my belly—his looks inspire. After what he said this morning or afternoon, or whatever time it is, I've spent the last two hours chanting a reminder in my head that he's just here for Ziselær. I can't let myself forget that.

"Z can feel Vulryn on the other side. He's going to get us across."

"How? He can't fly."

"He thinks he can jump." Ziselær growls behind him, a rumbling complaint, and Mikkael glances back and laughs again. "He's sure he can jump."

"And if he doesn't make it?"

"Then we'll all go for a swim," he tells me with a shrug, "and we'll find another cavern to chase after Vulryn." He pauses, his gaze flicking to Ziselær for a moment before he turns back to me. "He's as desperate to get there as you. We will find your dragon."

"This is a bad idea."

"It's the only idea we have. We're not turning around. She's too close. He won't leave her now."

Mikkael shoves the torch into the water—entombing us in darkness—and helps me climb into position and settle behind him. Ziselær grunts again and turns to stride back the way we came, as Mikkael reaches for my hands and wraps my arms across his stomach.

"You'll have to get a little closer. When he starts running, hold on. We need to hunch over his neck. He's gonna turn himself into an arrow."

I shove myself forward, resting my head and chest against his broad back as I tighten my arms. My nipples are stiff points, a flare starting to burn right where my fantasies about Mikkael always lead. By the gods, I hope this is over soon.

He laughs, one of his hands resting for a moment on the thigh rubbing against his. "Now you get it," he says without turning around. "I was so fucking horny every time we rode Vulryn. It's different when your cock or tits are digging into your mate's body. It's like they know they're finally where they belong."

That's exactly it. Mikkael and I fit. He's fighting against it because he hates me. I can't blame him, but I don't hate him. I've lived with the guilt over what I did for years, wishing I'd done something—anything—differently. I don't have many regrets. The attack that led to Mikkael killing his lover, his devastation at what he'd done because of me, are among the very few.

And it's not just the mating bond for me. It started there, sure. I've paid more attention to him, watched him, because of it. Like him, though, I've figured out how to distinguish between the mating bond and *my* feelings. Now, I watch him because he draws my eyes. He fascinates me.

I know that when his jaw tics, he's fighting emotions, or maybe arousal, he doesn't want to feel. I hide my smile every morning when he stretches out a clean shirt—as if he's grown overnight and will need more space in it—and then moves out of my sight to change clothes. I've realized that he hides his bare skin from me and I'm dying to know why. My gaze always follows his laugh because I'll get to see his smile. He doesn't wear his happiness nearly often enough.

I care for him. And it's moments like this that kill me. No matter how much he jokes with me or teases me, I realized a while ago that he'll never care for me.

I can enjoy this while it lasts, though. So I do. I clutch my mate and store this memory, the way I've stored so many others. But this one isn't a weapon I'll use to traumatize enemies. It's a treasure I'll pull out when I'm alone in my bed and need his body next to mine. When I want to remember what it felt like to believe, for a moment, that Mikkael could be mine.

Ziselær spins abruptly, dragging me from my thoughts, and starts to run toward the river.

He's so fucking fast. I was clinging to Mikkael before, but now I'm crushing myself to him. We're both leaning as far forward as we can, our bodies wrapped around Ziselær's neck. It's too dark to know where we're going, but that's probably a good thing. I don't want to see the river racing toward us. If we're going to fall into the water, I'll know it when we start to plunge.

A few seconds after Ziselær started racing through the cavern, he launches himself into the air, his wings plastered to his body. When I feel them start to flutter, though, my eyes fly open. They've adjusted enough for me to see dark outlines and I watch as the tips—regrown since Matthias's brutality but still not as muscular as they once were—flap frantically. As if he needs a few more feet to reach the other side.

We slam into the rock, Ziselær's wings flinging out against the cavern walls as his feet scrabble for hold. I can feel the spray of the river on my back and realize this massive blue dragon is nearly half submerged, the river acting like a powerful undercurrent as it tries to suck him in.

"Let go and follow me," Mikkael barks, grasping for feathers along Ziselær's neck to drag himself forward.

I do the same, wondering what the fuck he's doing, because if his dragon's going into the river, he's gonna wish to all the gods he'd gone with him. Within a few seconds, our feet hit the ground and Mikkael is pushing me toward one of the cavern's walls. And then Ziselær leaps—a frenzied, clumsy surge of his massive body that sends him flinging into the opposite wall.

And I take my first full breath since we saw the river, my heart starting to slow down a bit. I don't know how we'll get back across that monster, but I'm not going to think about it. Right now, we're a big jump closer to Vulryn, and I'm anxious to get there. This inability to speak with her is driving me mad.

"He told me to get off and away," Mikkael explains as he digs through his pack and lights another torch. "Z realized he'd need to fling himself out of the water and that he'd hurt us in the process if we were still astride him."

We watch his dragon rise and shake out his feathers, hues of the sky and sea shifting as he does. He still can't extend his wings because the cavern is so gods-damned small, but he manages a good jiggle.

I puff out a breath, my heart rate finally slowing to a steadier thump, down from the feverish pounding of a few seconds ago. "Well, that was fucking amazing," I breathe. "Ziselær's a good beast."

"The best." Mikkael's tone is unexpectedly sad.

I glance at him, surprised to see his eyebrows close together, a little frown on his lips. "What is it?"

"Vulryn isn't far." Mikkael's voice matches his expression, a melancholy so deep it draws out the raw parts of my heart, as if the mating bond wants me to join him in his pain. He glances at me, an apology in his eyes. "I know that's good," he says. "She needs us. But it still hurts to know this thing we're doing together is almost over. He'll be leaving me again soon."

Ziselær swings his head to look at us. But I can't see any of the anger and hatred he's worn like a cloak during so much of this trip. This glance is somber, speculative. His eyes are wide and don't hold the fire that usually flares when he turns to his rider. His snout is relaxed, mouth open just a touch. No flames flicker out.

"Let's just get through this and see what the dragons decide." I rest my hand on Mikkael's shoulder, bringing his gaze to mine. "Vulryn's surprised me more than any other being in my life. Maybe your dragon will do the same."

Mikkael scoffs, glancing at Ziselær and back at me. "No such luck for me," he mutters. Then he shakes his head, stepping away. "Let's just get the two of you to your dragon. Z's convinced she's close. He thinks we'll reach her in a few hours. And he's worried. He can't communicate with her and should be able to."

"I can't either. I haven't been able to talk to her. And it's freaking me out too because her presence is getting so strong, it feels like we'll turn a corner and find her."

"Then let's turn a few corners," he says, grasping my hand to tug me down the cavern. He drops it after we've taken a few steps, striding forward to take the lead. I follow in silence, struggling to stop my ridiculous heart from filling with a hope I know I can't let myself feel.

Twenty-seven corners and who knows how many hours later, we finally see her. Mikkael's torch casts enough light for me to really take her in—the copper feathers I've loved since the moment I saw her, flickering like the inferno that's consumed my heart; eyes glowing red that dance between Ziselær and me; a dragony smile that displays joy and victory. We've come for her, as she knew we would.

And now I see why she couldn't return to us. Her tail is trapped in the cave. Literally. It's as if Fhord came and used his power to embed it in the rock, like the grip swathing a sword's tang. I have no idea how she hid her pain from me. It must be excruciating.

Welcome, rider, she purrs, and my heart skips a beat. I'm so relieved to hear her voice. I have no idea why we couldn't talk before, but it doesn't matter right now. *I am pleased my drake brought you to me.*

He felt it when the monster trapped you, came immediately. He's been desperate to find you.

He is a good drake. Her gaze shifts to watch him stride toward her. He nuzzles his snout into her neck and up toward the horn highest on her head, grunting into it as he and Vulryn hold some conversation she doesn't share with me.

I'm aching to go to her, forcing my feet to stay planted where they are. She needs this desperately. Our reunion will come next. It's hard, though. I need to sink my hands into her plumage, feel her breath mingle with mine. Finally, Ziselær steps away, stalking to inspect her tail with an angry rumble.

Out of the corner of my eye, I see Mikkael walk in the same direction. But my gaze is focused on my dragon, and I can no longer stop myself from running toward her. In a second, I'm wrapping my arms around her neck, digging fingers into her copper feathers as I breathe in her scent.

I'm so fucking glad you're okay, I tell her. *Well, mostly okay,* I amend as I look quickly at her entombed tail. *You must be in so much pain.*

It is ... tolerable, she responds. *I will be pleased when you free me.*

But, how? Fhord isn't here and none of us can remove that much rock.

You will cut off my tail. She's so calm to be able to joke about something like this. My lips lift into a smile as I lean back to look into her eyes. And then they drop because she's serious. She expects us to cut off her tail.

Fuck, no, we won't. I'm aghast, my stomach launching into my throat at the suggestion. I dig my hands into her feathers, trying to calm myself because that idea is as fucked up as anything I've ever heard. *There must be another way.*

There is none, she tells me, her tone matter-of-fact. *The chatty male tried to free me, but the tricky male returned and trapped him too. We have been waiting for you to come.*

The chatty male? The tricky male? I demand, my gaze bouncing about the cave as I look for something else to talk about. I refuse to even consider the possibility of chopping off her tail. *Who are they?*

The chatty male sleeps, she tells me with a jerk of her chin toward a lump I hadn't even noticed. He wears colors similar to the rock around him, and he's trapped in the stone like my dragon, his entire leg encased in it. A shiver runs down my spine as I think about how miserable he must be, stuck lying on his side, his other leg twisted awkwardly adjacent to the rock holding him.

And who's the tricky male? You were taken by a sea monster. What the fuck happened to you?

That serpent brought me here and held me while the tricky male trapped me with powers much like those wielded by our male.

We really need to call Fhord something other than our male. He's Sifa's.

He remains our male. No other has taken his place. She pauses, her eyes piercing as she looks at me. *Shall I continue?*

And I laugh. I can't help it. She's so gods-damned precocious. Stuck here for days, proposing we saw off her tail unless we can come up with another plan, and she's still the same uppity bitch of a beast I love with every bit of my heart. *Yes, please,* I respond at last.

She huffs, leaning into Ziselær as he returns and his snout nuzzles into her neck again. He lays down next to her, as much of his body touching hers as possible with her tail trapped, and closes his eyes.

He is a good drake, Vulryn tells me, her wide eyes focused on Ziselær for a moment. She looks at me again and continues in the same sensible tone she adopted when she told me we'd need to slice off an enormous part of her body to break her free. *The tricky male and the chatty male speak of different worlds as the starry female does. The serpent who carried me here moves between those worlds, sometimes carrying the tricky male with him. The chatty male wishes to return to them but cannot.*

Why did they trap you here? And why is the chatty male in these caves, anyway?

The tricky male has not spoken of his reasons for bringing me here. I suspect he acts on the wyrm's orders, but we will do what we must to learn his reasons after you free me. The chatty male says the tricky male brought him to these caves, but he wandered through them freely until he tried to help me. The tricky male trapped him in the rock because of me. The chatty male has no magic in this place and believes the rocks around us suppress it. He does not know why the tricky male alone has power here.

I test his theory, trying to push my mind into Mikkael's for a moment. I can't. The spear of thoughts I've sent out a thousand times, that should work like second nature for me, evaporates whenever I cast it out. We're in deep shit if the tricky male returns.

"Finally." A deep voice interrupts my next question, and I spin to see the chatty male shifting himself onto an elbow—the most he can do to lift himself with his leg trapped the way it is. He's a handsome man, with lighter features that have darkened with the sun and aged like fine leather. He wears a thick beard and looks at me with eyes as blue as a sapphire.

"I was wondering when the dragon's rider would arrive," he says with a grin, kind eyes focused on me. "I'm Njörðr, and after you free us, I'm going to help you get back to your world. Then you'll help me get back to mine."

Great. As if we didn't have enough to do already.

MIKKAEL

I CAN'T DO THIS

"WHO THE FUCK ARE you?" My tone is harsher than I intended, but I can't help that shit. This Njörðr person just popped up like a fucking bunny emerging from a hole, and I need to know if I'm gonna have to kill him.

"As I said," he responds with a smile, "I am Njörðr."

Asshole. He knows what I'm asking. "And?" I prompt. When three gods-damned seconds pass and he still hasn't said a word, I try again. A little more direct this time. "What the fuck are you doing here, Njörðr?"

"The trickster Loki trapped me like this when he found me trying to help the dragon," he responds, turning to look at Vulryn with stark blue eyes. "He has power in these caves, more than he does in my worlds. It's probably why the trickster chose this place to hold your beast and me. I have no power or I'd have freed her already."

"But what are you doing in these caves? Even without magic, there are ways to get out," Dani points out. "Why are you here at all?"

"It is not so easy to leave," he says with a shrug. "The longer I'm here, the weaker I grow. When Loki first brought me here, he trapped me as I am now, rock holding me in place. He freed me from the stone only when he was certain I couldn't escape the caves, then trapped me again a day or so ago. Too many barriers stand between me and freedom." He glances again at Vulryn. "I know a path to fly away, but I couldn't free her. And I cannot fly," he adds with a smile.

"Why release you at all?" she asks. "Why not just keep you trapped in the rock?"

"I am mortal again," he tells us. "My body would not survive. The trickster wants me alive and constrained."

"How long have you been here?"

"Fate brought me to this land a decade ago."

My eyes grow wide as I realize he entered this world when Sifa and I did, which can't be a coincidence. I'll need to ask him about his worlds—my worlds—but we've got other things to worry about first.

"Loki found me within the last two months and bade Jörmungandr to carry me here. I had not seen the trickster in this land before then. He was ... displeased ... when I tried to help the dragon." He turns toward Vulryn, a hint of a smile playing on his lips. "What is her name, by the way? I cannot hear her words and would know what to call her."

"She's Vulryn," Dani responds, a world of love packed into that single word.

Vulryn growls, and I drag my eyes away from Dani to look at the copper beast. Dani and Z do the same, growing still, the way they always do when they speak with her. But they don't like whatever she's telling them. Dani's hands clench into fists, eyes brittle as glass while she watches her dragon.

Z's emotions fill me, although they're not reflected in his resigned expression—eyes dull and snout bowing down at the edges. He's bothered, even a little afraid, but not angry. He seems willing to accept whatever Vulryn is telling them, or suggesting, even if he fears it.

What is it? I ask him when he finally looks away from his draikana.

Go, he responds. Vulryn told him we need to leave before this Loki person returns. She believes he's powerful and could snare us all here.

How? Vulryn's trapped. We can't leave her, and I don't see any way to get her out.

Tail.

This response comes with only a few completely fucked-up words. She thinks we need to remove her tail. My gut clenches at the suggestion, the pain she'd live through twisting me inside, because what the actual fuck?

She can't be serious. We can't cut off her tail.

Escape. Vulryn's been thinking about this for days. She tried to chew through it, but her skin is so tough, and she passed out so often from the pain, she couldn't do it quickly enough. The wounds kept repairing themselves. She needs a sharp blade and a fast cut.

There must be another way.

Z doesn't respond this time. Instead, he looks around the cave, as if to point out that we have few options. Without Fhord here, there's not much we can do.

And I've never felt so gods-damned helpless in my entire life. My stomach is a rock, the weight of what they're proposing so heavy, it's a wonder I'm still standing. My gaze hops between the others: Vulryn's stoic acceptance of the torture she proposes, displayed in features that are much more relaxed than they should be; Z's quiet support of his draikana's choice, his eyes closed as his snout nuzzles into her neck; Njörðr's resolve, his eyes narrow and jaw clenched.

It's Dani's expression that stops my bouncing gaze, though. She's horrified. Her mouth hangs open, chin slack as she looks at Vulryn, then Njörðr, and back again at her dragon, her head shaking in denial the entire time. Her shoulders are tense, one palm clutching her neck. "She's serious," Dani mutters, almost to herself. And then she looks up at me, eyes flashing blue flames. "She wants us to cut off her tail," she snarls as she clenches her hands.

It takes every ounce of will I possess to stop myself from striding over and wrapping her in my arms.

The torture she's about to experience is going to destroy her. And Z. And maybe me too, because I'll get hints of it and it's going to be worse than anything any of them has ever suffered before.

The most terrifying part—for me, at least—is that I'm the one who'll need to wield the sword. Dani will be in too much pain to do it, and I would never let her bear that gut-wrenching responsibility. I'll be the cause of the agony that's about to rip through all of them.

Her anger spills into me like a waterfall filling the pool beneath it. "Are we cutting off your leg along with her tail?" I demand as I spin to glare at the male. I hate what needs to be done, and I'm not sure if I can do it twice.

"What is your name, dragon rider?" Njörðr's voice is calm, soothing. Centuries of wisdom and benevolence live in those simple words.

I inhale a few times before I answer, because I need to get my shit together. For Dani and the dragons. They're the ones who are about to suffer. "Mikkael," I rasp out.

"You feel so familiar to me, Mikkael," he tells me as his gaze holds mine. "Your spirit speaks to me, although I don't yet recognize its words."

I don't know what the fuck to say to that, so I keep my mouth shut.

"You can do this, Mikkael," he continues in the same timeless tone. "It is a necessary evil. We cannot be here when the trickster returns. Vulryn and I know this is the price we'll pay for freedom. It is a small thing, really. We've suffered before. It always passes."

"I don't know if I can," I admit. "Everything in me fights it. How can I hurt the dragon bound to my mate and my own dragon?"

"You can because you must. The trickster will trap us all if he returns. And he will return."

I let his words sink in, percolating as I focus on how fucked they are right now. Vulryn's tail might already be useless anyway. The rock must be compressing it—causing a shit-ton of pain—or she'd have been able to free it. The rest of her body probably is already starting to atrophy, trapped in the same position for days. Her tail will grow back, but staying like this would torture and kill her.

It's Z who gives me the final push. *Please*, he asks, not a single bit of the anger and hatred he's felt toward me evident in that single word. When I turn toward him, he's watching me with a fierce gaze as he shares his thoughts with me. He needs his rider to do this for his draikana.

He's right. This has to be done. I have to do it.

Finally, I nod. Striding over to Z, I dig my fingers into my dragon's feathers and rest my forehead on his neck for a moment. And then I unsheathe my sword with shaking hands and pull out one of my belts for Njörðr along with a long, thick rope for Vulryn. I stare at the wall for a minute or more, unable to look at anyone else as I try to work up the nerve to do this.

Dani's hand on my shoulder draws me from my stupor. It's comforting, and I desperately need comfort right now.

"You have to do this, Mik. For all of us." She's not angry any longer. She knows as well as me that this is inevitable.

I don't look at her, though. I can't. Instead, I respond with a quick dip of my chin and turn toward Vulryn and Njörðr. "Who first?" I grate out?

"Me," Njörðr responds. "I can see the bonds tying you to the female and the blue dragon, and those same bonds tying them to Vulryn. You will feel the pain that ripples through them when Vulryn is cut free. You may not be able to wield that sword again when you're done helping her."

He's right, I know. So I walk over and tie my belt around his thigh, just above where I'll cut, then stand above him, sword held high. "Will it grow back?" I hate the idea of taking his leg permanently.

"That I do not know," he tells me, not a hint of fear or regret in those words. "It would were I in my worlds, but I am weak in these caves. My magic won't be able to restore it until I am free of this place. By that time, it may be too late."

"And you still want me to do this? Why not wait and let Loki free you? Keep your leg?"

"I need my freedom more than my leg. The trickster will not release me from these caves. The world above us changes, and I must return to that fight."

"Well, you've run into the right people," I grunt. "If we get out of here, we'll take you to the fight."

"As the fates planned," he responds with an enigmatic grin.

"Fuck the fates," I tell him, "if this is the kind of shit they throw in our path." And then I slam my blade down, cutting through flesh and muscle and bone. Because anticipation is sometimes as bad as the real thing. His eyes grow wide in horror as his blood spews at the wall, little crimson fountains that escape the tourniquet on his leg. I step back to give him room to scramble away from the useless appendage.

"That ... was ... unexpected," he sputters. He hasn't screamed, which is gods-damned impressive. I'd have squealed like a stuck pig. But he's sucking in air like a man who nearly drowned, as he struggles to harness the torment of a cleaved limb. I have no fucking idea how he's planning to walk out of here, but we'll deal with that shit later.

"My thanks," he chokes out after a moment, finding a wall to rest his back against as his gaze finds mine.

I don't respond. If I open my mouth, I'm not sure what will come out. That was fucked, but it's nothing compared to what I'm gonna do to Vulryn.

She looks at me and purrs. Actually fucking purrs, like the precocious beast is happy about what I'm going to do.

"It's torture being trapped there," Dani murmurs from behind me, resting her hand on my shoulder again. "I can feel her pain. She wants this." She takes my chin and draws my gaze toward hers. "I want this," she tells me with a half-smile. "I know it'll hurt, and I still want it."

I exhale slowly, letting her truth settle into my bones. "I guess this is how I'll need to protect you sometimes, huh, my selfless, stalwart spy?"

"Agonizing things are necessary. Sometimes, they're the only way to get to the good."

She's talking about Vulryn and so much more. The tortured bonds that tie us all. The pain I've caused to the dragon and female the fates chose for me. The grievous things we've all had to do. My frozen heart starts to thaw again, just a little, as I wonder whether there might be good on the other side of all this agony. For Z and me.

And maybe, for Dani and me.

But I don't tell her that. Instead, I dip my chin again and turn toward Vulryn. Dani's already tied the rope around her tail. "Is it tight enough?" These words are a croak, but Dani understands them.

"It is," she assures me. "Just like with Njörðr," she adds. "I know you won't be able to do it with one stroke, but fast and resolute. We need this." She walks toward Vulryn's head, hugging her dragon's neck and resting her head against her feathers.

I nod again and trudge to her tail. My hands tremble, so I suck in a deep breath, and then another. When I'm positive my strike will be strong, I lift my sword over my head and bring it down.

The pain that spears into me stuns me for a moment. I spin my head to look at Dani and then wish the fuck I hadn't. She hasn't started crying yet. But she will. Her eyes are clenched shut, her back as straight as an arrow as she runs one trembling hand through her hair, the other shaking Vulryn's feathers from deep within them. She doesn't move, other than her quivering hands, as she moans, "Finish. Please."

I turn back toward the enormous gash I just cut into Vulryn's tail, thick blood bubbling out to cover the ground beneath her, and attack again. And again. And again.

Each cut shoots into me, and I'm only feeling ghosts of the pain Vulryn, Dani, and Z must be experiencing. Tears form in my eyes, but I don't stop. I can't. One part of my brain realizes that Vulryn's tail here is cartilage, not bone—thank the fucking gods, those gods-damned bastard—so I don't have to saw at it the way I'd feared. Still, I count twelve blows before I'm done.

Twelve agonizing, gods-awful, bloodcurdling blows.

When the last bits of flesh and feather wrest free of the rest of her body, Vulryn finally lets herself grieve her cleaved tail. Her keening fills the space around us, bouncing off the walls as if they mourn with her and share her pain. Dani drops to her knees, quiet sobs joining Vulryn's cry. Her face is hidden in her dragon's feathers now, as if she can't bring herself to look at anything else.

I look at Z and almost fall to my knees too. His eyes are closed, his mouth open as he pants slowly. Little flickers of his tail bounce off the nearby wall, but he's otherwise still. I want so desperately to go to him, comfort this dragon who doesn't want my compassion, but I don't. He's in pain. I can't add more.

But then his eyes open, and he looks at me. Really looks, as if he sees me for the first time. And with lumbering steps, he closes the distance between us. When he's close enough for me to touch him, he pauses. And then he takes one more step forward and rests his head against me. *Grateful*, he rumbles into my thoughts.

I can't stop the tears that fill my eyes. My knees buckle, and I fall into him, holding on for dear life. This may be the only thing I'll ever share with him, and I'll treasure it forever, fucked as it is. Like Dani said, sometimes agonizing things are necessary. I let myself remember our moments together, storing them with this one in that place I go when I want to feel close to my dragon.

Dani's hand on my lower back draws me back to this moment, this cave. "Vulryn wants her drake," she whispers.

"Right. Okay." I step back, holding his gaze for a moment and then watching as he turns and stalks toward his draikana. "Is she okay?"

Dani doesn't answer right away. Instead, she nudges me a bit, asking me—no, inviting me—to look at her. So I do.

She is the full moon on an autumn night, casting light on the oranges and yellows and reds that decorate the land. The flowers that emerge in the spring, bringing color to the land after a cold, long winter. The fire that melts hearts. And as much as I try to fight it, she's melting mine.

Maybe I shouldn't fight it any longer. I lift my hand to wrap it around her neck and finally—fucking finally—dig my fingers into those auburn locks. Swiping my thumb along her jaw, I hold her gaze and let myself really see her. The flawless skin, a random freckle decorating it. The eyes as blue as the feathers beneath Z's wings, shifting to the darker hue along his back as she looks at me. The lips that have parted. For me.

And I take them. It's the most natural thing in the world, kissing my mate. I knew it the first time we met, and I know it now. I'm supposed to do this, but I also desperately want to do it.

Me. Not the mating bond.

I want *her*. My strong, sexy, spellbinding spy.

She opens for me immediately, her tongue meeting mine as we explore each other. And the world stops turning. Nothing matters except the ecstasy, the euphoria, the utter and complete fulfillment that ripples through me. My entire body sings for her, because of her. Pleasure erupts in places I've never felt before as every part of me responds to the female I know belongs to me.

I tug her closer, holding her body against mine, her nipples pressing into my chest as my raging erection tells her exactly what effect she has on me.

But then she pushes away, moving backward as she lifts fingers to her lips. Her eyes are wide as she looks at her dragon and then back at me.

"We ... can't," she mutters, taking another step back. "It's not right. We can't be together. Not until Ziselær decides who will ride him."

"What the fuck are you talking about, Dani?" I reach out for her, but she lifts a hand, retreating from me even farther as her gaze skitters between Vulryn and me.

"I want you," she says, dropping her hand to her neck as she shakes her head back and forth. "Fuck, do I want you."

"I want you too," I breathe. "Like I want food or water. But not here. That's not why I kissed you. I would never take you in this cave. And not after everything you just suffered. Not with the pain you're still in. I just want ... fuck ... I want to be with you. To hold you."

It's so gods-damned hard to say it after everything we've been through. I'm admitting it to myself as much as I am to her. But it's true. And it's not the mating bond. It's her. I want to be with her.

She drops her gaze to the ground, her other hand laying across her heart, as if she'd put an end to whatever she's feeling. Whatever emotions drew her into my arms and then yanked her away.

Her words of a few seconds ago finally break through the haze in my mind. And the cracked ice in my heart freezes over again. Because I realize I was a fool for even considering letting myself trust this duplicitous female.

"That's not what you're talking about, though. Is it?"

"No." I barely hear this word, but it still seems to echo through the cave.

"You said you can't be with me until Z decides," I spit out.

She lifts her head, eyes blazing like a flame as she stares at me. Finally, she nods.

"You'll only be with me if I ride Z." The words are sand on my tongue, but they must be spoken. We need this truth between us so I never consider trusting her again. "You were with Matthias. You chose him over me. Because of the dragons. And if Z never forgives me, if he never accepts me as a rider, you won't accept me either."

Dani—my mate, the female the fates chose for me—nods again. And my fists clench.

"That's all this is, isn't it? You don't want me. You want Z's rider, whoever he might be." Now it's me who takes a step back, putting space between us. "And you don't think Z will ever choose me, so you won't let yourself get close. Won't let us explore this thing between us. Figure out if it could be real."

One more nod. To seal my fate.

I release my hands, forcing them to relax as I run them through my hair, trying to calm my racing heart. Storing this memory, too, so I don't ever let myself fall for this fantasy again.

"You won't get another chance," I tell her, my voice flat. "No matter what Z decides, even if he accepts me as his rider, I will never accept you. I will never choose to be with a female who doesn't choose to be with me." I glare at her, make sure she sees my disdain. "You've made your feelings clear," I tell her, not a hint of emotion in my words. "So I'm doing the same."

And then I turn to stride away from all of them.

I don't stop walking. There's nothing back there for me.

CHAPTER FIFTEEN

SIFA

THEY TOOK HER

"WE NEED TO GET the fuck out of here." I finally drag my gaze away from the dead males on the floor and turn toward Fhord. His eyes are as wide as mine must be.

"Sifa and I leave on foot," Fhord barks as he looks at the others. "We'll take back roads to get to the dragons and fly back to Revalle. The rest of you ride the horses. You'll be safer traveling without us. The Dróttning isn't looking for you but try to avoid soldiers anyway. Find someone to get you to Lumaria. We'll meet you there."

Torsten grunts and heads outside. He'll help Liv, Frida, and Toffer ready the horses while Leif, Jorunn, and Astrid gather things here.

"Ten minutes," Fhord says as he opens the pantry and shoves a loaf of bread and a few other supplies in a bag. "Be gone by then."

Leif nods. "Be safe, boss."

Fhord pauses, grasping Leif's arm. "You too, my friend. You too."

Spinning, Fhord gets our hats and cloaks, then opens the back door to gesture me out. I stride over to Toffer and Thor, giving the troll a quick hug and the cat a scratch on his ear.

"Home and hearth hearken," Toffer tells me. It's his favorite way of wishing me a safe return, and my heart always twists when he utters these words.

"I should be there before you. If not, it'll be soon after. Take good care of Thor for me."

"We'll fortify the fences for our friend."

"I know you will. See you soon."

I reach up to wipe a tear from his cheek as the corners of his lips lift in the saddest smile he's given me in a long time. After leaning forward to kiss his forehead, I turn to stride away, waving at Liv and Frida as I go. We need to leave, and I'm just a distraction right now.

Liv opens the gate as we cover ourselves, stepping out casually to look around before giving us a little nod. Fhord grabs my hand and drags me out—forcing me to jog to keep up with him—down the narrow street, and then two more. When we reach the corner that leads to a busier area we can't avoid, he pauses, looking back and forth before strolling forward. The goal now is to blend in, and nobody else is in a hurry.

Twice, soldiers glance our way, but thank the gods, their minds are weak. I'm able to delve into their thoughts and twist their memories of our descriptions. The focus and surprise in their eyes when they first see us melts away, replaced by bored inspection. Within a few minutes, we're moving away from the crowds, striding more quickly toward the outskirts of town.

The dragons are waiting for us when we arrive. Anxious. Ready to return to Revalle, and then Lumaria. We load them quickly and send out our thoughts to search the area around us. When we're confident nobody is close enough to see us enter the sky, we mount and fly.

Why are you and Tindera so restless?

My draikana's body demands the Dróttning's mash. She needs a safe place to rest.

Is she okay? I glance at Tindera and see her weakness. Her eyes lack the brilliance, the glow, they usually hold. The flaps of her wings are slower, more ponderous. She's still strong—for now. We need to get in and out of Revalle quickly.

She struggles and is anxious to swim in the island's waters. As they did with me, they will help rid her body of the wyrm's poison. His voice is tinged with worry, an emotion he rarely shows.

Is she speaking with Fhord about this?

Astarot's dragony laugh answers my question. Of course not. She's a proud beast and loath to admit weakness.

I'll talk to him. And make sure we do everything we can to get out of Revalle quickly.

As you must.

I smile to myself. He's a bit more chatty now but the same beast who captured part of my soul.

We fly in silence after that, Fhord and I constantly searching for other beasts. Nerthwaite is close to Revalle, so it doesn't take long before we start to sense them. I feel the change in

Astarot as he prepares to evade and possibly fight the dragons he once considered family. And my *need* to destroy the Dróttning—break the chains that have been binding these majestic beasts for centuries—grows.

Once, I'm able to enter a weak rider's mind and send him in a different direction. Only once. The half dozen other riders we encounter on our short trip have strong minds. I'd need more than the few minutes I have to control them. So we evade them, either by flying higher than any dragon ever should—forcing Tindera to dig for every last bit of strength she possesses—or by traveling far out of our way. Our two-hour trip takes five, but we make it.

We settle a couple of vikus out of town, where we'll leave the dragons while we go retrieve her. Fear for his draikana ripples from Astarot in waves, each stronger than the last as he realizes how fatigued she is after our flight. As soon as she and Fhord land, she trudges into the cave, ignoring the waiting goats as she drops to the ground.

Hurry. Astarot's plea drops into my mind. It's a single word, but it's all I need to understand his fear.

We'll return as soon as we can.

He dips his chin and settles next to her, nudging her neck lightly and then dropping his head to the ground.

Fhord watches her for a moment, his jaw clenched and nostrils flaring, and then spins and stalks out of the cave. I square my shoulders and follow. We need to get through this and get Tindera to Lumaria.

As soon as we're outside, though, my footsteps falter, shock rippling through me. Sagga is waiting for us, her brow wrinkled. Fingers bounce between the strands of long, gray hair she runs them through and the neck she pulls at. I've only seen her a few times—Halla and I always meet alone on the steps in Revalle's center—but my mouth drops open for a moment as I see how much she's aged. It's been eleven or twelve months since we last crossed paths, but she looks like she's been through ten grueling years.

"They took her," Sagga croaks as she throws herself into my arms. "I tried to hide her—to keep them from taking our Halla—but I couldn't. The Dróttning sent too many. They found our girl and dragged her to the Kastali."

My heart starts to race, a frenetic rhythm pounding in my chest, and the hands wrapped around Sagga's back break out in sweat. For a moment, I'm hyper-sensitive to everything: the trees standing guard as if they'll hide our dragons from harm; the birds singing above us, oblivious to the disaster Sagga's just laid at our feet; the harsh intake of Fhord's breath as he realizes what this means. What we need to do.

"Tell me exactly what happened," I urge as I step back from Sagga. If it were anyone else, I'd enter her thoughts, try to calm her down. But my magic fucks with Sagga's mind, I think because of her Seiðr. If I'm going to get anything rational from her, she'll need to give it to me.

"Let's get inside." Fhord's voice is low, and I flash out my thoughts to identify whatever threat he found. It's only two people, and they seem to be riding on a path that won't bring them here, but that will change if they get a hint of our presence.

"There's someone close," I tell Sagga. "We'll be safer inside."

When she enters, her eyes grow wide, and I realize she's probably never been this close to a dragon before. "They won't hurt you," I murmur. She's starting to calm down, and I don't want to do anything to change that.

"I know," she tells me. "The red one is yours?"

"Yes, Astarot." I try to see him as she would, marveling again at what a magnificent beast he is. "How did you know?"

"I feel your presence woven into the fabric of his. I would recognize your dragon anywhere."

She trudges toward him, less afraid than I would have expected, although I guess I shouldn't be surprised. Sagga's never predictable. Astarot opens his eyes as she approaches but lays still. When she rests her hand on his snout, he snorts in satisfaction and I realize Astarot craved her touch as much as she did his. She's an important part of my story—or, at least connected to an important part—and he wants to know her.

She's calmer as she stands with my dragon so I go to her, scratching behind his horn as I capture her gaze. "Tell me what happened, Sagga."

"A dozen of the Kastali's soldiers came to the house. The Dróttning knows what she means to you. I don't know how. I've told nobody. Halla was hiding in the basement, but they'd have found her wherever she hid. They were thorough."

"Did they say anything?" I can't keep the tremor from my voice. I don't know how the fuck we're going to get her if she's been taken to the Kastali. And we have to get her. She can't be punished for my sins.

"They demanded to know where they'd find 'the little girl the elf feeds'. I told them they were wrong, that we don't know you. They laughed and said the Dróttning knows better."

"When did this happen?" Fhord's pulling weapons from one of his bags as he asks this question. We were going in light, hoping we would draw less attention, but we'll need to be armed for what we're about to do.

"Two hours ago," she tells him. "My Seiðr drew me here. I knew I would find you."

"And you're sure they said they were taking her to the Kastali?" He pauses when he asks this question, staring at her as if he's angry at the information she's given us. I know he's not—he's just fucking intense—but fortunately, Sagga isn't easily intimidated.

"They were very specific about that," she tells him, straightening her back. "They want you there. And the Kastali is where you must go. If you don't free her today, you won't have another chance."

"How the fuck do you know that?" Fhord spits. I glare at him because he needs to calm his ass down. He nods quickly and returns his gaze to Sagga.

"Sifa knows," she responds in that mysterious way she favors. "I see what others cannot. This window to save Halla is small and getting smaller. It will be closed tomorrow."

Fhord opens his mouth, but I lift my hand, palm toward him. He scowls but stays quiet.

"Don't argue with her just to argue," I growl. "Would we go today if she hadn't said that?"

He leans back and crosses his arms, narrowing his eyes at me. And then he smirks. "We would."

"Then let's not fight about this. Do you have a way into the Kastali? And do you know where they'd be keeping her?"

"Yes to both questions." His voice is flat. He doesn't like this, but I'm going, so he's going too.

"Then let's gather what we need and go get Halla." I turn toward Sagga. "Nobody followed you, right?"

"I'm sure of it."

I look back at my stubborn mate. "Do you sense anyone else nearby?" I cast out my thoughts as he looks up, the way he sometimes does when he's searching. After a moment, he turns back to me and shakes his head.

"I don't either. She'll be safe."

Now he dips his chin once.

"We'll do everything we can to bring her here. If we're not back by sunset tomorrow, the dragons will take you to a place we know. Go straight there. You're never returning to Revalle again."

"Nothing is there for me except Halla." Her eyes are stern, little wrinkles at their corners and webbing out from her thin lips. "You will free her and we will go together."

"We will," I assure her, resting a hand on her shoulder. And then she drops to her ass next to my dragon and waves at me impatiently.

I guess I've been dismissed.

Within a few minutes, we've packed everything we need, sent our thoughts out one more time to confirm we're alone, and are stalking out of the cavern. Fhord leads us on an unexpected path toward the Kastali—one I never would have taken—but he gets us to the cellar we'll enter in less than two hours without crossing a single soldier. He knows Revalle and its surroundings well.

He drags open the cellar door then pulls a torch from one of his bags and lights it.

"How far from here?" I can see the Kastali, but it's probably not a direct line.

"We'll be in the tunnel less than an hour. Stay alert. It's used sometimes by Council members and others trying to hide from the Dróttning or disappear without being discovered. She's not here, so hopefully we won't have to kill anyone along the way."

"You've killed enough of the Dróttning's people for the day?" I smirk because I don't think there's an upper limit. Fhord will always be eager to kill more of the soldiers helping his bitch of a mother keep her iron fist around the dragons' necks.

He smiles and leans forward to give me a hard kiss. "Then stay alert so we know when to ready our swords," he grunts before kissing me one more time and leading the way into the cellar. I grab the door to close it behind me and follow him down.

It's a winding path, but not as bad as I'd feared. As Fhord predicted, within an hour we're moving into the tunnels beneath the Kastali. My thoughts find more and more people, but none down here. We make it to a ladder without having to kill a single soldier.

Disappointing, but maybe we'll get lucky when we're leading Halla out of here.

Fhord lifts a finger to his lips and then raises a palm. Within a few seconds, I hear the male and female voices he must have detected before me. They pass slowly, but they do pass. Perhaps five minutes after their voices disappear, Fhord climbs the stairs and pushes open a door in what is probably the floor above us.

Which squeals like Aksell when we relieved him of his paltry prick. Loud and never-ending, as if we've set every inch of his body on fire. I hold back my grin at the gruesome memory and watch Fhord pause while our thoughts flicker out to confirm we haven't drawn the chatty couple back to us. They're getting no closer, so Fhord pushes the door the rest of the way—prompting an even louder squeal—and then drops it with a heavy clatter.

"Way to keep a low profile," I mutter, smirking at him.

He shrugs and reaches out a hand to help me up, then closes the door with a little less clatter. "There's a storage closet near here," he whispers, perhaps realizing he should try to be quiet. "It usually holds uniforms. We'll go there first."

Fhord leads me slowly through the halls, pausing often to let voices pass before we enter another corridor. After ten minutes or so, he directs me into a large closet where we find clothes in our size. We're out into the hall again a few minutes later, hats sitting low on our brows as we walk more openly toward the cells Fhord thinks will hold Halla.

My stomach has been squeezing tighter and tighter—as if it's collapsed from the size of a grapefruit to an orange and now a grape—since we left the safety of the lower corridors. I'm trying to reel back my fear but can't keep images of Halla on the rack from bursting into my mind. I don't think the Dróttning would do something that horrific to a little girl, but I have no gods-damned idea how depraved she can be.

I'm so fucking terrified, I'm surprised I haven't gotten sick yet.

"We're going to free her," Fhord tells me as he rests a hand on my lower back, rubbing a bit to draw my thoughts away from the macabre pictures my mind keeps creating for me. "The Dróttning won't do to her what she's done to us."

"I thought I was done with this," I complain, forcing myself to breathe through the panic. A small group of soldiers enters the long corridor we're walking through a couple of dragon's-lengths ahead of us, so I straighten my back and stride, keeping my eyes straight ahead as they approach. "After we freed you and then were able to get the dragons out of the training grounds, I really believed I'd put this behind me."

"You need to protect her," Fhord says as he drops the hand that had been comforting me. I know why he can't touch me, but holy Helheim, do I need that grounding from him. "This fear for Halla is visceral and dredging up emotions you've learned to control when someone stronger's at risk or in pain."

He falls silent after that, nodding at the others as they approach and then pass us.

"How much farther?" I can't keep the tremor from my voice.

Fhord doesn't answer. Instead, his steps falter as his jaw drops, mouth open wide for a moment before he snaps it closed. "Shit," he utters, stepping forward to place himself between me and the male striding toward us, a dozen guards falling into place behind him.

I don't know who he is, but it's clear we're fucked. My mind darts out on the off chance he's weak enough to be controlled. A lash of pain flies back toward me as if he opened my skull and whipped me across my brain. I inhale sharply, struggling to hold myself up as the agony rises and then drops away.

"I wouldn't do that if I were you, elf," he warns, his voice low. Dangerous.

"Konungr Beron," Fhord says through gritted teeth. And now I'm sure we're fucked.

The Dróttning's husband found us. I have no idea how powerful he is, but if Fhord thought he could defeat him, he'd be striking now.

"Fhord," the Konungr responds, one side of his lips twisting up. "I thought you might come for the girl. Lucky me to have found you first."

He takes a single step forward, the half-smile growing to a full grin as his eyes land on me. "I've been wondering about you, elf," he tells me. "The female who took the Dróttning's son from her."

The grief and dread I'd been holding at bay consume me, my vision tunneling to nothing and nobody except the haughty male standing in front of us. I try to breathe, but I can't. In that moment, I'm back in the dungeons, body splayed on the rack, the Dróttning's knives slicing away every bit of my hope and resolve, as I turn to see sweet, innocent Halla hanging next to me.

I've failed her—I've failed everyone—and there's not a gods-damned thing I can do about it.

Chapter Sixteen

DANI

Whatever You Need

"Wait! Mikkael, wait!" My voice is sharp, but he's ignoring me and I need him to stop. Vulryn's pain is flowing through me in waves, and I'm not sure how much farther I can go.

Mikkael keeps walking—forcing me to jog to keep up with him. I can't blame him, but I also need him to fucking stop.

Vulryn barked at me when Mikkael and I kissed because I lost myself in him. The pain pounding inside me from her severed tail fell away as the feel of his lips on mine, his tongue dipping into my mouth to explore me, unleashed a river of bliss that flowed through my veins. I forgot about my dragon, bleeding out on the other side of the cavern, as I succumbed to a mate-induced euphoria.

He must ride my drake before you can claim him. Her anguish had whispered through her words. They were stilted, as if she could barely get them out.

I'd looked over at her, her demand filtering through the haze of my need for the male who finally was opening himself to me, taking a risk he swore he never would.

What do you mean? I asked, hoping she wasn't saying what I thought. What I knew.

My drake and I... our riders... must be mated, she'd told me. She was in so much fucking pain.

Devastation washed through me, eclipsing even my dragon's torment. I knew I'd never get another chance. If I rejected Mikkael again, he'd never trust me.

But that's what I did. Because my tortured dragon, whose tail he'd just cleaved off, demanded it. I'd never before wished she and I weren't bonded. Vulryn is everything. In that moment, though, I wanted nothing more than to be with Mikkael, even if it meant I didn't have her. And then a surge of guilt rose up, taking the place of the devastation.

I committed myself to Vulryn. I couldn't deny her demand. So I pushed him away.

"Please, Mik," I beg now, unable to keep my heart—or my pain—out of my voice. "Please stop."

His steps slow but don't stop. "What the fuck do you want, mate?" He spits the last word. He hates me again. Maybe he never stopped, and it was just this ridiculous mating bond cajoling us together when our defenses were so low. When we needed each other so desperately.

"We're not going that way. Vulryn's sure she can fly. Njörðr knows a way out. It'll be shorter, and we won't have to deal with the river."

He still doesn't stop. "I'm not going with you," he gripes. "I ... I can't."

I reach out to grab his arm, dragging him to a stop. He glares down at my hand and then at me. "Let me go."

"Just ... listen to me for a minute. Please."

My heart beats a dozen times before he responds, raven eyes spewing flames at me the entire time. Finally, he nods. "Speak."

"We need to fly out of here. Njörðr has explored these caverns. He said the only route to walk out is the way we came in. You won't be able to cross the river. You'll be trapped here, and that trickster Loki will find you. Or you'll die trying to cross it."

"What the fuck do you care?" These words are guttural, vibrating with anger. And some other emotion I don't want to contemplate.

"I can't be with you yet. *Yet*," I repeat because he needs to know how I feel. "I can't ignore Vulryn's wishes. Especially not when she's suffering so much. But it doesn't mean I don't care. Fuck, Mikkael, I care more than I ever wanted to."

Again, he's silent, this time for twenty beats of my heart. "I don't believe you," he rasps at last.

"I know." I shrug. What else can I do? "I don't know if I'd believe me either. I'm telling you the truth, but it doesn't matter. The only thing that matters is that you need to live. If not for me, for Sifa. She loves you. It would kill her to lose you too. Especially after Johan."

His eyes grow wide, brows bunching together, as his lips tip down. He spins and strides two male's-heights away, then stands and stares into the cavern, his back to me and hands fisted on his hips. I'm struggling to keep my shit together, the agony from Vulryn's severed tail threatening to consume me, but I can't let him go.

"That was fucking low, Dani." His words are a breath, so quiet they barely reach me.

"I'm not sorry. I'd never be able to face Sifa again if I left you here. Come with us for the friend who's been by your side for years, even if not for me or Ziselær."

"Fuck," he bellows. "Fuck, fuck, fuck." And then he turns and looks at me. "Your dragon is sure she can fly?"

"She is." I try to shut down the hope blossoming in my chest. He doesn't want to come, a thin thread pulling him toward Sifa and away from the isolation he needs right now.

"Can she carry anyone?"

"Ziselær can't carry all of us. She said she can carry Njörðr. We'll tie him on so he can stay mounted."

Mikkael's face falls. I'm sure the horror of what he had to do will stay with him for a long time.

"Will she carry me instead?" His words don't hold a hint of emotion.

My stomach clenches. He's devastated if he doesn't want to ride his own dragon. "I thought you'd want to take Ziselær," I murmur.

"I can't," he tells me. "I can't be that close to you, Dani. Not now. Not ever. I'll ride Vulryn alone. That'll be better anyway. Njörðr will be safer riding Z with you. She can drop me as soon as we get out of these caves."

"Whatever you need."

He jerks his chin down once, then turns back toward the dragons and stalks forward.

I'm not going to do what I promised. We can't leave him alone in the middle of nowhere. I'll tell Vulryn not to drop him off when we're free of this place. He needs to go with us until we reach the others. He'll be pissed but at this point, a little more anger and hate is just a drop in the massive bucket of his disdain for me.

Will you carry Mikkael? She's watching the angry male when I walk back into the cavern, her crimson gaze impossible to read.

Vulryn turns to me for a moment, her snout tight and feathers bunched around her eyes. I think she's going to refuse, but then she looks again at Mikkael and her expression softens. The tension in her mouth and lips disappears. *I will carry your mate*, she tells me. Not the angry male. My mate.

Vulryn is intentional about her word choices. I'm not sure why she called him that. The small, petty part of me wants to respond, remind her we rejected him. That she demanded it. But I don't. We'll talk about it later. For now, I don't want to add a bit of pain to what she's already suffering.

Can you make it to Lumaria? It's a long flight, and I don't know if Fhord will ever forgive me for taking this stranger to his island. But he tried to help Vulryn. If Njörðr's got any chance of getting his leg back, he needs to get into the water too. We can't just abandon him like this. Once we get there, we'll figure out if he can ever be trusted to leave the island again.

I will reach the pretty place.

We'll feed first. You must be starving.

I will feed in the pretty place after I bathe. I do not believe my stomach would tolerate a meal.

And you're sure you can make it?

She snarls in response. That's all the answer I'll get, so I accept it.

Turning toward Njörðr, I help him dress the stump for flight, tightening the belt girding his thigh and then swathing it in a gel we brought for wounds before wrapping it in his coat. When that's done, I dig through our packs to find a couple of the leaves he can chew to help with the pain. It's not much, but all we can manage with our limited supplies. Within a few minutes, he's good enough to travel.

And then I look at Mikkael. "Can you help get Njörðr onto Ziselær's back?"

He nods and strides over to the newest member of our group, helping him stand and then walk slowly together toward Ziselær.

The dragon makes himself as small as possible—not an easy thing for a beast that size—leaning over to give Mikkael and Njörðr the easiest path he can. Njörðr's secure within a few minutes and I settle in behind him—a better position for me to help hold him in place—doing my best to avoid any contact with his leg.

When I turn toward Mikkael and Vulryn, my mouth drops open. Mikkael is standing next to Vulryn's head, his forehead resting on the spot below her horn that she lets few touch. It's a sensitive area for her, and she typically only wants the feel of my hands there, although she'll tolerate it from close friends like Toffer. She looks relaxed, more at peace than she should be with so much of her tail missing, blood still oozing out.

He's whispering something to her. I can't hear the words, and I'm desperate to ask my dragon what he's telling her. I don't for now, though. I suspect he's voicing guilt for what he just had to do and she's letting him.

When he leans back, straightening his spine and stretching out a hand to scratch behind her horn, she snorts. Not an angry, growly snort, but a soft, accepting one. I didn't think she liked Mikkael. Now I don't know what to think.

And then she extends a wing and he mounts, settling on her back. They both turn to us—Njörðr needs to direct the dragons—and wait.

"Fly into that large cavern to the right," he says, loud enough for Vulryn to hear.

Neither of the dragons move. Vulryn barks at her drake, and he grumbles at her, almost an apology but not quite. Finally, Ziselær launches into the air and takes the lead.

What was that about?

My drake wanted to follow me. He fears I will falter. He wants to be able to see me.

He's just worried. Her voice is stronger now. Still weak, but much better than it was right after Mikkael took her tail. I can't blame Ziselær. I'm scared too and hate having to spin to look at Vulryn since I'll probably be doing it every few minutes. *Why didn't you want to go first?*

The chatty male rides my drake. He knows the path we must take. My drake must lead. I know there's more. Something is bothering her. But she's quiet for a moment, as if she's deciding whether to tell me the rest. Finally, she adds, *I wish I had not barked at you when your mouth met your mate's. I do not like the pain I caused you.*

And my heart breaks. My strong, valiant dragon, who's still bleeding from the trauma she insisted we inflict to free her, never apologizes. But she's apologizing to me, over Mikkael. *Please don't worry about me. I don't want to hurt you any more than you're hurting already.* And now I'm the one who's unsure whether I should say more. But I do. *You're right, I know. I need to be with Ziselær's rider, and it may not be Mikkael. We just need to make sure he picks someone good.*

If he does not, we will kill him. Her tone is light and she's sporting a dragony smirk when I glance back at her.

I huff out a laugh, my heart lighter because she's able to joke with me, even with all the pain she's in.

I love my dragon so fucking much.

Njörðr rasps directions to Ziselær occasionally—left into that cavern, straight through this one—but otherwise he's silent. I leave him alone for a while, but my curiosity is driving me a bit mad, and I'm desperate for something to take my mind off Vulryn and Mikkael's pain.

"You said you came here ten years ago from another world?" I ask, my voice loud enough to be heard over the steady beat of Ziselær's wings.

"I did," he confirms, not offering anything else.

"My friends came at the same time from worlds they call Midgard and Álfheimr. And a few others, I think."

His head is turned around so he can look at me when I say this, letting me observe his reaction. I've never seen such a perfect example of shock. His eyes grow wide, his entire body still for a moment, and then he blinks rapidly and shakes his head, before giving me a smile so full of joy, I can't help but smile back.

"I suspected there were others but had not yet found any. What are your friends' names?"

"Sifa and Toffer."

This look is somehow even more surprised, his pupils growing large as his mouth drops open. "Is Sifa an elf with dark skin who looks perhaps fifteen years of age?" he asks when he's able to speak again.

"She's an elf with dark skin, but she's not that young. My age, maybe a bit younger."

And now he's disappointed, his eyebrows drawing together as his lips tip down. He must know this younger Sifa, not mine. "I do not know a Sifa that age. The girl I know, a daughter of sorts to my son, Freyr, does not appear that old. She has lived a few hundred years, but elves age very slowly in my worlds. My Sifa is, no doubt, safe there, a better place for her kind. She's not exposed to the Dróttning's hatred of elves in this one."

"Which world do you come from?"

"It is easy to walk between worlds in that place. I spent time in all of them—Midgard, Asgard, Álfheimr, and the others. Even Helheim occasionally, if I had no choice but to engage with the trickster god Loki's loathsome offspring."

"Helheim's a real place? And it's run by someone related to the trickster who trapped you here?" I'm sure he can hear the wonder in my voice. I've been cursing about Helheim all my life but never believed it actually exists.

"Yes, to both questions. Loki's daughter, Hel, was cast to Helheim long ago. She has made it her own."

"I have so many questions about your worlds."

"Perhaps I can answer you another time. I am not myself. This body has grown tired."

"Of course. You're right. You need to rest."

"My thanks, dragon rider."

We leave the caves within an hour after that—at night, thank the gods—and fly toward the ocean and Lumaria. Vulryn started out determined to fly the entire way, but it's too far and I can tell already that she's too tired. Even her iron will won't give her the strength and stamina she'll need to travel so far.

We fly for a long time, though. The moon rises above us slowly, a near-perfect circle shimmering in a sky that I've always thought must have been painted for us by gods who disappeared long ago. It's more beautiful than it should be. So much more than *our* gods would ever give the mortals who walk this world.

I shake my head, trying to dispel my odd thoughts. All this talk of old gods—Sköll, Hræsvelgr and now Jormungandr, Loki, and Hel—has been fucking with my mind. Making me wonder if there really were benevolent gods in our world millennia ago, before the Dróttning and the Monarch and all the evil they unleashed on this land. But so far, all the old gods are evil too.

Maybe good gods have never existed and the beauty of this world is just a random act of fate.

The sun is cresting on the horizon when Vulryn reaches out. *We will land here. My drake knows of a cave.*

Thank fuck. She's so fucking tired. I can hear it in her voice, see it in the tight set of her snout, the struggle with every flap of her wings. I'm not sure if Ziselær convinced her to stop or if she gave in on her own, but I'm grateful.

I'm so glad, I tell her. *I'm exhausted. I was afraid I'd fall asleep on the way to Lumaria.*

Why did you not tell me? Her voice is layered with outrage, and I hide the grin I can't hold back.

You need the water. You're in so much pain.

I am fine. These words are angry. She doesn't ever want to be seen as weak.

I feel your pain. I want the water too.

You need sleep more. We will stop and rest. Perhaps I will feed. My drake knows of a herd nearby.

Relief ripples through me, my shoulders relaxing as I feel tension leave every bit of my body. *Food would be good, for all of us. You should feed.*

Perhaps, is her only response. But it's good enough.

Ziselær leads us to an enormous cavern, hidden at the base of a hill with an entry in the ground, concealing it from anyone flying overhead. Njörðr is wobbly when we land, so I don't move at first, watching Mikkael dismount Vulryn. Before he turns our way, he whispers something to her, quietly enough to not share it with anyone else, and reaches out to scratch behind her horn.

She leans into his touch, closing her eyes as she does when I caress her. Or when Toffer does, or one of the few other people she has claimed as family. It's a level of trust and acceptance I didn't expect between her and Mikkael. She doesn't like him.

He smiles as he turns away from her, and she opens her eyes, gaze following him as he strides toward the cave opening to remove the shrubs and bushes, usher us in, and then replace them all. When he climbs up Ziselær's wing, I realize the blue dragon is more comfortable around Mikkael too. And I'm dying to know what they've been talking about, because something changed on the way over.

I help Mikkael lift Njörðr up and over Ziselær's back and then support him as he makes his way down the wing, settling to lean against the wall next to the fire pit. As Mikkael drags our bags down from his dragon, I dig out a couple more leaves for Njörðr's pain but don't mess with his wound. It isn't dripping blood any longer, and we don't want to risk making it worse.

Then I go talk to my dragon.

You and Mikkael seem ... better.

He is more tolerable than he was. Her voice is contemplative, like she's considering her words before speaking them.

Did you speak during the trip? I mean, did he talk to you?

My drake helped us communicate.

A hint of hope sparks within me, but I try not to let it flare. We're all traumatized. Ziselær will go back to pushing Mikkael away when we get to Lumaria. *Z spoke with him?* I ask at last, making sure my voice holds none of the optimism I can't let myself feel.

My drake wanted to speak with his rider. Vulryn shares. *He sees your mate's strength and compassion.*

I wait for a moment, anxious for some detail about their conversation but none comes. My talkative beast has decided now's the time she's going to hold back information? I think not. *And?*

And we spoke.

You're not going to tell me what you spoke about?

I am not.

Why?

She doesn't get a chance to answer. Ziselær barks something at us, and Vulryn's head whips toward him, her snout a thin line as flames ripple from her nose. *Another dragon approaches. We will hide in the cave. Quietly.*

Fuck. I lift a trembling hand toward Mikkael, gesturing him over to Njörðr. "Someone's coming," I mouth when he's close enough. "We need to all go deeper." He nods, one arm ducking under Njörðr's shoulder while I do the same on the other side.

Vulryn takes the lead, creeping into the cavern as if her steps will draw this enemy toward us, so we follow her lead. It's painstaking because Njörðr is struggling to make any progress, but within ten minutes or so, we're far enough into the cavern to hopefully go undetected.

And we wait. And wait. And wait. My heart is pounding the entire time, my legs bouncing as if they need to be prepared to run when we're caught. Because I know we're about to get caught. I have no idea how long we're there, but it feels like half the day must have passed. I'm on high alert the whole time, too exhausted to face whatever might find us, but much too nervous to rest.

Finally, Vulryn lifts her head and looks in the direction of her drake. And she deflates. Whatever he says sends my dragon into a desolation so deep, I want to wrap my arms around her and take away all her pain.

What is it? I murmur, standing and resting my forehead against hers. *What did he tell you?*

He has been summoned to the Nest, she declares, each word a struggle, *and he will go. He belongs to the wyrm, and he returns to her.*

I dig my fingers into my dragon's feathers as my heart breaks for her and Mikkael.

And I send out a silent curse to the gods that are every bit as evil as I've always believed.

CHAPTER SEVENTEEN

MIKKAEL

GONE AGAIN

H E'S GONE AGAIN.

Z abandoned Vulryn—he abandoned me—to return to that evil bitch.

I'm not surprised he'd leave me. He's never let go of his anger and hatred, and I don't blame him one bit. A few weak moments, when it felt like he might be opening up to me, are nothing compared to the century he spent under the Dróttning's rule. Under that bastard Matthias's control. Whatever connection he and I might have been forming couldn't replace the utter devotion and commitment he had to them. He's still too broken.

But he's leaving Vulryn too. That, I never saw coming. I know how much he loves her. How dedicated he is to her. I thought she'd keep him here. That he'd help her get to Lumaria for the healing she needs.

Maybe Sifa and Fhord were right. Maybe he's not the dragon I thought he was.

And just maybe the fates were right, because I sure as fuck don't deserve the dragon I thought Z was. We might be perfect for each other after all.

"We're gonna stay here for the night," Dani says as she crouches down next to me, eyes kinder than they should be after I've been such a dick to her. She's clasping her hands together, as if they'd reach out to comfort me if she didn't stop them. "Vulryn can't fly like this. She's about ready to pass out from the blood loss and all the emotions this shit has dredged up."

I glance at her dragon, whose head is resting on the ground, eyes closed. Her lashes and cheeks are wet, and I realize I've never seen her cry. After everything we've been through—all she's suffered—it's this that shattered her. It hurts that Z could be such a bastard to her.

Everything is so fucked up.

"Njörðr needs to sleep more than us. We'll split the watch." Dani stifles a yawn as she says this, and I suspect she's about to offer to take the first shift. but I cut her off before she can.

"I'll go first," I tell her. "I won't sleep anytime soon. I need some alone time before my mind will rest."

"Are you sure?" Her voice is soft, and I can't hold back the sad smile that tilts my lips.

"I'm sure. Go be with your dragon. Sleep. I'll wake you in five or six hours."

"Thanks, Mik." She stands and turns toward Vulryn, but pauses before walking away. "I didn't reject you, Mik," she tells me in a quiet voice, still watching her dragon. "I just need to work this out with Vulryn. I need her to accept it."

Now she turns, her gaze holding mine. "But know that I would choose you if I could. For a moment, I almost did. I nearly told my dragon to fuck off and leave me alone." She smiles, but it's not a happy smile. "I couldn't, though. Not after everything she's been through. And I'm so fucking sorry."

I don't respond as she turns back toward Vulryn and strides forward, scratching behind her dragon's horn then digging her blankets out of a pack and snuggling next to Vulryn's stomach. Dani's asleep within a few minutes, snoring lightly.

I watch them for a long time, trying to work through my feelings. Everything's been so frantic since she and Z exploded into my life. My emotions have bounced around like a ball being kicked between teams, from fascination to fear, excitement to apathy, and everything in between. Maybe even from love to hate. It's been a constant struggle to keep the negative feelings from taking over, to maintain some hope in the midst of all the fuckery.

It's time to let it all go.

Z's made his feelings clear. He doesn't want me. That won't change. I need to accept it.

I'll never ride him.

Dani says she wants me, and I believe her. But it's not enough. It never will be. She'll always be the mate who chose everyone else ahead of me. I never knew I wanted a mate. Now that I've seen what the fates intended—what the Dróttning stole from us—I know exactly what I want.

I want someone who will choose me.

No, I *need* someone who will choose me.

I'm being an asshole. If I rode Z, I'd probably put his interests, his needs, ahead of Dani's too. But it still hurts like a bitch that my mate chose that bastard Matthias, again and again. And now she's chosen some unknown male that the Dróttning will pair with Z. Instead of me, her mate.

I need to stop hurting.

She's beautiful—exactly my type—and I've realized I like her. She's got the quirkiest sense of humor, and her love for and loyalty to Vulryn and the others is the kind of shit bards glorify in song. But the fates are wrong. She doesn't want me enough to push back on her dragon's demands. To kiss me when we both desperately crave it. I deserve someone who wants me that much, at least.

By the time I wake up Dani, I'm ready to touch her without being dragged into the bullshit the mating bond stirs within me. "Your turn," I tell her as I shake her shoulder, ignoring the tingles that burst in my fingers.

She opens her eyes and watches me for a few seconds, as if she's trying to get her footing. And then she lifts her hands to run them through her thick hair and yawns. "Right," she whispers. "My turn. Thanks. Sleep well, Mik."

I nod and stand to give her my back, walking over to my packs and pulling out my blankets. I don't turn around as I head over to Njörðr, lay down next to him with my face toward the wall, and close my eyes.

"Gorm? And Khanti?" Dani's soft words wake me from a restless sleep, full of all my fears about my mate and my dragon. I shake my head, trying to dispel images of Dani and Z leaving my side to run toward Matthias, who's just risen from the dead, decrepit and broken. Turning toward Dani's voice, I open my eyes to a dark cave with two un-expected figures standing between us and a soft glow from outside. It's sunrise, or close to it.

"Dani. Thank the gods. The message we got was odd, so we weren't sure who we'd find here."

Thank the gods, indeed. I stand to stride over, giving Gorm one of the half hugs men in this world share. I'm so fucking relieved. I passed most of my watch obsessing over Dani and Z, but I also spent plenty of time worrying about our fucked-up situation. I had no idea how in Helheim we'd get to Lumaria. Maybe we got lucky.

"How are you here?" I ask, releasing Gorm to step back and let Dani tug him into a full hug. Gorm's a solid male—another rider with a bond fucked by the Dróttning. His story about losing his pregnant mate is a good reminder that I'm just one of many people whose life the bitch has twisted.

"Let's get settled and I'll tell you," he says, wresting my thoughts back to what's important. "First, Khanti wants to feed. There's a herd nearby and no other dragons in the area. Will Vulryn join her?"

The hungry beast snorts and rises quickly, ready to hunt with the pink dragon.

Gorm's eyes grow wide as he sees the mangled stump that used to be a tail. "Fuck me. Who did that to her?"

"Me," I respond with one of those laughs that forces its way out sometimes, even though there's not a single thing that's funny.

He turns toward me and narrows his eyes, but not in anger or spite. His eyebrows draw together, and he cocks his head to one side as he watches me for a moment. He seems to be evaluating what I just told him, considering it. "Guess there's a story here to be told too, huh?"

"Fuckin' good one," I tell him. "Let's get some coffee and porridge going while the dragons hunt. We can catch up." I pause, reaching out to clasp his arm one more time. "I'm so fucking glad you're here, Gorm. Thanks for coming for us."

"We rebels gotta stick together," he responds as he grips my forearm with his other hand. "We will always come for you, Mikkael."

As we're cooking, Dani and I tell him about our travels—searching for Z, Vulryn getting dragged away by Jormungandr, and Z showing up to help us find her. Njörðr chimes in here and there, adding information about the serpent and her trickster god father, but mostly he listens, his hand on his chin, eyes contemplative. Gorm watches me as Dani tells him about our decision to cut off Njörðr's leg and Vulryn's tail, reaching out to rest a hand on my shoulder and squeeze when she describes the things I did.

But he's quiet, letting us finish, until we get to this cave and Z's visitor, explaining that we have no idea who came or how they convinced Z to leave. "This part, I know," he says with a half-smile.

"Then maybe you can tell us, because Vulryn is heartbroken." Dani casts her soft, blue eyes toward the cave's opening when she says this, shoulders slumping for a moment, before she straightens her back and turns her attention back to Gorm. "She thought Ziselær would choose her. It's killing her that he didn't. And she's already in so much pain."

"I don't think he had a choice," Gorm tells us. "Gunnar, the rider who found you, is a fanatic. He's as devoted to the Dróttning as they come. Everyone's been searching for Ziselær, and this rider never would have left him here. He spent a long time trying to convince your dragon to return. Gunnar and Matthias were friends—well, as close as either of them came to being friendly with someone else—and I suspect he wanted to save Ziselær from being taken back to the Nest by force."

"Don't they know what Z did?" The question comes out before I can stop it, my fear for Z driving me. "Won't he be punished for killing that bastard?"

"It was a massacre, Mikkael." His words are soft, dripping with a grief so deep, I wonder if it has any bottom. Dragons feel every death of a member of the Thunder—even those who we want dead because they fight for the Dróttning—as a painfully personal loss. "All the Dróttning's people, every dragon loyal to her, died. The rebels know, but none would share that information."

I exhale slowly, letting that worry dissipate. Knowing Z won't be in any immediate danger when he returns unleashes something within me. A rope that's tied around my spine, squeezing every time I try to take a breath, starts to unwind a bit.

"How do you know this?" Dani asks, her gaze spinning from Gorm to me and back to Gorm again. "Did Matthias's friend report finding Ziselær and what he had to do to convince him?"

"No, but his dragon did. To us."

"What do you mean?"

"Gunnar may be devoted to the Dróttning, but his dragon, Phorth, is devoted to us. The rebellion. He got a message to another ally as soon as he could—coded so the Dróttning wouldn't understand if she was listening in." He smiles, his eyes lighting up. "The dragons in the rebellion have created a way to communicate without disclosing anything to her. It's very clever."

"Phorth told you to come to us." Dani's voice is full of wonder.

"I knew friends needed help here. I didn't know who I'd find. That's more detail than they can relay."

"And, how's Z?" I can't keep the tremor from my words. I have to let him go. I know that. But I still need to know that he's okay.

"We don't know much except he didn't want to return but agreed when Gunnar threatened him." He's quiet for a few seconds, his gaze bouncing between us. "He surely knew

Phorth recognized your presence but chose not to reveal you," he says at last. "If Ziselær still felt Vulryn in the cave, Phorth would have as well. The mating bond's a different type of connection, but they'd be able to sense Vulryn at about the same distance. I suspect he feared for you. If other dragons came to force him to leave, you'd have been exposed. Too many of the beasts remain loyal to the Dróttning."

I'm surprised by my body's reaction to his words. I'm always so tightly wound, I've come to expect it. It's a normal state for me. But hearing that Z left to protect us—not because he was abandoning his draikana and me—soothes something inside me. An open wound, burning deep in my gut, starts to heal. The rope that's become a constant annoyance, crushing my spine, unwinds a bit more.

Dani and Gorm both look up toward the cave's entrance—smiles on their faces—a few seconds before Vulryn returns, followed by Khanti. Vulryn's ... better, somehow. She probably had the same conversation with Khanti that we just had with her rider. Like me, she seems more relaxed. Less distressed over Z's decision to return to the Dróttning.

"What happens to Z now?" I ask, although I'm not sure I want to know the answer. Gorm's lips drop into a frown and I steel myself for whatever he's going to tell me.

"The Dróttning sent him north," Gorm responds. "She'll order him to take a new rider soon, if she hasn't already. If he complies, they'll be in the northern Nest long enough for the trainers to oversee the pairing, make sure Ziselær complies with his new rider's demands. Sometimes it's a rough transition, especially so soon after another rider's death. If Ziselær refuses to take a rider, he'll go to the training grounds until he submits."

"Torture, like they did to Astarot before Sifa and Fhord saved him? Or what the dragons in the training grounds were suffering before we freed them?" The anger that fills me with his words spills into mine, turning them harsh and bitter.

"It doesn't start out so extreme, but yes, that's how the Dróttning trains disobedient dragons."

"Who?" I demand. "Who will ride my dragon now?"

"I don't know," he responds with a shrug and grimace. "The Dróttning always has several candidates for available dragons. It depends on who she's favoring at that moment in time."

"And the dragon has no voice in who gets chosen?"

"Dragons have no voice in anything the Dróttning does to them," Gorm grunts. "Some dragons get lucky, but the Dróttning prefers cruel vassals, so most riders are cruel. And with Fhord's betrayal, loyalty to her has become even more important." He looks up at his dragon, then stands. "Khanti thinks we should leave. Dragons often fly training runs in this area. We need to be gone before they start."

"Will you help us get to Lumaria? Vulryn and Njörðr need to spend time in its waters." My heart breaks a bit at the plea in Dani's words. She's not often as desperate for something as she is now.

Gorm turns toward Njörðr, one eyebrow quirking up as he cocks his head. "Have you been to Lumaria before?"

"I have not."

"You know that once you're there, they may not let you leave?" Gorm demands in a flat tone. "And if they decide they can't trust you, you'll be imprisoned until you convince them you deserve their faith. If you're able. The rebellion is trying its damnedest to make sure it can rely on everyone who goes there. They've realized recently how flawed their process has been. Too many troublemakers have slipped through. They're demanding more proof of loyalty before they let newcomers in."

"I realize this place is private and important, and that until I can convince them of my allegiance to their cause—and my opposition to the Dróttning—I will not be free." Njörðr's response is firm and direct, not a hint of uncertainty in it. "But I would go even were it not for this stump I'm hoping may be whole again. Your fight is mine, and your allies will find I have information that will help us all."

"That won't be our decision to make," I tell him. "But I'll champion your cause."

"As will I, for whatever it's worth," Dani chimes in.

Njörðr smiles, his kind eyes crinkling at the corners. "I couldn't ask for anything else."

We pack up quickly, loading our bags on Khanti for the long flight to Lumaria. I'm with Gorm now, while Vulryn carries Dani and Njörðr. It's a lot, but her meal gave her strength she desperately needed.

Within ten minutes we're airborne, flying as we always do in a nonsensical pattern, driven by the dragons' vague sense of other beasts approaching us. It's slow going, but the only way we can travel in this gods-forsaken place while the Dróttning lives. Finally, hours after we left the cave, we soar over the ocean, everyone relaxing a bit as the chances of being found drop drastically.

I've come here once before, so I know what to expect. Still, I'm surprised how quickly the island approaches. We're flying slowly—Vulryn is struggling after a long day of travel—but it still takes only a few hours. The dragons descend in unison, Khanti in the lead to hover less than a dragon's-length above the water. A surface that appeared calm and mild from far above is wild and choppy down here. Waves rise and crest, gashes of white ripping through the dark blue sea.

And then we're soaring into the thick fog that protects the island. The dread that comes with this mist fills me, and I'm reminded of the draugr forest. But that magic felt artificial—something the gods who revived those poor souls created to protect their monstrosities. This feels natural, despite the fact that like the forest, it inspires a desperate need to turn around, not delve deeper into the nothingness. The island does this on its own, and its magic is more primal.

I breathe in a deep breath when we break through the layer of muck, and Lumaria appears before us. It's so fucking beautiful. My gaze is drawn to Dani for a moment, as if something inside me needs to compare them, confirm my mate is even more stunning than this incomparable place. And fuck if she isn't, her eyes bright and the softest smile on her face.

But I force myself to look away, focusing on the calm blue ocean beneath us and the jade sculpture sitting in front of us.

It's exactly as I remember, a cone with a soft white cap, shifting shades of green along its side, and a ribbon of the brightest blue surrounding its base, leading to a massive cerulean lake sitting in the midst of the town.

Moments like this make me grateful I'm alive.

We're supposed to go to the field when we come to the island so we can be welcomed—really, inspected—by Birger and the others. But Vulryn's not an obedient beast, and she needs to submerge herself in the water. She flies low over the waiting emissaries, probably to let them see why she's not heeding their decree to all who arrive here, and then passes Khanti to head straight to the lake. Dani turns and waves at us—because Khanti is an obedient beast and we'll stay to greet the others—and then leans forward to say something to Njörðr.

Another piece of the rope around my spine unwinds as I watch my mate and her dragon drop into the water in the distance, safe at last, while we descend into the midst of the waiting group.

Chapter Eighteen

Fhord

Lead the Way

Fucking Beron. The asshole never comes out of his rooms. He's been holed up in there for centuries, only emerging when he must to wave at his peasants and prove he still lives. Today, of all days, he decides he's gonna be a hero.

The gods really are fucking with me. The bastards.

"I don't want to have to kill you and your soldiers, Beron," I tell him in my most threatening voice, "but I will. We're getting the girl and leaving, one way or another."

"No, you won't. Son." He spits out the last word, probably angry that he heard the news like everyone else after I revealed it in Lumaria. I wish I could have been here to see his face.

Beron's known since he married the Dróttning—giving her the title to go along with the power she'd amassed—that she and I are close. I'd only been alive for three decades when she took her place at Beron's side, after commanding his armies for nearly a century. I was still fully loyal to her and kept her dirty secret about my parentage, even from him. He had no idea my father's an elf who's either dead or trapped in one of the prisons.

Beron never realized she'd kept the strongest elf in Vanatia as a fuck-toy after caging the rest of them. She sent my father away, or just killed him, only when she'd gotten the child she wanted. She hoped to birth someone powerful who she could mold into a weapon to help keep her grip on power. And probably to keep her company, since she's been alone most of her miserable life. For too many years, that's what I was to her. But thank fuck, Sifa erupted in my world and broke me out of my idolatry.

It's about gods-damned time the Dróttning's hypocrisy is on full display. I should have told Beron years ago. Maybe he would have stopped her power grabs, if he could.

"You know how powerful I am, Dad," I respond with a smirk, "even if you've just learned the extent of it."

Beron smirks back, the fucker, then turns and smiles at the female to his left, who stares at us, her expression flat. "Jacinda here," Beron says in that better-than-all-you-peons tone I've hated since the Dróttning married him, "is a sieve, but she's not just any sieve. She's a netted sieve, and she's protecting all of us."

"The fuck she is," I snarl, because sieves are my greatest weakness. Immune to all magic, they deny me my most potent weapon—the ability to combine with my mate to control the minds of anyone who threatens us. "The Dróttning is still trying to pretend all elves in this kingdom are imprisoned," I point out to my asshole stepfather. "She doesn't have any sieves in her armies."

"Jacinda is sworn to me. Whatever you may believe about my relationship with your mother, I am still the Konungr in this land. I would not let such a valuable elf be sent to prison."

"And you just announce it? With all these soldiers to witness it? Aren't you concerned it will get back to the Dróttning?"

"Do you think I need to hide from my wife?" Beron demands, his voice rising as a tic starts to pulse in his jaw. I rarely see him and the Dróttning together, and I'm getting a better understanding of why with every word he says. He spewed out "wife" with the same malice as he spit out "son" a moment ago. "She knows what Jacinda is," he adds in a more neutral tone. "And these are loyal soldiers. They would not disclose my secrets. Ever."

"So you think you're going to imprison us? That I'll let that happen?"

"Oh no, my dear son"—again with a malicious twist to the final word—"I would never send you to a cage. That's your mother's ... fetish. You'll be protected, of course. I'll even let you and the elf share a room. My dear wife will decide what to do with you when she returns."

I can feel Sifa's fear—more for Halla than us—but I can't do anything except let her sense my confidence. Beron just told me exactly what I needed to hear to let him hold us. I don't know if he's a gods-damned idiot or if he's playing some game I don't yet understand, but it doesn't matter. We can escape any room he puts us in. So, we're gonna let him.

"Lead the way," I direct with a wave of my arm toward the hall that leads to the best rooms. "Sifa and I would be happy to be your guest for the evening."

Sifa turns to glare at me, but I just smile in response, caressing her mind with mine. She doesn't want Halla imprisoned a moment longer than necessary, but this is necessary. We might not be able to beat the dozen soldiers who surround Beron. No doubt, he's chosen some of the Kastali's best fighters for his entourage. Our best odds will come later tonight.

Beron turns on his heel and strides forward, his people parting to let Sifa and me pass, then falling into formation behind us. We travel a winding path that takes us where I hoped—to the royal guest suites. It's a secure area, but I know it well enough to be confident we can escape and find our way to Halla at last.

"You won't leave, of course," Beron says as he ushers us into a large suite. "I will call for food—can't mistreat my favorite son—and let you know when we can expect your mother to return." He pauses, smirking again. "Jacinda will stay outside while you're here. She'll make sure you don't try to change my plans with your magic."

And then he's gone, a hint of his unique smell—smoke and cherries, for some reason I've never understood—the only thing he leaves behind.

"I don't like this," Sifa growls at me as she inspects the room. "We need to find Halla and get out of here. What if the Dróttning comes back before we can free her?"

I stride over and plant myself in front of my rabbit, lifting a hand to caress her cheek. "You're so fucking sexy when you're mad. I'd throw you on this bed right now if I thought I'd have enough time before they barge in here with food."

Her eyebrows draw together in that cute, quirky way I love so much, her dark lips a fine line as one hand lifts to rub the back of her neck. "Why the fuck aren't you worried, Fhord?"

"Do you think this room can hold us?" I ask as my thumb tugs at her bottom lip. "Where's my ferocious warrior?"

"She's desperate to see Halla and make sure she's okay, not to mention eternally pissed that the Dróttning decided to target her. And that the gods-damned Konungr emerged from his hole to fuck with our rescue plan. Who in Helheim could have expected that?" She pauses, a little smirk twisting her lips. "Shit. I sound pathetic, don't I?"

"Maybe not 'pathetic'. A little crazy, but I like your crazy. Like I said, it's fucking sexy."

Her hand releases her neck and rests on mine instead. "Is there anything I do that isn't sexy?"

I watch my mate, unable to drag my gaze away from her deep brown eyes, as I cast my thoughts about for something—anything—she does that turns me off.

But there's nothing. Not one thing. She could roll around in the muck and grime and I'd join her there, happy to cake myself in mud as long as I can be muddy with her. Which sounds fucking amazing, now that I think about it. We'll give that a try when we get a little free time.

"Gods, you're incorrigible," she declares with a laugh as I shrug at her. "What now, then?"

"I'm starving," I tell her. "Beron won't poison us. Not before the Dróttning returns. When food arrives, we'll eat and wait until we feel the castle rest. Then we'll go get Halla and get the fuck out of here."

That's what we do. Beron sends a damn good meal but stays away. His sieve waits outside our door, and we wait inside. And wait. And wait. It was nearly sunset when we entered the cave to the Kastali, and it must be two or three hours past midnight by now. But the time isn't right yet. An hour before sunrise is our best bet. That's when we'll strike.

Neither of us expects the door to swing open and Beron to stride in, his entire retinue behind him—led by Jacinda, of-fucking-course.

"What the fuck do you want, Beron?" My voice is probably a little pissy considering the meal he fed us, but I've never liked the asshole, and I'm not gonna start being pleasant to him now. If he stays much longer, he'll fuck up our plans and Sifa will never forgive me.

"Silence, Fhord," he yips, finally letting go of the bullshit façade from earlier.

"Then tell me what the fuck you want. It's the middle of the gods-damned night. You should be tucked in bed, not stalking your prisoners."

"I just want to talk. Is that so hard?" He drops on the couch and gestures at us to sit.

When neither of us moves, he looks up at one of the soldiers and Sifa shrieks as a bolt of pain courses through her. My gut clenches, anger pounding through me like a gods-damned hurricane, when I see that fucking medallion in his hand. Our failure with Einar twists the knot that just formed in my stomach because I need to resolve this shit and make sure my rabbit never feels that pain again.

The soldier strides over and places the medallion in Beron's hand. He doesn't get a "thanks" in response, but I'm not surprised. The Dróttning doesn't tolerate kindness to her peons. She says it encourages laziness.

"I'm not above using my wife's favorite elf toy to get my way," Beron tells us in a flat voice. "I said 'sit', and I will do whatever I must to convince you to comply."

"I guess it's gonna be that kind of meeting," Sifa grits out, shaking herself a bit as the effects of the medallion whisper away. She drops onto a couch across from him and I join her, taking her hand. It looks like a gesture of support, but it'll amplify our connection.

"Leave us," Beron barks at the soldiers around us. "Jacinda, stand outside. Everyone else may go." He watches them bow deeply and then spin to stride out the door, the last soldier to leave closing it behind him. Then Beron turns to Sifa, a hint of a smile on his lips. "What kind of meeting this is, dear elf, is entirely up to you." He holds her gaze for a moment, an intense look in his eyes. "Or should I be calling you 'daughter'? You are mated to my son, after all."

"Stepson," I hurl, because I refuse to be more connected to this bastard than I already am.

But Sifa takes his pettiness in stride. She responds with that smile full of spite and spirit that always fills me with pride before her lips settle into the angry line she wears when she's dealing with assholes like Beron. She won't back down to anyone, especially not this jackass.

"Let's hold off on the niceties, shall we?" she purrs at him. "At least until you decide whether you're going to kill us or not."

"My dear girl, you misunderstand. I mean you no harm. I don't know what my lovely wife will do. She can be so unpredictable, and you've risen her ire. *I* won't kill you as long as you stay in line."

"What the fuck do you want, then?" My voice is somehow even more pissy than before, but he's fucking with my mate and it's taking every bit of will power I possess to not attack him right now.

"I want to talk about the girl, of course," he explains, as if it's the most natural thing in the world. "She seems so plain. Ordinary. Yet she's lived under your elf's protection for many years and Nerthus nearly tore my city apart searching for her. Not very ordinary."

"The Dróttning's just trying to fuck with me," Sifa declares dismissively as she leans back into the couch. She's bullshitting him, but she's good at it. If I didn't know her so well, I'd have no idea. It's the relaxation that gives her away. Sifa can settle into a story like none other. "She knows I've grown attached to the girl because I've been feeding her for a long time. She hoped to draw Fhord and me to her, and it worked."

Beron watches her for a long time, his expression flat. His eyes, though, are full of fire. He knows something and is trying to figure out how to get the truth out of us. "You're a good liar," he says at last.

"I'm not lying," Sifa assures him. "I expect you've already inspected Halla, so you know. There's nothing remarkable about her."

"Nothing obvious," Beron concedes, "but that is neither here nor there. She's more. I can feel it."

"Even if she were more, you're human," I remind the bastard. "You don't have any special senses that would discern it. So you're just fucking with us. You don't know shit."

"Do you think I can live this long without developing some sense of when people are lying? Or when someone is not what they appear to be?" Now Beron leans back, his hands splayed across his knees.

"You're human, but you've lived how long?" Sifa's voice holds a note of curiosity. I'd been planning to explore this once we kill the Dróttning, figure out how the Dróttning gives long life to Beron and so many of her acolytes. Sifa's right, though. Now's as good a time as any.

"Worried about your mortality, elf?" Beron's eyebrow cocks up. Fucker somehow knows about this too. There's no reason for Sifa to be aging as quickly as she is, but he shouldn't know that.

"I'm an elf," she responds with a shrug, that same bland expression on her face. "Why would I be?"

"Don't take me for a fool," Beron snarls at her. "I don't appreciate it."

"Then don't take *me* for a fool, my Konungr," Sifa snarls back. "If I had secrets—and I don't—why would I share them with you?"

"Because the enemy of my enemy is my friend," Beron responds with a shrug, feigning the disinterest he's been trying to wear since he entered this room.

"And I am your enemy." It's not a question. Sifa's voice is flat and emotionless.

"Or perhaps you are my friend." Beron lifts a single eyebrow, his gaze focused on my rabbit. Measuring her. Testing her.

"Friends don't treat friends the way you've treated me," Sifa responds with a shrug, gesturing at the torture device in Beron's hand.

"Not everyone in the castle is my friend," he tells her. "When loyalties might be questioned, I play the part the Dróttning would expect."

"You're telling me you didn't want to use the medallion on me? That you did it for effect?"

"I am," Beron responds with a nod. "Two soldiers I don't know well enough decided to join my retinue tonight. I suspect my beloved wife doesn't trust me. That she asked them to watch me while the girl is in the Kastali."

"Then why did they leave when you dismissed them?" I don't try to hide my qualms. I'm not sure what he's trying to do, but I don't trust the bastard as far as I can throw him.

"They're not supposed to let me know. When I sent everyone else away, they had no choice but to leave."

"Are you hoping to convince us you're an ally?" I demand. "Why in all Helheim would we believe that?"

"Because you have no choice." He shrugs, a smirk playing across his lips. "There are two possibilities for what will happen when you leave this room. You'll either walk out behind my soldiers to a cell, to await your adoring mother. Or you'll sneak out with me within the next ten minutes, to go break out the girl and get her away from here."

My jaw drops. Because that's the last thing I expected him to say. Now it's my turn to lean back in my seat, stretch out my legs and arms, and examine this male who made my mother the Dróttning all those years ago. He's more relaxed than I've ever seen him before, but I'm always with the Dróttning when Beron and I cross paths. Nobody can relax around her. Maybe he's grown to hate her as much as the rest of us.

Still, there's a nervous energy about him, as if he needs us to agree. I suspect it's a trap. He can't kill me outright, so he's looking for a way to lead me to my death, along with Sifa. If we try to escape, he'll have all the excuse he needs. I'll be damned if we give that to him.

"Let Sifa into your mind." I force my tone to be bored, but I sure as fuck am not as relaxed as I want him to think. "I don't trust anyone who won't open their mind to her."

"Would that I could," he sighs. "As you know, your mother has many ... talents ... and where she is lacking, her elves fill the gaps. They're all hidden in the Kastali, of course—like poor Einar—but she has tried to keep an elf for anything she might need. Shortly after we married, she decided she needed to protect me. She had her favorite elf, who sadly died shortly after, place a trap in my mind. I'd thought the trap would die with her, but I was mistaken."

"What kind of trap?" Sifa leans forward, her elbows on her knees as she watches Beron.

"It's a booby trap of sorts. If anyone pushes themselves into my brain, it ricochets against them and wipes their minds. They get a warning—a bit of pain to discourage their exploration—but you'd be surprised how many shove through it. Stubborn fools," he scoffs, a hint of a smile on his lips. "It's been a surprisingly effective tool to identify elves hiding in Revalle. You have no idea how many walked into my thoughts, only to lose all of theirs. Really fascinating to watch."

"I don't believe you," Sifa declares. "I've never heard of such a talent."

"Are you so arrogant as to believe you know everything possible among your kind?" Beron's pulled out his condescending tone for this tirade, mimicking our stances as he leans back to rest his arms on his chest. "You've been here a decade and you know all about this land's elves? Impressive."

"Don't be an asshole," I sneer, giving him my fuck-you face. "It doesn't suit you."

"It's a learned behavior. I suspect we both got it from the same source." He keeps his eyes focused on Sifa the entire time but she doesn't back down. She's relaxed as she holds his gaze, not a hint of fear in her.

Fuck, do I love this female. She's not afraid of anybody or anything.

Except losing Halla. Or Astarot or me. And I sure as fuck am not going to let her lose any of us. Especially not that little girl.

"I have something for you," Harald says as he stands and walks over to open a drawer in a table near the window, digging for a necklace with a large opal in the center. "A talisman of sorts. It's the antithesis of the medallion. While you wear it, the Dróttning's favorite weapon can't hurt you."

"Why would you give me this?" Sifa hasn't moved. She doesn't trust it, and I don't blame her.

"A gesture," he tells her as he walks over and places it in her hand. Then he takes the medallion out of his pocket to activate it. And Sifa just sits there, not a hint of pain rippling through her.

I jerk my chin at it. I wouldn't be surprised if the damned thing had poison hidden in a secret compartment, scheduled to release in a few hours and kill my mate, or some other concealed threat. When I examine it, though, I see it's whole—no hidden levers or doors—and I can't identify any risk Sifa would face from wearing it. I hand it back to her after a few minutes with a nod.

"Do you have another?" Sifa asks, as she puts it on. "For Dani," she explains when I quirk an eyebrow at her.

Beron dips his chin once and strides over to open the same drawer and pull out a ring. "They're a matching set," he explains as he slips it on one of Sifa's fingers, "for appearances. One is enough to protect you."

"Thank you," Sifa murmurs, her brows lowering as her lips relax, no longer the thin line she's been wearing since Beron entered our room.

"It's a start," I concede. "But I need more. Send Jacinda away. We'll need to be able to access our magic as we travel through these halls. I don't trust you, and I don't think I ever will."

Beron stands to stride over to the door, opening it wide so we can see Jacinda standing alone. "Go to your room. I won't need your services tonight."

She drops into a deep bow and turns to stride away, never looking back.

"How do you know we won't kill you?" Sifa's tone isn't threatening. It's a reasonable question.

"The girl isn't where you'd expect, and the escape routes Fhord might use aren't available to you. I might have sent some soldiers there when we got into the room."

"Why?" I notice the lift in her voice—something I wouldn't even sense if I didn't know her so well—but she's still got a tight net containing her anger and fear.

"My insurance policy," he tells us as he waves us into the hall. "You won't kill me while I'm your only hope for finding and freeing her. When I take you to the tunnel that will lead you out, you'll see I'm an ally, in this at least."

"Why?" Now it's my turn to ask, because this makes no gods-damned sense. "Why the fuck, after all these years, have you decided to help me on something like this?"

Beron looks at me as if I'm stupid, shaking his head as a heavy sigh bursts through his lips. "When did you betray your mother, son?" He doesn't spit out the last word this time. He's trying to make nice, but I still don't trust that shit one little bit.

"Recently." We both know the answer to that question. No reason to hide it.

"Exactly." With that, he turns and stalks down the hall.

Sifa shrugs and follows after him and I do the same.

Guess we're gonna find out if we can trust him.

Chapter Nineteen

Dani

Best Thing Ever

Thिस water is the best thing ever. Better than an oyster bursting in my mouth—or something else bursting in my mouth. Better than my hand wrapped around my favorite fruit—or wrapped around something else. Better than riding my dragon—or riding something else.

Okay, it's better than mind-blowing sex. Everything leads back to sex because I need to get laid. Desperately. And this water is reminding me how fucking good it would feel to orgasm here. Again. And again. And again. I hated Matthias, and I'm glad he's dead, but I miss his cock. Although what I really want is Mikkael between my legs, or in my mouth, or my ass. And I'll never have him.

I drag my thoughts away from the lunacy of my sex-starved brain, focusing on the dragon who is finally relaxing. She's been holding all her emotions in tightly since Mikkael cut off her tail. She refuses to show weakness, but I think she also wasn't sure if she'd be able to reel herself back in if she let go. Now, she's releasing the grip she had on her pain, letting herself feel her tail regrowing. To experience—work her way through—the agony and hopelessness and anger that wanted to consume her.

The physical part is a strange sensation, a mixture of pain and irritation that has me constantly scratching my ass. It's annoying but not close to the torture of having her tail cut off, or the initial agony as Vulryn's body struggled to control the bleeding and grow on its own. That hurt like the worst of Helheim the whole trip back here, and I still can't believe Vulryn flew in so much pain.

She's fucking strong. My badass bitch can survive anything.

We're in the water for a long time. It can heal injuries in seconds, rid someone of disease in minutes, and restore health to a badly battered body in less than an hour. Regenerating a massive tail is a whole new beast. Every once in a while, I look over and watch the progress. It's slow—compared to the other miracles I've witnessed here—but steady. If I keep my eyes on her for a few seconds, I can actually see the change.

A gods-damned miracle.

Njörðr's leg looks like it will be whole sooner, but it'll be a race. I smile to myself, wondering who will win.

An hour, perhaps more, after we dropped into the water, a handful of horses and riders emerge from the town, riding in our direction. Even from this distance, I recognize Mikkael. There's something about the way he carries himself—shoulders back and head up, comfortable on the horse but fully in control—that I see every time I watch him ride.

And I watch him a lot.

Which pisses me right the fuck off, but there's not a gods-damned thing I can do about it.

The angry male may come with us when we go after my drake.

What the fuck? That's not the first thing I expected my dragon to say to me, after everything she went through. *We're going to get Ziselær?* I ask, trying my damnedest to keep my surprise—and worry—from my voice. *And you want Mikkael to come with us?*

Of course we will go to him. The wyrm took him from us. He went only to protect me ... and you and the angry male. We will free him from her clutches. And the angry male will ride him away.

I have so many questions. Something changed between Mikkael and the dragons when he rode Vulryn. I'm dying to know what they said to each other, but she hasn't told me yet and maybe she won't. She's allowed to have some secrets, even if it drives me a little nuts.

I start with the most important question, though. *What if he doesn't want to come back?*

He will.

How can you be so sure?

He is mine now and I am his. He will not reject me for the wyrm.

Déjà vu. I can't argue with her. So we'll go, and hopefully we'll survive this time too. *When are we leaving?*

Tomorrow. We must rest first. When I fight for my drake, I cannot lose.

Why take Mikkael with us?

She's quiet longer than I expected and I'm not sure why. All my other questions rise in my brain—demanding answers—as I wait for her reply. Finally, she tells me something I never expected. *The angry male must ride my drake. He is yours. He must also belong to my drake.*

I didn't think you liked Mikkael, I tell her, my heart in my throat. I've never loved my dragon as much as I do in this moment. She knows what I want, and she's decided she wants it too.

You like the angry male. I think you may need him. That is enough. And I have realized he is ... tolerable. Then she says something that cuts through the heart of whatever anger I'm still nursing toward Mikkael, because she's right. *Perhaps he would not be so angry if he was chosen by the dragon and mate the fates chose for him.*

I don't respond right away, letting her truth sit within me before shuddering out a heavy sigh to fill the space around us. My dragon sees this world and everyone who walks it so clearly. I wonder if her desolate life—devoid of the expectations others place upon us every day—left Vulryn with eyes that can see what too many miss.

Or maybe she's just wicked smart. My brilliant beast.

And if Ziselær rejects him? I ask at last. *Or us?*

Then, we will kill him. That has not changed. These words come with her laugh, because we both know we're well past that. She'd kill herself before she did any harm to Ziselær or me. But it's all the answer I'm going to get and I'm okay with it. We'll figure it out. We always do.

Mikkael's gaze holds mine as he gets closer. He's smiling, but it's not a happy smile, more wistful, as if he's given up on a long-held dream. It sends a shiver down my spine. We may have to work to convince him to go with us. He's let go of Ziselær. And me.

Although, he probably never included me in his dreams anyway.

"Come to bathe with us?" I ask with a smile that I hope will draw him out of his pensiveness.

"Can't pass up on the chance to dip in this water," he responds. But he's looking away as he drops off his horse and pulls his tunic over his head, leaving a thinner shirt that still hides his skin from me. His shoulders slump and the discontent in my gut grows.

"It's as good as I remember," I breathe. I'm trying to talk to him, but I get the sense he doesn't want that. I'm not sure why he's here. He could have gone to another source of the water, or waited until we were done. But the lake is best, and we'll be a while, which he probably realizes.

"It's different—better—than the other sources of this nectar in these lands," Njörðr adds, his voice spearing through my distraction.

I spin to stare at him. "You know of the places in Vanatia with water like this?"

"Of course. I'd have withered away and died years ago if I hadn't found them." His tone is matter-of-fact, as if he's stating the obvious.

"Why would you die without them?"

He watches me for a moment, his eyebrows tugging together at first, then loosening as his eyes brighten and a smile plays at his lips. "You don't know of the connection between our worlds, do you?"

"I have no idea what you're talking about," I tell him. "I mean, of course there's a link because you and others have come here. But I didn't know they were linked in other ways."

He nods, his smile growing broader. "I shouldn't be surprised. Nerthus knows, but she ever has been ... particular ... about who shares her knowledge. She's only gotten worse over the centuries."

"You know the Dróttning?"

"Better than you might imagine. But that is a story for another day. For now, know only that a tree grows in Asgard, my world. We call it Yggdrasil, and it is the source of all life in every world. There are many others like me, and we cannot survive without its fruit. That tree's roots are deep, and they touch the wells of water in this world to give them some of its magic and power. This island is rich with Yggdrasil's essence and must have bloomed out of its largest root in the area with smaller roots leading to other pools."

"Would everyone who spends time in these waters have a longer life?" Mikkael's voice is broken, as if he's afraid of the answer but desperate to hear it nonetheless. When I turn to him, he's holding his breath, leaning toward Njörðr with his eyes focused on him.

"I don't know why not," Njörðr responds with a shrug. "The places I found have given me the life I wouldn't have without the tree's fruit. I'm alive and strong, powerful, because I drink the water, just as I would eat the tree's apples at home. It should do that with others."

"Well, fuck me," Mikkael mutters, his gaze finding mine for a moment. But then he shakes his head and looks away, sucking in a deep breath, and another.

And I realize that Njörðr's words unleash something in me as well—a fear I've carried since realizing I'm mated to a human and developing a strong bond with an elf aging far too quickly. I should live much, much longer than them, but maybe Mikkael and Sifa already have the long life I want for them both. I can't hold back my grin. I wish I could be here when Sifa returns and learns what Njörðr discovered.

"I know now what it is," the enigmatic male says as he looks at Mikkael, a twinkle in his crystal eyes. When my grumpy mate just stares at him, confused, Njörðr smiles. "Why I recognize your essence," he explains.

"I don't even know what that means," Mikkael responds, little wrinkles forming on his brow and around his eyes.

"I sense someone familiar in you. I barely recognize his presence—it's been so long since I've come across any of his progeny—but this water amplifies everything magical within us."

"I have no magic," Mikkael scoffs, shaking his head. "I'm as human as they come."

"You don't recognize your magic, but I do. Hœnir, a father of the Æsir gods, lives within you. I believed his line had died out. I see now that it hasn't." Njörðr's grin somehow grows even wider as he watches my bewildered mate.

"Fuck off," Mikkael laughs as his eyebrows draw together. "I'm not descended from a god."

"Not just any god," Njörðr declares. "Hœnir was one of the most powerful. He fathered, along with his brothers, the first humans. It's why I can sense him, although I suspect dozens of generations separate you."

"You're fucking with me." Mikkael shakes his head, glancing at me as if to get my support.

"I've wondered how I could be mated to a human," I tell him as I lift my palms toward the heavens. "It would explain a lot."

"Tell me," Njörðr continues, "do you have good intuition?"

Another shrug. "Sure, but what does that have to do with anything? Lots of people have good intuition."

"I suspect yours is better than most," Njörðr says. "Hœnir had the gift of prophecy. Intellect and reason as well, but his ability to see the future was startling. Search inside for that kernel of his power. You'll find your answer there."

Mikkael watches him for a few more seconds in silence, his eyes wide as one hand lifts to scratch at his jaw. Finally, he jerks his head back and forth a few times and drops into the water, turning away to stare at the mountain.

Tell him, Vulryn urges after a minute or so, an unexpected hint of a plea in her tone.

Tell him what?

She responds with an impatient snort, turning to stare at me with narrow eyes. *Tell him that we will leave tomorrow to free my drake, and he is to join us.*

Shouldn't I wait until he's alone? Give him a minute to get over the bombshell Njörðr just dropped on him?

The chatty male will agree with us. He will help convince the angry male to join us.

I watch her for a moment, unable to hold back the smile that's forcing itself free. *What will we call Mikkael if he stops being the angry male?*

She holds my gaze and then spins to stare at Mikkael, who is noticeably ignoring us, every ounce of his attention focused on the peak in the distance. *He may always be the angry male*, she tells me at last. *We will wait and see what he becomes if he allows it.*

Fucking wise. That's what my dragon is. She's so fucking wise.

And she's right. Now's as good a time as any. I cross the distance between us and place my hand on Mikkael's arm, ignoring the warmth that blooms there. He doesn't twist away like I'd feared, and when he turns to me, his expression is more open and hopeful than it has been in a while.

It's probably the water. It'll suck the negative emotions out of anyone.

"We're going after Ziselær," I tell him as I drop my hand but hold his gaze. "Tomorrow. You should come."

He's quiet for the longest time, his jaw clenching but no other sign of whatever emotions rage within him. Finally, he sighs, relaxing into whatever decision he's made. "No, I shouldn't," he murmurs as he turns to stare at the town.

I wait for him to say more, but he doesn't.

"It would be good for you, Mik. Good for Ziselær."

He shakes his head once, still watching the lights flickering in the distance as he clenches his jaw again, his shoulders tight. "I'm done, Dani," he tells me quietly. "You and Z told me how you feel, and I finally listened. I won't chase him any longer." Now he turns to me, his eyes flat, not a hint of emotion in them. "And I won't let the mating bond drag us together. We both know how our bodies would respond if we rode Vulryn together. I won't be a slave to my urges. I can't be."

He turns, pushing his way through the water toward the shore. "I'm done here," he mumbles without looking back. I can only watch as he mounts his horse, kicks his heels, and gallops away.

You will try again with the angry male, Vulryn tells me as she drops me off after we leave the lake. Njörðr left a couple of hours before us—his leg fully restored—so we're alone. Exactly what I need right now.

He told me how he feels. I need to respect that.

She's quiet longer than I would expect, but I know she has more to say. So I wait. Finally, she speaks again.

My drake must see him.

Did he tell you that?

He did not. He has not admitted it, even to himself. But I know. He is bonded to the angry male. The angry male should ride him.

I think Mikkael's been hurt too much by Ziselær. And me. I can't blame him. I don't know if I'd try again.

Vulryn's eyes narrow, her newly-formed tail flickering in the dimming light. She spits out a little puff of fire, rising to her full height to look down on me.

You do not know if you would try again? Even with me?

That's not what I meant, I tell her, reaching forward to rest my hand on her stomach. *I will always fight for you. No matter what.*

Yet, you believe the angry male possesses no such fight? You think so little of him?

And that's not what I said. Although, it is. A little bit. Okay, maybe it is what I said, but it's different. He never fully bonded with Ziselær. We've both hurt him so badly. He doesn't want to give either of us the chance to do it again.

You will go now to speak with the angry male. He will leave with us tomorrow.

With that, she spins and stalks away, extending her wings with two hard flaps to propel her into the sky and toward the closest herd.

And I go in search of Mikkael. Because she won't take "no" for an answer and maybe she's right.

Before I can find him, though, Jorunn finds me.

"I thought I'd missed you," she says as she strides toward me, a rare grin emerging on her lips. Her long, auburn hair is tied back in the braid she always wears, giving her a fierce look. With sharp blue eyes and a muscular build honed by decades of training, it's no surprise she leads Fhord's Ætt.

"What are you doing here?" I ask, my gaze bouncing around as I search for Astrid and the others. It's just her, though. We don't embrace—Jorunn isn't a hugger, and I'm good with that—but her eyes are bright and welcoming. I can tell she's as glad to see me as I am her.

"I'm here with the rest of the Ætt, Liv, Frida, the troll, and the cat," she responds with a smirk, resting her hand on a beautiful hilt sitting on her hip. It's made of some dark wood—mahogany, maybe—inlaid with a brilliant copper and I can tell already that it's part of an extraordinary sword.

"What about Fhord and Sifa? I thought they were going to meet you."

"That lasted about a minute. We got split up. It's a long story, and I don't have much time. I need to report to Birger, but I heard you were on the island and leaving soon, so I came to find you first."

"Alrighty. What can I do for you?" My gaze drops to the sword again as memories of my last visit here—Jorunn's pledge in the tavern—fill my thoughts. I drag my eyes back up where they belong. This could relate to anything.

But her smile grows as she unclasps the belt from her waist and holds the scabbard out to me.

I can feel the blush rising to my cheeks as warmth fills my chest. I don't know what I did to deserve this family that's somehow become mine, but I'm gods-damned grateful to have them. "You didn't have to do this," I whisper, not quite sure if I can trust my voice.

"I don't *have* to do shit," she agrees, shaking the sword a bit as I stand and stare at it like an idiot. "I want you to wield this when we face the Dróttning. Maybe it'll be the blade to take her life when that fierce beast you ride carries you into battle. Her or the horse Torsten found for you. I've met him, and he's quite the mount. Torsten asked me to tell you he's waiting for you in Vanatia."

"I don't know what to say." I also don't think I could speak if I tried. My heart's in my throat, and I'm struggling to contain the tears that fill my eyes.

"Thank the gods," she declares, reaching out to lift my hand so she can rest the scabbard in it. "I'm not one for conversation." Her expression softens, light entering eyes that rarely show any emotion, as she rests a hand on my shoulder. "Use it well," she says, before turning and striding down the hall, never looking back.

I watch her for a few seconds, reining in the emotions trying to spill out of me—bursts of joy and gratitude that leave my knees weak. And then I grasp the hilt and pull the blade from its sleeve. My eyes grow wide, releasing the tears I tried to stop, as I gaze at copper dragons etched on steel, their intricate designs the most exquisite homage to my dragon I could have imagined. They're soaring away from the hilt, as if unleashing Vulryn to attack, and I see now that copper beasts adorn the mahogany too, embedded so precisely my hand can't tell where wood ends and metal begins.

Nothing could give tribute to Vulryn's swagger and viciousness and feral beauty as perfectly as this.

I can't wait to show Vulryn. And then use it.

First, though, I need to finish the task she's given me and find my asshole of a mate. I suck in a few deep breaths, wiping my eyes to make sure I don't share any of my emotions with him, and turn toward the tavern I'm told is his favorite.

He's here, a cup of ale in his hand and a female on his lap.

Because he is the wanton male. In Lumaria, at least.

He watches me, a sneer on his perfect lips, as I enter the room and stride over to plop myself on the other side of the table

"Go away," I snarl at the bitch sitting in *my* spot, pushing an image of my most disgusting kill into her thoughts. She stares at me for a moment, eyes wide and jaw hanging nearly low enough to service the cock she's too fucking close to, then stands abruptly to race away. She doesn't look back, probably terrified of what I'd show her next.

I enjoy my gift a little too much sometimes.

"Come to fight me?" Mikkael demands, smirking at the sword on my belt before his gaze roams upward, pausing at my breasts and lips, and finally settling on my eyes.

"We're not taking no for an answer," I tell him, hands on my hips and back straight. His eyes dip to the nipples that decide to announce themselves under his inspection, a smile lifting his lips.

"No," he says, as if he's telling them off instead of me. Bastard.

So I reach out and tuck my fingers beneath his chin, dragging his smoldering gaze up where it belongs. "Talk to me. They've got nothing to do with this."

"But that's it, Dani. They've got everything to do with this—them and the cock that rises every time I catch a whiff of that citrus and sandalwood soap you love. This thing between us fucks with me. I can't let it."

"You're giving up. You are not a male who gives up."

"I'm letting go. There's a difference."

"The fuck there is," I growl. I meant to be a little nicer about this, but he's being a wuss. And Mikkael is not a wuss. "You barely gave Ziselær a chance. He was warming up to you. We both know it. Vulryn knows it. He didn't leave us. He left to protect us. We need to go get him."

"Why in all of Helheim would I do that to myself? Again?"

"Why would you risk losing him, when you might be able to get him back?" I yell this at him. I'm failing miserably at this whole "nice" thing, but maybe a kick in the ass is exactly what he needs. I suck in a deep breath, though, determined to try to be reasonable with this headstrong male.

"Look," I say in my most persuasive voice, "you have a short window of time. The Dróttning wants him to take another rider. If he refuses, she'll torture him. We've seen what her dragons suffer. And we know what kind of rider he'll get if she chooses. He has a bond with you. It's probably throbbing inside him right now, forcing him to acknowledge your connection. What if Ziselær's in the Nest wishing he was with you? Because you were getting closer! We all saw it."

"And what about those?" he demands, staring again at the nipples that refuse to rest. "And this?" he asks, looking down at the enormous bulge in his pants.

"Maybe don't bring along the harlot," I suggest as I turn to glance at the female who's still staring at me with wide eyes, her chin trembling.

"She didn't do this, Dani," Mikkael murmurs, drawing my gaze back to him. And now I can't look away. He's wearing his emotions in bright eyes and a smile so sad, I feel like my heart is breaking too. "This is all you," he says. "Ever since you dropped back into my life, it's been you. I can't take it any longer. There's no us. There can never be an us."

I don't know what to say. I want him, but I've rejected him so much, he won't believe my words. He needs to just come. I need to show him. If we can work it out, we will. If not, we'll go our separate ways.

"Don't let that stand between you and your dragon," I urge him. "If you refuse to leave with us, you may lose him forever. He'll be forced to take another rider, and you'll have to watch someone else on his back. It'll be a repeat of what happened with Matthias. His rider will demand your death, and Ziselær will be caught in the middle again. Your bond will endure—it'll grow—as long as you both live. You can't let your dragon be stuck in that position. Not after everything you've gone through."

He leans back, dropping his hands to his knees as he watches me, and I wait. He knows I'm right. I can almost see the fight fizzling out of him, his expression relaxing as his shoulders droop just a bit. Finally, he dips his chin. "He could be miserable with another of the Dróttning's riders," he says.

"He *would* be so fucking miserable," I agree. "Gorm said the Dróttning's gotten worse in recent years. She wants her dragon riders to be cruel and loyal to her, without fault. He'd never have been joined with Khanti if she was like this before."

"I owe it to him to try again."

"You owe it to him and to yourself. You deserve to be together."

"You're not getting laid, though. You know that right?" He grins at me, the old Mikkael emerging as he lets his decision settle into his soul.

"Not by you," I tell him. "But who knows what might happen along the way?"

"Fuck you, Dani," he responds with a smile. This one's forced though. The mating bond can be a real bitch about others touching what it considers ours. His must be roaring inside him at the thought of me with someone else.

"Not this trip, Mikkael," I say with a smirk. Standing, I watch him for a moment, relief filtering through me. "It's good you're coming," I whisper, not trusting my voice enough to say anything else. Because this day has been way too fucking emotional. "We leave at dawn."

And then I turn and stride away, trying my damnedest not to think about the harlot that'll probably be sashaying back to Mikkael's lap as soon as I'm out the door.

Chapter Twenty

Mikkael

A Long Flight

She's waiting with Vulryn when I get there, both their backs to me. So I stop and watch them.

I'm so fucking conflicted about this. I've been telling myself I'm only going because of Z. When Dani pointed out the obvious—that if the Dróttning hasn't already forced Z to take another rider, she's gonna torture him until he does—a rock dropped into my gut, landing with a thud that would have doubled me over if I let myself show Dani one hint of emotion. I don't know if I can stop it, but I know I'll never forgive myself if I don't try.

I'm willing to die for my dragon. I sure as fuck better be willing to fight for him too.

But as I ogle my fierce mate, I admit it's more than that.

I want Dani. I think I need her. The thought of her leaving without me might have hurt more than the thought of Z taking another rider. I don't know what the fuck I'm going to do about that. Because despite what Vulryn relayed to me through Z on the flight out of the cave—that Vulryn's demand is the only reason Dani pulled away in the cave—I can't escape the fact that Dani has chosen someone else every time she faced a choice. And like it or not, I need to be with someone who chooses me. Dani's not that person, regardless of what the fates have decreed. Fuckers that they are.

I'm going anyway. I know that I'm setting myself up for heartache, but I can't seem to care.

She's slapping her palm against her thigh, the way she does so often, her other hand scratching Vulryn behind her horn. When I first noticed how busy her hands are, I attributed it to her being a bitch. She couldn't control everyone, and it frustrated her. I see now how wrong I was. She doesn't want to control people. She wants to help them. Now that she's escaped Harald's iron grip over her life—free to live the way she wants—that nervous energy fills her. I think she's always looking for the next battle she can wage to improve this fucked-up world for Vulryn or Sifa or Fhord or even Toffer and the gods-damned cat.

She and her dragon are so alike in that way. Always the first to leap into the fray. Protecting those they love. Embracing enemies who might become lovers, like Vulryn did with Z.

And I wish Dani would do with me.

"I know you're there," she says without looking back, her voice light. The playfulness in her words feels forced, but I'll take it. She wants to start this trip the right way and so do I. "If you're going to leer at me, at least have the decency to hum in approval, or grunt, or something."

"What makes you think I like what I see?" I ask, making sure my tone's flirtatious, no hint of my desperate emotions seeping through.

She turns and stares directly at the cock that's tenting my pants. Like it always does when she's around. Then she smirks, and the fucker twitches. She doesn't say a word, but she doesn't have to. She won this argument.

This is gonna be a long flight.

But I don't need to hate it. I've been making myself miserable, erecting and holding an artificial barrier between us. The mating bond's going to trigger my body's response, no matter what I do. I don't have to fight the inevitable. I like it when my cock rides a woman's ass, even if that's all it rides. Maybe I should let myself savor riding my mate's ass, while it lasts.

That's what filled my thoughts when I pushed Bodil off me and left the tavern alone, a few seconds after she gathered the courage to come plop herself on my lap again. I shoved the idea away last night, convincing myself I need to keep a wall between Dani and me. But it landed right back in my brain when I woke up this morning, hard as a rock, hours of flight clinging to my mate stretching in front of me.

What if the demanding bastard throbbing in my pants is right? My cock's led me into some ... questionable ... situations, but he usually manages to make it worthwhile. That could be the secret to flying with Dani.

Besides, fucking with Dani has somehow become one of my favorite things to do, and she's stuck with me.

I adjust myself—because holy Helheim, now the fucker is straining to feel the ass I'm gonna let him ride—and stride over, my mood lighter. Winking at the precocious female fate paired me with, I aim for the horn on the other side of Vulryn's head, scratching her in the spot she loves.

"Thank you for taking me with you," I tell the copper dragon. I'm pretty sure she used to hate me. Chopping off her tail seems to have brought us together, somehow. That was the most fucked-up thing I've ever done, but Vulryn needed it, and I think she felt worse for me than I felt for her. The ride out of the cave connected us in a way I never could have expected.

She purrs, leaning into my scratch for a moment, then rises up, pulling her head away from Dani and me.

"She's ready to go," Dani says with a smile. "We've already waited too long, and she needs to get to her drake."

"After you," I tell Dani with a flourish. She responds with narrowed eyes and a wrinkled brow but doesn't ask whatever question is on the tip of her tongue. Turning, she mounts her dragon and then watches me do the same.

"This is gonna be such a long flight," she mutters as I wrap my arms around her, digging my erection into her ass. I don't try to hold back the moan that starts in my cock and erupts through my system.

Yup, this feels good.

"What are you doing?" Dani whisper-shouts, spinning her head to glare at me. "Scoot back."

"Nope," I respond with a smirk. "You wanted me to come and this is what you get." I thrust my hips forward just enough to emphasize my words.

"I didn't ask that to join the party," she exclaims in a shrill voice, her eyes slanting down to look at the bulge wedged between us.

"But you knew he'd come. He's always here when we're this close. So I'm gonna enjoy the ride. You should too. Maybe it'll help both of us. My cock riding your ass could be exactly what you need."

She holds her scowl a few more seconds but then sucks in a deep breath as her face relaxes a bit, like it always does when she talks to her dragon. Finally, she huffs out an exasperated sigh and turns, scooting forward enough to put some space between us. But that won't do at all. I tug her back, settling her where she belongs.

"What the fuck?" Her tone is even more shrill, and I can't hold back the laugh.

"You'll be here as soon as Vulryn takes off," I explain in a very reasonable tone. "May as well get used to it."

"Fuck. Me." These words are a breath on the air, just loud enough to reach me.

But I did hear them, so I lean forward, my lips nearly touching her ear, and rumble, "You wish."

She shakes her head, a little sigh escaping as she pats Vulryn on the neck. And off we go. The pressure pushes Dani back a bit farther, drawing another moan from me.

This is definitely the right way to ride Vulryn with Dani.

As we fly higher, my thoughts shift to the utter joy of flying on a dragon's back. I don't think this excitement will ever go away. Lifting into the air, feeling the dragon's power between my legs as the earth drops away, is unlike anything else in the worlds. Beneath us, a land that's harsh and rugged in the muted morning sun becomes soft and smooth, greens melding together to create a brilliant shamrock, caramel streaks breaking the surface with pops of fuchsia and crimson and sunflower dotted throughout.

So fucking beautiful. I tighten my arms, breathing in her scent, as I sigh.

And she lets me.

Maybe life can be good after all. At least in moments like this.

We fly in silence for the first few hours. I'm ignoring the lunacy Njörðr launched at me yesterday, pushing it out of my thoughts every time it tries to bubble up like it'll blow up if I give it space in my head. I sure as fuck am not descended from a god, despite what the crazy old bastard claims. Instead, I focus on the female in my arms. She feels so much better than I expected. Every part of me has been craving this for a long gods-damned time. Her touch is feeding my soul. It may be all I'll ever need.

Even if my cock would like a fuck of a lot more.

The sun is high in the sky when Vulryn shifts her wings and starts spiraling down to a bright emerald field with a river as blue as the sky shimmering through it. Without even thinking about it, I pull Dani closer, giving her protection she doesn't need. When she responds by leaning into me, her breaths mirroring mine, something in my gut—or perhaps a bit higher and to the left—calms. By the time Vulryn is flicking out her wings to soften our landing, my mind's more at rest than it's been in a long time.

"Thank you," I murmur with one last inhale of Dani's scent as I lift my leg over Vulryn's back and climb down. I don't know what I was thanking her for and I suspect she doesn't either. But I don't offer an explanation and she doesn't ask.

"Will we be here for long?" My gaze is dancing about, worries about being found by the Dróttning's guards sneaking in to steal away some of my peace.

"I need to find some privacy and then eat something. Thirty minutes, maybe?" It's a question, but just barely.

"That'll be enough. Let's go different directions. I could use some privacy too."

She smirks as she looks down at my bulging pants. She's not wrong. Fucker needs some relief before we go again.

"Have fun," she purrs before turning to sashay from me. I watch her a few seconds, unable to drag my gaze away, then stride in the opposite direction.

I'm quick this time, memories of Dani's ass rubbing my cock, her scent wrapping around me, carrying me to one of the best orgasms I've felt in a long fucking time. Maybe ever. When I'm done, I take care of other business, then dig out some soap to wash up and head back, hungrier than I realized.

But again, I find myself stopping to stare before she can see me.

The sun's harsh rays bathe her in bright light, and I might like this image of Dani more than any of the others bouncing in my head. She's calm and still, her forehead resting against Vulryn's to give me a perfect view of her profile. Her shoulders are loose but not in resignation. They seem relaxed, as if some weight has been lifted from them. With her eyes closed and her lips tipped up just a bit—like she's trying to hold back a smile—she looks more content than I've ever seen her.

My smirk emerges unbidden. Riding my cock was as good for her as it was for me.

She turns just as my lips tip up, her shoulders rising as her mouth forms a thin line. My gut twists a bit at seeing her erect a wall between us, but I get it. I'm doing the same. We can't let our guard down.

"I'm starving," I announce as I stalk toward my mate and her dragon, reaching for the pack that should hold food. "I'll lay out a few things on the rock," I add, pointing behind Vulryn.

Dani nods, grabbing our water skins and striding toward the nearby creek. She returns as I sit down beside the food I've laid out, reaching for some bread and dried meat.

"What changed?" she asks after we've eaten in silence for a few minutes, one eyebrow rising in the charming way it does sometimes.

I don't have to wonder what she's asking. This flight was different for both of us because I was different. But I don't get a chance to answer her question. Before I can, Vulryn warbles a warning, spinning her head to watch twenty or more warriors emerge from the trees on the other side of the clearing. The dragon's crimson eyes blaze, a fury rising within her that's intense enough for me to feel, even through the tenuous bonds that link us.

"What the fuck?" Dani mumbles, standing to rest her hand on the hilt of her sword. I do the same, ready to fight whoever the fuck is approaching us.

These aren't the Dróttning's soldiers. Their uniforms are nothing like what they wear in Vanatia—more ornate, as if they're designed for looks rather than function. But they are fighters, carrying themselves with purpose, a lethal resolve in their stiff spines and unblinking glares. The male at their lead is the gaudiest of the group, but it doesn't detract from the power he wears like a cloak. He moves like a king, and I wonder if that's exactly what he is.

"What are you doing here, Monarch?" Dani demands, answering my question with her own. Vulryn stalks forward, placing herself right behind us. She's on edge, ready to attack, and I realize this could be very bad. Very, very fucking bad.

"Dani, my loyal warrior," the male declares, waving his arm toward us in a gesture that would look inviting in any other circumstance. His gaze flicks to the soldier just to his right, holding a dragon bolt aimed directly at Vulryn, and then back to Dani. "Imagine my surprise when I learned of the northern beast causing trouble in Vanatia, being ridden by a female rumored to be sworn to me."

"You're looking for me?" Dani's tone is higher now, a hint of fear finding its way into her words.

I want to reach out, rest my hand on her shoulder, but I know she wouldn't welcome the support—both because I'd be the one offering it, and because I can tell already she needs to face this male on her own.

"Of course I'm looking for you," Harald proclaims, a laugh in his words. "Why else would I be tromping through this gods-forsaken land, hiding from the bitch who rules it, two dozen of my best guards in tow?" He turns toward the soldier threatening Vulryn, adding in a low voice as he looks back at Dani, "With my best dragon-striker at my side. He never misses, you know? Worth his weight in gold for an outing like this one."

"Why? This must be dangerous for you. Why would you come for me?" Dani's tone triggers something within me, and I can't stop myself from stepping forward, my hand reaching for her. But she spins, glaring at me for a moment, before turning all her attention back to Harald.

Harald's eyes darken, mirroring the bark of the nearby trees, as he takes a single step forward. "Did you think I sent you to claim this beast for yourself?" he whispers. He's still a dragon's-length away, but his words are clear and concise, strong magic carrying them to us. "Did you truly believe I would shrug my shoulders and go about my business when I learned you betrayed me and escaped to this place with one of my dragons?"

"I had no choice," Dani insists, throwing her shoulders back as she lifts her chin.

And I'm so fucking proud of her in this moment. I have no right to be. She's not mine. But something stirs deep inside me when she stands up to this bastard.

"There's always a choice, soldier," Harald responds. "You chose to break my trust."

"You would have killed me. And her." Dani's voice is sharp, her love for her dragon animating her. "I couldn't let that happen."

"You don't know what I would have done." Harald snarls these words, finally showing us some of the anger that must have driven him here. "You've served me for many years, yet you know nothing at all about me."

"I know we'd have been dead *because* I served you," Dani yells, one hand flinging up as the other grips her sword more tightly. "You ordered us to torture these beasts, never letting them form the bonds they crave. Vulryn's life was miserable before me. You wouldn't have allowed our bond. I'm as sure of that as I am of this dragon's love for me."

"You know nothing," Harald shrieks back, several soldiers around him turning in surprise as he does. But then he sucks in a deep breath, glaring at the ones by his sides before focusing again on Dani. "It matters not what you believe," he mutters. Then he lifts his chin, barking his next words. "You'll return with me to Njordheim."

"The fuck we will." Dani's voice is firm, not a hint of fear.

She turns to Vulryn and the copper beast spits out a single line of fire, which ripples with red and gold flames as it flies directly at the male holding the dragon bolt. The blaze, nearly as straight as an arrow, spears through his throat, dropping him to the ground, as all Helheim breaks loose.

Not for me, though. I stand there like a fool, staring at the dead male, astounded by the magnificence that is Dani's dragon. I've never seen anything like that in my life, and I am utterly, completely awestruck.

Thank fuck, though, Vulryn has a good head on her shoulders. Before Harald's people can recover the bolt and aim it at the dragon they're probably desperate to kill now, she's in the air, her claws reaching for Dani and me. I'm swept up in her cage, holding on for my life as she throws herself into the air and races away.

I can only watch as we escape another powerful enemy, who's now more determined than ever to destroy my mate.

SIFA

NJÖRÐR

NOBODY ELSE CROSSES OUR path as we follow Beron through winding halls to a door that reveals a staircase spiraling down farther than I can see.

"Is this your way of getting us into the dungeon without a fight?" Fhord demands, planting his feet as he throws his shoulders back.

Beron shakes his head, as if disappointed by Fhord's distrust. "If I wanted you imprisoned, I'd have thrown you down here when you arrived. Instead, I fed you. Now, I'm leading you to the girl." He's quiet for a moment, his features relaxing other than a little tilt of his lips and the smallest crease between his brows. "I am not your enemy, Fhord," he says quietly.

Fhord scoffs, his eyes shards of emerald beneath heavy lashes. "You are the rightful konungr. The Dróttning holds power only because of you. When that changes, maybe I'll grow to trust you."

"It is not so easy," Beron insists, casting his eyes down for a moment before lifting his chin high to huff his next words. "She covets power and has learned to wield it like a knife, even against me."

"Then tell us something to prove you're on our side. We know she sent Einar away because she found someone even more powerful. Who is Jarl and how do we reach him? If you turning against her isn't some bullshit story, you must agree we can't let him live if he'll make her stronger."

Now it's Beron's turn to scoff. "Even if you could find him, it wouldn't matter. Jarl is not of this world. He can bring you to your knees with a touch. Nobody will defeat him. Not even you."

"What do you mean, he's 'not of this world'?" I demand, my skin prickling at the suggestion.

"I believe he's like you, elf," Beron responds in a voice full of scorn. "The walls between your worlds and ours have weakened, letting too many creatures pass through them. Or perhaps he came with you and has been hiding, gathering strength and allies. I know not when Askell found him, only that Jarl helped that weasel and Knut amass power and used them to worm his way into the Dróttning's cabal."

"Aksell and Knut have been working together?" I can hear the anger in Fhord's voice, sharp as the blades he'll use to split the throats of our enemies.

"Of course they were working together," Beron exclaims with a bitter laugh. "Aksell's a fool, but he's a well-positioned fool. He needed someone like that crafty bastard Knut to manipulate the rebels the way he did. And Knut needed Aksell's resources." But then Beron straightens, his expression and posture shifting as he again takes the mantle of the imperious ruler of this land. "I don't know where to find Jarl but would warn you to stay away. You shall see," he says with a shrug, "if you survive long enough. Let's finish this."

"Gladly. You still haven't explained why we're coming here, though. You told me she's not where I'd expect, yet you're leading me directly to the dungeon—the first place I planned to search."

"Be patient. This is a large place, and she isn't in one of the cells you'd anticipate."

Fhord seems to be weighing his response—deciding whether we can trust Beron—but I've had enough of the bickering between these headstrong males. "We're wasting time standing here arguing about nothing," I exclaim as I stride past Beron to take the lead. "Let's get Halla and go. She's a little girl and wherever she is, she's been there too long."

I feel them on my heels as the door slams, a torch that one of them must have grabbed casting dim light to flicker off the walls. We descend for a while, nothing but bricks around us. Finally, longer than I would have expected, we near the landing. At first, I don't see much else, but when I'm ten or twelve steps away, the room starts to open up in front of me.

It's fucking horrific, I realize as I take the final step down. The cells at the Nest are bad. These are so much worse, and my stomach twists thinking about Halla spending time here. The smell hits me first, a mix of shit and vomit that wrenches a gag from me, the meal we ate bubbling in my stomach as I gasp an inhale, trying to hold it down. I bend over, breathing slowly, until it passes.

And then I stand and really look. The brick that surrounded us in the staircase continues down here and at first, I don't see anything out of the ordinary. As Fhord shifts the flame he's holding closer to a wall, though, I realize I'm wrong. Everywhere I look—every single surface, the floor beneath our feet, even the ceiling above us—is covered in dried blood. Now that I'm focusing on it, that smell joins the crap and puke I recognized at first.

Fuck. Me. I can't believe that bitch would hold a ten-year-old girl in this place.

"Ignore it," Fhord commands, reaching out a hand to draw my gaze to him.

"Is that ... blood?" My voice is so soft, I wonder if he'll hear it.

"Ignore it," he repeats, a thumb stroking my cheek. "Let's just get the girl and go."

I'm too stunned to speak for a second, fear for Halla ripping away every rational thought I can muster, but that fear brings me back to this moment and Fhord. Shaking myself—literally—I nod and rest my palm on his hand. "She doesn't belong here. We need to get her away and make sure the Dróttning can never bring her back."

Fhord jerks his chin down, leaning forward to kiss me, hard, then turns toward Beron. "Take us to her."

Beron drops into a mocking bow before turning to stride down one of the three halls that lead away from this central area. We walk, and walk, and walk, my gaze bouncing occasionally to glare at the crimson walls and doors we pass. Part of me wants to ask Fhord and Beron why the fuck she would do something so horrific, but I don't really need to ask. I know the answer to that question.

She's evil. She wants the blood of her enemies around her when she indulges her dark impulses.

If I weren't already committed to her overthrow, I would be now. This is bad enough. Bringing a child down here, holding her in this place, is almost more depraved and demonic than I can comprehend.

Finally, Beron pauses in front of an iron door, no window or hole disturbing its solid surface, and pulls a key from his pocket. Turning to give us an odd smile, he spins the lock and pushes.

I don't see her at first. It's black in this hole, flickers from the torch the only thing to pierce the darkness. I take a single step in, my eyes adjusting quickly, and cast my gaze through the room. I'm on the verge of spinning and punching Beron—or something much, much worse—when she moves, sitting up on whatever bed they gave her. And my breath catches in my throat.

"Ms. Sifa?" she croaks, and the rock in my gut disappears. I've never felt such relief in my life.

"I'm so sorry," I mutter as I stride forward, pulling Halla into my arms to lift her away from the bed as she wraps her legs around my waist. I tug her face into my neck, a need to protect her from the filth and depravity of this place consuming me, a fire that starts in my toes and burns everything in its path. "I'm so, so sorry."

"Why are you sorry?" she asks, leaning back to look at me with her brilliant, clear eyes. "You came for me. That's all that matters."

I can't hold back the sob that erupts at her words. I kiss her cheeks and then her eyelids, clinging to her even more tightly than she's clinging to me. "You never should have been here at all, my sweet girl. I should have protected you."

"But you did, Ms. Sifa, just like you always do. You're here. You're taking care of me again."

I nudge her head into the crook of my neck again as I stride toward Fhord and Beron, sucking in one deep breath after another, until I feel my racing heart start to slow a little. "You're so smart," I tell her, releasing my hold so I can look at her again. "You see everything so clearly."

"You do too," she proclaims, the wisdom of a child animating her features. "You were just scared. That's all." She smiles again, lifting a hand to wipe my tears. "But you're better now. Right?"

"I am so much better," I assure her, relieved when a laugh escapes me instead of a sob. I look up, my heart warming when I see Fhord's smile. "Much better," I whisper, only a small catch in my voice this time.

He reaches out a hand to caress my lower back, dropping a kiss onto my head. "We should go," he murmurs. "It must be close to daybreak by now. I want to get back to the dragons before the sun rises if we can."

I nod, gathering my frantic thoughts as I push down the guilt that's been weighing on me since I learned the Dróttning had taken Halla. She's right. We got here. We're taking her away before that bitch can harm her. That's what matters.

So I spin and stalk out, turning into the hallway we took to get here. Beron extends a hand, though, grasping my arm. "There's a better way," he says as he points his chin in the opposite direction.

I still don't trust him. Twisting, I cock my eyebrow at Fhord.

"He's right. We'll get out quicker that way."

Dipping my chin, I wait for Beron to take the lead and follow, Fhord on my heels. I don't let go of Halla. I don't think I could even if I tried. But they were right. Within ten or fifteen minutes, Beron stops and reveals a trap door in the floor that I wouldn't have found, opening it with a squeal.

Fhord goes down first, leaving Halla and me with Beron while he confirms it's safe. I'm surprised for a moment, but Fhord must trust Beron more than he admits. When he returns, he grunts, "We're good," then reaches up for me to hand Halla to him.

A wide smile splits her lips, and she clutches Fhord as soon as his arms wrap around her. I can't hold back the grin. She's never met Fhord before, but somehow, she knows she can trust him as much as she trusts me.

When I drop next to them, she refuses to let go. "His turn," she tells me with a giggle as she squeezes his neck more tightly.

A soft warmth fills me, my chest growing light as I feel Fhord's emotions flare in response. He's already besotted by this little girl who means so much to me. I didn't realize before how desperately I need that.

Fhord smiles, a gentle look in his eyes. "I've got you," he assures her, one hand reaching up to stroke her silver hair. But then he looks at the Konungr and his eyes shift into sharp stones. "You'd better not be fucking us, Beron," he says, his tone deep.

Beron just smirks and drops the grate, its screech echoing in the hall for a few seconds.

"Do you trust him?" My voice is wavering again, and it pisses me right off. I can't protect Halla if I can't keep my emotions in check.

"Not for one second," Fhord declares. "But we have what we came for, and this should get us back where we started. Might be time to start."

"We'll see," I say as I turn and stride forward, anxious to mount Astarot and put this land behind me.

We get back to the dragons quickly, thank the gods. Sagga's exactly where we left her, sitting next to Astarot, watching the cave's entrance like a hawk. When we enter, her eyes grow wide, and she gives one sharp nod of her chin before standing to walk over to Fhord and Halla.

"Did they harm you?" she asks, drawing the girl into her arms.

"No, Mama. Ms. Sifa got me before they could. I'm safe." Halla finishes with an enormous yawn as she finally turns her gaze toward the dragons, a small smile lifting her lips. "Will we ride them?" she asks, turning to me.

"We will. Which would you like to ride?"

"I get to choose?" Now her smile is huge, creasing her cheeks and crinkling her eyes.

"You do," I assure her, doing my damnedest to keep my voice serious. "It's an important decision—who will carry you on your first dragon ride? And you're choosing for yourself and your mama, since she'll ride the other, and I believe it will be her first ride as well."

Halla looks at Sagga, her expression growing as serious as mine. "Will it be your first too, Mama?"

"It will," Sagga tells her with a nod.

"Which should I choose?"

"That, my dear girl, is completely up to you. I would not take that decision away."

Halla's gaze bounces between the dragons, her eyes bright. Finally, she focuses on Tindera. "I think I have much to learn from this one," she says. "What's her name?"

"She's Tindera," I respond. "Fhord rides her. The red dragon—who I ride—is Astarot."

"Perhaps I'll ride Astarot the next time. Today, I should ride Tindera."

She's so sure of herself. But she'll need to be with what she's about to face.

I help Sagga mount Astarot and watch, unable to stifle my grin, as Fhord sets Halla on Tindera and settles behind her, whispering in her ear the whole time. Little hands disappear into the dragon's golden feathers as the little girl readies herself for her first flight. We cast out our thoughts, making sure nobody is close enough to see us leave the cave or launch into the sky, and then Tindera leads us into the pre-dawn morning.

It's still dark, the trees like ghosts watching us as the dragons saunter out to join them. But hints of color shimmer on the horizon as the sun positions itself for its trek through the day. I feel lighter than I have since Nerthwaite, relief that we're taking Halla and Sagga to Lumaria—the safest place possible for them—helping lift some of the weight and hopelessness I've carried the last few days.

Tindera spins her head to glance at her drake, puffs out the smallest burst of fire, and then runs the few steps she needs to lift into the air. Astarot gives me a little caress through our bond and follows his draikana, stretching out his wings to propel us up and away from the cave as Sagga hums in delight in front of me.

"Thank you, my dear child," she sighs, barely loud enough for me to hear, before relaxing into me. We've never been close—Halla and I have a much stronger bond—but it still soothes part of me to have her here. She's devoted herself to Halla, laying the groundwork for what will come, and my need to protect Sagga as well as Halla rumbles in my chest.

We don't speak during the flight, and I'm glad. My thoughts bounce around between so many things—the impossible tasks we face to defeat the Dróttning, everyone who might get hurt in this fight that Fhord and I have started, how tough it will be to rebuild even if we do succeed—and I don't want to talk about any of them. I'm nervous and so conflicted for the first half or more of the flight, finally relaxing a bit as we soar over the water, letting the slow rhythm of the waves calm me.

Hours after leaving Revalle, we descend to soar above the water, and then finally enter the fog that surrounds Lumaria. Sagga's whole body tenses, the island's natural protection filling her for the few seconds it takes to get through, and then she relaxes and sucks in a deep breath.

"Stunning, isn't it?" I ask as I turn to see her expression. She just nods, her eyes wide as she takes in the majesty that is Lumaria.

A handful of people wait for us in the field, and as we get closer, I recognize Birger and two of his advisors. But then we get closer and my mouth drops, memories of my worlds spilling into my thoughts to push out everything else.

Njörðr—Freyr and Freyja's father—is in Vanatia. He's in Lumaria.

My mind stalls on these facts, everything else dissipating like a dense fog that's burned up by a sudden burst of sun and heat, condensing and falling to the ground below. I know others have come from my worlds—Mikkael, as well as the old gods who have been appearing over the last few weeks. It makes sense that Vanatia would draw in somebody I know. But I'm still speechless, too stunned to think of anything else as questions fill my mind. I have no idea why he's here or what this means.

Do you know the bearded male? Astarot's voice drops into my head, pushing aside the puzzle of Njörðr's presence.

I know him well. He's from my worlds, the father of Freyr, the male who saved me after my parents were killed and always treated me as a daughter. His daughter, Freyja, is the shifter hybrid I mentioned, who can sprout wings and fly. I'm sure I don't keep the wonder from my voice, because I am astounded.

Fhord turns to me, my message to Astarot reaching him as well because my mind is too splintered to hold a wall between my dragon and mate. A spark of surprise ripples through me before I remember that Lumaria enhances our mating bond, letting me speak to Fhord in our thoughts even without the strong emotion that connection usually requires.

Is Freyr who you mentioned when we were talking just before Sköll's attack? He sounds worried, as if he distrusts whatever we're about to learn.

He is, I respond, filling my words with the love I still feel for Freyr and his family.

You're sure this is his father? he asks, a crease I can see even from here forming between his brows.

Positive, I tell him. *His appearance is exactly the same, but it's more than that. I can sense him, beyond how he looks. He feels like the home of my youth.* Now that the initial surprise is dropping away, I'm filled with relief—tears spilling into my eyes as my chest expands—and a joy that's different from anything Fhord or others I love inspires in me. It's as if I've come home after ten years, bringing everyone and everything I need with me.

Astarot lands as close as he can to the others, snapping out his wings so I can dismount. I force myself to help Sagga, although I want nothing more than to run to Njörðr. When Fhord strides up next to us and takes her arm to draw her away, I smile at him in thanks. And then I spin to face Njörðr, positive I'm grinning from cheek-to-cheek.

He doesn't recognize me at first, but I'm not surprised. I looked fifteen when I last saw him, and the difference between fifteen and twenty-five years is a big one. But as I close the dragon's-length between us, I see the realization lighten his expression. His stoic regard shifts to surprise—eyebrows shooting up toward his hairline as his mouth falls open—and then joy. By the time he's throwing his arms open, his eyes are dancing and his grin is wide, strong cheekbones taking over his handsome face. And then he's wrapping himself around me, pulling me into an embrace I melt into.

"Your friend spoke of an elf from Midgard named Sifa, but I could not imagine it would be you." Njörðr's voice ripples with emotion, the love of a grandparent for his long-lost progeny. "It is so, so good to see you, my child. If I had any idea you shared this land with me, I'd have turned it inside out and upside down searching for you."

I'm still speechless, my thoughts bouncing randomly, without the order I'd need to voice any of them. Finally, I lean back to look at Njörðr, the question that rose in my mind when I first recognized him slipping from my lips. "How are you here? In Lumaria, and Vanatia?"

He laughs and I'm home again, memories of dinners in Asgard with Njörðr, Freyr, and Freyja filling my mind. "Those are two different questions," he tells me, "with very different answers."

"How are you in Vanatia?" That's what matters. Everything else can wait.

He shrugs, his features relaxing as he watches me with a small smile. "When Ragnarök cracked the barrier between worlds, it reopened a passage that I thought forever closed. As had been foretold long before the Vanir ever walked Midgard alongside humans, Vanaheim called me home to my mate."

My thoughts splinter, Njörðr's words dragging up memories of the histories of our peoples and the tales of Vanaheim, the original home of the Vanir. I shouldn't be surprised that Vanatia and Njordheim are Vanaheim—and I feel silly for not making that simple connection—but I always believed this world didn't exist. "Freyr said Vanaheim and Asgard were the same place," I point out, "which just had two different names over the millennia."

"So we told those who served us in Midgard," Njörðr explains. "It was a simpler explanation than the real one, and eventually, we treated it as the truth."

"And what is the real explanation?" My mind's still spinning. but I think I'm catching up. I'm finally ready to release my tight hold on Njörðr, moving to relax into Fhord's side as he wraps his arm around me and tugs me close. I barely notice the others, watching this unexpected encounter in shocked silence.

"The Vanir lived on Vanaheim in the days of my youth, before even Freyr and Freyja were born. Our magic grew of its lakes and streams. Eventually, we discovered Asgard and Yggdrasil—the tree of life."

"You're saying that Vanaheim's lakes and streams carry magic?" I've seen this in my worlds, but it doesn't seem right here. I've lived in Revalle for a decade, aging the entire time.

"Some waters do," Njörðr clarifies. "This island most closely connects these lands with Yggdrasil, so every drop holds the tree's magic. It's more sporadic in Vanatia and Njordheim. Only some of the water touches one of Yggdrasil's roots, imbuing those streams and ponds with its power."

I let this explanation settle within me as a spark of hope ignites. Maybe I already have the answers I've been seeking. "Why would you leave Vanaheim, pretend that it doesn't exist?"

"We learned we could carry Yggdrasil's fruit with us for sustenance, no longer be so closely tied to our homeland. And so we moved there. We lived in Asgard when Freyr and Freyja were born, and eventually, we stopped returning to Vanaheim. Then enemies came to try to wrest Asgard from us. Many of the Vanir chose to abandon Asgard and return home. Freyr, Freyja, and I stayed, eventually embracing those foes as family."

Memories of this history—the Norse myth embraced by Midgard's residents for so many years—fill in the details of Njörðr's story, convincing me of the truth of his words. Freyr and Freyja never spoke of their mother, not even mentioning her name. It was as if they wished they'd been borne of Njörðr alone, no part of her running through their veins.

"Freyr and Freyja's mother was one of those who returned to Vanaheim," I say. "Is she your mate?"

"She is," Njörðr tells me, a shadow passing over his features as he holds my gaze. "I suspect our conflict with the Æsir led her to become the tyrant she is today, lest she lose another world she'd claimed." He's quiet for a moment, watching me as his words settle, telling me who he's talking about before he says the words. "You know her as the Dróttning," he confirms, "but she was simply Nerthus to me. I did not know she'd had another child until this world pulled me here and I realized who my wife had become in the millennia since she left us."

A chill rolls down my spine as I realize just how porous the walls between our worlds have become. "How long have you been here?"

"I left Midgard on the heels of Ragnarök. The mate bond yanked me here but not to bring us together. I may have loved her in my youth, but I soon learned to see her for what she is." He pauses, his gaze shifting to look at everyone gathered around us. "I'm here to destroy her," he adds when he looks at me again. "And I suspect you are as well."

And now I'm truly speechless.

Njörðr has been in Vanatia—Vanaheim—as long as me, and I had no idea.

So much of what I believed has shifted on its axis.

But I know, deep in my soul, that Njörðr is right.

We're all here to destroy her.

Maybe the fates really are on our side.

CHAPTER TWENTY-TWO

DANI

MAGNIFICENT BEAST

"**F**UCK, I LOVE YOU, you magnificent beast." I can't hold back my joy. It pulses through me, sending shivers into my toes, legs bouncing as I cling to Vulryn's neck.

We're a few vikus from where the Monarch found us, hiding in the forest another half-viku from the small field Vulryn landed in. We're probably being paranoid—they couldn't possibly follow us after the twisting pattern my dragon took to get us here—but I sure as fuck never expected the Monarch to track us down in Vanatia. We're not taking a single chance.

"How the fuck did she do that?" Mikkael asks, his voice every bit as energized as I feel as he paces a man's-height away from us. "That was abso-fucking-lutely amazing."

"We've been practicing," I tell him with a shrug. A wave of embarrassment washes over me as he continues to gaze at me like I should get some credit for saving our asses. But this was all Vulryn. My magnificent beast.

"How did she even think of that? Because let me tell you, it's gods-damned brilliant. Even better than what Z did with the spiders."

"That's what gave me the idea." I push aside the memories of hundreds of spiders crawling all over me—that experience was beyond fucked and my skin crawls just thinking about it—and smile at Vulryn. She's preening her feathers as she watches us talk. She's so fucking proud of herself, and she has every right to be. "I was blown away by what Z did with those spiders and wondered what it would take to shoot fire like that at a distance. I asked Vulryn, and she started experimenting with it."

"I've never seen another dragon do it," Mikkael declares. "You need to hide that from the Dróttning until we're ready to use it. Vulryn could train the other dragons and shock the shit out of that bitch." He finally stops roving and stands still, sucking in a deep breath and giving us one more enormous grin. Fuck, he's handsome when he's like this—excited about something, none of the walls he's erected standing between us.

But I can't let myself get dragged down that path. This is a moment of weakness for Mikkael, nothing more. He'll be pushing me away again soon enough. Instead, I just nod because he's right about Vulryn's new trick. We had to use it this time, but with any luck, the Dróttning will never find out. Harald hates her enough to keep it a secret. He won't tell her anything that might save a few of her soldiers' lives.

"Let's finish what we started," I announce, digging my hands into Vulryn's feathers for one more scratch. "Z needs us, even if he doesn't realize it yet. Let's go get your dragon and go home."

Mikkael's responding smile takes my breath away. The part of me that belongs to him flares to life, an intense craving I'll never be able to satisfy. So I drag my gaze away, focusing on my dragon. *Time to go*, I tell her.

My drake will take him as a rider, she responds, staring at the mate I wish I'd never met.

It doesn't matter. I've pushed him away too many times. The damage is done.

She snorts, swinging her head to watch me as I stalk up her wing and climb to her back. *It is never too late*, she assures me in that know-it-all tone she uses sometimes. *When my drake claims him, he will see that we all belong together.*

And what if Z never claims him?

She's quiet longer than I would have expected, her gaze still fixed on me. I'm aware of Mikkael climbing up behind me, settling in with his chest pressed to my back as I try my damnedest to ignore the shiver that rolls through me, but my focus is on my dragon. Finally, Vulryn responds. *My drake will take him as a rider*, she insists before spinning her head to the path ahead and striding out of the forest.

I want to push for an answer to my question. I love Vulryn, but I despise this bullshit. We're chasing her happiness. Why can't I chase mine too, even if I do think it's too late and he'll never take me.

But I don't ask that question or any other. We still have no idea what we're going to do once we get to the training grounds. I should quiz Vulryn about her plans—whether she thinks he'll come out to her if he can, or we'll need to track him down, trapped somewhere inside. I can't bring myself to talk to her, though. This thing between us is growing larger in my mind, and I'm not sure if I want to let it go.

Mikkael clings to me the whole time and as much as I hate to admit it, he was right about flying together. I decided to follow his lead and stop fighting this *need* my body has to feel him. It's drawing out emotions I should ignore—part of the reason my frustration with my dragon is growing with every flap of her wings—but the contact with my mate calms me. My body craves his and it feels good to give in and feed this hunger.

The sun is setting when Vulryn starts to drop from the height we chose to lift us above other dragons who might be in the area. Our eyes scan the skies above us for anything that might be a threat. Vulryn can sense other dragons, but we've learned that's not enough, 'cause who knows when an eagle shifter's gonna show up and try to carry someone away? But we're alone in the quiet sky as we spiral down to a cave Fróðr told us we'd find in this area.

Vulryn stalks in as soon as she lands. Her mood is as dark as mine, probably because our emotions are so attuned. She casts a mean side-eye at me as she watches us dismount. *My drake will take him as a rider*, she tells me again when she jerks in her wings and spins around. *I will hunt*, she adds in a voice that's a bit less pissy—the uppity beast—before tromping outside.

Fuck me. My dragon can be such a bitch when she wants to be.

Mikkael and I don't speak as we work together to prepare dinner. But it's not uncomfortable. We both know what to do without having to talk about it. It's a pleasant camaraderie that does even more to calm and feed the mating bond.

Vulryn returns as we're sitting down to eat, gazing at me as she stalks in. Her bad mood is gone and I realize mine is too. I smile at her, sending a soft caress through our bond, and she rumbles in response.

I love her. That'll never change, even if she does piss me off occasionally.

I will rest, she tells me in a soft voice.

Sleep well, my love, I respond, making sure to infuse my words with all the affection I feel for her. I'm exhausted too after our emotional day and find my blankets soon after Mikkael and I clean up our meal, dropping into sleep quick-ly.

Vulryn's keening drags me from a dream about my mate and me riding our dragons, happier than any of us thought possible. I'm lost for a few seconds, immersed in the joy of our bonds, but then my eyes fly open and I spin my head to search for her in the dark.

We're not alone.

Two enormous dragons stand at the cave's entrance, the remnants of last night's fire casting just enough light to see their dark forms. No color breaks through the gloom that's settled on the cave, but I can sense Z, my connections to Vulryn and Mikkael flickering with their erratic emotions.

A chill runs down my spine, filling me with ice even under my warm blankets. I can't grasp the blue beast's thoughts, but my dragon and mate can. And they both are overwhelmed by a mix of fear and despair that feels like it will suffocate them.

Standing, I reach for the coat I left next to my bed last night and wrap it around me, then stride over to stand in front of the intruders. "What are you doing here?" I ask Z, ignoring the other dragon for now. For a moment, his eyes soften, as if he wants to tell me.

But he doesn't. Instead, a sharp voice pierces the silence as the dragon's eyes grow hard, all the light in them slipping away. "We've come to take you to the Dróttning," the male explains in a conversational tone, like we're about to sit down to dinner. I drag my gaze away from Z, wishing I could read the emotions behind those dark eyes, and look at the male on his back.

He's thin and even with the dim light in the cave, I can see that his hair is wild, as if he woke up dragging his hands through it and never bothered to tame it. He sits like most riders, a pompous air to him that suggests he likes perching high on his beast, looking down at everyone else. I suspect his expression would be cruel if I could see it—a sharp contrast to his words, which seem almost welcoming.

"Who the fuck are you?" I don't try to keep the anger from my voice. Hiding it won't do shit and it's already boiling inside me.

Because Z took another rider.

He's always been Ziselær. We were lying to ourselves that he'd changed, become something other than the heartless beast Matthias molded over a century of cruelty.

I fucking hate the Dróttning, that vile bitch.

"I ride Ziselær," the male explains with a half shrug, as if I just asked the stupidest question ever.

I want to ask Vulryn to shoot one of her arrows at this asshole. Fuck knows he deserves it. But I bite my tongue and keep my ideas to myself. We can't let the Dróttning know what Vulryn can do. And Ziselær isn't alone. The other dragon probably would take my life in return, and I'm not ready to die yet.

"You're sitting on Ziselær's back," I point out to the prick, "but that's not what I asked."

"His name's Knut," Mikkael mutters as he parks himself next to me, his gaze focused on his dragon. "He's the bastard who pretended to be with the rebellion but turned on us when we rescued Fhord and Tindera." He spits, his fists clenched tight and shoulders thrown back. "Fhord should have killed you when he had a chance."

"But he didn't. And here I am. I warned the Dróttning—tried to save a lot of lives, including Matthias's—and the Dróttning rewarded me well. When Ziselær learned who the Dróttning had chosen for him, he embraced the bond. He's mine now. Which means you will be too, Dani."

Knut's head dips down, his gaze roaming over me, and I'm fucking relieved I had the presence of mind to grab my coat when I got up. His scrutiny feels lecherous and dirty, as if every spider that's ever attacked me has transported here to weave their webs around my body. But then Knut pauses, cocking his head to the side. "Well, probably not," he says. "You're still alive only because the Dróttning demanded it. She's very excited about your punishment. You have some ... unpleasant ... days ahead. I doubt you'll survive."

"Fuck you, Knut." Mikkael's words are sharp, but the hand he lifts to caress the small of my back is soft, gentle. It sends a warmth rippling through me that I desperately need.

"You are a handsome creature, aren't you?" Knut's voice is playful now. "And you are my type. But then, everyone is my type. I'm not picky. Alas, though, it's not meant to be. The Dróttning hasn't asked for the pleasure of your company, and I don't think we'll bother taking you back." He's quiet for a moment, as if he's pondering his plans, then turns toward the other rider, a female who's been silent so far. "What do you think, Aslaug? Our liege doesn't want to play with him, but should we?"

I can't see her smile, but I can sense it. It feels like the air shifts in the cave, suffused with the casual cruelty of these riders. "It would seem a waste not to," she responds in a cold voice. "I'd enjoy that game."

Knut claps his hands, triggering memories of the Monarch. They're similar in a superficial way—both gaudy and extravagant. But Knut's arrogance is a front. I've just met him and already I can tell he's a power-hungry prick, pretending to be important.

Fucker doesn't deserve to ride a dragon like Ziselær. It's gonna kill Vulryn to watch him destroy her drake.

Maybe I *should* ask Vulryn to shoot a flame through the bastard's heart.

Before I can, though, Vulryn strides forward, her head high and flames billowing from her snout. She barks at Ziselær, rearing up over him as if to attack.

He does the same—Knut's laugh spewing into the midst of the dragons' squawks and squeals—rising to his full height and staring her down. But she's not intimidated by Ziselær's size. The temper that washes through her surrounds me, digging in to set fire to my bones and every bit of muscle and sinew and flesh beneath my skin. I couldn't escape the onslaught of emotions wafting from my dragon if I tried.

She's the baddest beast in either of these kingdoms and she is pissed.

Not just angry.

Furious.

Enraged.

Frenzied.

Vulryn has done everything for her drake. My dragon let herself be caged by that mother-fucking wyrm, suffered the indignity of pretending to cower to her and eat her slop, subjected me to lecherous guards, all to save this ungrateful beast from her clutches.

He is her drake, but he does not deserve her.

And she will end him.

Her attack is lightning fast, a lunge forward to wrap her teeth around his jugular. He whips back, drawing her with him and sending Knut tumbling to the ground. Out of the corner of my eye, I sense the other rider reaching for a weapon—probably a dragon bolt, the bitch—but she won't be able to use it. Vulryn and Ziselær are spinning too fast for her to get a clear shot.

I can only watch as Vulryn and her drake brawl. There's no other word for it. They are vicious and ruthless, and I don't see any way for both of them to leave this cave alive.

"A little help," Mikkael screams, sucking me out of the dread I'd been wallowing in. I spin my head to see him clashing with Knut and the female, his sword flinging wildly as he tries to defend against two very fucking good fighters. My heart drops to my feet, but I drag the bastard back up where it belongs. Because we've got work to do, gods dammit. Racing to my pack, I pull out the sword Jorunn gave me, eager to paint its edge with somebody's blood, and then run toward Mikkael and the others.

The other dragon is in my way, but it's focused on Vulryn and Ziselær, its teeth snapping as it seems to be holding itself back from attacking. I don't know why the fuck it's not helping Ziselær, but I can't waste time on that shit right now. I dart around that massive beast and fling my blade at the female. She must sense me, though, spinning just in time to deflect my blow.

She's good, I realize at once, and I'm impressed Mikkael managed to fight off her and Knut. We clash for a long time, her blows pounding at me, biting my flesh more often than I'd like. But my sword takes her skin just as often, the copper dragons that soar across the blade glowing red with her blood.

It takes me too many seconds to gather my thoughts—drive out the clamor of the onslaught in this cave and the fact that we're not all leaving here alive—but I finally manage to find the focus I need to attack her mentally. Dragging up images of Vulryn destroying the beasts still loyal to the Dróttning, I twist them a bit to make it look like her dragon is falling to mine and push into her mind.

She freezes as they land in her thoughts, her lips dropping into a slight frown as she lets her guard down just enough to give me the opening I need. Lunging forward, I shove my sword into her chest and then up, nearly slicing through her heart. It's fucking sharp, and a laugh bursts out of me as I think about how grateful I am to Jorunn for this remarkable weapon.

The female stares at me for a moment, eyes wide as her mouth drops open. Neither of us moves—both waiting for the death we know is coming—until blood starts to bubble from her mouth. I yank my sword away and puff out a shallow breath as she drops to the ground.

Her dragon's wail jerks me from my shock. It's hysterical and filled with so much pain, I almost feel sorry for the beast. I twist toward it, watching in horror as it flings its head back and forth, the pain of losing a rider so intense, even I can feel it. For a moment, I'm sure I'll be dead soon too. I just took its rider's life. If it's anything like my dragon, it's a vengeful beast.

But it doesn't attack me and I don't know why. Instead, it barks a command and I jump back, knowing instinctively that this dragon wants me far away from the female. Leaning forward, it lifts her into its mouth, more gently than I would have thought possible, and runs toward the cave's entrance. As soon as its wings are free, it extends them, soaring into the sky.

Almost immediately, Ziselær flings himself away from Vulryn. Vulryn pauses and I feel her uncertainty. The shields she normally keeps between us have collapsed, all of her focus on Ziselær's betrayal. But as he draws away, I feel a pang of hope erupt in her, wondering if he'll act differently without the other dragon here. Whether it was all a ruse. Ziselær backs away, though, flames flickering from him as he snarls at Vulryn and then howls at Knut.

I spin my head to see that bastard still fighting with Mikkael. But something's changed. They're not as vicious as they were a few minutes ago, maybe because the dragon's agony is sucking them down too. Knut jumps back and away from Mikkael's blade, parrying with him as he retreats to Ziselær.

When he gets close enough, Ziselær rams his snout between the males, giving Knut a few seconds to mount the blue beast. Once more, the dragon's eyes seem to soften as he looks at the rider he rejected. Only for a moment, though. As soon as his new rider is settled, Ziselær twists and sprints toward the cave entrance, flying away as soon as he can fling out his wings.

I don't move for a long time, my thoughts vacillating wildly as the chaos of the last few minutes bounces in my mind. Thank the gods, Mikkael has his shit together.

"We have to go. Now," he yells, dashing to the packs to grab them and then back toward Vulryn.

I shake off the shock and glance around the cave quickly, then follow him. We mount and Vulryn is in the air in a few seconds, soaring away as fast as she can.

It's quiet for a long time, Vulryn's wings the only noise to disturb my spiraling dread. But I need to know if this is as bad as I think it is. Where we go from here. *What happened with Ziselær?* I bring myself to ask at last, my heart in my throat.

My heart beats a dozen times before Vulryn responds. But then she sighs and I know we're fully fucked.

He chose the wyrm, she says, her voice a whisper that barely reaches me. More silence follows these words, the heaviness of her grief crushing me with its intensity. After a few minutes, she shakes herself, feathers rippling frantically as I grip her more tightly, holding myself up. Mikkael's doing the same, but I'm not as focused on him as I should be. Vulryn's devastation is all I can take in this moment.

Why didn't the other dragon attack you? It makes no sense that it would just stand there and watch. Vulryn might have been in trouble if she had to face both of them alone.

My drake claimed the right to kill me. The wyrm's beast heeded his demand. She's quiet again, finally adding, *My drake forgot that I am not easy to kill.*

Why did he stop and leave?

I am not easy to kill, she says again. This time, though, I feel the disgust in her words. *When the other beast left, my cowardly drake chose to escape with his life.*

Fuck. I don't know what else to say. Nothing will help my dragon right now.

We've flown for an hour or more when I sense her emotions shift from the despair and disgust that was beating her down as she threw us into the air into an angry resolve. *We gave my drake a chance to prove himself worthy*, she declares in a haughty tone. *He did not. So now, we will kill him.*

These words are firm, not a hint of regret or uncertainty in them.

Still, my heart breaks. Because my brave beast isn't admitting it to herself right now, but she will soon. This is gonna kill her. And Mikkael. Neither will be the same again.

And there's not a single gods-damned thing I can do about it.

Chapter Twenty-Three

Mikkael

Empty

Now I know. He belongs to the Dróttning. That won't change.

Ziselær chose that bitch over his own draikana. Took that bastard Knut, of all people, as a rider and then carried that fucker to the cave we were hiding in. He tried to kill Vulryn, and when he couldn't—because Dani's beast is ferocious—he carried his new gods-damned rider away.

I should be surprised, but I'm not. Matthias fucked him up and he hasn't had nearly long enough to repair all the damage that bastard did. Ziselær told me again and again, in so many different ways, that he couldn't ever let himself accept me. That I'd never ride him. I should have believed him.

But fuck, it hurts. A blade has pierced my chest, slicing through more sinew and muscle with every beat of my broken heart, and nothing will ever be able to yank it free. In my head, I know why they did it. My soul, though, doesn't give a shit about that. My dragon joined my mate in rejecting me.

The cavern that formed within my body when they shoved themselves away from our bond will never fill. I'm empty and I always will be.

Dani settles more deeply into my chest, wrapping her arms around mine on her stomach, and I should push her away. I should rebuild that wall between us, especially now. But I can't bring myself to do it. I need my mate's touch more than I need to protect my broken heart. So I hold her, resting my cheek on her head and inhaling her scent. It calms me. Maybe even fills that gaping hole in my gut, just a bit.

The sun is sinking, almost gone, when Vulryn heaves in her wings and starts to spiral down. When we're close enough, I see the plateau she's aiming for, which looks like a flat rock, nowhere to hide. But I trust her, more than I ever could have trusted my own dragon. She's strong enough to protect us, even though she must be as heartbroken as me. Probably more, because she thought he'd chosen her. She lost something she believed she had.

We don't speak as Dani finds the hole we'll climb into, dragging away a bush and watching Vulryn and me enter before she puts it back in place. The silence continues as she unpacks Vulryn and starts cooking a meal for us. I just watch as my mate cares for me. It soothes me in a way I didn't realize I need, but desperately do.

When we're done eating, she pushes a glass of whiskey into my hands, giving me a half smile before she gathers the dishes and a few other things and heads deeper into the cave—probably toward a pool. She returns a few minutes later with clean dishes and packs everything before striding over to kneel in front of me.

Her gaze holding mine as she reaches for my hand. "You should sleep, Mik. It'll do you good."

I nod. I don't know if it'll do me good, but I do need to sleep. It'll be nice to escape into oblivion for a little while. She already spread out my blankets and I lay down, pulling one over me. But then she tugs her blanket over to place it next to mine and drops beside me. She's so close, I can smell her freshly scrubbed skin, feel the heat of her body, see the goose flesh on the bare arm resting on top of her cover.

When she scoots back—not touching me, but inviting my touch—I reach out and drag her into me. The moan that rustles through my lips catches us both by surprise, drawing a little laugh from her. I just hold her tighter, taking what I can from my mate in this moment. Sleep takes me sooner than I expected.

Dani and I are still wrapped around each other when I wake up. Her back is pressed against my chest, close enough for me to realize we're breathing and our hearts are beating in sync. I must have slept a long time. It wasn't long after sundown when we got here last night, but light's already starting to filter in through the bushes that protected us from any searchers. I needed it. I think we all did.

I still feel empty, the loss of Ziselær a wound that will never close, but I'm better. Dani's here and she filled some of that void. She's awake, waiting for me to move, but I'm not ready yet. So I cling to her for a bit longer.

"Why didn't you go to Vulryn last night?" I ask at last, voicing the question that's been teasing my thoughts for the last few minutes.

"I wanted to be with you." Her voice is soft, and I wonder if I hear a hint of guilt in it, as if she feels like she betrayed her dragon by comforting me.

"She probably needed you as much as me."

Dani scoffs, lifting her chin, and probably her gaze, toward Vulryn. "Have you met my dragon?" she asks with a laugh. "She's pissed and resolved. She shoved aside her heartbreak while we flew here yesterday."

"Maybe she's just putting on a strong front," I mutter. She knows her dragon better than I ever could, but I have to believe Vulryn's hiding her grief. That she's as achingly desperate as me. Still, she survived so much in the North. Maybe she already is more focused on rage than anguish.

Dani spins over, lifting her hand to rest it on my cheek as her gaze holds mine. Her eyes are so blue, as if the gods chose the purest parts of this world—the sky and water—to supply the perfect hue to this glorious female. She's fully open to me and I think if I followed our bond, I'd see into her soul. My heart starts to throb as I raise my hand to caress her soft skin with my thumb.

"I wanted to be with you," she repeats, and I believe her. "I told Vulryn and she agreed, but I would have come to you even if she didn't. I let her push a wedge between us. I chose her when I should have chosen you. I won't make that mistake again. She knows now. Even if you don't want it, you're as much a part of me as she is. When you need me, I will be here for you."

I don't cry. Ever. They beat that shit out of me when I was young, removing every hint of weakness if I made the mistake of revealing it. But fuck if Dani isn't finding tears I didn't know I could shed. My heart has never needed to hear words as much as it needed to hear those.

And I kiss her. It's as pure and perfect ... as undeniably right ... as before, leaving me wondering why I don't do this every day, all the time. She's still, and for a moment, I think she's not going to kiss me back. I couldn't blame her. I've been a bastard to her. Every day. All the time. But then her lips part and her tongue tangles with mine. Warmth spills through me—my cock standing to attention, hoping he's gonna be involved—filling me with the knowledge that I am home.

Dani is my home.

Which scares the fuck out of me. Because I don't think I can let myself go down that path. Losing Ziselær was hard. But I never really believed I'd have him. He made sure of that. Dani's different. And opening my heart to this captivating female, only to have her cast it aside, would destroy every beautiful thing I hold in my soul.

She pulls back after a few seconds, leaning away so she can look at me. "Now's not the time for me to take advantage of you," she tells me with a smirk.

"It's exactly the time," I respond, pushing away my macabre thoughts as a grin splits my cheeks. "Get 'em when you can, I always say. Maybe you'll get lucky."

Her gaze tracks down to my bulging cock, eyes crinkling with her smile. "Somebody wants to get lucky," she points out. I can only shrug. She's not wrong. "I want it too," she says as she looks up at me again. "But not like this. You need to trust me, and you don't yet. I don't blame you. I wouldn't trust me, either. Let me work on it. Before we take a step you might regret."

I watch her for a moment, an argument at the tip of my tongue, but she's right. "I told you once," I respond at last, "that if I ever take you, it'll be because I want it. Not the bond. Me. And then I'll make love to you. You'll be mine, and I'll be yours." I'm quiet for a moment, just watching her eyes, waiting for her to stop me.

She doesn't, so I say what's been pushing its way from the darkest recesses of my mind since we lost Ziselær, demanding that I acknowledge it. "I realized on the flight over that I want that—more than I've let myself admit. But you're right. I have no idea what would happen if I trusted you, only to have you leave me the way Ziselær did. It would change me. I don't know if you'd like whoever emerges from those ashes. I don't know if I would."

"I don't think you have it in you to become someone I don't like," she tells me, her lips curving up in a little smile. Then she pauses, casting her gaze down as she murmurs, almost to herself, "Someone I don't love." Before I can chase that thought, she shakes herself and looks up again. watching me as my mind catches up with hers—still focused on the word she whispered to herself a few seconds ago.

Dani loves me, and I think I love her too. Which blows me the fuck away.

"I agree, though," she says. "We can't explore this right now." She leans forward for one more kiss, a quick press of her lips to mine, and then stands. "Let's go to Lumaria, spend some time together. Decide where we go from here. If we go from here."

She reaches out a hand, one eyebrow arching adorably, an unspoken question in her eyes. Will we pursue this thing between us in Lumaria? And I know she's right. We need to chase this, but now's not the time. Reaching up, I take her hand and we both laugh as she tries to drag my heavy ass off the floor.

It feels good to laugh with her. The hole in my gut isn't quite as cavernous.

We bathe in the pool that was hidden farther in the cave—separately, to the disappointment of my throbbing cock—and eat a hurried meal. We're in the air again within an hour. The wall we both erected between us is shorter, thinner, and as I mount Vulryn behind her, she leans into me, feeding my soul even more. It's a long flight, but it goes quickly. Soon, Vulryn is soaring across the ocean and into the fog bank surrounding Lumaria. And then we're through it, descending to the field where Birger and others will greet us.

My heart thumps a bit faster when I see Sifa and Fhord waiting for us—Sifa smiling from ear-to-ear as we draw closer, and Fhord glowering like he usually does when I'm near. But he's not quite as dour as he was the last time I saw him. I think he's warming up to me.

As Vulryn starts to spiral down to land, I tighten my hold on Dani, leaning in to inhale the citrus and sandalwood that she always wears. I'm not sure when she'll be this close again, and I want her scent in my nose as long as I can have it. "Thank you for the ride," I purr in her ear before grinding my stiff cock into her ass one more time, for good measure.

She laughs, filling the hole inside me a bit more, and wraps her arms around mine. "Anytime," she hums as Vulryn's feet hit the ground.

I suck in one more whiff of her enticing-as-fuck aroma and swing my leg over Vulryn's back, dropping to her wing and jogging over to Sifa. And I pull her into my arms, grateful to be with my oldest friend again.

"I missed you, you cranky asshole," she tells me as she hugs me as tight as I'm holding her. "But I thought you'd be gone longer." She leans back, her lips dropping into a frown as she looks at me with sad eyes. "And I hoped you'd have Ziselær with you."

"He chose the Dróttning," I tell her, my voice flat. "She gave him a new rider—fucking Knut, of all people—and he came with another dragon to take us to the Nest. He and Vulryn fought, but he's not strong enough to take her down. I killed the other dragon's rider, so Ziselær and Knut left. It was ... so fucked ... but we're alive."

"Ziselær," she asks, "not Z?"

"He's always been Ziselær. It just took me too long to admit it. He was never mine." Fuck, it hurts to say that. The more I give it voice, the more real it is. I thought I'd accepted his choice but telling Sifa about it just reminds me how big of a hole Ziselær created inside me when he chose gods-damned Knut over me.

"I'm sorry." Sifa's voice is so sad. She understands. "I really thought he'd make the right choice."

"Me too." I step back, suddenly anxious to escape the pity that's rolling off Sifa. "I let him go," I say, trying to convince myself as much as her. "I've been holding out hope, but I'm glad to know. He doesn't want me. I've accepted it."

She nods, lifting her hand to hold my cheek as her eyes, brimming with her kindness, gaze at me. "It's good to know, so you can let go." She glances up and then turns back to me with a smile. "Astarot tells me that Vulryn wants to hunt and she's going to carry Dani to the lake. Do you want to join them?"

"Yeah, I do." I should put distance between Dani and myself right now, but I can't think of anything I want more than to drop into those healing waters with my mate. "I'll see you later, yes?"

"We'll eat together," she assures me. "I'll send a message to your chambers once you're back there and settled."

Tugging her closer for one more hug, I nod my agreement. "Thanks," I respond before spinning and jogging to Vulryn. Dani's mounted and waiting for me, so I climb up and settle next to her for the short flight.

We don't waste any time when she drops us at the lake. We both came prepared to swim as soon as we got here, wearing bathing clothes underneath our shirts and pants. Tossing everything else to the ground, we end up racing into the water, splashing and diving in as soon as we're deep enough. And fuck, it feels good. For the first time in a long time, I can see a happy future. One with Dani and Vulryn. I'm surprised how right it seems, even without Ziselær.

I'm floating on my back, staring up at the clouds drifting across the pale blue sky, when I see them.

"What the fuck?" I mutter. "That's a shitload of dragons. I didn't think the rebellion had so many allies in the sky."

"What?" Dani stands and spins to look at me, then follows my gaze up.

"Fuck!" Her voice is shrill. I watch as her face goes slack, like it does when she talks to Vulryn, then she focuses on me again.

"Vulryn will tell the others. We need to go."

"This is an attack?" A chill rolls down my spine as I realize what that means. "Did we lead them here?"

"I don't know," she responds, tears filling her soft blue eyes. "I hope we haven't fucked up royally."

She starts pushing her way through the water to the shore and I do the same, moving as fast as I can. They're getting closer, and we need to get back to the city, figure out what we can do to defend it.

The horn that blares in the distance confirms what we feared. They didn't expect these beasts. The Dróttning found Lumaria. We might have led them here.

Fuck. Fuck, fuck, fuck. My stomach is in my throat and I have to hold back the gag that shoots up from my gut. I've fucked up a lot in my life, but I've never fucked up this badly, put this many lives at risk, endangered a place that matters so much to the people I love.

"Snap out of it," Dani barks at me. "I can feel your guilt. It could be just a coincidence. This is a large force to be pulled together at the last minute. I don't think it's our fault."

"It's a pretty big fucking coincidence," I growl back. "But it doesn't matter. We'll deal with that shit later. Right now, we just need to get back to the city. Figure out how we can help."

"Vulryn's coming to get us. She'll take us to Fhord and Sifa. They'll tell us what they need."

We towel off quickly and throw on our clothes, then start running. Vulryn spirals down less than a minute later, landing with a thud and flinging out her wings. We're in the air a few seconds after that, racing toward the city, almost as fast as my heart is beating in my chest. Shame pounds through me, the certainty that we caused this forming a rock in my gut, but Dani's right. I can't get distracted with what-ifs. The only thing that matters now is the fight.

Vulryn shoots like a spear toward the city center as people scatter away, creating enough space for her to drop us next to where Fhord and Sifa are meeting with some of his advisors. We jump down as soon as she extends her wing, my stomach hurling into my throat again when Fhord turns toward us with flaring eyes.

"Fuck, I'm sorry if we did this," I tell him, my gaze holding his.

He just shakes his head, not a hint of reproach in his expression. "Not your fault. I know how she works. This was planned before you came. Maybe she followed you to make sure she had the location right, but she knew enough to gather her forces in advance. She'd have found us soon anyway."

"We're not here to toss around blame," Sifa interjects. "We have to hold them off to give our people as much time as we can to get underground." She turns toward Dani. "We'll lead the dragons but avoid combat if at all possible. The goal is to draw them away. Others on the ground will try to stop them from dropping their riders. We need to push them away from homes, try to keep them over the fields."

And then she spins toward me. "You'll do something much more important. Halla's in Fhord's rooms. Someone will take you. Your job is to protect her, at whatever cost. She's the most important being on this island. The Dróttning wants her back and we can't risk losing her. Everything depends on it."

I nod my head, grateful for this task. I've known for a while that Halla wasn't just someone Sifa fed and had grown to love. She's special in a way I don't understand but can feel deep in my gut. If I have to give my life to save hers, that's exactly what I'll do.

But I can't leave yet. I turn toward Dani, my heart in my throat, and close the distance between us. Grasping the back of her neck, I tug her toward me and take her lips. She's the birth of the stars at the dawn of time, the caress of your lover as you cling to each other under a full moon, the sweetest piece of fruit I've ever tasted. Dani is the beginning and the end for me, and I've been a gods-damned jackass to take so long to admit it to myself.

Breaking away and stepping back—my hand still holding her neck tightly—I capture her gaze, letting her see the resolve in my eyes. "My sexy, savage, spectacular spy," I rasp, wishing to any gods left in this gods-forsaken place that I'll have more time with her, "you are every bit as badass as that beast you ride. Don't you dare die."

She smirks and my cock twitches, reminding me I've been a bastard to him too. "I'm not done with you yet," she says. Then she leans into me, pressing her lips to mine. "See you soon, Mik," she tells me with a wink. Turning, she strides toward Vulryn, throwing one last smile at me over her shoulder before she mounts her dragon and they launch into the sky.

CHAPTER TWENTY-FOUR

MIKKAEL

MINE

I DON'T BOTHER KNOCKING on Fhord and Sifa's door when one of their people points me to it. We're lucky the Dróttning's dragons aren't already attacking the city, and this building's a big target. I need to get Halla and Sagga out.

"Finally," Sagga declares as soon as I swing the door open. "We nearly left without you. We're not safe here."

"I came as fast as I could," I explain as I wave my hands to beckon them toward me. "Let's go."

Halla stands and reaches for me, but Sagga doesn't move from the chair she's sitting in.

"I'll slow you down," she explains, her gaze fierce, when I swing an arm from her to the door. She sure as fuck doesn't need directions but maybe she'll take the hint. Instead, she shakes her head. "Halla's what matters. Go without me."

"I can't do that, Sagga." My tone is too brusque, but I can't help it. I don't have time for this bullshit. "Halla needs you. We won't leave you to be killed."

"You can and you will." Her voice is firm, not a hint of doubt in it. "I've seen two paths. You only survive in the path that leaves me behind. Halla is all that matters. Go. Now."

"We already said goodbye just in case, Mr. Mik," Halla tells me, her words small, drawing my gaze to an expression I've never seen on this typically carefree girl before—brows together, eyes bright with unshed tears, and lips tight. "She'll be safer if we leave her here. Our path is dangerous, and it'll be worse if Mama goes with us. We have to go without her." She turns to smile at her mother, her free hand lifting to wave goodbye.

"You're wasting time, boy," Sagga snipes at me. "Go. Keep her safe."

I dip my chin because I can't do anything else. Halla's my focus and we won't get far if I have to drag Sagga with us. Pulling Halla's hand, I lead her downstairs, my heart ratcheting up—pounding in my ears—when I hear the screams that tell me the Dróttning's dragons have arrived.

Halla's hand tenses in mine, but her steps don't falter as I tug her out of the building. I hate to expose her like this, but we need to get below ground and I know of only one place in the city to do that. I start to run but realize quickly that her little legs can't move fast enough. I could lose her in the madness the city has become—people pushing and shoving as they flee in different directions, nobody here yet to take charge, give order to their exodus.

Dragging her toward a nearby building for cover, I drop to a crouch. "Climb on my back," I tell her with a smile, my gaze scanning the sky above. "We'll move faster."

She nods and throws her arms around my neck as I grasp her legs. After taking another quick check of the area, I push back into the street, look one more time for anything I might have missed, and start running. My heartbeat kicks up but just barely. It already was hurtling inside my chest, an allegro to accompany our escape. I have to force my way through the crowd, but I realize that's a good thing. The Dróttning could be looking for a little girl with silver hair and the more cover Halla has, the better our chances.

That and the hat I steal from a passing display. Better on Halla's head than in ashes on the ground.

The first dragon to soar over the city, spitting fire at everything in its path, draws terror like blood, thickening the air. Too many people pause to stare up at the beast, their eyes wide, mouths hanging open in shock. Roofs and trees and a few of the homes explode into flames, the inferno spewing from the beast's mouth consuming everything it touches. He's soon joined by another, and then another, the death and destruction that gushes from their mouths ravaging vast swaths of the city.

For a moment, my heart breaks. I'll never be able to share this with Dani—not the way we should have if I hadn't been such a fucking idiot. I won't swim with her again, stroll these streets hand in hand, or picnic in the park. This island should have been ours. I took that from her.

But I can't think about that shit right now. I'll grieve later. One thing matters now—the little girl on my back—and if I get anything right in this life, it sure as fuck better be this.

"Go there," I yell, aiming a nearby male and female toward the stone buildings a block over, wondering where the fuck Fhord's advisors are. "Tell everyone to hide in places without a wood roof," I demand. "The riders won't come after you. This isn't that kind of attack. Just do what you must to escape the dragon fire."

They nod, their faces relaxing just a touch as they get the direction they desperately need. And thank the gods, they take charge, moving the crowd in the right direction, because we can't get sucked into this morass. I start pushing my way through again, anxious to get out of the street and away from the dragons' sharp gaze.

We don't make it.

We're still two dragon's-lengths away from the door that will lead us underground when one of the beasts stops his razing of the city, slowing to pivot in the air above us. I feel Halla's fear, a shiver rippling through her as her arms tighten around my neck. Before I can hide, the dragon's gaze finds mine. He pauses, holding himself aloft a dragon's-length away, and his face shifts into one of those dragony smirks I used to love. This one, though, sends a chill down my spine, my barreling heart slowing for a moment as I realize we are well and truly fucked.

"Shit." Spinning in place, looking for anything that could protect us in our final lunge toward the cave that's our only escape, I find an alley that might work. It's got enough cover to protect us part of the way, and it'll get us close. "Hold on," I remind Halla. And then I run.

My heart is already pounding in my chest. I've been racing through this town, forcing my way through the throngs searching for refuge, for ten minutes or more. Now I'm sprinting, jumping over any obstacles in our path, trying my damnedest to hide beneath the occasional awning or canopy sprinkled along the way. My breaths rasp through my throat, ragged and harsh, but I will not let these bastards win. I will save this child, if it's the last thing I do.

The dragon who's been following us—a massive black beast with eyes as red as rubies—lands in front of the alley, crushing everything beneath him and blocking our route to safety. I turn, desperate to just get away now, and fuck if there isn't a blue dragon there. My mind fills with images of the corpses dragons leave behind when they focus their fire on a single victim, but I push that shit aside. We will not die here.

Ziselær slips into my thoughts next, trying to replace the macabre images my mind showed me, but I shove that crap aside too. It's not him. He chose Knut. Bastard's back at the Nest, fully committed to the Dróttning now. He rejected me, and there's not shit I can do about that.

It still hurts like fuck.

I expect the dragons to light us up. I'm not sure how or why, but I know Halla's too important for the Dróttning to risk losing again. They don't, though. Instead, the riders drop from their beasts, stalking into the alley with shit-eating grins on their faces.

Dropping Halla, I point toward an alcove that'll provide some cover—maybe even protect her from a claw swiping in to pull her away. "I just need to take care of them," I tell her, keeping every hint of fear or doubt out of my voice. "You wait there, and I'll get you when I'm done." I smile, making sure it reaches my eyes.

"You can do this, Mr. Mik," she tells me, her voice strong and sure. She smiles back and turns to run where I pointed her. And I draw my blades.

"You don't have to die today, reject," the black dragon's rider tells me with a sneer. "We can save you for Ziselær, let him kill you himself, if you give us the girl and step away."

"Z's not gonna kill me," I tell them with more confidence than I feel. "He's had plenty of chances and he hasn't done it yet. But I'm not giving you the girl. And I'm gonna take your head for trying."

I lunge for him first. He's closest, and I already can tell he's a fucking asshole. He's the reject, a petty part of my mind reminds me. The fates chose me for a dragon. He probably rides only because he's sworn fealty to a malicious bitch. I wouldn't take that life, even if I could.

Bastard's also good with his blade. He jumps aside, flinging his sword up to crash against mine, then bringing it down in an arc that would have taken the head of a lesser fighter. But I'm not a lesser fighter.

I throw myself back, the blade barely missing my neck, and lunge toward him, opening a gash in his side. Crimson spews from the fresh wound to paint the ground beneath us but he doesn't slow down. Grinning like the lunatic he probably is, he thrusts toward my neck, sending me backwards just in time to see the other rider jump into the fight.

Fuck. Me.

The next few minutes are a mindless flurry of swords and pain. I hold my own—stop these bastards from killing me and taking Halla to the Dróttning—just barely. Three times, one of their blades nearly guts me or takes my head, but I'm able to dance away just in time. They've opened gaping wounds on my side and a gash on my neck, but I will not die easily. And these fuckers won't be the bastards to do it.

I'm struggling to breathe when the gods finally give me a fucking break. The blue rider misses a step, leaning into the other's sword. A cackle spurts from me as I shove him hard from his side, watching as he falls onto the black rider's blade. The pupils of the soon-to-be-dead asshole blow out, his eyes bulging as his mouth falls open. For a moment, they watch each other, both too surprised to move. And I finish the job, slashing my blade down and through the neck of the black dragon's male.

I feel the dragons' rage before I hear it, a grief and anger so strong, it blasts toward nearby beasts and spills into me through my connection to Dani and her dragon. They are hate and grief and wrath, their only goal in this moment my destruction. They both rear back, walls of black and blue, as flames gush from their mouths and nose. I twist in place, looking for an escape that won't expose Halla to their vengeance, even though I know I won't make it. I'm gonna die in this gods-forsaken alley, and there's not shit I can do about it.

When I see a cavity that might provide enough cover, perhaps three man's-heights away—in the direction of the black dragon—I start sprinting, although I have no fucking idea how I'm going to get there. The ebony beast sucks in a deep breath, as if he wants to make sure the flame he shoots at me will burn me to ashes, and I prepare myself to die. Pictures of Dani and Ziselær erupt in my thoughts and I embrace both of them. They'll never be mine, but I'm relieved as fuck to have their images with me as I go to my death.

I'm running, nearly to the hole I'm hoping to fling myself into, when the flames start to shoot from the dragon's mouth. My mind scrambles to drag up Dani's image, the feel of our bond, but instead, it's my tenuous, barely-existent, bond with Ziselær that pushes its way to the surface. For a moment, it feels like he's coming, like my desperate mind has convinced itself he'll save me again.

And then he's there, throwing himself between the black dragon and me, pushing the other beast aside with a screech full of scorn. *Mine,* he shrieks at the heartbroken beasts who want nothing more than to punish me for their pain. They growl in response, wings spreading behind them as they rise to their full heights, demanding my death for themselves.

The next few seconds are tense as fuck, and I can only watch as these three massive beasts squeal and bark at each other as they decide which one has the better claim to my life. I see Knut on Ziselær's back—the grin on his face a slap to mine—and my gut twists with the knowledge that fucking

Knut is going to come out of this shit as the victor, riding my dragon back to the Nest.

But my gaze keeps pivoting back to Ziselær's eyes. His rage and grief and resolve are all I can see.

Finally, the other beasts give in, their angry roars turning into discontented grumbles as they lean away, giving Ziselær space to land. Knut drops from his back, striding toward me with his chest and chin held high, a smirk on the smug bastard's lips. He's a man's-height away when he stops and spits in my direction.

"Ziselær convinced them," he says in that friendly tone he always uses when he's trying to fuck someone over, "and he's given me the right to take your life."

"Gods-damned generous of him," I respond with a smirk, "considering how badly he wants to take it himself. But what the fuck makes you think you have any hope of beating me in a fight?"

Now, Knut plays his ace. He turns toward Halla, crouched in the alcove a dragon's-length away, and then looks back at me. "The Dróttning wants the little girl alive, but she doesn't give a single fuck how much she's bleeding when she gets there. Or how many limbs or eyes she's lost along the way. I can take her like this, or I can let one of these dragons work out its grief on her first. They'd be happy to oblige."

"I always knew you were a monster," I snarl at him, my chest growing so tight, I can barely breathe as bile spills into my throat. "But this? That would be fucking depraved. You really gonna hurt a little girl like that, Knut?"

"I'll do whatever I must to please the Dróttning." Somehow, the bastard looks even more smug as he says this. His sneer and crossed arms twist in my gut like a knife. This asshole winning—fucking Knut, of all people—may be the worst part of this. The fates truly are fucked.

"I'm not gonna let you take her," I declare, raising my sword to stand between us. "And I'll be gods-damned if I'm gonna just bend over and offer my neck to you. You want to kill me, you'll have to work for it."

Knut watches me for a few seconds, the smile taking over his expression again. And then he looks at Ziselær and dips his chin. "My dragon has changed his mind. He'd like to be the one to take your life. I'm feeling generous today—and I like this jacket too much to let it be stained by your blood—so I think I'll give him this. I made him promise he'd use flame, and he agreed. He's a good beast and happy to finally have a rider worthy of him."

"Fuck you, Knut." My voice is hoarse, the grief that ripples through me at his words too overwhelming to hide. I know my dragon hates me, that he craves the vengeance he'll only find with my death. It still hurts to have it thrown in my face. "Z's known a long time that my life is his to take. If he wants it, I give it freely."

Ziselær rears up, drawing my gaze toward him. And I can't hold back the grin. Because if anything good came out of my bond with this amazing beast, it's the knowledge that the fates chose me to ride him. The Dróttning and that gods-damned usurper fucked him up too badly for him to recover—and that breaks my fucking heart—but he started as my dragon. I'm his perfect rider, and I'm gonna cling to that when he takes my life.

That, and the memory of Dani's lips on mine, the body that was created for my touch—just as mine was made for hers—pressed to me. I wish we'd had more time, that we could have explored this bond between us. But maybe this is better. She won't grieve me the same way with our bond incomplete. I want her to live and love again. I want her to be happy.

I'm ready, Ziselær. These words are for him alone, although I suspect Knut can hear them too. The fucker.

Z, he corrects me with a dragony smirk, and I swear to all the gods above, the cheeky bastard winks. The full meaning of his response ripples through me, sending shivers up and down my spine.

He's mine. He's been mine since he chose to leave the cave we were hiding in, to protect us. Guilt and regret fill him at the pain he's caused me, overlaid with a promise to never hurt me again. He has so much to prove to me in the days and weeks and years to come.

And then he spits out flame.

Directly at Knut.

The bastard's face slackens, his mouth dropping open and eyes growing wide as he's completely consumed by Z's fire. The other dragons shriek, rattling the nearby windows with their rage, but before they can attack Z, Vulryn and Tindera are there, throwing themselves between Z and the others.

I don't even look at them, though. My eyes can see one thing—the majestic blue dragon the fates tied me to, who's reaching to me through the bond that's been flimsy and fragile since we found each other. He's gazing at me, love softening his features, and my heart is expanding in my chest. It explodes out, filling the cavern in my gut that opened when I thought he'd rejected me, every crack and crevice brimming with his commitment to me.

He's dropped his shields, opening himself to me completely to let his memories flow into mine. It's the strangest thing I've ever experienced, as if they've been there all along and I can examine them as I would my own. I understand why he left. I even agree with the sacrifice he made returning to the Dróttning, despite what it cost me. Every ounce of doubt and fear inside me evaporates.

Sending my mind toward his, I grasp the bond that will help make me whole. And then I *feel* it solidify inside me, an unbreakable line forming between Z and me, anchored in that place that used to be achingly empty and barren.

Mine, my dragon says, his voice full of pride and adoration.

And now that word means something very different than it did a few minutes ago.

Z has claimed me as his rider. And I've claimed him.

Maybe the fates don't hate me after all.

CHAPTER TWENTY-FIVE

SIFA

THE GIRL IS SAFE

THE GIRL IS SAFE.

Astarot's message drops into my thoughts, and I take the first full breath I've managed since the Dróttning attacked Lumaria. I don't know how he did it, but I owe Mikkael an enormous debt. If the prophecies are true, we all owe him.

Where can I find her? I let Astarot hear the relief and gratitude in my voice. He knows how much she means, how terrified I was when I realized the Dróttning sent the dragons to capture Halla, and destruction of Lumaria was an added boon for the bitch. After her dragons retreated, we came to the field used to greet visitors to the island. We're alone, waiting for Fhord and Tindera to join us before we venture into the city.

The angry male and his dragon bring her. He's quiet for a moment and I can almost feel his humor slipping through the bond to wash over me. *Although I suspect he will no longer be the angry male.*

I didn't understand a single thing you just said, I tell Astarot, spinning my head to stare at the smirking dragon. *Who is the angry male, why won't he be angry any more, and why the fuck would he and his dragon, whoever that is, have Halla?* I cock my eyebrow at him, sending frustration back through the bond.

Vulryn calls him the angry male *and I agree, that has been a good name for him. You call him Mikkael. Do you prefer that name?*

I don't try to hide the shock that ripples through me, my eyes growing wide as my mouth falls open. Astarot laughs, the little shit. His expanded vocabulary is a source of great joy for my mischievous dragon. *Mikkael and his dragon are bringing Halla here?*

As I said, he tells me with a playful flick of his tail.

Ziselær?

What other dragon would accept the angry male as a rider? Only the fates could make such a choice.

Now I turn my entire body so I can stride over to my dragon. Maybe I'll get more information from him if I get a little closer. *What is Ziselær doing here?*

Astarot watches me approach, leaning forward to offer the horn he loves to have scratched. *The blue beast chose his rider and draikana*, he tells me, a smile in his voice. *I believe he has shared his story with the angry male. I will let him tell you about his dragon's choice.*

You're enjoying this way too much, I declare as my fingers dig into that spot behind his horn, earning a low rumble from my roguish beast. The calm that filled me when I learned that

Halla is well seeps into my fingers and toes, relaxing all the parts that have been tense and rigid since the Dróttning's dragons attacked.

It is a happy apostasy. The blue dragon played his part well. Although I suspect his draikana knew.

And kept it even from Dani?

Perhaps she is as resilient as she claims, Astarot muses, *but losing a drake or draikana is a ruinous wound. Still, she did not suffer long. She is a crafty beast. She may have realized all was not as it seemed.*

I watch him for a few moments, stunned by the depth of his perception. I shouldn't be, though. He's always been the smartest in our pairing, by far.

They come, he says as his snout lifts toward the sky.

And then I see them. Ziselær, Vulryn, and Tindera—all with their riders—lead the pack. And it's a massive pack. Dozens of dragons follow those three, some with riders and some without. I recognize a few. Gorm and Khanti soar next to Aquina and Sunni, close on our dragons' heels. But many, many more are strangers to me.

"Mikkael has quite a bit to tell me," I murmur, my lips twitching into a broad grin as I realize what this must mean. Ziselær went back into the Nest to gather support, and perhaps intelligence. When the time was right, he rallied his forces and followed the dragons the Dróttning sent to attack us. He even was able to take out Knut, the treasonous bastard.

These beasts have committed to a side. Ours.

Holy fuck. We might just win this after all.

Mikkael doesn't dismount right away, and I wonder if he wants to savor the joy of his first ride as a bonded pair a little longer. Despite the devastation to a town I know he's grown to love in a short time, he's happier, more relaxed than I've ever seen him. His shoulders are usually tight with the anger that's been boiling inside him since the fates gave him a mate and dragon who weren't yet ready to embrace him. Now, they're loose as he leans forward and digs his hands into Ziselær's feathers, scratching *his* dragon. His smile is bright, drawing out the crinkles around his eyes that he doesn't share nearly enough.

Ziselær's different too. I never focused on it before, but when Matthias rode him, he always seemed tense, as if he was anticipating anger or punishment or disappointment from his asshole of a rider. He twitched, often moving his snout or tail, or shuffling in place. The occasional unexpected touch he received—rare, because most people stayed away from the massive beast—drew a flinch or shiver from him, as if he found the contact repugnant. It felt like he couldn't allow himself to relax, ever. Now, like his rider, he's calm, at peace.

Mikkael drops his head to Ziselær's neck, planting a kiss on his feathers, and then whispers something. The blue beast spins his head, eyes bright and wide, and dips his chin once. Extending a wing, he snorts before turning to look at his draikana. My friend gives his dragon another good scratch and turns to say something to Halla, who's been waiting patiently. She climbs onto his back, and he dismounts and kneels to drop her to the ground. And then he rises, turning to watch Dani climb down from Vulryn.

I breathe out a sigh of relief, because that look is charged with emotions I've been hoping to see between them. Smiles emerge on both of their faces as their eyes meet, and for a moment, they're still, perhaps enjoying the anticipation that must be filling them. Dani's face relaxes and her lips part, which seems to break the spell. Mikkael takes the first step, but then they're striding toward each other, and she's in his arms.

I turn toward Halla, loath to intrude on this moment, and walk to her, while Fhord does the same. *I have someone checking on Sagga*, he tells me through our bond as Ziselær and Vulryn rise into the sky to our side. My insides warm with the knowledge that he chose her. She's a strong, resilient beast, but I'm sure she needs her drake just as much as all dragons need the other pieces of their souls.

Astarot launches up next, followed by the rest of the dragons, but he leads them in a different direction, toward the nearby herd. I sense his caress as he goes, Tindera at his side, and I wrap my arms around Halla, letting my relief that she's safe fill me. She hugs back but seems much less troubled than me, as if she knew all along that Mikkael would protect her. I wish I had her faith that everything would be okay. I hope she's able to keep it, in spite of the challenges she'll face sooner than I'd like.

"Fhord has someone checking on your mama," I tell her as I give her a good squeeze. "But I think she's okay. She's very hard to kill."

"She is," Halla assures me, stepping back and resting her hands on my cheeks. "I can feel her heartbeat, right here," she says as she places one hand in the center of her chest, the other dropping to her side. "We'll go to her soon."

"Very soon," I agree, standing to lean into Fhord, drawing him toward me as I luxuriate in his scent.

We'll also grieve soon, and figure out if we can rebuild or will need to abandon Lumaria to find someplace else to hide from the Dróttning. Right now, though, we can let ourselves savor this moment. We've been joined by dragons and some riders who abandoned everything they know to support our cause. They threw themselves into the fray, and our chances of destroying the Dróttning are exponentially better because of them. I have more hope than I've had in a long time.

Mikkael and Dani stride toward us, hand in hand, like it's the most natural thing in the world. I'm dying to ask them about this change in their relationship, but I hold back. That's their secret to share, or not. For now, I'll focus on the bigger picture. "Astarot tells me you have quite the story to share," I announce. "We can't wait to hear it."

He nods, a grin splitting his cheeks as he looks toward the blue and copper beasts spinning around each other in the distance. "He knew when he went back to the Nest that we belonged together," Mikkael relays in a tone filled with awe, "but couldn't do anything about it then. He risked exposing us if he refused. So he went and realized while he was there that he could help. He started gathering allies, learning as he did that every beast who's committed to our cause had already given up the slop. They were starting to break her grip over them. He pretended to eat it too, and he was already ahead of the others because he'd been away from the Nest for so long."

"And thank the gods," Fhord interjects, squeezing my hand. "We'd have been fucked if they hadn't come when they did."

"But why attack Vulryn in the cave?" I ask. That's the part that doesn't make any sense, even now. "It sounds like the battle was fierce, vicious."

Dani answers this question, glancing at Mikkael as one side of her lips tips up quickly. "He had no choice if he wanted to keep up his ruse, but his heart wasn't in it," she says. "I think Vulryn realized that as they fought. They were brutal at first, and I was sure one of them would die. But once I got dragged into the fight with the riders, I couldn't watch them. Vulryn felt Z draw back, and he left as soon as the other dragon did, rather than stay and fight."

"He was playing his part," Fhord mutters, his head cocking to one side.

"He was," Mikkael concurs. "He knows a lot about Knut and sensed even more when that bastard opened his thoughts to Z. He realized the link would give him access to information we'd need, but that he'd be able to protect himself—resist a true bond—without the slop's hold on him. He'd heard rumors by then about the Dróttning's plans, so pretended to accept the asshole as a rider."

"Knut was always gathering information that might help him scrape his way up," Fhord spits out, his voice low and angry. "He was smart, too. If he even suspected Ziselær was still loyal to you, he'd have demanded your death."

Mikkael nods, another little smile playing at his lips as he looks up again toward the distant dragons. "Z couldn't risk speaking with me. Their bond was new enough to be unpredictable and Knut might have heard it. He also assumed the Dróttning was paying more attention to him than normal. She might have been able to listen in at the wrong time, if there's still enough slop in his system for her to hear his words."

"He'd have given up his cover," Fhord agrees, "and we'd have lost Lumaria completely."

Now, Mikkael turns back to Fhord, no hint of the animosity that used to ripple between them. They're not friends yet, but maybe they will be.

"Z says the Dróttning's wanted this island for a long time," Mikkael says, "to destroy it, but mostly to deny you this refuge. She got the opportunity she's been looking for with Halla. She decided to take a chance and let you rescue her, but give you something she could follow. She'd send enough dragons to get Halla back and destroy your sanctuary in the process."

"Beron helping us was a ruse?" Fhord snarls these words, his hatred for the Konungr turning his voice brittle and cold. "No wonder I despise that fucker."

"But we were careful. Fhord didn't trust him. We only brought back Halla." A shiver runs down my spine as Mikkael's words dig into my skin. What if we did this? Are we responsible for all these deaths? My stomach twists at the thought, vomit pushing its way into my throat.

"Nothing else?" Mikkael's eyebrows push together, one of his hands rising to dig into his long hair, pulling a few strands out of the strap that ties it back.

Fhord draws my attention back to him as gentle fingers reach out to touch the necklace at my throat, Beron's "gift" to protect me from the medallion's pain. And I feel my heart sink. With hands that have started to tremble—a weakness this strong male at my side *never* shows—he unclasps it. The bile in my gullet rises even higher, threatening to spew to the ground below.

I turn to look at him and feel his heartbreak in my soul. His gaze is on me, but his eyes are vacant, unfocused. He's smaller than I've ever seen him, chest caved in and shoulders rounded. "We did this," he whispers, each word broken.

"I'm so fucking sorry, Fhord. I had no idea." I don't try to keep the grief out of my voice.

"This is all on me," he insists. "I know the bastard. I *know* not to trust him. I should have seen through him, realized he'd never betray the Dróttning. I don't know what the fuck I was thinking. I just wanted to protect you." His finger reaches out to catch the tear that's rolling down my cheek, then tucks a strand of hair behind my ear. "I did this," he says, his own eyes filling with evidence of his grief.

The silence that follows Fhord's words is heavy, almost suffocating. It feels like the air was sucked from the space around us, leaving everyone bereft and empty. When Mikkael speaks again, his voice is low, full of the pain that's weighing all of us down.

"I know it's little comfort after all you've lost, but this attack is what drew these dragons and riders to your side. They know that this place—these people—are key to defeating the Dróttning. And that they matter to you. I don't know if Z would have been able to gather this force otherwise."

Fhord looks up, his gaze scanning the assembled riders, dipping his chin and giving a sad smile to the many he knows. "Thank you for coming," he tells them. "You've helped save a place and people that mean more to me than I can say. All our supplies and plans are here, not to mention the elves who've spent years exploring their magic and honing their skills. If they'd been killed, we'd have no hope of destroying the bitch who's been controlling the lives of us and our beasts far too long."

"She'll need some time to regroup," I add as my thumb caresses the back of his hand and my free hand reaches for Halla. "It'll give us a chance to do the same, figure out where we go from here. For now, let's see how bad it is, then start planning our next attack."

Lumaria lost lots of buildings, but more importantly, the Dróttning's dragons killed many, many people. When we reach the outskirts of town, we see the dead being gathered and join the procession of wagons carrying them toward the city center. They're covered so we can't see their injuries, but from the size and shape of the bodies, we know that men and women, children, even infants, took their journeys to Valhalla today.

The dragons were ruthless, incinerating everything in their path. Half the city is destroyed, and its leaders are just starting to figure out what can be salvaged and what can't. Fhord releases my hand and strides toward Birger and a small group of his advisors while I stand on the outskirts and try to get control over the rage and grief and hopelessness that are battling for dominance within me.

"Have you told him?" Njörðr's voice draws me out of my stupor, and I feel my eyebrow cock as I look at him in confusion. "Have you told him about Freyr and Freyja?" he continues. "He knows his mother is my mate. Does he realize he has siblings in our worlds?"

"I haven't told him. The attack interrupted us before I could. But ... why does it matter right now?" This seems like it should be the last thing on our minds. I'm not sure why Njörðr tracked me down to ask this question.

"It's time to attack her," he says in a low voice. His jaw is tight, brow furrowed. I've known Njörðr long enough to recognize his resolve in whatever he's about to propose. "All the pieces are in place. Your mate is connected to our worlds in exactly the way we need. The blue dragon has accepted his rider, the girl is ready to play the role the fates established for her, and her mate approaches. We can use these bonds to destroy Nerthus."

"I don't understand."

"Come," he mutters, taking my hand to drag me toward Fhord, Halla in tow. "I'll explain it to all of you."

Fhord gives me a tight smile when he sees us, reaching for me as soon as Njörðr releases his grip. "We have no time to waste," Njörðr announces as he captures everyone's attention. "The Dróttning is weaker than she's ever been with the loss of so many dragons. And you are stronger than ever, now that all the bonds have been embraced. We have everything we need to defeat her."

"How can this be the right time?" Birger demands as he waves his arm toward the devastation. "We are sitting ducks. She could attack again at any time."

"No, she couldn't," Fhord murmurs, his gaze fixed firmly on Njörðr, who nods his agreement. "We've ripped a hole in the Dróttning's most stalwart and dangerous fighting force. Even with the loss of Tindera and Astarot, she couldn't have expected this many beasts to defy her. She wouldn't have thought it possible with the control she's always had over them. That must be why she accepted Ziselær without hesitation. His return convinced her that her chains on the dragons held strong."

He turns toward me, his smile vicious this time. "She has no contingency plans. She'll need to test every dragon's allegiance before she moves again. Now's the perfect time."

"But even with all these dragons, we're no match against her army." This is from one of Birger's advisors—the older female, Girta—her words sharp. "If we gathered all the rebels together, we'd still have only a fraction of the people she does."

"That, my dear, is where you're wrong," Njörðr declares with a broad grin. "Fhord is her weakness and our strength."

"I'm just one male," Fhord grunts in an exasperated tone. "I can only do so much."

"It is your blood that will give us what we need," Njörðr explains as everyone stares at him with flustered expressions. "Do you know our history?" he asks after a moment. "Has your mate told you about our home and your family in our worlds?"

Fhord's eyebrow cocks up, one side of his lips dipping down. "She hasn't," he responds, a question in his tone. "And I have no family, other than the bitch of a mother the gods gave me."

"You are so much more than you realize," Njörðr says. He stands straighter, throwing his shoulders back as he lifts his chin. After a quick grin toward me, he turns back to my mate. "Nerthus and I are two of the pantheon known in our worlds as the Norse gods, and you are a member of that group. You have siblings—Freyr and Freyja, the Norse god and goddess of love—and they are powerful beings."

He pauses, for emphasis I think, as his gaze spins around the circle of onlookers, catching each eye. When he looks at Fhord again—whose confusion ripples through me—I can feel Njörðr's excitement about what he's going to tell us. "You, though, are more powerful than all of them, and even more than Nerthus, because you are half elf. You were born of a female who'd consumed Yggdrasil's fruit *and* the water of its root, and you have bathed in and drunk those waters for your entire life."

Now, Njörðr looks at me, his smile somehow growing broader. "You are mated to an elf with strong ties to that world," he says before turning back toward Fhord. "You ride the dragon the fates chose for you. All the other bonds are in place but one," he adds with the briefest peek at Halla before his gaze finds Fhord again. "Because of your connections to our home, we can use your blood to force open the portal to our worlds that was fractured during Ragnarök."

Now, Njörðr flings out his arms, capturing everyone in the spell he's weaving. "We will pull home the elves who belong in this world and with them, end Nerthus's reign here forever. They wait in Helheim for our call. It is time to call them."

Chapter Twenty-Six

Mikkael

You Knew?

I WANT TO GET Dani alone.

A huge part of me is devastated about Lumaria—and I'll grieve about the destruction very soon—but the rush of joy from bonding with my dragon and standing here with my mate has shoved aside every other emotion. I embrace it because I know I'll never feel anything like this again. And because I don't have a choice. I couldn't ignore the calm and peace and pure fucking bliss that's rippling through me even if I wanted to.

I'm listening to Njörðr blather on about the paths between the worlds and bringing home a bunch of elves who disappeared centuries ago—blah, blah, blah—and that is some interesting shit. But at this moment, with my mate's hand in mine, I have exactly one thing on my mind. Well, maybe two, but one of them has captured every part of my body. Each cell, the blood racing through me, my pounding heart exist for this purpose alone.

I need to claim her. I've never needed anything more. The mating bond knows we've embraced it, that we've finally admitted to ourselves how desperately we crave each other, how empty our lives are without this connection. It can't snap into place, though, without this final thing. Our souls will fully connect when our bodies do. It's a greedy bitch pulsing inside me, and even though it feels more right—purer and truer than any other bond in my life except for Z's—it will writhe and thrash until Dani and I fuse it in this one primal way.

My mate and I need to talk too. I have to tell her I was wrong. That I should have admitted to myself—and to her, which matters a fuck of a lot more—that she's a part of me I'll never be able to live without. That I've changed. That I know what a gods-damned bastard I've been.

But holy Helheim do I need to fuck her first. I'll give her the words after I tell her with my tongue, and my hands, and the cock that hasn't relaxed since our dragons started flying toward this field together. It may never be soft again, always ready, at my mate's beck and call.

My mate. A burst of warmth ignites within me to spill through my limbs as I let the term tumble through my thoughts. Even with the bond pulsating within me, I'm at peace for the first time in my life.

I turn toward her, letting her feel everything I am, and she smirks and steps in front of me, wrapping my arms around her waist as she settles her perfect ass right against my throbbing cock. *Should I tell you what I'm going to do to you when we finally can be alone?*

If she didn't turn and wink at me as the question dropped into my mind, I'd be sure the mating bond took over and sunk me into a fantasy deep enough to conjure her voice. But she's an elf who knows how to do this shit. And Sifa told me she and Fhord can communicate in their minds while they're in Lumaria. Maybe Dani and I already are close enough to do that too.

For a moment, I'm not sure if I can respond. But then the memory of the dead king in the forest pops into my thoughts, and I realize I have all the knowledge I need. *Fuck, yes*, I rumble, hoping my voice tells her how desperate I am for exactly that. *What are you going to do to me, my spicy, sultry spy.*

What am I not going to do to you? she purrs. Drawing me close enough that I think I could come from just this contact, she says, *I'm going to taste every inch of you, exploring with my tongue as I find each place you like to be licked. I'll start inside your thighs, since I know that's where you want to see me, move up oh-so-slowly to your hip bone, drag my tongue along your stomach and chest, and then nibble my way from your collarbone to your ears.*

I hold back the plea that tries to shove its way out, because these people do not want to hear my need for this female in my arms. I'm stiff, but I'm gonna be a fucking stone before she's done.

You'll want to reach for my tits—don't think I haven't seen you watching them, she adds with a smirk, *but when I claim that glorious body of yours, you're not allowed to touch mine. Not yet, at least.*

Wicked female, I grunt, my thoughts now fully focused on the image she's painting for me. *Why would you deprive me?*

Because this is all about you, she tells me with another nudge of her ass into my desperate cock. *But don't worry. I'll let you caress me when I'm done with you.*

I can't hold back the snarl. A few surprised glances look our way, but I also can't bring myself to give a single fuck. They'd understand if they had this utterly irresistible female in their arms. *My sinful spy*, I rasp. *You'll be the death of me, but I will die so fucking happy. And so gods-damned hard for you.*

I'm just getting started, she hums, moving her palms down to rest against my thighs and then drift up far enough to send a twitch rolling through my cock. *I'll work my way back down to where you really need me—and where I'm desperate to spend some time. I'll start by running my tongue over your tip, tasting that little drip of desire I know will be waiting there for me, then licking up and down the veins on that long, thick shaft.*

Fuck. Me. I try my damnedest to stifle the growl that surges from my gut—or maybe my groin, the demanding bastard—but still get a few raised eyebrows and smirks. If I had a fuck to give, I'd apologize, but again, I cannot find even one fuck inside me to give.

Oh, I will, she promises with a squeeze before she starts to move her hands slowly along my inner thighs. *But not yet. I'll go slow. Ease you into it. I'll be on my knees and I'll let you stroke my hair, dig your hands in so you can take some control, see how deep I can take you, while I savor my mate, wrapping my lips around your dick as you plunge into my throat.*

I thought I was hard before. Nope. Now I'm a steel rod, a diamond forged deep in the soul of this scrumptious female. And I can't help myself. My palm lifts to rest on my bulge for a moment before squeezing it just a bit. We're in the midst of a large group of people, but I don't think they give a shit. Anyone I care about knows what this mating bond has been doing to me. *What next?* I groan, my hand gripping my cock again.

I'll spend some time there, she assures me. *I'm going to suck you until you're almost ready to come and then I'll push you back onto the bed and fuck you until you do.*

I can't hold back my laugh as Dani turns her sultry eyes toward me. *You're as turned on as me, aren't you?*

I want to take it slow, but once I have you in my mouth, I don't think I'll be able to wait long to feel you inside me. She shudders out a breath and looks back at the others, growing quiet. I let the image she's painted for me dominate my thoughts, not yet willing to give in and listen to Njörðr and the others plan the attack that could take her from me.

A cry from above us draws our gaze, and Dani and I look up together to see our dragons dancing in the sky. She leans farther into me as her mood shifts, growing serious. *I was so relieved when I realized Vulryn didn't feel like she'd been rejected*, she says in a pensive tone. *That she suspected Ziselær was playing a role but had already committed to us.*

I'm still lost in the fantasy she spun, but then her words trickle through me like a cold rain as I understand what she just said. *You knew? After Z left, before you laid down with me that night—before you said the things you did—you realized Z may have already chosen me as a rider?*

Not for sure, she explains, lifting her shoulders in a light shrug. *Vulryn didn't say anything. But she didn't feel heart-broken, and even her anger seemed manufactured. I started thinking about what had happened, how little damage their fight did to either of them, how he left right after the other dragon. It was so tough to believe Ziselær would reject Vulryn. It just made sense.*

Why didn't she tell you? Or you tell me? I rasp, my voice warbling with the ache that erupts inside me at her words.

Dani spins her head to look at me, her brows drawing together as her lips droop. Eyes that had been blown wide with lust a few minutes ago now are cloudy. *Neither of us was sure. I wouldn't get your hopes up like that on such a thin reed. And I think she felt like she needed to protect him, if he was playing a role. She couldn't risk it getting back to the Dróttning, if there's another traitor hiding somewhere in Lumaria, so didn't tell anyone.*

The joy that felt impenetrable disappears, my shoulders collapsing, suddenly too heavy to hold up. Dani chose Z's rider after all. She's happy, or maybe just relieved, that it's me, but she didn't really choose me.

I shouldn't care. The end result is the same, and we can all live happier ever after now. If we survive.

But the boy inside me who's been desperate for love since he landed in this gods-forsaken place needed my mate to choose me, for me. It's ridiculous—I know it's fucking ridiculous—but I also know I need something I'll never have and I have no gods damned idea what the fuck to do about it.

What's wrong? she asks, holding my arms on her stomach again as she undoubtedly senses the change in my mood. I don't try to hide it.

"Right, Mikkael?" someone asks, yanking my focus back toward the conversation happening around us.

"Fuck, sorry. I didn't hear what you said," I mutter as I glance up, looking for whoever saved me from answering Dani's question.

Birger smiles, and I wonder if he's perceptive enough to see that I needed a distraction. Or maybe it was obvious from my expression because I sure as fuck don't try to hide that, either. "Ziselær said something to Tindera and Astarot about others in the Nest who will continue as our eyes and ears. Is that right?"

I cast my eyes up, plunging through the bond to my dragon. *Did you tell Tindera and Astarot that other allies remain in the Nest and will help when they're needed?*

Sad? He ignores my question for now, worried about the devastation that consumed me a moment ago.

Let's talk about it later, I urge. I don't really want to think about this and should get my shit together and participate in planning the most dangerous thing any of us will ever do.

He's quiet for a few seconds, as if he's not ready to let go, but then I feel his assent. *Friends*, he confirms, the word arriving in my thoughts with all the nuance I need to answer.

I give Birger a quick smile and nod. "Z says we have friends still hidden wherever we need, including at the prisons. If we call them, they'll do what they can, even if it means revealing themselves or risking their lives."

"We hope it won't come to that, but it's good to know." Birger's responding smile is full of sympathy—or maybe pity. It turns my stomach a bit, and I'm suddenly anxious to get in the air and away from this island.

"The dragons will carry as many as they can," Fhord adds. "Everyone else can stay here and rebuild our home."

"We're rebuilding?" I probably should have bitten my tongue since they must have talked about this while I was lost in the nirvana Dani was spinning for me, but I'm too fucking surprised to do that.

Sifa responds with a smile that tells me she knows exactly where I was when I should have been listening. "We won't cede this place to her," she declares, her voice ringing in the air around us. "Here and everywhere across Vanatia, if we care about it, we will claim it, hold it to our hearts, and fight to our last breaths to keep it. The time is now. The struggle is here. The days are ours. We take the battle to her, and we don't let her rest until we finally condemn her putrid soul to Helheim and toss her rotting body in the ground."

I nod, my dour mood giving way to the *need* to throw myself into this conflict. I still haven't avenged Johan. Like Sifa said, the time is now. "When do we leave?" I ask, not trying to hide my grin at the thought of a long flight on my dragon.

"Today, this hour if we can," Njörðr responds. "The sooner we attack, the better our chances. We go straight to a place Fhord knows near the largest elven camp. Tomorrow, we free the elves."

"I thought we were going to try to bring some elves back from Helheim first," Dani points out, her spine stiffening a bit. "When does that happen?"

Njörðr's eyebrow cocks up, a playfulness in his expression I didn't expect. "While we're freeing the elves the Dróttning has trapped," he says with a smirk.

"What the fuck?" I bark, because that sounds like a very bad fucking idea. "I thought we needed their help to defeat the Dróttning. How can a ragtag band of rebels hope to invade a place that's more impenetrable than the Dróttning's steel trap of a heart?"

"You shall see, dragon rider," Njörðr proclaims like he's a gods-damned soothsayer. "The power we will harness and unleash there will be unlike anything seen before in this land—even the fabricated magic borne by my deviant mate and her latest toy. All the pieces are in place. It is time to play the game."

I shake my head, nothing else to say. This may be a gods-damned game to him, but it sure as fuck isn't to me. My dragon and I just found our way to each other, and I need to figure out my shit with Dani before I let death take me. But Sifa knows him—she trusts him—and there's no way I'll miss this. It may be my best chance to avenge Johan. I'm going, and

I hope to all the gods above and below that Njörðr knows what he's doing.

Life, Z tells me with a reassuring caress through our bond as I shove aside my insecurities for now, squeeze Dani, kiss her on her temple, and stride with her toward our dragons. Z and I have a long life to live together. We won't let it end so soon.

Fuck, it feels good to talk to him. The funk that wrapped around me while I stood with Dani dissipates, the warmth and glow of my dragon's love burning through it. There's so much I want to say, even more I want to know, and I wonder if he feels the same. *I didn't think we'd ever have this,* I tell him as I give Dani a quick kiss and climb aboard my dragon.

Be safe, Mik, she tells me as she catches my gaze from atop Vulryn. *Don't you fucking die before I have my way with you,* she adds with a smirk.

I wouldn't dare, I drawl with a wink. *This body won't be able to rest, even in death, until it claims yours.*

Promises, promises, she purrs. And then she blows me a kiss and pats her dragon, who launches into the sky.

Z and I watch them for a few seconds before he flings himself up to follow. We've flown for a minute or so when he speaks to me again. *Inevitable.* My dragon's still thinking about my words before we left Lumaria—that I doubted I ever would ride him. He knows now that we couldn't have escaped this, much as he tried. Like with Dani, it's the bond, but it's so much more than that. The bond reveals and strengthens something that existed when we both were born. Our perfect match was out there. We just needed to find each other.

You were so tightly fettered to Matthias, I remind him, the memories of his commitment to the usurper, all the emotions their connection inspired, bouncing in my thoughts. *After so many years together, everything he meant to you, I didn't think you could ever want me enough to sever that bond.*

Inevitable, he says again, this time with a slightly different meaning. He realized as we hid in the cave, Z alone standing between us and capture, that he couldn't subject me or Vulryn to the Dróttning's brutality. Once he allowed a thread to form between us, he was bound to me. It's why he couldn't kill me, despite that bastard's demands. More importantly, he recognized how much trauma he'd endured. The years of abuse by Matthias crystalized into an awareness—for the first time in his life—that he deserves a better life.

That he deserves his draikana and me.

It kills me to know what you suffered, I tell my dragon, letting him sense the heartbreak that fills me whenever I think about the wing tips that bastard sawed off, how much pain Z must have suffered in the century they spent together. *I wish I could take every bit of pain he inflicted on you and make it my own. Or better yet, torture that fucker the way he tortured you.*

Z's quiet for a long time, a mix of emotions rippling through our bond. Finally, he voices his thoughts. *Torn*, he tells me in a ragged tone. Z's love for Matthias hasn't disappeared. Matthias was cruel, inflicting pain on Z to satisfy his own needs, but never his dragon's. But he also could be kind, and they had some good days. Z didn't hate all of it. He's conflicted about the male who rode him for a hundred years and still feels tremendous guilt for killing him, even if he knows now he made the right choice.

What you did isn't your fault, I snarl, making sure he feels the conviction that has my heart racing, every bit of me pulsating with the need to rip this guilt from him. *That bitch did this. She has fucked up this world for too many years, playing god as she rips apart the fates' plans, twisting the bonds she was never worthy of earning for herself.* I pause, resolve growing inside me.

We have a role to play, I tell him. *I have no gods-damned idea what we're supposed to do or how we're gonna do it, but I know we're here, we're together and joining this battle for a reason. And there's nobody I'd rather fight with than you. Everything we've been through, all the doubts and questions and suspicions, have brought us here, with these beasts and their riders. We can win this. We will win this.*

Z doesn't respond right away, his emotions shifting from the friction that fills him when he talks about the fucker that used to ride him to a peace I don't think I've ever felt from my tormented dragon. Finally, a single word fills his thoughts, no explanation needed.

Fate.

Fuck yes, I growl. Because he's right.

Everyone gathered together, every bond between us, each piece of this puzzle falling into place, is fated.

And I have to believe the fates aren't gonna fuck us this time around.

That the moment has come for all of us to fight for what we need.

A chance—a single chance—to build a life worth living.

Chapter Twenty-Seven

Fhord

I Always Will Be

Tindera carried four riders. And not just any riders. She carried four large men and all their weapons. It was a shitload of weapons, too.

Every dragon carried a heavy load. We spent the time we needed to figure out who could fight and brought them with us, leaving just enough people behind to defend Lumaria while the survivors retreat to the underground caves in case the island is attacked again. They'll get the tunnels stocked within the next day. I can't imagine the Dróttning would waste her dragons' time because she'll know we wouldn't stay after that attack, but I won't risk more lives. Too many have died already.

Not as many as I feared, thank fuck. The city turned out to be the safest place on the island, and it took me a minute to figure out why. The Dróttning sent them for Halla and wants her alive. The dragons didn't know where they'd find her, so they couldn't burn indiscriminately. No young girls died. Everyone my people carried in from the farms and ranches was male or older. In the city, the beasts couldn't risk accidentally killing Halla, so they torched buildings, giving people time to escape as they pushed them into the open.

Ziselær and the others arrived and forced them to retreat before they had free rein to kill everyone in sight.

It could have been so much worse. Bringing Halla here exposed her to danger—and thank fuck Mikkael kept her safe—but it also prevented the Dróttning from destroying everyone and everything on the island.

The gods must have decided to step back and let fate run our lives today. And thank fuck for that, too.

We're huddled in a massive cave about twenty vikus from the large elven prison, trying to rest. It's barely big enough for all of us. Fifty-two dragons joined our cause, each giving Sifa access to their minds to confirm their allegiance. She's doing that now while Dani and I give her as much of our power as she needs to get through it. We'll rest tonight and make sure we're ready to fight tomorrow, but this is important. We won't risk welcoming a traitor into our midst.

I can't keep my gaze away from my mate. She's the strongest person I've ever known, and I find myself constantly in awe of her. Despite being ripped from her home and everything she's suffered at the Dróttning's hands, she is a bright spot in the gloomy days of each person who crosses her path. She sees the good in everyone—even that pissy bastard Mikkael, who somehow is growing on me—and knows what to say to bring out the best in all of them. And for reasons I can't understand, she seems to think I'm worthy of her.

I will never be worthy of my little rabbit, but I sure as fuck will spend my life trying to be.

As if she senses my gaze, she looks up from the dragon she just examined, finding me across the cavern. She smiles, and my cock twitches at the same time as my heart. They both exist for her. They don't deserve her either, but she treasures them like they're the most precious things in this world other than her dragon.

My savage and I are lucky bastards.

Everything about her feels lighter now, a weight she's been carrying for a decade lifting with Njörðr's presence and the information he shared. We've talked about it some but I don't need her words to understand. Sifa can stay with us forever, live the long life she should have as an elf. The water will give her what she lost when she left her worlds and the tree that sustained her there. And she learned the fate of the male and female who have loved her like their own child since she lost her parents—my half-brother and sister, of all things. It warms me inside to know my rabbit and I have been connected for centuries, without even realizing it.

Holy fuck, do I wish I could take her someplace private and show her how grateful I am to have her love. There is no private place, though. This cavern is big enough for the dragons and the two hundred people they carried, but it doesn't have a single arm or even a short tunnel. We're all here together, and after the fuck-fest Dani and Mikkael shared with us on Lumaria, we'd be run out of the cave if we tried that shit. Their grunts and moans were so loud, you'd think they were actually having sex, not just using their strengthening mate bond to chase some fantasy as they stood fully clothed in our gods-damned midst.

So it's blue balls until we get to our next stop. I've got something to fight for, beyond fucking with my bitch of a mother as much as I possibly can.

It takes Sifa more than four hours to finish. Four exhausting hours. She nearly collapses as she draws away from the last dragon, but I'm there to catch her. I always will be. She responds with a groggy smile as I tug her into my chest and is asleep by the time I cross the cavern to settle her into our blankets. I climb in behind her, wrapping my body around hers, and I'm out almost as quickly.

The noise drags me out of a heavy sleep. Sifa's still in my arms, and I don't think either of us moved last night. I should get up and join the others in getting us ready to go, but I can't bring myself to disturb my exhausted mate.

Okay, that's not the reason.

I can't bring myself to leave her. My demanding cock needs to stay right where it is, tucked against her delectable ass, as long as possible. The intractable savage inside me craves this physical contact with our mate, which will steady and calm us before the most dangerous day of our lives. My pounding heart won't beat the same once she leaves my arms and refuses to squander any of our time together.

Everything else can wait. It'll be dawn soon. I'll drag my ass up when the sun's rays find us.

Before that happens, though, Sifa stretches. And my fucking cock jerks, joining with my savage to demand that I strip her underwear down and take her now. I ignore both of them. We'll have plenty of time with our little rabbit after we liberate the elves. We have work to do first.

"This feels so fucking good," Sifa murmurs, linking our fingers together. "I wish we could stay here forever."

"I'd give anything to be inside you right now," I groan. "Well, anything except the fight we're about to take to that bitch. We've been waiting for this day for too long to miss it."

"So gods-damned long," she agrees. She's quiet for a minute or more, before finally giving voice to the thoughts weighing her down. "I'm afraid," she whispers, drawing my arms more tightly around her. "We've lost Johan and Khirta and their deaths hurt, but I feel in my bones that something terrible is going to happen today. I don't know if it will be terrible for us or her, whether the worst is yet to come or the best. I don't know who will die today, but I'm so fucking scared it will be even worse than losing Johan and Khirta."

I inhale her lavender and rosemary scent, focusing on our hearts beating together, breaths rippling in and out of us at the same time. And I open myself to her, letting her feel my confidence and optimism, but most of all, my utter devotion to her. We don't move, our only motions completely synched, as we both drink in the touch of our mate.

Finally, she sucks in one last breath, holding it for a few seconds, and exhales slowly. "Thank you, Fhord. I needed that."

"Anything. Anytime. Anywhere. All that I have is yours. And tonight, every inch of me is yours. I can't wait to celebrate liberating the elves and bringing the Dróttning one step closer to her destruction."

"Today will be a good day," she tells me, her voice more confident now.

"A very good day," I declare. And then I stand and pull her up to stand with me. We stride over to the others, hand in hand, to make the final preparations for our battle.

Two hours later, we're plunging to a field a viku away from the prison in stages, the dragons all stalking into the surrounding forest as soon as their feet hit the ground. They drop the fighters with their weapons and lead the way through the trees. We want them free to fly as soon as I call for the charge. They'll maneuver better without anyone on their backs while we join the strike on the ground.

Our plan is simple. Brute force. The Dróttning will know we're attacking within seconds, so I've got nothing to hide. I'll rip the prison in two—through the barracks, not the cells—if that's what it takes to get us in. We'll kill everyone who fights for the Dróttning and free the prisoners, carrying those who can't walk to safety. At some point, Njörðr will take my blood to bring back the missing elves, but I'm not thinking about that. He'll let us know when the time is right. Whoever doesn't fit on a dragon will disappear into the trees with instructions on where they can go to find the refuges we've set up in the area.

The Dróttning's people aren't expecting this attack, unless someone betrayed us. Whatever they throw at us, though, won't stop our assault. This is the best shot we'll get at either prison. It's now or never.

It takes thirty minutes to get into position. We don't encounter any sentries, but we didn't expect to. The prison is well-guarded from within and bound by so much magic, it'll take Sifa and me to puncture it. Nobody else in this world, other than possibly Harald, would have a chance.

The prison is vast, at one time holding thousands of elves. Hundreds remain, every one of them imprisoned since the Downfall because the Dróttning hasn't allowed a single elf to be born in captivity. They've been kept apart, cells separating them except when they're allowed time in common areas with sentries watching every move, for each one of those years. The Dróttning has ordered the death of the very few females who managed to conceive. Not a single captive has seen sunlight since they entered this Helheim centuries ago.

The physical space hasn't gotten smaller, though. It's built into a mountain that, like the Nests, is riddled with a natural cave system. From the outside, it's nothing but a hole in the mountain, just like any other except for the dozens of soldiers standing guard. By the time I was born, the Dróttning had modified the caves to add cells, each of which then held ten or twelve elves instead of the two or three who occupy them now.

The captives have more space, but their conditions are much worse. Water that long ago ran clear and fresh now is polluted, the waste of so many years having nowhere else to go. Blankets are threadbare, replaced only when they've deteriorated completely. Wounds sometimes never heal, the bodies unable to harness the energy needed, although the injuries are incapable of killing the suffering elf. Each death in this Helheim came at the edge of a sword, usually years or more after the elf grew too weak to eat the meager meals provided.

Shaking my head, I focus on the task at hand. It all rests on me now. As it should. I'm her son, and I've done more than anyone else to help her hold the power she'd claimed by the time I was born. Too many people suffered by my sword or knife to maintain her grip on the necks of everyone across Vanatia. Too many victims lie deep in the ground—most in massive graves, their bones mingling together over the centuries—because I gave my power and strength to her. Too many mates, riders, drakes, and draikanas have been torn apart because I couldn't see past her thirst for power.

I don't deserve redemption, but I'm gonna claim it anyway. That's the only path to a life with my rabbit, and I won't let anything or anyone get between me and that life.

Sucking in a deep breath, I reach for Sifa's hand, squeezing it gently as my mind caresses hers, clinging to the love and support I find there. Digging deep in my gut, I grasp the magic that waits there, writhing in anticipation. It's always ready when I need it, waking from its rest—just as my savage does—when my adrenaline starts to flow.

And then I cast out my will.

Not much happens at first because I've started deep underground. I've been here enough on the Dróttning's errands—overseeing the torture of one elf or another—to know that when we attack, the guards will herd the prisoners into the tunnels and out of reach if I don't shut down those escape routes. My thoughts reach into the cave system, finding the handful passages they might use, and I squeeze them. When avalanches that I trigger rumble the ground around us, a bell rings deep within the prison.

That's our signal. The battle cry rings out and I truly get to work. Drawing in some of Sifa's power, I rip open the entrance, flinging my rocks at the waiting guards. My power and focus are fresh, so I kill them quickly, each boulder a direct hit. Einar's magic lashes toward me in response to my assault, and it would destroy a lesser being. Sifa and I should be writhing on the ground in agony, our attack abandoned as we search for breath.

We came prepared, though. We had an elf in Vanatia cloak those fucking medallions Beron gave us. He made sure they disappeared from the Dróttning's perception before we left Lumaria, probably convincing her I destroyed them or buried the bastards so deep, they'll never emerge again. She'll feel their power now that we've put them to use, but we're not hiding any more. The Dróttning would have learned of our attack within seconds of her soldiers ringing the bell anyway.

Beron's "gift" doomed us in Lumaria, but we've turned the fucking tables on him and the Dróttning. Sifa and I are untouchable. We left Dani and Halla in the cave, and Vulryn will get them when it's clear. My rabbit hated the idea of bringing Halla, but that fucking prophecy is as vague as they always are. If there's any chance we'll need the little girl here, we sure as fuck better be prepared.

The rest of the elves stayed in Lumaria. Everyone else is human, no elf magic for the medallions to manipulate. Well, almost everyone. That bloodthirsty troll and the cat are here too—Toffer sure as fuck wasn't going to miss this chance to take as many lives as his soft little heart desires—but the medallion won't affect them either. We've neutralized the prison's best defense.

Still, we're far from safe. The prison is close to the Nest so that dragons can defend it in the unlikely event someone is foolish enough to attack. They're not well-trained—the Dróttning has gotten sloppy, avoiding conflict through her cruelty for a long gods-damned time—but with their weapons, they don't need to be. And many have learned some of Vulryn's tricks.

Be safe, I cast out to my dragon, hovering with the others between here and the Nest, waiting for the assault.

Always, she responds, a hint of exasperation in her tone. She still isn't through the pains she's suffered because of her need for the slop—as Vulryn insists we call it—but she's better. And she wouldn't miss the fight for anything.

And then I turn to Sifa. "I'll see you on the other side," I mutter, leaning forward to take her lips. I spear my tongue into her mouth, needing to taste her again before we go. It's fucking hard to drag myself away, but I do.

"On the other side," she agrees with a smirk. And then we start running.

The guards haven't come out, but we didn't expect they would. After the pummeling I gave their friends, they wouldn't dare. When I ripped open the entrance, I destroyed the passage that they've relied on for centuries to stop anyone who tried to force their way in. It was brilliant—close to a dragon's length of rock, passable by only one or two people at a time, lined by holes just big enough for a pair of eyes and a sharp arrow. Nobody had ever entered without permission. Before us.

As soon as we step out of the sun, we're attacked. The next ten minutes or twenty or thirty—who the fuck knows?—is an all-out brawl. They're fighting for their lives and we're fighting for our freedom, so everyone is motivated as fuck to kill their opponent. I'm back-to-back with Sifa, and my heart jumps every time some asshole flings a blade in her direction.

I need to focus on the swords aiming at me, but I can't stop my eyes from searching for my little rabbit every time I lose track of her. Sifa doesn't give me one single reason to fear for her, though. She's vicious, centuries of training behind each thrust and swing. It'd take someone with a lot more skill than these lackeys to best her.

I, on the other hand, am not nearly focused enough. Three different times, she huffs a warning at me as one sword or another comes too close to something I don't want to lose. So I finally drag my thoughts away from my ferocious mate and fling myself into the scuffle. For now, I'm just using my blade and the occasional fist. We're packed too tightly together to start flinging stones around. The time for magic will come soon enough.

We'd been fighting longer than I expected when the Dróttning's soldiers throw themselves into the fray. The guards we've been brawling against are the first wave. Anyone who gets past them faces warriors. Now, I can't spare one bit of attention for my rabbit because these bastards are fucking skilled.

Four surround me as soon as one of the assholes sees who's attacking them and calls to his buddies. They're not stupid. If they can kill me, this assault will fall apart. And it's a gods-damned grind to stay alive. I'm spinning in place, struggling to avoid the weapons that are trying their damnedest to end me. My sword is everywhere, but it can't do shit except block. Whenever I see the smallest opening into one of the soldiers, someone else fills it and then shoves his fucking blade back at me.

My breath is rasping through my throat within a few minutes, every inch of flesh and stretch of muscle working to protect my body from the death these fuckers want to claim. Finally, just as I'm wondering whether I'm even gonna make it into the prison, one of them stumbles, falling toward me with his throat exposed. I block a blade aiming toward my own neck and slice his, then spin again because I can't spare even a second to make sure I managed to kill him.

Now, I've got a shot. I'm still defending against their thrusts and swipes, but I can fling my fucking sword at them, too. It's still a gods-damned grind because these bastards know how to fight, but it doesn't feel impossible. My savage is snarling at me, desperate to be unleashed, but I can't do that yet. I'm gonna need my hands and my voice, but he'll get his chance soon enough.

The second soldier's mistake drags a laugh from my parched throat. He changes hands with his sword, holding it backwards for a moment as he tries to plunge it into my side. Before he can, I twist and crash my blade against his, sending it flying to the ground. And I thrust, digging my blade into his unprotected gut. A fucking snort bursts from me as his eyes grow wide in shock, but I can't spare the time to watch him die.

I kill the last two quickly, taking one's head and the other's hands, before shoving my sword directly into his heart. And then I lean over, hands on my knees, and fucking breathe. I don't know where my next attack is coming from, and I have to find my rabbit, but before I can move, I need to just fill my lungs, which are sucking in air like I've been trapped underwater for the last ten minutes instead of fighting for my life.

Sending out my thoughts, I find Tindera, relieved to confirm she's alive and winning her battle against some beast or another. When I can finally stand up and look around, I realize we've done it. I see a handful of fights, but our people don't need help. They'll take down the last few soldiers soon enough.

And then I find Sifa, and my heart finally unclenches. She's smiling as she fights the bastard who captured her all those weeks ago. Asshole rejected my command to stand down while I saved Astarot's life and took her to the Dróttning to be tortured. Fate has given my rabbit a gift, offering up this fucker's life, and she's taking what's hers.

Sifa's covered in blood, her brilliant eyes dancing, and she's never been more beautiful. When she sees me watching, she tosses a smirk my way and puts the asshole out of his misery, dropping to her knees to shove her sword up, through his balls straight to his neck.

I almost drop to my knees, because holy fuck, that was the sexiest thing I've ever seen. And I'm the luckiest bastard in any of the worlds, hers or mine.

The pain erupts from nowhere, every part of my body exploding in flame, and I collapse, unable to hold myself up. This isn't the torture Einar created, a twisting of his victims' muscles as he took control of their bodies and wrenched them. I'll never forget the mind-numbing agony from the medallions he created for the Dróttning.

This is somehow so much worse, as if every cell, each span of bone and hunk of flesh, has burst into flame, a conflagration that will eat me alive. And there's not a single gods-damned thing I can do to fight back. Even if I knew what the fuck was attacking me, my mind is chaos, its only focus escaping this agony.

I manage to spin my head and find Sifa, but she's not looking at me. Her gaze is fixed on a male standing a dragon's-length away from us, a wicked smile on his face. "Jonathan?" she croaks, confusion managing to shove aside the agony for a moment. "You're Jarl?"

I twist to look again at the male, my heart splitting in two as understanding washes through me. This is the bastard who captured and was torturing Sifa in Midgard before she got dragged here. He's got her again and I can't find the strength or power I need to protect her. My body turns cold, ice joining the fire in my veins, as I'm buried under a hopelessness so deep, I'll never be able to dig my way out.

The fucker laughs, his ugly cackle breaking through the clamor around us as if it's aimed directly at my rabbit and me. And then he takes one step forward, staring at her alone. "I've been waiting years to get you back, elf," he hisses. "Fucking Loki and his useless spawn couldn't do it, so I'll do it myself." He pauses, his lecherous gaze roving over my rabbit. And my savage roars his devastation, his *fury*, that he's not strong enough to protect her. "You're worth it," the bastard crows. "You'll be in Midgard where you belong soon enough."

He looks at me for a moment, the fires cascading through me somehow flaring even hotter, and cocks his head. "I'll have fun killing this one before I go," he adds in a low tone. "You can watch," he continues as he turns back to Sifa. "Because you're mine, Sifa. You've always been mine, and I'm gonna enjoy destroying the bastard who thinks he can take you from me."

He steps forward again, his magic rippling out in waves to send everyone in this vast cavern crashing to their knees. My savage is keening inside me, the torture of this male's power crushing his magic as effectively as mine, our mind unable to harness even the minimal focus we need to shift.

If I wasn't already on the ground, I'd plummet to it now. My heart is bursting, pounding in my chest as every other part of me goes numb. My savage and I are trapped within this useless body, unable to even move toward the bastard who came here to take our rabbit. He's going to kill us and there's not a single fucking thing we can do to stop him.

CHAPTER TWENTY-EIGHT

MIKKAEL

PARTNERS

I GET IT NOW. My body is a gods-damned inferno and I finally understand what all the bitching about medallions has been about. These fuckers *hurt*. If I could move, I'd shove a blade into my heart, but I'm fighting just to breathe. There's no way in Helheim I'll find the strength to put myself out of my misery.

I'm grateful that this cocksucker probably will stroll soon through the pathetic group of losers cowering at his feet—trussed by his magic like gods-damned hogs—and eliminate us one-by-one. I don't know what the fuck we were thinking, believing we could beat the Dróttning. We deserve the death we're about to claim for being such stupid fucks.

Thank the gods Dani isn't here. She hasn't had nearly enough time with her dragon. At least she'll survive.

Fight! Z's voice drops into my thoughts and I cast out another thanks to the gods, this time because Z and I bonded before I die. I know they don't give a shit about me, but I gotta thank someone, and the fates seem to have fucked us this time. So the gods get my gratitude today. Bastards that they are.

This thing is burning the fight out of me, I pant to my dragon, glad I can cast my thoughts toward him because I wouldn't be able to open my mouth and form words if I tried. Even thinking at him almost takes more energy than I possess. But if I use my last inhale to respond to Z, it'll be well spent.

Dani's image spills into my thoughts and a wave of regret pushes aside the pain for a moment. I fucked up so badly with her, letting myself get sucked into childish fears that don't mean shit, and ignoring the sexy-as-fuck female the fates somehow decided to give me. *Tell Dani I'm sorry,* I mutter to Z, anger at myself taking the place of the guilt. *Tell her I know how gods-damned stupid I've been.*

No. His response is sharp and short, a single word without a hint of nuance. He's pissed at me or the situation—I can't tell which—and his petulant attitude cuts through the torture racking my body just enough to pull a guffaw up from my gut, sending it spurting through my lips.

No? I demand, a shaky laugh in my word. *Why the fuck not?*

Fight, is his answer, this time with the explanation I need. I'm human, or mostly human, but I have access to his power and I've never used it before. Whatever is happening to us isn't happening to our dragons. Plus, I might have some god essence in me, if Njörðr's right. Z thinks that quirk in our pairing—the blood of some ancient god in my veins, along with the high that will come the first time my dragon's magic infuses me—could give me what I need to escape whatever this bastard is throwing at us.

I could fight back. And I'm the only one here who might have a chance.

How in all the gods' names do I do that? I groan. Even if he's right, it won't matter if I can't access his magic.

Relax, he says, his tone so full of love and comfort, the pain wanes for a moment.

I try to do what my dragon says, struggling to drag my thoughts away from the fire consuming me. But I can't with that bastard holding a torch to every part of my body. And then I feel Z. His power seeps into me, a gentle tide that starts in my gut, rolling out and through my arteries before it stretches to my veins and then every little capillary that branches into my toes and fingers.

And fuck if the pain doesn't start to filter away everywhere his magic touches. My body craves it so desperately after being denied so long—through all the fears and disappointments and heartache we've both felt since we recognized each other's presence—that nothing else is strong enough to displace it.

Not even this douchebag's power.

I stand, throwing my shoulders back because there's no reason to hide from him. He'll know soon enough that I've escaped his grasp, and if he's gonna send an extra burst of his devilry at me, I want it to happen now, not when I'm in the middle of killing him. His head whips up, shock twisting his features. His eyes bulge out and I don't hold back the laugh. I've never before seen someone so fucking surprised that their eyeballs actually swell like gods-damned balloons. Then his jaw drops like he's craving my cock—not that I'd ever drop trou for this prick—but he's otherwise completely still.

I stride forward, ignoring everyone writhing around me because I do not need to be distracted by the agonized faces of the people I love. When I'm a dragon's-length away, he shakes himself out of his daze, a quiver rolling through his body as his eyes narrow. And then I feel his power spear at me. Something shifts in the cave, and I get the sense that he's less focused on everyone else as he tries to regain his hold on me.

Z's magic within me shivers, and I wonder if he can feel the pain that's intended for me. The strength he's giving me seems softer than before, like the initial rush is dissipating, so I start running, gripping the sword that somehow is still in my hand, even after this ratfuck's attack. If I've got a time limit, I'm sure as all Helheim not gonna waste a single second walking.

He pulls a blade from a scabbard at his waist when I halve the distance between us, but I can tell already that he's not a swordsman. His hold is too tight, stance too rigid. His magic has been all he's ever needed. He may have gotten the basics—although I suspect nobody even taught him that—but he's probably never had to fight for his life.

His power, though … that's some impressive shit. The closer I get, the stronger its push. Somewhere inside me, I can feel Z fighting to hold his magic in place, waging a battle with this shitgibbon I can't even comprehend.

As soon as he's close enough, I swing my blade, aiming for his neck.

And then he really attacks. I'm vaguely aware of the movement and sounds in the cave behind me, a wave of relief washing through everyone. Because he's abandoned his hold on them to focus every ounce of his sorcery on me. Even my rock-solid dragon can't stand against this assault. The bastard's torture pushes back into me, my beast's magic strong enough to provide some relief, but not capable of fully protecting me.

Despite the agony, the hole in my gut fills, just a bit, when I realize I can move. The pain isn't debilitating like before. I *want* to lie down and cry like a baby but I don't *have* to. I should be able to push through this shit and kill this cunt, once and for all. So that's what I'm gonna do.

When he sees me take another step toward him—eyes bulging for a second time, to my delight—he shifts his magic again. A collective gasp fills the space behind me, and I hear a fuckton of people collapse to the ground. Tightening his grip on his sword, he snarls at me. And I laugh. This buffoon has one trick and without it, he's a useless piece of shit.

I swing at the dickhead's throat, and this time, he doesn't raise his sword in time to stop me. The moment slows as I watch my blade slice through his neck, dislodging his head, which topples to the side before his body catches up. For a split-second, he looks like a fucking zombie, body alone standing there as if it might amble off into the caves. Then it crumples to the ground and the seconds start to roll along just like they're supposed to.

Z's relief washes through me. He's still in the sky above us, fighting against one of the Dróttning's beasts—somehow holding his ground against the dead fuck's impossibly strong magic while he survived a fight for his life—and I'm overcome with awe at my dragon's strength. *Thank you, my glorious beast*, I rumble through our bond. *Every person in this cave owes you their life.*

Partners, he purrs at me. We did it together. For the rest of our lives, we'll do everything together.

Partners, I echo. *Now destroy the beasts who still fight for that wyrm while we finish down here.*

He grumbles his assent, still hating the fact he has to fight dragons he's considered family for a long time, even if he knows they're enemies now. That bitch has given us no choice but to destroy everyone and everything that stands by her side.

Sifa's touch on my arm drags me from my macabre thoughts, and I spin to grin at her. She throws her arms around me, tugging me into a fierce hug. "Thank fuck," she says as she releases me and steps back, her eyes bright. "Astarot told me what Z did, and he's gods-damned impressed with your dragon. He said the beast Z's fighting above us is vicious, but Z managed to give you what you needed anyway."

Fhord's hand lands on my shoulder before I can respond, and I turn to see something I never thought I'd see from the bastard. He's smiling like we're friends or something, giving me a look reserved for Sifa and his Ætt—and occasionally, Toffer and Thor. "Glad you were here, Mik," he tells me as he drops his hand from my shoulder and extends it in a peace offering.

"Fuck yes, you are," I declare as I take his hand in mine, pulling him into a half-hug. "Me and my dragon," I add as I release him and step back.

"You and your dragon," he agrees with a nod. "Ready to go free some elves?" he asks with a smirk.

"Nothing I'd rather do," I proclaim, extending my arm to wave him forward. "After you."

He dips his chin and strides forward, Sifa and me falling into position behind him as the rest of the fighters trail us. It looks like we've killed all the Dróttning's guards by now, or they're hiding somewhere, not willing to make some suicidal stand against the inevitable. The elves are ours, and everything's about to change.

Njörðr joins us behind Fhord, a smile playing at his lips as he reaches for Sifa's hand and walks by her side. He's here to do the impossible—open a portal between this world and Helheim and drag hundreds of missing elves back here. He thinks he'll take their place in Helheim and I have no idea why he wants to do that. But Njörðr's a gods-damned enigma, and I've decided not to question shit like this. Maybe he feels guilty that his mate is responsible for all the pain this world has suffered and this is his penance.

Whatever the reason, he's convinced we'll have the power we need to defeat the Dróttning if we free these elves and pull the rest of them where they belong. So that's what we're gonna do.

We're halfway through the prison—hundreds of shocked faces watching us like they think it's an elaborate trick—when

Fhord's muttered "Fuck" darts at us from down the corridor, just as Z seems to flinch in our bond.

What's going on? I probably don't keep the fear that's washing through me from my voice, but I think I'm right to be afraid. Whatever has both of them anxious must be bad.

Wyrm, Z tells me, his tone firm as he sets aside his worry to focus on what matters. Tindera, through Fhord, thinks the Dróttning shifted as soon as she felt Fhord's magic and started racing here. It's the only way she could have covered so much distance so quickly.

How close is she?

Close. A hint of fear sneaks back into this word because he's not sure how many of our allies will be able to resist her call. They've all stopped eating her slop, but some for longer than others. Nobody's tested when her control slips, so nobody knows who might turn against us when she's close enough to wield her full power against them.

Well, fuck me. This should be interesting.

"What do we do, Fhord?" I demand as I stride toward him. I know he said it's now or never, but he didn't expect that bitch to get back in time to stop us.

"We free the elves," he grunts at me, gesturing at a cell that hasn't been unlocked yet. "We'll deal with her when she gets here."

"We've done a lot," I remind him. "Shouldn't staying alive be at the top of our 'to-do' list for today?"

"I said we do this today or not at all and I fucking meant it." His voice is harsh, angry, and fuck if I don't believe him. "Free the gods-damned elves or get on your dragon and leave. Those are your choices."

"I guess I'll go free some fucking elves, then," I grouse, spinning to unlock the cell he gestured at, my heart picking up in my chest like a bloody drumbeat. We were moving fast before, but now we're flying, even the rescued elves working to draw weaker elves from their cells as those of us with keys release lock after lock.

"Now," Njörðr barks as soon as Fhord flings open the last cell and drags those males into the central room we began gathering in a few minutes ago. "You're with me," he says, pointing at Fhord. "Everyone else, form rings around us, one hand on the shoulder in front of you and the other on the shoulder to your right. When I tell you, dig deep to find your magic. Give it to me." When several of the freed captives mumble their confusion, he looks up, his gaze floating across the hundreds of beings encircling him. "You're exhausted and drained. I know it won't be much. But together, it should be enough."

We do as we're told, shuffling into place and linking our bodies as Njörðr directed. And then he starts murmuring in a language I've never heard. Sifa has, though. Her shoulders relax and I turn to find her smiling. I can't help but smile in response. Her calm seeps into me, like it does so often, and I'm a little less terrified about the Dróttning and whatever the fuck is about to happen.

It starts small, a vibration that disturbs the air near Njörðr and Fhord, which trembles in response to whatever he's doing. I've never thought of this strange male as powerful but I was wrong. He's the Dróttning's mate. His life began millennia ago and he's walked every world we know to exist. He might be as strong as her, and I suspect his power would put even Fhord and Sifa's to shame.

Thank fuck he's on our side.

The quiver expands with the volume of his words, a fucking earthquake by the time Njörðr's yelling his spell into this vast space. And then he slices a blade down Fhord's hand, splashing blood to the rock beneath them. It sizzles like rain losing itself in an inferno, crimson smoke frolicking between the males in our center.

Now, the magic is stifling, as if I'm sucking in Njörðr's conjury with every breath I take. It's frightening and also oddly exhilarating. I don't know if I want to drop into a fetal position or find my mate and fuck her until we both collapse. Since I can't do either, I just stand here, half of my brain examining all the sensations rippling through my body while the other half clings to the spot inside me where my bonds to Dani and Z reside, holding tight to those connections.

I'm surprised when it starts to happen, although I shouldn't be. The space around Njörðr seems to fold in and he disappears, my human eyes unable to see through the havoc in the center of the circle. Or maybe he's gone. I have no gods-damned idea how this is supposed to work.

Without warning, my head whips back as an explosion fills the space where Njörðr stood, my entire body following like a ball on a fucking string. I'm saved from the ground by bodies and hope the bastard at the bottom still lives. Every part of me aches, as if I've been beaten senseless, and I was lucky enough to land on top of this pile. Shaking my head, I lean forward and look up. And my chin drops like a rock to my chest.

I'm dizzy and weak as fuck, but it's not because of the blast that just took us all down.

It worked.

It fucking worked.

We freed a few hundred elves and several hundred *more* stand in the space we just were blown out of. They're dazed—because who the fuck wouldn't be?—but they seem stronger than the ones that were trapped in the cells here. They're all pale as ghosts, but the new ones don't look starved. They either had access to food in Helheim, if that's where they really came from, or they didn't need to eat.

This rescue is about to get very interesting.

CHAPTER TWENTY-NINE

MIKKAEL

HALLA'S MATE

ONE FEMALE STEPS FORWARD, her gaze scanning those of us who are still scrambling to our feet. She has coloring like mine—tawny skin, dark hair, and brown eyes. If I wasn't completely besotted by my mate, I'd find her attractive, with her generous curves and full lips. Now, her beauty is something I notice and dismiss.

Her power and the authority I already can tell she wields are much more important. "Who leads here?" the female demands, although she seems to answer her own question when she finds Fhord and Sifa. Nodding, she steps forward, extending her hand to Sifa first, as she continues to hold Fhord within her eyesight.

"We do," Sifa confirms. "I'm Sifa. What's your name?" Her voice is gentle but firm. She's not sure what this female needs and, as only Sifa could do, is relaying with a few words that she'll respond in whatever way she must.

A hint of a smile flickers across the female's face. "I am Finaan, but niceties must wait, Sifa. Nerthus approaches. We've spent centuries preparing for this day. We'll fail, though, if all the pieces aren't in place." She glances up, dipping her chin again as she seems to confirm something. "The girl will reach us in time, but her mate yet is too far."

"Halla's mate?" Sifa demands, her eyebrows lifting halfway up her forehead. "How are you more aware of what's going on in this world than we are?"

Now, Finaan's smile is broad. "That is my gift. I'll explain after Nerthus falls." Turning to Fhord, she asks the most un-fucking-expected question possible. "Do you have a dragon who can retrieve the northern monarch? None will survive if he's too late to join his mate in standing against Nerthus."

"Wait, are you saying Harald is Halla's mate?" Sifa's as shocked as me. Because that might be the craziest thing to happen on the craziest day ever.

"I can only sense his power and hers, and the link between them. If Harald is the northern monarch and Halla is the girl, then yes, they are mates."

"Fuck, no," Fhord snarls, launching into his grumpy protector mode. "Halla's ten fucking years old and Harald has lived longer than me."

"Keep them apart after this," Finaan responds with a shrug. She's still sharp as a fucking sword but it's a dull edge now as she tries to appease the large male glaring at her. "When the fates decree, they'll find each other. But today, they *must* create their initial bond. The full bond will come later, when the girl has aged. Right now, it will be enough for them to be close together, breathe the same air. Their souls will find each other."

She pauses, glancing around at the stunned faces staring at her, not a single person acting on her demand. Then her eyes and lips narrow as she turns back to Fhord. "The girl is too young yet to access her powers," she growls. "Her mate's presence and magic will give her the push she needs to become what she was born to be. We will not defeat Nerthus without the strength of their pairing. Send a dragon for the Monarch. Now."

"I fucking hate this," Fhord mutters, reaching for Sifa's hand as if he's the one who needs strength to get through it. Sifa doesn't seem nearly as pissed. She seems to have accepted whatever fate might throw at Halla when she agreed to bring her here. She knew she'd despise some or all of this shitshow, so she's just rolling with the punches at this point.

"Do you have a dragon who can retrieve him?" Finaan repeats in a flinty tone. "He is close, perhaps twenty vikus to the northeast. A fast beast will bring him in time."

"I'll send Z," I offer. He's as quick as anyone else and I think he'd welcome a chance to break away from the battle that somehow is still raging outside. He fucking *hates* having to kill former allies. Drawing up Harald's image, I cast it toward my dragon. *This male, the northern monarch, is twenty vikus north and east of us. Can you go get him? Fast? It might be the most important thing in this world.*

Capture?

If you must, I concur. Z won't have any way to speak with him so grabbing him and racing away might be his only choice. Harald'll be pissed, but hopefully we'll all be alive and that's what matters.

Now, he responds. The fighting is slowing enough for him to break away without endangering the other dragons. He pivots in the air, abandoning an assault he dreaded with a beast he once called friend, and throws himself into flight.

"He's on his way," I tell the others just as Dani and Halla stride into the cavern, their eyes growing wide as they see the hundreds of elves gathered in our midst.

"My thanks," Finaan says before turning to Halla as Dani walks over to stand with me.

I reach out for my mate's hand, a wave of calm washing through me when I feel her touch, and watch Finaan. I already can tell that she's a serious elf, but at this moment, she seems downright giddy. Whatever she sees or senses in Halla must be exactly what we need. I still have no idea what that might be—and I'm pretty sure I'm not alone in my ignorance—but I suspect *this* will be the most unbelievable part of an unbelievable day.

Dropping to her knees, Finaan stretches out her hand. Halla looks up to Sifa, a silent request for permission, and in response to Sifa's nod, places her palm in Finaan's. Something passes between them, and for a moment, the silence is loud enough to drown out the pounding in my ears. Then Halla nods and smiles before turning to me.

"Is yours the blue dragon, Mr. Mik?" Her voice is low, but I have no doubt everyone in this cave heard it as her question echoed around us, no other noise to disturb its path.

"He is, Halla."

Now her eyes close and her face relaxes. If I didn't know better, I'd think she was talking to a dragon. I realize it's probably Harald, though. Somehow, Finaan showed her how to reach through the mate bond and speak with him. I wish I could see his face. He's probably more shocked than any of us to have a child's words suddenly appear in his thoughts.

If I wasn't so freaked out about everything happening right now, I'd laugh at the lunacy of this world we live in.

A minute or more passes as we all watch Halla in silence. And then she nods again and opens her eyes to look at me. "My mate will come with your dragon. He's confused. We both are confused," she adds with a nervous giggle, "but he knows it's important. He agrees to help us."

"Well, fuck me," Dani chirps by my side. She glances over, one side of her lips ticking up just a bit. "That might be the biggest miracle of the day," she whispers.

"Not the biggest, not yet," Finaan interjects with a glance at Halla. But then her head springs up and she stares in the direction of the prison's entrance. "Nerthus will be here soon," she declares, her tone low and fierce with warning. "We have a minute, maybe more, before she arrives."

Harald's expecting you, I tell Z before I get too distracted by whatever is about to happen in these caves. *He should go willingly.* I feel his acknowledgment, even without a word in response, and focus on Finaan.

"We'll hold her back as long as we can," she's telling Fhord, "but it won't be long enough. You'll need to shift and fight until the girl's mate arrives." She pauses, a smile playing at her lips. "Thank the gods Nerthus's mate left this world," she adds. "We would have no hope if she had his power to draw from."

"How do you know that?" Sifa asks, shock rippling in her voice as her gaze bounces between Finaan and Fhord.

"I felt his presence as we changed places," Finaan responds with a shrug. "He is a righteous male, and wise to leave this world before he did more harm than good." Her head lifts with a jerk as she looks again toward the entrance. "She has arrived," she says in a flat voice.

Fhord turns toward Sifa, lifting his hand to caress her cheek. "Stay the fuck alive," he grunts, before leaning forward. I look away, loathe to steal their privacy, and don't hear whatever Sifa murmurs in response.

But then my gaze is drawn back to them and I watch in fascination as Fhord shifts, turning quickly into a massive wolf. He doesn't do this often, and I've never seen this side of him before. He's fully animal now, but something about this beast continues to remind me of the grumpy male I've somehow started to think of as a friend. Maybe it's the obvious love he shows for Sifa. Whatever it is, I feel safer in his presence. He can stand against the Dróttning's wyrm and might be the only being in this world who can.

I sense her presence before I see her, a wave of enmity and hate rolling toward us. When she slithers into the cavern, my skin prickles, memories of the spiders that covered Dani crawling into my brain, making me feel like I'm the one trapped in their web. I'm told the Dróttning is pretty in a cold, heartless way. Her wyrm form is not. It might be the most disgusting thing I've ever seen—a baffling mishmash of green and black that looks like it was spewed from Hel's gut.

Fhord's probably gonna have to wrap his maw around that vomit personified and I've never been more thankful that it's him, not me, who stands between the wyrm and Halla.

She laughs, but I don't see it. Instead, it's a feeling that washes through me, dirt and waste permeating my bones for an instant. Before she can get too close, though, the elves that Njörðr brought back from Helheim step forward. They link hands and send out their power, building a wall between the wyrm and the rest of us. The wyrm's disdain grows thicker, her malevolence filling the vast cavern like a sludge saturating the entire space.

I prevailed once against you, and I will again. These cold words drop into my head like Z's do, but they're not from my dragon. They're brittle and angry and somehow worse than the feel of her magic. Everything in me tries to shrink away from her power, but I'm trapped, stuck here along with everyone else to witness the fight for control of this land.

The Dróttning's magic spears out like an arrow, almost doubling me over, and I feel the elves harness their own energy and fortify the wall between us. For a minute, maybe more, nothing physical happens. Everybody is frozen in place, harsh breathing the only movement anywhere in the cave. The battle that they're waging is fully mental, the Dróttning's ridiculous power holding its own—maybe evening winning—against the collective magic of her enemies.

When she releases her hold, moving faster than my eyes can follow into the cavern, I think the elves have won and the wyrm is searching for a better position to attack. But the devious serpent has something else in mind. Before any of us can move to protect her, the wyrm's tail lashes out to grasp Halla's ankles, dropping her to the ground as the cunt starts to drag her across the cavern.

Fhord's wolf responds nearly as quickly, launching himself at his gods-damned mother, his enormous jaws clasping onto her neck. She flings herself up—dragging Fhord as he swings around her like a gods-damned flag—and at first, I'm convinced she's going to break free. But then he seems to find a well of power, twisting to force her neck into a freakish bend that would break anyone else.

Not the Dróttning, though. It'll take a fuck of a lot more than that to kill her.

For a few seconds, it looks like he's won. She doesn't move, and I half expect her to release Halla and escape while she can. Because I'm a gods-damned fool. The Dróttning doesn't fall easily.

Halla's low gasp breaks through my delusion, and I realize the wyrm's grip is tightening, squeezing her little body harder and harder. I don't even think. My sword is in my hand and

I'm launching at that fucking shrew before I can stop my-self, Dani and Sifa running at my side. We're at her tail and hacking furiously within moments, but her shell is solid as a fucking rock. We're not even breaking her gods-damned skin.

We must be annoying her, though, because she finds the strength to fling up her head—hauling Fhord's enormous ass with her—and seize Dani's gut, tossing her to the other side of the cave like she's a bug being flicked away.

Black rolls over my vision, the fury that consumes me shoving out every other emotion. The fear, anxiety, and hate that had driven my thrusts as I tried to save Halla are gone. I am anger and wrath and a thirst for vengeance so fierce it parches my throat.

The wyrm's open maw is whipping toward us again, aim-ing for Sifa this time, but I'll be gods-damned if I'm gonna let her take my friend too. I throw myself in her path, blade up as her jaws snap closed around me, and shiver in satisfaction when my sword draws blood and a spine-chilling shriek from the bitch. But then she's throwing me too. I'm a bag of bones, weightless as I soar to the far wall and slam against the rock, tumbling to the ground.

Fuck me.

Now, I wish I'd died when that bastard Jarl tried to stop us all. I've never experienced pain like this, a vise that seems to have encased every inch of bone and bit of flesh and squeezed.

Hold, Z demands. He's close and felt the pain that con-sumed me. He needs me to hold on a little longer.

Holding, I grunt, pushing myself up to search for Dani. She's in better shape than me, I realize as my mind catches up, reminding me how stupid I was to throw my human body between the wyrm and an elf she almost certainly wouldn't have been able to kill, who would have healed quickly if she'd been hurt.

I'd do it again, though. The thought of that bitch's teeth drawing a drip of Dani or Sifa's blood twists my insides, and I don't think I could stand aside and let her hurt either one of them.

I feel Harald's presence before I see him. I know he must be powerful—he's the northern monarch, with a firm grip on his people—but when he found us before, I didn't sense his magic. I do now. It's a massive ship pushing through pounding waves, an inexorable force that will not be stopped. Even the Dróttning seems to recoil at his strength.

When he stalks in, the flamboyant, angry male we encountered in a field is gone. This is the elf who rules a country, holding his land against the threats of the Dróttning. This is Njordheim's leader.

"She's mine," he declares as he glares at the wyrm who's probably surprised as fuck to see him here. "Release her and we'll leave without harming you."

I've never wondered what a wyrm laugh sounds like, but now I don't have to. A croak spews through her teeth, something hovering between a snort and a cackle, as she rises up, towering over Harald and everyone else, her clamp on Halla tightening.

Harald doesn't back down though. He stands, unyielding, as the wyrm breathes down on him. But then I feel a movement in his power. It's aimed fully at Halla now, and I wonder if he's protecting her in some way, giving her the strength to withstand the unbelievable pressure the wyrm's coils are creating.

That's not it, I realize, as I sense another shift. It leads to what can only be described as an exchange between Harald and Halla and then a moment infused with magic so pure—so beautiful—that I don't think I'll experience anything like it ever again. It feels like Asgard opened its doors for a single beat of their hearts and poured its blessing on them.

The ripple that follows throws me backwards—again—but this blast isn't destructive. It's the opening of a door, the whisper of a promise, the first drop of rain to flood a parched field. Pushing myself up, I can only watch in fascination as Halla becomes what she was born to be—an enormous silver dragon, so fucking majestic I'm dumbstruck just being in her presence.

The truth of it ripples through me. Halla's a dragon shifter, and I know deep in my gut that I'll never see anything as beautiful. Only my commitment to Dani and Z could compare to the utter devotion I feel in this moment toward this astonishing creature.

Her attack is sharp and swift. Before the Dróttning can shift—before she can move—Halla's wings fling out, breaking the wyrm's paltry hold on her, and Halla launches herself into the sky. Her jaws open and she clamps onto the wyrm's neck, pushing down to hold her in place.

For a moment, I think it's over. Halla's grip is a vise, her dragon impossibly strong, I can't imagine the Dróttning breaking free.

But that bitch is tough to kill.

We're all still frozen, staring at Halla's dragon, when the Dróttning shifts to her normal form, falling to the ground below before morphing into her wyrm again. And then all Helheim breaks loose, every one of us pulling our heads out of our asses to launch at the wyrm. She and Halla are a blur, flinging each other as they try to take control, end their enemy quickly.

The wyrm has lived for gods-damned millennia, though, and Halla is ten fucking years old. Already, I can see the difference in how they fight, the old witch using her power and centuries of manipulating chaos to take control in their battle. As the rest of us search for an opening to help the silver beast—the speed of their brawl holding us back, 'cause a strike at the wyrm could easily hit the dragon—the maggot finds the opening she needs to grab Halla's legs with her tail, hurling the silver beast to the ground.

Which is exactly what we need. As one, we throw ourselves forward, swords raised high to attack where we can. Her skin, though, is a fucking rock. Swipes of my blade don't do shit, not even scratching the surface of her granite hide, so I try shoving the tip into her. From the corner of one eye, I see silver wings flapping frantically, trying to stop the crush of the serpent's tail working her way up Halla's trapped legs to her body. But I push that image aside. We need to hurt the wyrm to help Halla.

When the Dróttning's foul maw shoots toward me, aiming for my neck to slice my head right off my shoulders, I barely dance away, one sharp tooth scraping across my skull. Blood spills down my face, dripping into my eyes as a fire spears across my crown, but I wipe that shit away.

I'm tough to kill too. And she won't be the one to end me.

Definitely not before I've taken Dani.

I'm sure as fuck not gonna die without feeling my mate's legs wrapped around my naked ass at least once.

Jumping back into the fray of elves struggling to harm the wyrm, I see Sifa and Fhord crawling up her neck, aiming for the eyes that may be her only weakness. The hag realizes it too, flinging her neck up and down as she tries to throw them off. And I don't know how the fuck they'll cling to the disgusting serpent. She's tossing them like gods-damned balls, their fingers grasping onto whatever they can to hold on.

But that drags her attention away from the rest of us. She's not as focused on her tail as she needs to be, giving Halla's massive dragon the chance she needs to free herself, just a bit, from the wyrm. She wrests out the parts of her wings that the tail had trapped, stretching them wide to lift herself into the air and toward her enemy's head. Once more, Halla's mouth opens and circles the witch's neck, pinning her to the ground. The rest of us follow, launching ourselves toward the bitch, clutching whatever we can to help hold her down.

Time seems to slow as my gaze finds Fhord and Sifa. Even from here, I can see the accord that whispers between them. Fhord leans back to move out of Sifa's way, and she climbs the male's-height that remains between her and the Dróttning's head. As the wyrm fights to break free, every muscle working to fling herself up and throw us off, Sifa reaches one of her eyes. Lifting up onto her knees, she positions her sword just above the wide orb, casts one more glance at her mate, and then smiles and plunges her blade as deep as it will go. The monster's black blood spurts out, coating Sifa in the vengeance she finally claimed.

The wyrm and the dragon howl at the same time. The Dróttning erupts in a torment so deep, it seems to have been dragged up from Helheim to spew into our midst, her agony pummeling us with hatred and anger and eternal pain. Halla's yell is a demand to the rest of us, trembling with the victory that's within our reach. And I've got no gods-damned idea how I understand her, but I do.

I toss myself as far away from the wyrm as I can—along with everyone else—and the dragon tightens her grip to lift the Dróttning's head up. My heart is pounding in my ears and I'm frozen in place as the wyrm's writhing increases, her *need* to break free unleashing a final burst of panic and power. But it's not enough.

Halla's jaws tug together as she oh-so-slowly rips through the dense hide, bones and sinew, unleashing another torrent of black raining down on us. And then they snap closed, every bit of resistance gone as she severs the wyrm's head from its body. Lurching forward, she catches the bloody skull and flings it to the other side of the cave as the rest of the wyrm drops to the rock below. Finally, she turns to shriek her victory at Harald.

Fuck me. I think Sifa and Halla just killed the Dróttning. While Harald, that fucker, stood around and watched.

My mind is starting to catch up to the enormity and impossibility of what just happened as I stare at Harald, who raises a single eyebrow, his lips twisting into a smirk. The bastard's gaze follows Halla as she drops to the ground in front of him and shifts back. Almost as if it never happened, she's a child again, looking up at the asshole who doesn't deserve to kiss her feet.

"You're my mate?" Halla's voice is small but strong as she watches Harald.

"Don't get any ideas," he declares dismissively. "I didn't come for you. I saw a chance to defeat the Dróttning and took it. I have no interest in a mate. Certainly not a child shifter. Our paths won't cross again." He turns to Dani, his eyes narrowing as his lips thin. "Don't ever return to Njordheim. You're not welcome there."

If he were within my reach, I'd take his head or die trying. Dani just lifts a finger to wave her disdain at him, and Halla seems to take it in stride, shrugging at his petulant little outburst. They're both stronger than me, watching with smiles playing on their lips as Harald spins on his heel and strides out of the cave.

CHAPTER THIRTY

DANI

WITH MY LIFE, ELF

W E'RE DONE. AND ... we won. I think.

Nobody's said a word yet. They're probably all in shock, like me. My mind is still trying to grasp what I just saw. What Halla became. What she did. That Halla and Harald are fucking mates, and the Monarch rode in like a white night—instead of the mercurial and often cruel leader I've always known—and saved the day. Before he turned back into the bitter, hateful ruler I escaped when I came to Vanatia.

The Dróttning's dead. We came to free the elves and somehow, we freed the whole fucking country. Not that it'll be easy. I know it won't be. Beron's still technically the king, but that can't last long. Fhord and Sifa are the most powerful beings here now. They won't let him cling to power after everything he's done.

They won't be the new konungr and dróttning, though. Fhord's said more than once that he doesn't want to rule. But they'll make sure Vanatia's next leader is focused on the people who live here, not their own power.

Fhord and Sifa are good elves. The best. A ruler they support, who's backed by their magic, should be a fantastic gods-damned—or maybe, finally, gods-blessed—ruler.

Njörðr's gone, replaced by hundreds of elves, most of them still dazed as fuck. We all escaped into the sunshine as soon as we shook ourselves out of our shocked stupors, and they're glinting against the light like they haven't seen it in weeks. I suspect it's been centuries. They'll have quite the story to tell if they really did come from Helheim.

Mikkael's voice breaks the silence. Because of course it does. "Holy fuck," he yells, spinning to find me. And then he's striding forward to pick me up, cupping my ass in his arms as my legs wrap around his waist. "We made it," he rasps, his head tipped up so his gaze can hold mine, a sexy smile playing at his lips. "You know what this means, right?"

I stretch closer to his ear, because this is between us and I don't want to share it with anyone. "You think you're gonna fuck me?" I purr, running my tongue along the shell of his ear. "Or did you have something else in mind?"

He leans back, his smile growing all the way to his eyes, drawing out the crinkles at the corners that somehow make him even more sultry. "Is that what you think I'm going to do to you, my so-fucking-sexy siren of a spy? You think I plan to fuck you?"

He scoffs, his dark gaze *smoldering*. "That'll come in the days and years ahead. This first time, though, I will worship you. Like I said, I intend to make love to you. Every drop of blood that pulses through your veins will vibrate with my devotion to you. I have a lot of groveling to do. I'll start by kneeling at your feet and then draping your legs across my back so I can savor you while you come on my tongue."

"That's a good fucking start, Mik," I mutter, his words sending a flame straight to my core, that branches out to fill me with a warmth I never thought I'd feel with this male.

"That's enough, you two," Sifa laughs as she strides up next to us, her hand in Fhord's.

Mikkael turns to smirk at her. "You were here once too," he says. "You remember."

"Which is exactly why we came over to interrupt," Fhord declares, his eyes narrowing. "We all heard you in Lumaria. You need to get a bed and give the mating bond what it needs. Fuck each other, already. Just ... no foreplay near us. We don't need to hear that shit again."

My mate turns his smirk to me, but this one's different. It's a promise of things to come—wicked, filthy things that he won't voice with our friends standing right next to us. Releasing his grip on my ass, he sets me on the ground, leans forward to press his lips against mine—drawing a groan from me, because, fuck, his kiss feels so right—and then wraps his arm around my waist to tug me into his side.

"You knew Jarl," Mikkael says, pulling my attention back to Sifa. "Is he from Midgard?"

"I'm so fucking glad that asshole is dead," Sifa snarls, her nostrils flaring as she lifts her chin. She takes a deep breath like she's wondering what to tell us, then nods. "You know the Dróttning fucked with Toffer and me when we got here, right?" she asks, her tone flat.

We both nod. She's told me a little bit about what happened when the Dróttning captured her, but not much. I've never pushed. Seeing what the Dróttning did to Fhord, I'm sure it's not something Sifa ever wants to relive.

"What I never told you is that he and I were imprisoned and tortured in Midgard, before we got here. We called him Jonathan there, and he came into his power in the days leading up to Ragnarök. Like others who developed magic in those days, he was stronger than the old gods." Her gaze lifts to Halla, who's sitting on the ground next to Tindera, as she adds almost to herself, "Ragnarök made everyone powerful."

"Anyway," she continues as she shakes her head, "he captured me early in the fighting, and I'm pretty sure nobody even knew. He did it to get back at Freyr, who he hated. Jonathan found a perverse joy in torturing me. He reminds me a lot of Matthias, that bastard."

Sifa's so stoic as she explains her connection to Jonathan, it breaks my heart. She suffered horribly but is still one of the brightest, most loving people I know.

"One day, he brought in some of Freyr's blood. I recognized the scent and knew he wasn't lying about that. Jonathan claimed he'd killed Freyr, who was like a father to me, and I've spent ten years wondering if he was telling the truth. It wasn't until Njörðr arrived that I learned he'd been lying. Thank the gods." She shakes her head, her eyes casting up as if she could see her friend if she tried.

"That's the day Toffer and I came to Vanatia," she says at last, glancing for a second toward the troll standing with Astarot, his fingers scratching the dragon's favorite spot. "And Halla, I learned years later, although she was still an egg at the time. I realize after what Njörðr did that it was Freyr's blood, his connection to Fhord and the Dróttning, that opened the portal we came through. I still don't know how, but it must have been the magic that was everywhere when Ragnarök ripped open that world."

"Halla's from our worlds too?" Mikkael's voice ripples with surprise, his eyebrows nearly high enough to blend with the hair falling onto his forehead.

"I knew at the time that something else had come with us," Sifa responds as she looks at Halla again, then turns back toward us. "She hadn't hatched yet. Apparently, dragon shifters are more dragon than human, or at least she is. The egg disappeared, and I had no idea why or where it had gone. But some instinct told me it was important—that I had to hide it. So I did."

Sifa looks down, a hint of a smile lifting her lips, then back up. "Sagga knew, though. She's more powerful than anyone realized. She lived in Harald's kastali and felt the egg's arrival there, since our mating bonds dragged us all to our mates. At the same time, Sagga received a vision about her future and our need for her. That stubborn female tracked down the egg and found a way to get to Revalle. She waited until Halla was old enough to create an innocent reason for our connection. She set it all up. And thank the gods she did."

"Had Halla shifted before?" Mikkael's voice is full of wonder. He's grown nearly as close to Halla as Sifa has over the years.

Sifa shakes her head, her gaze once more finding Halla before returning to us. "My guess is she didn't even know she could. Sagga kept a lot from her. She wanted her to feel like a normal child but also was afraid Halla might say something—innocently, of course—and draw the Dróttning's attention." She grins, shaking her head as her eyes glitter. "I had no idea what she'd become, and I'm still astounded how powerful she is. But she was born during Ragnarök. Like Jonathan and the others I mentioned before, everything Yggdrasill created in those days has a shocking amount of magic."

She's quiet for a moment, shadows spilling into her eyes, and I wonder if her thoughts have snagged on Jonathan or Jarl or whatever that asshole called himself. "If she hadn't changed before, why now?" I ask, hoping Sifa will focus again on the child she loves.

"I don't know much about dragon shifters," she says, her expression softening. "Our worlds haven't seen one for a long time. But I think it's like Finaan said. They can't shift until they mature unless they get close enough to their mate for their powers to mingle. Halla and Harald aren't fully bonded, thank the gods, but something about accessing her mate's magic triggered her first shift."

"So, she came to this world because of Harald. Does Toffer have a mate here too?" I can't hold back the laugh that bubbles up with my words. I hope he does. He deserves that happiness.

"Or maybe a dragon," Sifa tells us. "Either bond could have pulled him here. I have no idea who, but they must have been in or close to the Nest, since Toffer didn't disappear the way Halla did."

"And I was attracted to you," Mikkael murmurs, lifting my hand to kiss my wrist, sending little flares into my veins to warm every single part of me. He watches for a moment, the barest frown tugging down the corners of his lips. "I wonder why I landed in Vanatia instead of Njordheim."

"I was probably here on a job for the Monarch," I respond with a shrug. "I've come here a lot over the years."

"But, ten years ago? You'd have been a teenager too." Now, Mikkael lifts his free hand to rub his thumb across my cheekbone. It feels like he can't keep his hands away from me, now that we've both embraced our bond, and I don't think I've ever enjoyed his touch as much as I do in this moment.

"You think I was born twenty-some years ago?"

When his eyebrows slam together, I can't hold back the *guffaw* that spills out of me.

"You weren't?" A little rasp finds its way into his question, prying another chuckle from me.

Fuck, it feels good to laugh. I'm free for the first time ever, and I'm about to join this delicious male in exploring a life together. With our dragons. I don't know how I got so gods-damned lucky. "I'm an elf, Mik," I remind him. "I'm almost two hundred years old."

His eyes grow wide as saucers, mouth dropping open as he watches me in silence. And then his lips lift into the smirk I've grown to love, and he leans forward to kiss me, plunging his tongue into my mouth. A flame whips through my body and I can't do anything but kiss him back, every part of me consumed by my mate.

"C'mon guys," Sifa mutters to our side, breaking through the hurricane spinning inside me.

Mikkael leans back, his gaze locked on mine. "My seasoned spy," he purrs, wrapping his arm around my waist and pulling me into him. His mouth finds my ear as he whispers, "I've always loved older women. Our mate bond must have been preparing me for you."

And I take a couple of deep breaths, willing my heart to calm the fuck down. "Who's Loki?" I ask after a moment, trying to focus again on the friend standing in front of us.

Now Sifa shakes her head, glancing at Fhord and then back at Mikkael and me. "Loki's a Norse god too—the trickster god. He sired Sköll and Jörmungandr—the wolf who took Thor, and the serpent who attacked Vulryn and carried her to the cave where Loki could trap her. Hel too. Helheim's ruler is his daughter. He's always used the snake to carry him and his offspring between worlds and has probably been the Dróttning's go-between for a long time."

"But why is he here?" I ask, my gaze bouncing across the group as I try to understand why Vanatia's been inundated with "old gods" that have caused so much havoc lately. "They seem to be working for the Dróttning, but that doesn't make any sense."

Sifa shrugs. "I'm not sure," she says. "Before you got to the cave, Jonathan said he would take me back to Midgard since Loki's spawn couldn't. That doesn't explain how he knew I was here, though, unless the Dróttning told him. Maybe she asked Loki to get rid of me and Jonathan was eager to oblige."

She pauses for a moment, her gaze moving toward the cave and then back to us. "Jonathan was human until the trickster started feeding him Yggdrasil's fruit on the eve of Ragnarök. Loki had no idea Jonathan would be as powerful or cruel as he was. He created a monster he couldn't control. Maybe he used me as bait to trap Jonathan here," she muses with a shrug.

"You think the Dróttning agreed to take Jonathan if Loki got rid of you and Vulryn? And Njörðr, I guess. She'd want to send him away too, if she knew he was here." I could see that. The Dróttning considered herself untouchable and probably thought she could control Jonathan like she does everything else.

"Maybe," Sifa responds with another lift of her shoulders. "We can ask the trickster god the next time he drops by," she adds with a rueful laugh and a shake of her head.

"So, he'll be back? He's gonna keep coming to fuck things up until we kill him?" Mikkael's tone is light, but I feel his angst. We haven't even met Loki and he's already more of a threat than the Dróttning ever was.

"He's hard to kill," Sifa responds with a grimace. "But let's worry about one thing at a time. We've got a lot of work to do here, to ferret out everyone loyal to the Dróttning."

"You had no idea what you were in for when you got dragged here," Mikkael remarks, a teasing note in his voice.

Sifa looks up at Fhord, a smile lifting her lips. "And thank fuck I did," she declares as she turns her gaze toward Astarot, standing next to Tindera, and then back to Fhord. "It brought me here and I wouldn't trade my mate or dragon for anything."

"Me either," Mikkael says, pulling me even closer into his side. "What's next?" he asks, lifting his head to look over the hundreds of elves we just led from the prison.

"Fhord and Tindera are leaving with Leif and Torsten to go to the draugr forest," she begins.

"We should go," Mikkael spurts out. "I promised to come back, too."

"They'll take care of it," Sifa responds with a shake of her head as her hand rests on his arm. "The draugrs will rest tonight. I'll return to the cave and tell Mótsognir the Dróttning is dead. But first," she adds as she turns to me, a playful smile brightening her features, "we've got something important to do in Lumaria."

"Why do I think I'm gonna hate this?" I ask, already uncomfortable with whatever she has in mind.

"Do you trust me, Dani?"

It's the simplest question, but in this moment, it means so much more than five little words. It's the product of a relationship borne in anger against an enemy, tested through the machinations of a wicked smart dragon and battles for the fate of a country, and refined through a stalwart friendship I never knew I wanted but now couldn't imagine living without.

"With my life, elf," I murmur.

"Then trust me in this," Sifa urges, adopting that persuasive tone she always uses to get her way. "Come with Astarot, Halla and me to Lumaria. Astrid and Jorunn will go too. We have something to show you. If you don't want to stay, you don't have to."

"You had me at Lumaria," I tell her. "I can't think of any-place I'd rather be right now." I look up, bouncing my gaze over the many, many people surrounding us. "But what about them?"

"They'll be well cared for. Gorm and the others already had plans in place for the imprisoned elves. They have to adjust a bit for the others, but they knew what Njörðr planned. They're prepared to find homes for them too. They're looking forward to helping everyone figure out where they belong and what they want to do—and to figuring that out for themselves, now that they're free of the Dróttning."

"We've got a lot of work ahead of us," Mikkael says before turning to me. "But first, rest. Lumaria?"

"Like I said," I respond with a laugh, "Sifa had me at Lumaria. If you're with me, there's no place I'd rather be."

"If I'm with you," he mutters, his voice so low, it almost sounds angry. Turning to stand in front of me, he lifts his hands to cup my face, brushing his lips against mine once before drawing back and holding my gaze. "Fate brought us together. It brought our dragons together. But this thing between us isn't just fate. I've been fighting these feelings for years because I'm a gods-damned stubborn bastard."

"So fucking stubborn," I huff, bringing my hands up to rest them over his.

"Too fucking stubborn," he agrees with a sharp dip of his chin. And then he looks at me with so much love in his eyes, I suck in a deep breath, holding it while I wallow in this moment. "I thought I loved a female once, but I didn't know what the fuck I was feeling. This is love. This thing between us isn't just the lust the fates created. It's sunrise at the end of a dark night, a breath of air after being trapped underwater, the warmth of a fire to dispel the cold of a long day of travel. It's everything good in a fucked-up world." He pauses, his thumbs reaching up to catch the tears that have started to trickle from my eyes.

"I don't know how I got so lucky," he adds after a moment, "but I realize now what a fool I was to not seize this thing between us from the moment I recognized part of my soul inside yours. You never need to ask again if I'm going to be with you. If you'll have me, I'll always be with you. Wherever you travel, every step of the way, each moment of the day. I'm yours, Dani, and I thank the fucking gods that you're mine."

I feel the truth of his words deep inside, where my bond to him and Vulryn resides, a warmth that starts there and flows out to blanket me in his devotion. "Thank the fucking gods," I echo, rising to my toes so I can taste his love too. This kiss isn't hungry or fierce. It's gentle, our lips and tongues exploring each other with the knowledge that we have the rest of our lives to sate this need we both have for our mate.

Will our male be returning to the pretty place with us? Vulryn's voice drops into my thoughts just as Mikkael leans back, his eyes going distant as they do when he speaks with Z.

Fhord's going back to free the dead guys in the forest, I tell her. *We'll go with Mikkael, Sifa, Jorunn, and Astrid to Lumaria. And Halla, Sagga, Toffer, and Thor, of course. They'll go where Sifa goes.*

The sun beast's rider is no longer our male, Vulryn announces dismissively. *You have accepted my drake's rider and he has accepted you. He is our male. There will be no other.*

I can't hold back my grin at her words. I knew she'd welcome him as soon as I did—her feelings about Mikkael have been changing for a while—but it soothes something within me to hear my dragon embrace my mate this way. *And what is Fhord now, if he's no longer our male?*

He is the grumpy male, Vulryn explains as if to a child. *I have watched him. When he is with the starry female and a few others, he is happy. When he strays from them, he becomes… unpleasant. The name suits him.*

She's right, as she always is. Fhord loves a handful of people and they see a side of him he rarely shows. But he is, at his essence, a very grumpy male. *The grumpy male, it is,* I agree with a smile. *Our male will come to Lumaria with us. Are you ready?*

Her excitement whispers to me through the bond. She's nearly as eager to swim—and then fly—with her drake as I am to finally embrace my bond with Mikkael. *I am*, she affirms. *Are you?*

This is another simple question with a deep meaning. My wise dragon understands. Everything between Mikkael and me will change in Lumaria.

I'm so ready, I assure her. And I am.

Mikkael and Z must have had a similar conversation. He smiles at Sifa and declares, "I guess it's time." And then he takes my hand to walk with me toward our dragons. We're in the air within seconds—Toffer and Thor with us, as Vulryn prefers—then flying through the fog into Lumaria hours later. My heart soars when I see the island, which already feels like home. I send an unspoken question to my dragon as she ignores the field where Birger and the others *always* meet visitors, falling in behind Astarot to fly to the other side of the city.

The fire beast asked me to follow and I agreed, she explains in that voice that tells me she knows more than she's sharing.

Why? I don't think I keep the nerves from my voice. I don't like when people make a fuss about me and something about this is making me uncomfortable.

We shall see, she responds vaguely, a little laugh in her words.

Now I'm sure I'm not going to like this. Whatever they've planned can't be good.

Within a minute, we're spiraling down to a large field with a home at its center. And it might be the prettiest home I've ever seen. It's in the style of a cottage—its dark roof sloping up at a sharp pitch—but it's not a small space. I suspect it holds several sleeping rooms in addition to its common spaces. It's as blue as the feathers that cover Z's belly, a crystal lake on a sunny day. With lush bushes and flowers everywhere—and even an adorable picket fence surrounding it—it's perfect.

When we land, Sifa spins to find me, her smile broad and carefree. And I understand. She plans to give this to me. She promised a place on this island if I wanted it, and she intends to make good on that promise now. I shake my head because this is too much. But she just nods, mouthing a "Yes" as she turns to follow Jorunn in climbing down her dragon's back, then helps Sagga.

I spin to find Mikkael and realize he already knows, probably from Astrid on the ride over. He smirks, waiting for her to dismount before blowing me a kiss. Halla wraps herself around his back and he drops to his dragon's wing, then to the ground.

"No," I tell them as I join them in front of the house. "Whatever you're thinking, the answer is no."

"You can't say no," Mik says, wrapping an arm around me to haul me into his side. "I'm heading back to Revalle tomorrow to get my things. Z and Vulryn would never forgive us if we refused them a home on this island."

"We can get a place, but this is too much." I turn to Sifa, my heart in my throat. "It's too much."

"It's not enough," she insists, her hands on her hips. "Everything we have is because of you and your dragon—and your mate and his dragon," she adds with a smile at Mikkael. "We can never repay you. This is such a small token for all that we owe you."

"Besides," Astrid says as she moves into position beside Sifa and lifts an arm to gesture to the north, "Sifa and Fhord—with Toffer and Thor—are moving in there. Your dragon would be angry if you refused a home right next to that bitchy cat your beasts all love so much," she points out with a wink. And then she spins, aiming east as she adds, "Jorunn and I will be there. I'm not sure where Torsten and Leif will land. I suspect they'll be in the city. They like to be closer to everything, but Jorunn and I want our privacy."

Now she pauses, her eyes growing soft as she watches me for a moment. "You've been running non-stop since you came to Vanatia with us, you haven't had a moment to rest and settle into your new life. You'll need your friends as well as your mate and dragon in the days ahead. Let us be here for you."

"It's already done," Sifa interjects, "and too close to our land to let anyone else live here. If you don't take this house, it'll sit empty. It's for you," she offers in a softer voice, "because you're part of our family and we want you close as we all work together to figure out what the future looks like for Vanatia."

"Don't decide now," Jorunn says as she strides over to stand with Astrid, throwing her arm around her lover's shoulders. "We're gonna go home and fuck," she adds as she gazes at Astrid, her eyes brimming with adoration, "because it's been much too long. You two should do the same."

Mikkael's answering growl in my ear tells me what he thinks about that suggestion.

Jorunn smirks as she tugs Astrid away. "Let us know tomorrow what you decide."

Sifa smiles with a nod and spins to head north with Astarot, Halla, Sagga, Toffer, and Thor as Mikkael pulls me closer.

"No harm in looking," he says as he starts to lead me toward the entry. "And I think this is a perfect place for what I plan to do to you tonight," he adds in the rumble I feel in my core.

CHAPTER THIRTY-ONE

DANI

HOME, AT LAST

MIKKAEL PAUSES ON THE porch, turning to give me that smile that launches a kaleidoscope of butterflies in my stomach. "Are you ready, my splendid spy?" he asks as his tongue finds my ear, dragging down the edge to pause and suck on my lobe.

"Yes, please," I gulp, a flame already igniting in my core as my body reacts to my mate's touch.

He leans away, gives me a lingering kiss on the lips, then swings the door open. I can't hold back my gasp. "It's perfect," I murmur as I drink in the dark wood and soft colors they chose for the furniture and decorations. A sense of certainty billows through me when I walk in, like I really do belong here with Mikkael at my side.

The entry opens to a spacious room, a fireplace on the right with plush couches and chairs positioned perfectly, a round dining table for ten in the center, and a large kitchen to the left. I can see right away that it was built and decorated for us by friends who know me better than I know myself. It's home, and I couldn't refuse their gift if I tried. I'm speechless, filled with a deep sense of belonging and sisterhood. I find myself wandering to the window, wishing I'd told them how loved this gift makes me feel. How much I appreciate all of them.

"Good things come when you give your trust to people who care about you," Mikkael whispers, his voice low and sexy as fuck as he tucks his hands under my shirt and splays his palms across my stomach, resting his chin on the top of my head to look out the window with me. "Do you trust me?"

"I do," I tell him. "I'm yours. Today, tomorrow, always."

"I told you I want to make love to you," he purrs as his hands grip my waist and he spins me. "Will you let me take control and worship this body that has consumed my fantasies for as long as I can remember?"

The fire that ignites in my core at his words darts up and out, capturing every part of me in its flame. My pussy is pulsing already. I have no idea what he has in mind, but whatever it is, I need it. I dip my chin. "I'm yours," I repeat, "for anything and everything you want."

His responding grin is the hottest thing I've ever seen, eyes crinkling around dark eyes that are burning for me. He's so fucking beautiful. I can't wait to run my hands over his warm tawny skin, free his long, dark hair from the cord that always ties it back. And then he lifts me up to toss me over his shoulder and stride for the bedroom. He groans as he takes a deep inhale, probably scenting how ready I am for every single thing he wants to do to me.

When he sets me down in the middle of the room, I'm confused for a moment. He glances up toward the rafters, his smile even broader now. "I'm sure they didn't have this in mind, but these are perfect for what I want to do to you." He leans forward to kiss me, hard. "Stay put," he demands as he heads back to the living room.

He returns a minute or so later, a rope in one hand and a soft cloth in the other. He flings the rope over the wood beam above us, testing its strength as he yanks down, and sets the cloth on a nearby table. And then he slowly, deliberately, strips me, lifting my shirt up and over my head as his lips and tongue taste the skin he's exposing, unclasping the band across my breasts before bending to suck one nipple into his mouth, then the other, and finally tugging down my pants and underwear, teasing me as his tongue goes everywhere except where I want it.

"What are you doing to me, Mik," I mutter, my head thrown back as I let the sensations he's igniting within me take over, pushing out everything except the feel of my mate's lips on my skin.

"I'm worshiping you, my sultry spy," he hums as he steps back, his heavy gaze moving slowly down my body and then up, that wicked grin back on his face. "Should I tell you something I've learned about what will make a lover scream my name and beg for more?"

These words trigger another flare at my core, because fuck, yes, I want to know. "As long as you don't name any names," I manage to croak out, my body a throbbing mess already.

He wraps his hands around my waist, drifting them up toward my breasts as his gaze follows them, pupils blown wide. "When someone tells you what they'd like to do to you," he tells me, "they're usually describing what they want done to them. I couldn't fuck you properly when you started this," he adds, his hand dropping to circle my clit with his thumb a single, tantalizing time, the bastard. "Now I can, and I'm going to finish it."

He leans forward for another kiss, his tongue exploring my mouth for a few seconds as I try to stop myself from orgasming at the mere thought of what's coming. He's not wrong. I fucking love the idea of being tied up and completely at Mikkael's mercy.

"Ready?" he asks, cocking his head to the side. I hold his gaze and dip my chin, unable to restrain my grin. Grabbing the cloth, he extends a hand to take mine, wrapping one wrist and then the other gently before twisting the rope and tying a knot. "Too tight?" he asks, one eyebrow lifting.

"Perfect," I respond, wishing he was naked too, but so fucking turned on by the fact that I'm completely bared to him. I'm his, and I know in my soul he'd never abuse the trust I'm giving him.

He pulls the rope to stretch my arms above my head, leaving me comfortably standing on the ground but unable to do anything except experience what he's about to do. He ties the rope to the headboard and stalks back over to stand in front of me. And then his finger drops down to my pussy, gathering the arousal he finds there. He plays with my clit for a couple of seconds, circling it with his thumb and pressing against it with his palm, before lifting his hand to lick every drop, his gaze never leaving mine.

"So fucking delicious," he groans as he leans forward to kiss me. This time, his kiss is demanding, full of passion and need. His lips and tongue are voracious, consuming me as I let myself settle into the feelings he's igniting inside me, experiencing every spark that bounces through my body with his touch.

His mouth breaks free of mine, kissing and nipping along my jaw and down my neck. When he reaches my breasts, he stops his slow descent, wrapping his hand around one to tweak and pinch my taut nipple—which I love so fucking much, I think I might come just from this—while his mouth laves at the other one. He's launching sensations inside me I didn't think I could feel, my body fully at his mercy as he seems to know instinctively exactly what I need from my mate.

The orgasm he's drawing from me is cresting, about to wash over me, when he abandons my nipples, kissing his way down my stomach. "But that was so good," I moan. Because he has me bound, unable to finish what he started, and I *need* him to do it.

"Do you want to come, my spicy spy?" he drawls, pausing at my hip bone to look at me with glazed eyes.

"So, so much. Please make me come, Mik."

His growl at my words sends a shiver down my spine. He smiles—a feral grin that I feel in my core—and dips his chin once. "Since you asked so nicely," he says before lifting one of my legs over his shoulder and *feasting* on me. His tongue and lips and teeth are all over, lapping up every bit of arousal he's finding in my body. Within a minute, I'm riding the wave that will carry me into the abyss of ecstasy he's promising, and then he plunges two fingers inside me, finding the perfect spot, as his mouth focuses on my clit.

My orgasm rips through me, wave after wave of pleasure that seem to go on forever, leaving me trembling and boneless as I hang in front of him. Before I can pull myself up again, though, he's wrapping my other leg around his shoulders, lifting me up enough to take all the pressure off my arms, as he continues to eat me like I'm a delicacy he's coveted his entire life. His groans are nearly as loud as mine, which somehow turns me on even more than his fingers and tongue.

It's not enough, though. The mating bond is writhing inside me, demanding everything. It's a hole that can only be filled with my mate's cock, growing needier and needier with every swipe of his tongue and pump of his fingers. "You have to fuck me, Mik," I tell him as the bond pulses inside me. "I've never wanted anything more. Please."

He stops for a moment, his heavy gaze lifting up to find mine. "Do you trust me, mate?" he asks, repeating his question from earlier.

I smile, because there's only one answer. "I do," I tell him, my body vibrating with the emotions that ripple through me at the knowledge that I'm utterly at his mercy and there's nowhere else I'd rather be.

"Then trust me in this," he demands. "Let me worship you a little longer. It'll be worth the wait, I promise."

With one more inhale to calm my racing heart—and the bond that craves him like I crave food and water—I dip my chin again. "I'm yours."

"Mine," he declares, and his head drops again, fingers plunging into me as he continues to feast on my pussy. Now, he's a male on a mission, dragging two more orgasms from me—swallowing everything he draws from my body like it's his last meal—before he slows. And then he's licking me leisurely while he holds me up, my thighs still wrapped around him, as I come back to my senses.

I feel the satisfied laugh that rolls through him as he moves one leg and then the other, arms supporting me as I find the strength to stand on my own. I am a mess of nerves, every single one spilling pleasure into my veins as the echoes of Mikkael's devotion wash through me. I've never felt so complete and sated, but it's still not enough. I *need* him. Nothing else will satisfy the bond that's twisting and wriggling in my gut.

Slowly, Mikkael works his way back up my body, caressing and stroking me with his tongue and hands. When he's standing in front of me—still fully clothed, his cock bulging in his pants, he smiles lazily, resting his palms on my cheeks as he parts my lips with his. I taste my arousal and respond with the thirst pulsating inside me, my tongue spearing into his mouth to tangle with his, drinking up every bit of him I can get.

"My seductive spy," he purrs. "Are you still hungry for me?"

"I need you to fuck me, Mik," I beg, wishing I could wrap my arms around him and drag him to the bed. "Since the moment I saw you, I've needed this. You hated me, but I never hated you. This started with lust, but when you dropped into my life, pissy as fuck and pushing me away every chance you got, I knew it was so much more than that. I love you and I *need* to embrace this bond between us. I need you tied as firmly to me as I am to you."

"Fuck, do I love you," he rumbles, kissing me leisurely before releasing my cheeks and reaching for my wrists. He unties me quickly, lifts me into his arms, and strides over to the bed to lay me down. And then he holds my gaze and starts to strip, a tremble rustling through me as I watch my mate expose himself to me for the first time.

He's everything I want in a male, hard planes and rippling muscles covered with elaborate designs. Plus an enormous cock. I'm gonna be thanking the gods for that for years to come. "Did you get the dragons after you found Z?" I ask as my gaze is drawn to the many tattoos dedicated to the beasts, almost all of them blue.

Mikkael laughs, a release of pleasure and awe as he glances down. "I started adding blue dragons years ago," he tells me. "I didn't know why. It just called to me, and once I'd done one, I needed more. I understood when I saw Z. Something inside me knew all along that I belonged to a blue dragon."

Then he spins and shows me the female on his back. She's not exactly me, but pretty gods-damned close—thin but muscular, with fair skin like mine and auburn hair as close to my color as ink could get. "This," he says as he twists his head and looks at me, "is one of the first ones I got, years before you landed in my life. I described what I wanted to the artist and he gave her to me. I understood this, too, when we met, although it pissed me off for a long time."

My heart is pounding in my chest, every beat for this magnificent male in front of me. "You've worn me for years, even before you realized what we'd mean to each other?" I'm stunned—so awestruck by the depth of our bond, I don't think I could move if I tried.

"It's always been you, Dani. I fought against it, tried my damnedest to push you away, and I'm so fucking sorry for all the heartache I've caused both of us. I'm gonna spend the rest of my life making it up to you."

I reach out a hand, my body coming to life again as his love fills me. "Start by making love to me, Mik."

And he does. Taking my hand, he lays next to me and starts exploring my body again as I explore his. His touch is gentle at first, soft caresses and tender kisses as we relish the feel of our mate's naked body. Soon, though, the passion flares again, his lips and fingers growing more demanding. When I wrap my hand around his cock, capturing the pre-cum on its tip and squeezing as I stroke him, he moans, lifting himself to hover over me. He's motionless for a second, drinking me in with his eyes, before positioning himself at my entrance.

And then he plunges in, filling me in a way I've never experienced before, our collective groans echoing in the room. We're both still at first, luxuriating in the joining we've denied ourselves for so long, and then he grins. And my world lights up for the first time in my life.

He starts to thrust inside me, a slow, leisurely screw—making love to me, like he promised, as he kisses me gently—and I feel his presence in my gut, where my bonds to him and my dragon reside. It's as if he's pouring his soul into mine, filling and binding me to him with every surge of his hips. I've never experienced anything like this, his body so perfectly fitted to mine that it's drawing out pleasure I had no idea I could experience. Spots he finds in my core explode with every poke and prod of his massive cock.

Soon, though, we both need more. He throws his head back, a low, throaty growl rumbling through his lips, and starts to truly fuck me. He's pistoning in and out, dragging sensations from me that don't seem possible, as our bodies work together in a hurricane that soon will sweep us both away.

"I want to come with you," he mutters, leaning down to give me a frenzied kiss. "This bond needs us to fall off the edge together." Diving his hand between us, he finds my clit, circling it with his thumb as he continues to thrust inside me, almost frantically.

I was close before, but now I'm there, ready to dive headfirst into wherever his body is taking me. "Now, Mik," I scream. "Come with me now."

And he does. I feel his cock expand, but the rapture from those sensations pales in comparison to the ecstasy that fills me when our bond fuses together. In that second, as he spills into me, the world seems to stop, my mate and me the only beings in the vastness we're floating through. I sense our dragons—those bonds will always be there—but every bit of me is consumed by the joy of connecting, of tying myself to, my mate.

He shivers, the bond impacting him as deeply as it did me, and falls to my side. "Thank you, Dani, for being mine," he murmurs as he kisses my hair and wraps his arm around me, tugging me to lie on his chest.

I'm on the edge of sleep when he speaks again, his voice groggy but calm. Sated. "I used to hate this land, wonder what the fuck I was doing here," he whispers as he digs his nose into my hair, inhaling deeply. "I know now. Vanatia's changed, but I've changed more. It took you and Z for me to realize I belong here. I belong with my mate and my dragon." He laughs, a low rumble. "Fate might know what the fuck it's doing after all."

His words bounce in my head as I snuggle into his embrace, listening to the low snores that start a few seconds later.

He's right. Mikkael and Vulryn are as perfect for me as I am for them.

This is where I belong, too. With my mate and my dragon.

Fate definitely knew what it was doing.

I have no idea what I did to deserve these gifts from the gods, but I'm gonna cling to them with everything I am.

Epilogue; Ziselær

Together Forever

I COULD NOT HAVE known I would find such joy in my life.

For so long, I knew nothing but pain and guilt and fear. I loved my rider. I still do, in some depraved part of my soul, that clings to the belief that I deserve everything he gave me. But my fate-ordained rider—our male, as my draikana calls him—is helping me see that I am worthy of more.

I deserve the happiness and love the fates have given me.

Like my draikana and me, my rider and I will be together forever. As it should be.

Our riders' offspring—a male and a female, born together—squeal in delight across the field as they frolic with my draikana and the male born to the starry female and angry male. He is not so angry these days, but my draikana finds joy in vexing him. She is heavy now with the eggs she soon will lay, but she still relishes playing with the littles. The closer she gets to her hatching, the more time we spend with them. There is no place she would rather be.

Life has not been simple since the silver beast killed the wyrm. The land still seethes with unrest. But that tumult cannot reach us here. The leader has neither dragons nor ships to cross the water. Our beasts destroy any he tries to build.

The dragon shifter visits more often now, her draw to my draikana growing along with the brood my draikana soon will bear. The silver beast is young but wise. She will join the sun beast when the eggs come. The sun beast's own hatchlings have aged enough now to be left with the fire beast. He is eager to have time alone with his offspring, as I will be in the months to come.

Together, the sun beast and the silver beast will protect my draikana, as always. They love her nearly as much as I do. Everyone who knows my draikana adores her.

I stretch, luxuriating in the sun's warmth.

I am a lucky beast, and I thank the gods every day for their gifts.

And I'm starting to think I truly do deserve them.

The End.

This world has more tales to tell!
Sign up for my newsletter or follow me on Facebook or Instagram to get updates on the duet I'm writing, starting with *Foul Faith*, coming Spring 2026.

Thank You

Thank you for reading *Mythical Menace!*
I hope you enjoyed *Tales of the Vanir*,
and I would appreciate it so much if you would
take the time to leave a review on Amazon,
Goodreads, or wherever you review books!

Author's Note

I'M SO LUCKY TO be able to do what I love, supported by family and friends. Thanks to my hubby Al, our boys Albert and Stephen, and the amazing friends who have been cheering me along.

Thanks also to everyone who read *Mythical Menace* and shared their thoughts with me, starting with my alpha reader Cynthia, who's read all my books and given me great feedback.

With this series, I relied heavily on beta feedback.
Many thanks to Cindy Ray Hale and Keele Publishing,
Kaitlin Slowik, and Keeya Marquez
for all of their comments and suggestions.

And last but definitely not least, thanks to everyone who gave this book a try. I fell in love with this world and hope you do too. As an indie author, your support means everything. I'm grateful to everyone who talks about my books, through a review or on social media, and just as grateful to everyone who reads them. Thank you!

Also by Rochelle Wilcox

The Road to Ragnarök
(mostly closed-door portal romantic fantasy;
Heavy Heart has one spicy scene)

Fickle Fate
(the spicy prequel, available to subscribers
to my newsletter at RochelleWilcox.com)
Lost Long
Enemies Eternal
Alive Again
Heavy Heart

About the Author

Rochelle Wilcox is happily retired from practicing law, focused on writing what she loves to read. You can find Rochelle at rochellewilcox.com and at any of the social media sites below:

amazon.com/stores/Rochelle-Wilcox/author/B007PEWME6

goodreads.com/author/show/6951175.Rochelle_Wilcox

bookbub.com/authors/rochelle-l-wilcox

facebook.com/TheRoadToRagnarok

instagram.com/rochellewilcoxauthor/

tiktok.com/@rochellewilcoxauthor